A CURSE OF GEMS

A RETELLING OF TOADS & DIAMONDS

THE CLASSICAL KINGDOMS COLLECTION
BOOK SEVEN

BRITTANY FICHTER

LIKE FREE STORIES?

Sign up for a free no-spam newsletter with free short stories, exclusive secret chapters, and sneak peeks at books before they're published . . . all for free.

Details at the end of this book.

In loving memory of Helen Bennet, one of our own shining jewels who is now singing with Jesus where your beautiful soul shines brighter than ever before.

Everywhere you went, you left the sparkle of joy and the love of Christ in your wake. Your presence at my book signing was one of the greatest honors I've ever received. When we lost your beautiful smile and sweet heart, it left a hole on this side of Heaven. But in the view of eternity, it'll only be a little while before we're there singing along with you once again.

CHAPTER 1
DISCOVER THAT MAN

Lucas bit his tongue as he tried again to scrub the blasted spot off his left boot. What good was a strict exercise regimen if one couldn't rub hard enough to get a spot off a shoe? If his kingdom's resources were more recovered from the war, he would have bought a new set of boots a year ago. But since Maricanta was still healing, his five-year-old boots would have to do.

"There is a correspondence for you, Sire."

Lucas froze briefly. Then he dropped the cloth he was using to take the letter from the servant's tray.

"Would you like me to finish your—" the servant began.

"Thank you, Nelson," Lucas said as he took his foot from the table against which he'd propped it and tore the envelope open, not even bothering to find his letter knife.

Nelson paused slightly and then nodded before giving a short bow and turning out. Lucas's hands trembled as he pulled the thick, crisp parchment out and opened it. And there, in the earl's thick, blocky handwriting Lucas had come to recognize, was the letter he'd been longing for and dreading for a fortnight.

Your Highness,

I would usually begin such letters with all sorts of vain pleas-

1

antries and flattering compliments to someone of a rank such as yourself. But as I have come to know you, I have learned that you have little time for such folly, so I will bring myself to the point in the most delicate and practical manner of which I am capable. You have asked for my daughter's hand in marriage. And I regret to say that I cannot in good conscience give it.

My family is most honored by your attentions, namely to our daughter, Vittoria. While I cannot say I am surprised, for she has always been a girl of unusual spirit and beauty, we were most gratified when your gaze was turned in her direction. Furthermore, your request for my blessing, humble as it is, further evidences your sense of honor and good humor.

I will admit that the speed with which you seek my blessing of my youngest daughter's hand did take me a little by surprise. For though we have been familiar since you were young, there has been very little intimate communication between our families and between yourself and Vittoria in particular. I pray I do not overstep my bounds when I risk speaking honestly in saying that I struggle to see whether each of you know enough of the other's nature to ensure your happiness throughout your years.

LUCAS STOPPED. A feeling much like he'd eaten bad fish began to pool at the bottom of his stomach.

I was curious as to the nature of your interest...and if I'm honest, hers, the last time we visited you in your home. And while I was impressed at your gallantry and your treatment of her, for your treatment was nothing short of what any father would want for his daughter, I was struck by an observation I have not been able to shake or chase from my head.

I will preface this by mentioning that Vittoria is our youngest, and my wife and I have admittedly spoiled her. I had hoped, however, that the good sensibilities with which you are known to handle your military would guide her well, that you would be a grounding force for her, and she an uplifting one for you. When I

observed you together, however, I noticed a difference between you
that I cannot reconcile for your good, hers, or that of Maricanta as
a whole. For whoever you choose as your bride will affect the
welfare of the kingdom, and though her happiness is by duty a
concern of mine, I do not wish to grant it to her at the cost of thou-
sands of others.

Lucas couldn't breathe. And yet he read on.

When you were in the market together, as is her habit, my
daughter spotted a lovely piece of jewelry. It was a necklace
encrusted in gems and more expensive than any piece of jewelry
that I have purchased for my wife. She begged it of you, assuring
you it would bring her great delight.
    I could see from your expression that this request of hers was no
mere trifle for you. I can only see how such a demand would put a
strain on you, as the kingdom is only beginning to recover from its
financial depression. From what I have observed of your family, you
dress respectably, but there is little excessiveness or gaudy living.

Little excessiveness. Everyone in the kingdom knew which royal
family member kept that number from being none.

I nearly interfered to remind my daughter to be sensitive to
your financial situation, as your coffers are those of the people. But
then I held myself back. For I thought it would be beneficial to see
how you would react to her in such a situation, and she to you. For
if nuptials were said, I would not be present to remind my daughter
on a daily basis to curb her desire for trinkets of gold and jewels. So
I watched. And I was first impressed by the slight pursing of your
lips and the furrow of your brow, for I could see that you did not
approve of such a purchase. But where I had hoped you would

gently offer her something else of lesser value, or better yet, convince her to place her hopes in something other than trifles for her happiness, you finally nodded at the merchant and paid him from your pocket. And though it pains me to say it, I have seen this behavior from both of you more times than I can count in the short months you have been giving her your attentions. She asks, and though you balk, you do her bidding. And every time I hope you shall call her to her senses, you capitulate again, and she glories in your generosity.

I don't know if you're aware of it, but I knew your father, even before he was prince regent. And while you are far my superior, for his sake, I would be remiss if I failed to admonish you with the same love I know he held for you.

LUCAS'S CHEST squeezed even tighter than he knew possible, old pain mingling with the new, doused with a generous bucket of shame, though for what sin he did not know.

You are such a pleasant young man. Even through the war, every time I saw you, you were striving to do what might please others and put them at ease. And as the stresses of war were heavy on your household, no one could hold you to blame for such a desire. But as you are a man now, perhaps it is time to strive to find who the Maker truly has made you to be in both deed and action. You were given much strength and repose, but if you cannot find it within you to stand your ground on and off the battleship, you will begin to lose that man within, and the world will lose the worthy soul the Maker has placed within you. Accommodating the needs of those around you is heroic, but capitulating to them for the sake of peace is detrimental to you and the other parties.

Denying you my blessing truly does grieve me, for I would have been delighted to call you my son. But just as my daughter wanted the jewels you bought her but did not need them, so you wish for her. As her father and a friend of yours, I cannot in good conscience recommend you to life together, for I believe you would be a hindrance to one another. She must learn to put others' wants before herself, and you must discover the man you were made to be rather than the man others wish you to be.

Please forgive any pain I bring you in this correspondence. I have shed no small amount of tears myself while writing, but it is with a clear conscience before you and the Maker that I am refusing your request for my daughter's hand in marriage. Perhaps one day, after you've found that man inside you, and my daughter has discovered that woman within her, you might be united yet. But until then, I pray fervently that the Maker bring you what you need in this life and that you find true joy along with it.

In your service and the Maker's,
Lorenzo Di Stefano

LUCAS PUT the letter down and stared blankly at the wall. He'd been refused. After planning and praying and scheming all the perfect ways to propose to the woman of his dreams, he'd sent the letter to her father almost as an afterthought. Of course, it was customary to seek the lady's father's blessing before requesting her hand. But never in his wildest dreams had he thought the man would say no.

Lucas put the letter in his pocket, though why he did so, he had no idea. His chambers were suddenly far too confining, so he stepped out to wander the palace halls, his boots' luster forgotten.

It wasn't as if he was unaware how quickly he'd tried to bring about such a match. In truth, he hadn't even been looking to find love. There was more than enough to do around the palace and the shipyard, trying to rebuild the kingdom his grandfather had so successfully dismantled during his unholy war on the merpeople. But after his brother and his wife had finally admitted their love and gotten married, he'd very quickly realized his own longing for what they had. For though they were often apart, Michael piecing Maricanta back together, and Arianna seeing to the recovery of the merpeople, their happiness every time she came home or he went out to her raised the spirits of the entire palace.

Perhaps even better than their long gazes at one another or their quiet teasing or the way he kissed her temple when she wasn't expecting it was the way they could depend on one another. Whenever one needed help, the other was there. And though their crowns were heavy, they bore the weight together, their determination to be faithful providing a foundation which their people so desperately needed.

Lucas, of course, entertained no delusions of marrying someone like Arianna. Not only was it highly unlikely for a prophesied mermaid to show up at his door, begging for his help, he was also aware that love was far more than simply falling prey to one's attractions. It took determination. A decision to love would eventually lead to love, he had heard. And so, when Vittoria had crossed his path several months before, he had known instantly that she was meant to be his. The moment he'd laid eyes on her, he'd envisioned the life they could lead together. Her golden curls blowing in the wind on the pier as she welcomed him home from his naval excursions. The way her cheeks would dimple as she laughed at their children playing in the sand. Falling asleep with her in his arms at night, relishing the sensation of being home before his brother sent him to sea once again. That she was terrified of the ocean, as he soon learned, was slightly concerning, but Lucas knew from watching his brother's marriage that fear could be overcome by love.

Never in all the weeks since sending the letter had he entertained the thought of being denied that future.

Though he usually loved the way the palace windows caught the early afternoon sun and threw it against the glass columns, shining floors, and the pearls which hung from the ceiling above, today it was all too bright. As a headache already threatened to send him back to his room, he moved away from the west side of the palace toward the south, where the light wasn't quite so strong, and the walls were made of slightly more practical materials, such as stone, like a palace's walls should be.

He tried to push past the numbness, which seemed to have overtaken his senses, to understand why her father had said no. Lorenzo Di Stefano had been a dear family friend since Lucas was small. Or, according to this letter, long before. Lucas had half expected the man to come to the palace personally to congratulate Lucas and Vittoria for finding one another. From what Lucas understood, most families who were close were overjoyed when their children married one another, ensuring allies and good humor for years to come. So the refusal felt all the more like a slap in the face. It came from a man about whose opinion Lucas deeply cared.

He did remember the incident when Vittoria had asked Lucas to buy her the necklace. And Lorenzo hadn't been too far off in noting Lucas's true feelings about the matter. He spent very little on himself, as his coffers were tied to those of the crown. But half the reason he'd bought the necklace had been to assure Lorenzo that he cared for Vittoria and that he meant to see her happy for the rest of their lives.

Instead, it had done just the opposite.

Before he could continue to pointlessly mull, for his thoughts were flying in circles around his head, Lucas heard the sound of shouting coming from down the hall. As he got closer, he realized the shouting was his brother's.

"Mother, I mean it. You need to leave Arianna alone." Michael's voice, though muffled through his study door, was louder than Lucas had heard it in a long time. He took a step closer to hear better. Would it be best if he let his mother and brother figure this out on their own? Or did his brother need reinforcements?

"But it's been six months!" came their mother's shrill protest. "And Arianna hasn't even shown any interest in getting with child! I'm saying this as a queen, Michael—"

"Queen mother, Mother. You are the queen mother. Arianna is the queen."

What Lucas wouldn't give to see the look on their mother's face at that jab. He put his ear to the door, his mulling temporarily pushed to the side.

"All I'm saying," she said in a low, flat voice, "is that you need an heir. And Arianna is so busy, constantly waltzing off to sea, that whenever she's home, she's too tired to attend any of the parties or balls I've been trying to give." She huffed. "It's not as if she can have any life left within her to attempt bringing about an heir—"

"Mother!" Michael roared. "What my wife and I have time and energy for is none of your business!"

As much as Lucas wanted to continue his moping, this was the most interesting conversation he'd heard in weeks. Or perhaps it was that he didn't have the strength within him now to puzzle out the reason his father's friend had chosen to dismantle the life he'd hoped and prayed for. Besides, now that the merpeople had control of the seas again, thanks to Michael and Arianna's marriage, there was little, aside from training their new naval officers, for him to do while his ships were being rebuilt.

"You admit that you know little of what it takes to run a kingdom," Michael snapped. "And if that's the case, why in the depths would you try to tell me or my wife how to run ours? Or our family, for that matter?"

"Lies. I've never admitted such a thing."

"You've said so numerous times. Ask anyone in the palace! Really, what have you done for our kingdom, Mother? Other than suck our treasury dry when we were penniless and find ways to torment my wife."

"I raised you!"

"No, Bithiah raised us, as did the rest of the servants. Now, I suggest you go find something productive to do before I really lose my temper."

"You ungrateful, spoiled—"

"Michael," Lucas opened the door and dredged up a smile as though he hadn't heard what everyone in the palace must have heard by now, "I believe you needed to see me?"

Michael threw him a grateful look while their mother looked as though she might cry or go on a rampage. She might do either. Or both.

"Well, I can see you don't need me." Drina sniffed. She whirled around, nearly colliding with Lucas as he approached his brother's cluttered desk. She didn't even glance his way as she stomped out the door. "If I disappeared, you probably wouldn't even shed a tear!"

"Goodbye, Mother!" Michael shouted as she slammed the door behind her.

Lucas let out a whistle. "That was louder than usual."

Michael sat in his chair with a thump. "She won't quit hounding Arianna about having a baby. We've been married for six blooming months, and the woman won't desist!"

"So what are you going to tell her when Arianna does get pregnant?" Lucas flopped into the chair across from his brother. "You know she'll want to run every inch of that child's life from conception on."

At this, Michael smiled slyly.

Lucas leaned forward. "Arianna's already pregnant, isn't she?"

Michael's grin widened. "Why do you think we haven't told Mother?" He started to look down at some parchment but stopped to peer more closely at Lucas. "Something's wrong. What is it?"

For a brief moment, Lucas considered showing Michael the letter. If anyone would understand his desire for companionship, it would be his big brother. But the dark circles beneath Michael's eyes stayed his hand, and he pretended to scoff and shook his head.

"Nothing pressing."

But Michael hadn't kept the kingdom together by being unobservant, and to Lucas's dismay, he put the paper down and came closer to study him. "Something's wrong," he said again. "What are you not telling me?"

Lucas drew in a breath through his nose before forcing a smile and shrugging. "A missed opportunity, that's all. There will be more in the future." He nodded at Michael's desk. "Now what have *you* been up to?"

Michael watched him for a moment longer before returning to his desk. "Actually," he said, rubbing his eyes, "I did need to see you."

"About?"

Michael frowned as he sorted through the paper piles on his desk. When he finally found one with a blue seal, he handed it to Lucas. "The last of Grandfather's debts needs to be paid."

Lucas scanned the page. "I thought we'd made enough after the wedding to pay everything back."

"We did. The problem has been getting the payments where they need to go. Destin was the first kingdom I paid after Tumen, then all the smaller debts here and there. Unfortunately, repaying this one has been more...difficult."

Lucas gave a start when he read the name at the bottom of the page. "Terrefantome?" He looked up at Michael then back down at the page, sure he was seeing double. "How in the depths did Grandfather manage to get a messenger over to them? Let alone get their money?" He handed the parchment back. "Do you have to pay it?"

"Grandfather was creative if nothing else." Michael shook his head. "Unfortunately, the Maker knows we gave them our word, even if they are degenerate thugs."

"But what about when you tore up the treaty with the pirates?"

"Going back on our word to kill merfolk is one thing. Borrowing money is something else." Michael looked as though he was going to say something more, but then he stopped and began shuffling papers around on his desk instead.

"What is it?" Lucas asked.

Michael grimaced. "What do you know of the place?"

Lucas shrugged. "What everyone else knows. Criminals of heinous crimes have the choice of being executed or exiled there, along with whatever family members wish to come with them. But before the criminals go in, they're branded so everyone knows what they did and where they're supposed to be."

Michael studied him. "What else?"

"They're landlocked with just a few miles of open beach. Everything is surrounded by a huge wall, with the exception of the beach, which is guarded by the merfolk." He scratched his head. "Aren't children of the branded criminals allowed out?"

"If they can prove their intentions are good, yes." Michael went to a shelf, pulled down a map, then returned to his desk and unrolled it. "The land originally belonged to the *Taistille*, a group of deadly nomads that can suck an entire village dry of resources in less than a day. The land is hardly hospitable, and they can't grow much due to the constant rain and fog. It's basically a swampy wasteland with just enough resources to sustain them. As it is, I can't for the life of me figure out where they got the money to lend in the first place." He huffed. "But somehow, they raised just enough to tempt Grandfather, and now we're reaping the rewards." His mouth tightened. "Again."

"Didn't the kingdoms start dumping criminals there several hundred years ago?"

"Yes. But here's the interesting part." Michael's eyes gleamed. "Criminals hid there before the place was even used for exile."

"Why?"

"They discovered that the land grants its residents a strange kind of power."

Lucas blinked. "The ground has power?" He'd heard of many of things that had power, but dirt had never been one of them.

Michael gave him a strange look. "The ability to become invisible to outsiders. And as soon as this became well known, those who wanted to hide from the law began to flock there."

"And the kings let them?" Lucas scoffed. "I can hardly imagine Everard's ancestors being satisfied with that." Not that he understood everything about the famed Destinian power, but there was a reason their neighbor kingdom had been known as the fiercest, most powerful kingdom for centuries.

"By the time the monarchs realized what was happening, it was too late. Searching for the missing criminals was dangerous because they could disappear and attack the kings' search parties or merely slip away to do whatever dastardly thing they wished in the world."

Lucas shivered.

"So," Michael continued, "it was finally decided that the neighboring kings would erect a wall around the land to keep the criminals inside without hope of escape. Now it's common practice to allow criminals who would otherwise be executed or imprisoned for life the option of going to Terrefantome instead."

"The Taistille must have loved that."

Michael grimaced. "One can only imagine."

"Which means..." Lucas said, "it's basically a cesspit." He paused. "But how do people get out?"

"Guards of the highest merits are chosen to stand at the gates. Once they've been exposed to the land, just like the people who live there, they have the ability not only to gain invisibility themselves but to see others who are doing the same. We're continually sending new guards there to make sure we have a large pool with the ability to see those who try to escape while invisible."

"I thought they would lose their invisibility once they crossed the wall."

"If only it were that easy. Most, from what I'm told, can only hold their invisibility for several minutes but no more than an hour or two. But once they're rested, they can do it again and again and again."

"So the ability stays," Lucas mused, and Michael nodded.

"Their invisibility proved to the kings the most dangerous of traits, and it was for that reason that they walled off the place so as to keep the villains in one place."

Lucas stared down at the long brown wall that encircled the small patch of land on the map. Well, not small. It was far wider than Maricanta. But the thought of being stuck in a land so dreary, penned in by walls his entire life, made him shudder. "You said children are allowed out?"

Michael picked up a quill and pointed at the four exit and entry gates. "The guards are also trained to judge and inspect those requesting to leave. They're encouraged to let out families, young couples, and women first."

"Who would take their families to such a rotten place?" Lucas leaned closer to study the location of the gate that led into Maricanta.

"Many do. Unfortunately, this means their children are raised in a land of evil and slavery."

"Slavery?" Lucas found himself leaning forward.

"Women are often treated like chattel." Michael snorted, shaking his head at the paper in his hand. "The land has marshals and laws protecting people from slave trade. Supposedly."

"But they don't," Lucas guessed.

"To be considered untouchable, a woman of marriageable age must be claimed either by her husband or another *protector*, someone who can claim responsibility for her."

"Wait...What?"

"If she has a father or brother or husband," Michael said, "she's supposed to be safe. But if she loses her father, she's seen as a woman living unprotected. And even the marshals will insist that she's better off if someone claims her."

"Just anyone can claim her?" Lucas asked incredulously.

Michael nodded. "She can be taken as a wife or personal servant, and the so-called crown will do nothing."

"Why do I get the feeling that a protector is the opposite of what it sounds like?" Lucas said, unable to get past what he'd heard a moment before. He tried to imagine his little nieces, Claire and Lucy, being raised in such an environment, but not even his imagination could take him that far.

"It depends on the individual. Some protectors, such as fathers and brothers, will do their best to keep the women they care for safe. There's even talk of using somewhat...unsavory methods to make them less attractive to other men. Unfortunately, some young women, and even some who aren't so young, are used for personal gain by the very men who are supposed to protect them." Michael shook his head. "Not that we plan to send in hordes of young maidens to deliver the money, but it's one more reason to dread this assignment."

Assignment. So Michael was sending him in. Not that Lucas was surprised. "If anyone can become invisible, I don't see why this is a problem," Lucas said, studying the map.

"The land will accept one as its own only after they've resided there seven years. And it's only to outsiders that they appear invisible. They can see one another just fine." He squinted at the map. "The castle that the current king, if you can call him that, resides in, is on the far east side of Terrefantome, so it's a good two weeks' journey on horseback from the gate in Maricanta. Not to mention two weeks back." His jaw tightened. "And now their self-proclaimed king..." Michael squinted at a parchment, "*Bartol*, is threatening us with disaster if we don't pay them back soon." He stepped back and rubbed his eyes. "Not that I haven't been trying. But no matter how carefully we plan, as soon as they cross the gate, they're never heard from again."

"Then send them in groups."

"I have. We've lost four envoys. The first one traveled with the royal crest. The second, third, and fourth were undercover."

"And none survived."

"We had exactly one from each group return. And each man said the same."

"The criminals?"

Michael nodded. "For the most part, yes. They set traps on the road for new arrivals. There's a sort of honor code that keeps most of the robbers focused on those who are just entering. Everyone new is open game."

"Why can't the gate guards be sent in?" Lucas asked. "If they've been there long enough to be invisible."

"We've tried that already. Every single envoy has included gate guards. But for some reason, we never hear from the guards themselves again. And the sole survivors who return are always separated from the party without knowledge of what happened to the rest of them." He leaned forward. "So even if any of the parties did make it all the way to the king, we would have no way of knowing. Bartol could have taken the money and killed them, for all we know, and demanded payment again, and no one would be able to prove otherwise."

"And what exactly is he going to do if we don't deliver yet another payment?"

Michael leaned on his desk and looked straight into Lucas's eyes.

"He's threatening to break down the wall and release the exiles into our land if we don't pay them back in three months' time."

Lucas let that sink in as his brother scratched his head and grimaced at the map.

"And the criminals aren't even the worst part," Michael continued. "When our men aren't being attacked by gangs of criminals, they're trying to survive the land itself."

"But I thought it was just a barren wasteland."

"If only that were true. The land itself is full of what we can only gather to be Sorthileige."

Lucas sat straight up. "From the ground?"

"The land barely produces enough to keep everyone alive. There are hidden tar pits, animals of mixed proportions, and all sorts of strange ills that can cost a strong man his life within days. Many of the people are dangerous, but the land itself is just as likely to kill you as the people are."

Then Michael surprised Lucas by cracking a tired smile. "But after much searching, I've finally found a weakness. Against the people, at least." He opened the lowest drawer in his desk and pulled out a small velvet drawstring bag. He opened it and tipped it upside down, and three gems, purple, red, and white, rolled out.

Lucas gaped. "Diamonds?"

"If any of the natives are touching diamonds or wearing them on their person, they can't become invisible," Michael said.

"So one would have to force the diamonds upon his enemies before the gems could be of any use to them."

"Precisely." Michael rubbed his stubbled chin and sighed. "The more I learn about this place, the more I loathe asking anyone to take on this task. But it must be done, and I'm afraid doing it myself would—"

"Are you insane? Of course you're not going to do it yourself." Lucas scowled at his brother. "The Sun Crown can't go gallivanting about because of our grandfather's stupidity. Especially now that you're a father—"

"Would you keep it down?" Michael hissed. He ran a hand through his short black curls. "I know I can't, which makes it all the worse that I have to ask you."

"I would have gone even if you didn't," Lucas said, glaring at his older brother. "Do you really think you could have kept something like this from me? I've known you were up to something for the last month. I would have discovered it sooner or later."

"I know." Michael gave Lucas a wry grin. "But that doesn't mean I have to like it."

"What else should I know before I infiltrate this bastion of darkness?"

Michael stood and went to one of the windows, rubbing his neck and watching their nieces playing in the garden. When Michael stood that way, he reminded Lucas of their father. Not that he remembered as much as he would have liked. But there was something about the stance and profile that made Lucas's heart ache just a bit, as if he were missing something grand without even knowing what it was. Michael was like their father in so many ways. Honorable to a fault, careful, thoughtful, considerate.

And though everyone swore that they could be twins, as they shared the same dark, curly hair and hazel eyes, Lucas felt often like he'd taken after his mother in every other way. Poor judgment included it seemed.

"Beauty is coveted in Terrefantome," Michael finally said quietly. "Diamonds are their weakness, but they hoard them when and where they can. Women become toys. Many girls, the daughters of the exiled criminals, will run away and sell themselves as wives to those wishing to leave if it means crossing the wall to the other side."

"Why don't they cross it themselves?"

"The trip to the wall is too dangerous."

"Why aren't all the innocents being let out?" Lucas asked. "It seems wrong to hold any."

"Simple. The criminals are being exiled for the rest of their lives, and they want to keep their families. And as much as I'd like to set that all right, I can't." He rubbed his eyes. "Not now while we're still just recovering from the war."

He went back to his desk and opened one of the drawers. "But back to your assignment and our missing convoys, I've had the coins stamped this time with our crest so that their king," Michael sneered, "can't take the gold and insist it was already his."

"Very well."

"And if you're not home within six weeks of entering Terrefantome, I'm coming after you."

"You are not!"

"I will." Michael leaned on his desk, eyes glinting wickedly. "So if you don't want your big brother running in to save you, you'd better watch yourself."

Lucas rubbed his face and groaned. Then he changed the subject. "And just who is this Bartol?"

Michael rolled his eyes. "Kings have risen and fallen for centuries in Terrefantome, but no one can seem to keep a running monarchy. From what we can gather, there are uprisings every few years. The strongest triumphs, and the weaker one dies off." He looked unhappily at the coin he'd pulled from the drawer. "Unfortunately, this recent claim to the throne, however, has run longer than most."

"You said we have three months to get this done. That doesn't leave us much time."

Michael put the coin away. "I've found two men who were released from Terrefantome when they were young. They've agreed to act as your guides and guards while you're there. As soon as we have two more, that's when you'll go."

"I can't imagine anyone ever wanting to go back after escaping that."

Michael drew in a deep breath. "To say I'm paying them handsomely would be an understatement."

"How are we going to get out at the gate?"

"I've been thinking about that." Michael paused and scribbled something on a parchment. Then he looked back up at Lucas. "We're going to use a staining ink on your necks to give you criminal marks."

"Will they come off?" Lucas gave his brother a wry smile. "I'd prefer not to be a marked criminal for the rest of my life. That's just my preference."

"It'll come off in time. But in the meantime, I've already had Roberto draw up a new emergency crest, and the gate guards will be notified long before you need it." He searched his desk again and pulled out a square of parchment small enough to fit entirely in Lucas's palm. In blue ink was a sun lily with a merperson's tail. The flower had five flourishes like hair, and there were six different kinds of fish swimming around it.

"Indigo ink," Lucas said. "This stuff isn't cheap."

"I wanted to make sure it couldn't be copied if it were found."

Lucas continued to study the drawing. Roberto, their cartographer, was not only in charge of creating the royal maps, but he also worked for the crown in a more secretive service.

Every so often, Michael would commission Roberto to create a new drawing with expensive inks, a combination nearly impossible to reproduce. The individual with the secret would then carry the square of paper with him, and when he needed special help, he could give the square of parchment to the guard, who would notify the crown. Whenever a new image was created, the gate guards and those who were in charge of guarding the kingdom's borders would be shown the card long enough to know what to look for if they were presented one. There were no words or names that might be used to identify the individual or their kingdom. It was the crown's most secretive way of being contacted by those who were protecting its secret interests.

Lucas sat up straighter and put the card in his shirt. "I'm not worried about myself. No need to look like you're sending me to the gallows."

Michael's smile faded as he met his brother's gaze. "I know you're a good fighter. But don't get cocky. If something happens, your guides will at least be able to hide from the newcomers, because they're natives. You won't."

"Well then," Lucas said, standing and stretching, determined to chase the fear from his brother's face, "I'd better start helping you look for more of those escapees."

Michael arched an eyebrow. "And why would that be?"

Lucas forced a grin. The last thing he wanted was for Michael to know about Vittoria. Not right now at least, while he had so much else to worry about. Because if he did find out, he would worry. So he wriggled his eyebrows and straightened his shirt. "It sounds like they have so many pretty women. It would be a shame to miss out on one."

Michael's eyes went wide. "Lucas, I swear, if you come home with some—"

Lucas only laughed as he left his brother's study, shutting the door behind him in time to block the wad of paper his brother had thrown at him.

"I'm getting something to drink," he called over his shoulder. "Then I'll come back."

It was good to see his brother smile, Lucas mused as he made his way toward the kitchen. During the war with the merfolk, Lucas felt as if he'd gone years without his brother's grin. He couldn't help teasing just to see that smile. When Michael smiled, it felt a little like they were carefree boys again. But when he rounded the corner and was out of sight of his brother's study, his own smile faded as he fingered the folded parchment in his coat. He wasn't going to be coming home with a girl anytime soon. And it was his own blasted fault.

MICHAEL AND LUCAS talked of strategy late into the night. When Michael finally noted how dark it had grown outside, Lucas bid him goodnight and promised to return the next day to begin preparations. Though the mission had caused his brother a good deal of lost sleep, judging by the dark circles beneath his eyes, Lucas found himself ridiculously relieved by the distraction. Maybe this was what he needed to keep himself busy until he could get past the shock of Lorenzo's letter.

He didn't have time to continue his musings, however, because as soon as he was out of his brother's study, he realized he hadn't had supper and made his way to the kitchen. Once he'd pieced together a platter of stolen leftovers from the pantry, he began to make his way up to his room to eat. A flash of color, however, caught his attention at the end of the dining hall.

"Did Michael keep you all this time?" Arianna's clear voice rang out through the hall like a silver bell. Lucas took his load of food and sat down across the table from her.

"I kept myself."

Arianna just smiled, though it looked slightly pained, and shook her head. As he drew closer, in the light of the torches and fireplace, Lucas realized she was a bit pale. Even for a mermaid.

"Congratulations, by the way," he said in a low voice, offering her a slice of pineapple. "How far along are you?" Not that he knew anything about pregnancy or childbearing. But it was a question he'd heard other women ask enough to know it was appropriate.

She smiled and took the fruit. "Thank you. And not nearly as far along as I'd like. The physician said I have six months left, but Bithiah says it's probably another seven months at least."

"So you're listening to our head housekeeper now, instead of the physician?"

Arianna gave him an ornery look. "Would you contradict Bithiah?"

"No," Lucas laughed. "I can't say I would."

Arianna grinned. But instead of taking a bite of the fruit he'd given her, she put it on her untouched plate of rice and studied him instead.

Lucas squirmed. Though she'd had her voice for months now, Arianna still had a way of watching people that made one feel as though she could see inside his soul. Her pale blue eyes sometimes spoke louder than her words. And now those eyes connoted concern.

Great. Another person to be concerned.

"Michael's worried—"

"I know."

Her eyes softened. They already had that look of a mother. Well, every mother but his. He couldn't remember the last time his mother had actually been concerned about one of her children in a way that involved something other than the wealth of the kingdom.

"I'm worried, too." She leaned forward. "What's wrong, Lucas? You've been on edge for weeks now."

He stared back at her. What was wrong with him? According to Lorenzo, a lot.

"You don't seem like yourself," she added.

"How do you know what I'm like?" He dragged up a teasing smile. "You're not even there half the time."

She arched an eyebrow. "Bithiah is, though."

He rolled his eyes, but she pressed.

"Is this about Vittoria?"

"For a mermaid who couldn't speak for most of her life, you sure don't waste words," he said, taking a big bite of a roll.

Arianna gave a little laugh and leaned back, resting her hand on her still flat belly. "I suppose I'm always afraid my voice will disappear in the morning. But back to you, you were on edge, but you seemed...hopeful, even this morning. What's changed?"

Lucas looked out the window at the ocean, silver in the moonlight as it crashed on the beach with its hypnotizing rhythm.

"What do you think we would have been like if there hadn't been a war?" Would he have felt the need to do what Lorenzo accused him of, pleasing everyone at the cost of...how had he put it? The cost of his true self?

Instead of being annoyed by his abrupt shift, Arianna only

nodded slowly. "I think our generation was cheated a great deal by our parents. And I mean more than just growing up and doing without." Then she tilted her head and studied him with that soft smile again. "But that doesn't answer my question."

Tired of the nagging thoughts circling through his mind, Lucas let out a gusty breath and pulled the folded paper from his coat. After staring at it for a moment, he handed it to her. She opened it and read for a moment before her eyes popped.

"You proposed?"

He just gave her an unhappy grin.

"Almost."

She went back to reading. When she was done, she handed the letter back.

"Well," she said, shaking her head, "that's quite a letter."

"What are your thoughts on it?" He tried to sound casual, but inside, he was suddenly dying to know.

Arianna sighed. "If I'm honest?"

Lucas leaned back and rubbed his eyes with the heels of his palms. So Lorenzo had been right.

"Don't be like that," Arianna said, leaning forward. "Let me finish."

Lucas gave her a scowl.

"To be quite honest, I was never dearly attached to Vittoria."

"Because she's royalty?" Arianna wasn't known for her great love of royals. Although, his mother's behavior when Arianna had first arrived in the palace the year before might have had something to do with that.

She punched his arm. "No, you dunce. Because she treats you like a coin purse. But more than that, I think that her father may have a point."

"So I'm a spineless pushover." Lucas pushed his food around his plate, appetite gone.

"That's not what I said either. Besides, you stand up to Michael. I've seen you do it."

"When we're discussing military logistics. That doesn't count." He had stood up to him in one other regard, but that had worked itself out quite nicely, and not a word had been said about Arianna's well-being since.

"What I mean is that from what I've seen in my short time here, you strive to serve as the peacemaker. And that's not a bad thing. The only problem is that you've allowed your chosen role as peacemaker within your family to expand so that you often sacrifice what you *need* to say and do to achieve what others *want* at all costs." She twisted her mouth thoughtfully. "And like Lorenzo, I can't help wondering who that man is inside of you, waiting to be discovered. If only you'd give him a voice."

He rolled his eyes, but smiled slightly. "There you go with voices again."

"Well, I was without one for most of my life." She grinned. Then she leaned forward once more and squeezed his hand. "I have been praying for you, and I will continue." She started to rise, then stopped and sat back down in her chair. "But before you go, I wanted to give you this." She removed a leather thong from around her neck. On it hung a miniature whelk shell that swirled delicately up to the place where a hole had been cut for it to hang.

Lucas held it up to his ear but immediately had to pull it back. The merpeople were known for storing their magic in shells. If they wished to grow legs to come ashore or wished for the humans to come down to them, they would often sing songs directly into shells. The song inside this particular shell was fierce and urgent. He looked at Arianna in surprise.

"If you find yourself in trouble," she said, "throw that in the ocean."

"Michael says I can't bring anyone with me to act as a runner." The beach was in Maricanta. How was he supposed to get it there if he was in Terrefantome?

"I know that. But there is a short stretch of beach that belongs to Terrefantome that opens up to the ocean."

Lucas looked through the window wall at the ocean now. Storms were rolling in, and the gray, foaming waves were dark and choppy.

"Since they have access to the coast," he said slowly, "why can't we just sail in and skip all the tomfoolery of getting in through the gates?"

Arianna frowned at the shell in Lucas's hand.

"The water off that beach is dangerous. Whether naturally or in response to the land itself, there are dozens of sea vents close to the shore that put out high amounts of Sorthileige."

Lucas shivered in spite of himself.

"I can guide my people in and out of the area, but it will take a great amount of control and power." She looked down at her stomach. "And in my..." she paused and lowered her voice as several servants walked by before continuing. "*Condition*, I'm not certain I'll have the power to guide many in and out more than once." She tapped the shell. "Try your best to escape the way you came in. But should there be an emergency, and you can't get back to the gate, all you must do is throw this in the water, and my people and I will come. In fact, we'll be waiting until we hear that you've returned."

"Thank you," Lucas hung the shell around his neck. "But I won't need help."

Arianna gave a delicate snort and opened her mouth as if to speak, but before she could, her eyes grew wide as her face turned an odd shade of gray, and she threw the back of her hand over her mouth. Lucas stood to help, but she waved him back down. After a moment of what looked like great discomfort, she stood, squeezed his shoulder, and took a deep, shaky breath. "Enjoy your meal and eat some for me. Because at this rate I'm never going to eat again." She began to shuffle back down the hall, all hunched over like a little old woman with her hand still over her mouth and the other wrapped around her stomach. But before she reached the door, she turned back once more.

"Lucas?"

"Yes?" he answered.

She gave him a half-smile. "Take care."

He looked back down at the shell. "I will."

CHAPTER 2

OUTSIDE THE WALL

Y ou gonna buy something or stand there all day?"

Jaelle whipped around to face the butcher again. There was no hint of a smile in his dulled blue eyes, not that she expected any. His left whiskers twitched slightly as he glanced again at his growing line of customers. The woman behind her cleared her throat loudly as she glared.

Jaelle apologized and finished her stepmother's order. Then, as she waited for it to be prepared, she couldn't help glancing across the square again. Sure enough, the man was still staring at her. His gaze was so strong that when she'd first seen it as she stepped up to order, she'd forgotten quite why she'd come. Instead, she was recalling how the last time she saw someone stare like that, her sister had forbidden her from ever going to the market alone again. That had been six weeks ago. But when word had gotten out that morning that the butcher was slaughtering one of his pigs, her stepmother had insisted Jaelle go at once to get them some ham. And when her stepmother gave an order, Jaelle knew better than to disobey.

Jaelle quickly paid for the bit of pork and stuffed it in the bag she wore over her shoulder as she mumbled an apology. Then she took her brown paper package and hurried in the direction of home. But she could still feel the man's eyes following her as she went.

Which way should she take home? The back streets would be faster than the highway, particularly as the market was unusually full today. But the way the man was looking at her made her hesitant to walk anywhere that wasn't in the public eye.

Glancing at the man again, she saw now that a marshal, conspicuous in his red and brown uniform, had stopped to talk with him.

Fantastic. Just what she needed, the old marshal giving the man information about her family and where she lived.

Jaelle quickly scanned the crowd. Only a few yards ahead of her, plodding along in the thick of the throng, was a family with four daughters. Even better was that their hair was nearly as black as hers, not quite as dark or as shiny, but almost. She pressed forward until she was quite near them. Thankfully, they seemed not to notice her walking close on their heels. She followed them that way for a block before she let herself shudder. And when she could no longer see the man or the marshal, she allowed herself a moment to take a deep breath.

That was close.

But she let down her guard too soon. A heavy-set man was suddenly to her left, and without so much as glancing at her, bumped her hard enough to send her sprawling into an alleyway. She struggled, as the mud into which she'd fallen was quite slick, to stand up. As she did, though, the large man left the highway as well and stood at the entryway to the alley and blocked her path. Jaelle's heart jumped into her throat as she turned back toward the square, only to find the man who had been staring at her turn the corner as well. She was trapped.

The side street was narrow, and too late, Jaelle chastised herself for not walking closer to the middle of the road. It had seemed good to stay on the opposite side of the road to the marshal. But now, as she looked back and forth between the men in front of and behind her, she knew she'd made a mistake.

The man who had been staring stalked toward her. Jaelle tried to run, but she slipped and fell in the mud. The gray sky above gave his skin a nearly colorless hue as he reached toward her where she'd fallen. Grabbing her wrist, he flipped her hand over. His grin widened.

"Not spoken for, eh?" His voice was deep and scratchy. He dropped her wrist, then stepped back. "Well, Tobias. What do you think we ought to do with this one? She obviously needs someone to protect her."

"She's got a mask," the man called Tobias called back.

"Yes, but no mark." The man tapped her bare wrist and turned his head to stare hard at her mask.

"I'm a bit surprised." Tobias grinned. "This one seemed feisty enough to try."

"You know the punishment for a false marriage mark," Jaelle spat. Her voice was appropriately biting, and for once, Jaelle was glad for the mask. Without it they might see just how frightened she was. "And I'm not unprotected."

"We could always convince her to take the mask off," the first man said, smiling.

"I'm Chiara's stepdaughter." She stood slowly. "And you need to let me go." With her peripheral vision, she tried to measure the distance between herself and the nearest corner. She was fast, but was she fast enough?

"Chiara." The first man mused as he rubbed his chin. "I don't think I know that name." Then he shrugged. "Sounds like a woman. Not that it matters. You see, we're new here in town. Just moved here from the eastern wall. And we think you'll make a lovely addition to our house, spoken for or not." Our house? Did they live together? Then it struck Jaelle. They must be brothers, which meant, should they be successful, she would be living with not just one man, but two. She had to get away.

The man called Tobias didn't smile. He was taller than the first man, and though he wasn't largely muscled, he would be able to overpower Jaelle easily.

"You've still got a wife," he grumbled. "This one's for me."

"I don't know." The first man cocked his head. "I kind of like this one. Kind of makes me want to start over."

"You do, and I'll tell the king you're hoarding—"

"She is spoken for, and you'll do kindly to go your way and leave her be."

Jaelle nearly melted with relief when a young woman appeared at the edge of the alley. She had long, black hair that fell down her back in large curls, and her blue eyes cut back and forth between Jaelle's attackers. When they didn't move, she took a few steps forward. "In case you weren't aware, that girl is the stepdaughter of Chiara Barese, the only healer you'll find in this town. So if you'd like to live the next time you injure yourself, I suggest you not jeopardize your chances by taking her assistant."

Jaelle took the men's looks of confusion as an excuse to run to her sister. She had to pass Tobias, but he was too busy sharing a long look with the other man to make more than a half-hearted attempt to grab her. Selina brushed Jaelle behind her as she continued staring the men down.

"And," Selina added, taking Jaelle's hand, "if I ever see either of you in the tavern, keep your hands to yourselves, or I'll make sure Higgins never lets you set foot inside again."

The first man looked as though he was about to say something, but Tobias put his hand on his shoulder.

"Let's leave them be. Not worth the trouble."

The first man glowered briefly at Jaelle once more before following Tobias. Only after they both looked away did Selina yank Jaelle back onto the highway.

Jaelle could feel her sister's anger rolling off her in waves as she dragged Jaelle down the muddy highway through town. So she chose to remain silent and hope her sister's anger cooled by the time they reached the edge of town.

The highway, Selina always complained, was a ridiculous overstatement for the town's main street. The fact that two carriages could ride on it simultaneously going in opposite directions, she said, did not constitute a highway. But Selina didn't rant about the definition of streets or the shanties that lined those streets or the village size or the lack of civilization as she pulled Jaelle along. She only bristled, her mouth set in a straight line. That was never a good sign. Sure enough, as soon as they were nearly out of town, Selina sat Jaelle down on a tree stump and stood back to glare at her.

"Have you lost your senses?"

Jaelle twisted her skirt between her fingers. Her heart was still hammering in her chest, and her skin prickled. Her wrist felt as though the man's clammy fingers were still wrapped around it, and her hands trembled no matter how hard she squeezed the fabric.

"That man almost claimed you!" Selina's voice went shrill.

"I'm aware of that," Jaelle muttered. After all, she'd been the one to tell Selina all about Terrefantome's dangers when they were young and Chiara had dragged Selina with her to this horrible place. Back then, when their parents had married, Jaelle had been Selina's protector. But Selina was older, and as soon as she reached marriageable age, she'd taken up the cause of Jaelle's safety. And it was a role she still took seriously. Serious enough that Jaelle kept her mouth shut now, as she was still too shaken to argue.

"Either one of them could have taken you." Selina began to pace. "Right now, you might be in the back of someone's cart on the way to who knows where! Or in a shack on the far side of town." She turned to glare at Jaelle. "You could very easily be in that alley with that monster's filthy hands—"

"I know!" Jaelle burst out, angry tears running down her face. Why did she have to cry every time she was frustrated? And the more furious she was, the faster the tears seemed to spill. She sat taller and tried again. "I know. But Chiara caught wind this morning that the butcher would be selling parts of his old sow." Jaelle tried to control her breathing. "She told me I had to go."

Selina cursed. Then she put her hands on her hips and turned in a circle before facing Jaelle again.

"Look. I'll talk to Mother. Whenever she wants meat, I'll get it for her."

"They could decide to take you."

Selina just waved her off. "If those low-lifes ever show their faces in the tavern, they know better than to touch me. Old Man Higgins will throw them out in a heartbeat. In the meantime, though, please don't go out by yourself. Please." Selina gathered Jaelle's hands in hers, her blue eyes searching.

"I'm nineteen years," Jaelle retorted. "I'm not a child." But her retort lacked conviction.

"You could have fooled me." Selina smirked.

Jaelle scowled and fingered the cracks in the stump she was sitting on. "This is all Seth's fault," she muttered.

Selina sat beside Jaelle and hugged her.

"I know," she said into Jaelle's hair.

"If it hadn't been for him, we would have been out of here by now." Jaelle bit her lip, her voice catching slightly in her throat. "I could have had my own healing shop." She tried unsuccessfully to give her sister a smile. "You'd be married. Maybe I'd be, too."

"Jaelle..." Then Selina sighed and stood. "I need to get to work." She pulled a handful of coins from the little pocket she'd sewn into her dress. "Give Mother three, but put the others—"

"In your stocking. I know." Jaelle put the money in her own pocket and leaned forward. "Do you have to go?"

"You know I do."

Jaelle shook her head. "I hate how they treat you there." She sat back. "You don't have to stay. You could quit anytime. There has to be some other way to make enough money to satisfy your mother."

"You and I both know it's not that simple." Selina gave a poor chuckle. "Besides, it could be far worse. Tavern work certainly isn't my first choice, but Old Man Higgins won't let anyone get too close to me. He'd lose his best tavern girl if someone whisked me away." She shrugged. "And because everyone knows they'd lose their ale if he kicked them out, they leave me be." She tossed her hair. "It's almost better than being claimed. No husband, and I get paid to carry drinks around all day."

Jaelle arched a brow, refusing to be distracted. "As simple as telling Chiara I won't fetch her meat?"

"Point taken." Selina gave Jaelle a wan smile, her long, thin face lovely even when she stuck her tongue out.

"I'm telling the truth, though. Maybe you'll find someone one day who you *will* want to marry. Or I will. And we can all leave together."

Selina turned. "Excuse me?"

Jaelle blushed, but continued anyway. "Surely not all men are like Seth. Particularly outside the wall." She tried to garner a smile from her sister, too. "Maybe one day you'll find one who you want to call husband."

Selina sighed and sat back down, taking both Jaelle's hands.

"How many times do we have to go over this?" Selina studied her for a long moment before something in her eyes hardened. "We don't need a man to get us out of Terrefantome. We don't need the Maker." She leaned forward and forced Jaelle to meet her gaze. "I promise you this, little sister. I am going to do whatever I can to get you out of here forever. And we are going to be happy. Just us. No one else to hold us back or tell us what we can't do or hurt us ever again." She kissed Jaelle's forehead before letting go.

But before she could turn toward the tavern, the foot traffic, which had been light as they'd talked, changed from a crawl to a run. Women shouted at their children to hurry, and men prodded their animals along with all sorts of colorful language.

"Judith?" Selina called out to the woman who lived half a mile from them. "What's going on?"

Judith, a skinny woman with a sallow face and sharp chin, turned to face them, her skin an unusual shade of white.

"Taistille have been spotted not a mile east of town!" she called as she dragged her two sons by their ears.

"Go!" Selina practically shoved Jaelle back onto the street. "And don't wait up for me tonight!"

Jaelle didn't have to be told twice. She wove her way in and out of people until she reached the familiar grass knoll. Still, even as she hurried from the town, she wished with every step that just as she'd escaped the predators a few minutes before, her sister could leave the tavern behind forever.

And, she promised herself as she reached the front door, she, too, would do whatever it took. She and her sister would leave Terrefantome forever. No more Chiara or Taistille. No more men who crept through the streets looking for unclaimed women. And never again would either of them work a tavern job. Because when she and her sister finally did leave, they would never look back.

CHAPTER 3

MASK

As she stepped inside the house, Jaelle let out a shaky breath. Her resolution on the steps, however, added the bounce back into Jaelle's step as she dropped the package of ham on the table, along with Selina's coins. After glancing around to make sure her stepmother didn't see, she ran to the room she shared with Selina and put the rest of the coins in one of Selina's stockings. It was an odd hiding place, but the only one that Chiara hadn't discovered yet. Then she put her apron on and grabbed her scissors and herb basket. Before she could escape to the quiet solitude of the little garden behind the cottage, though, she found herself in the hall, face to face with her stepmother.

"That took an awfully long time." Chiara looked Jaelle up and down carefully.

"I ran into some men," Jaelle said, holding her stepmother's gaze. Any normal woman in Terrefantome, stepmother or not, would have been terrified by such a statement. Jaelle had talked enough with the other girls in the town to know that much. But Chiara was not a normal woman.

"Did you get the ham?"

Jaelle pointed to the package on the table, wishing very much to slap the satisfied look off her stepmother's face. But her intentions must have been clear in the set of her shoulders because

Chiara grabbed Jaelle's chin and leaned down until she was inches from Jaelle's nose.

"Before you get defiant with me, girl, let me remind you that I am the reason those men left you alone today. If it weren't for my protection, you would have been long gone with them by now."

"Selina protected me," Jaelle snapped. "You weren't there."

"And they let you go for the same reason they leave Selina alone at the tavern." Chiara leaned in closer. "All I have to do is give the word, and your world will come crashing down."

Jaelle yanked her face out of Chiara's grasp. "You won't do that. You need me too much." She allowed herself a smirk as Chiara's face turned red. "And my herbs." She nodded at her stepmother's withered hand. "You'll also need a good deal of luck setting bones with only one good hand."

"Don't get smart with—" But before Chiara could finish her threat, someone banged on the door.

"What is it?" Chiara bellowed.

"My arm!" A man's raspy voice replied. "A log fell on it."

"Jaelle!" Chiara snapped, but Jaelle was already moving, grabbing supplies from the medicine cart. Chiara let him in, and Jaelle helped him up on the long wooden table her father had hewn out for patients. While Chiara prepared her supplies, Jaelle set to cutting the man's sleeve from his arm and rolling it back for Chiara to see.

Chiara studied the arm for a moment before poking it in several places, making the poor man cry out. Finally, she stood back and nodded once to herself.

"Not badly broken. Won't need surgery for this one." She looked up at the man. "How much do you have?"

A bead of sweat rolled down his face as he used his good arm to fish several coins out of his pocket. Chiara snatched then up and counted them. "You're a bold one, coming here with this." She chuckled.

"It's all I've got." The man wheezed.

"And if that's true, I'm sure my daughter will be able to tell me that you're never seen frequenting the tavern?" Chiara smiled.

The man stared at her for a minute before finding a silver coin in another pocket. Chiara nodded to herself smugly as she took the coin and rolled up her own sleeve.

"No spirits for this one, Jaelle. He doesn't seem to want them."

Jaelle looked at the man's face again, which was turning a funny shade of green. She vacillated for a moment, as Chiara slowly made her way around the room, looking for her gloves. Jaelle knew what she wanted to do...what she should do, but if her stepmother saw, Jaelle would probably lose her supper. When the man let out a groan, however, Jaelle's decision was made.

"Where is the rag?" Chiara called as Jaelle darted back out to the garden.

"Coming!" Jaelle called back as she snatched a rag from the line where it had been hung to dry. On her way back to the front room, she took a bottle of wine from her father's old stash and splashed the rag with it. Hopefully, not enough for Chiara to smell, but enough to distract the man from Chiara's work.

As soon as she was in the main room again, she shoved the rag in the man's mouth. "Bite down hard," she told him.

Jaelle always hated working with Chiara, which was sad, considering how much she had loved working alongside her father. Perhaps it was because Chiara wouldn't touch a patient unless they had money. Or maybe because it felt, on more than one occasion, as though all Chiara had ever wanted was to replace Jaelle's father, to erase him from the memories of all those he'd helped. And in six years, she had done just that. His medical tools, this table, the house, even their patients, now all belonged to the cruel woman beside her. And no one even questioned it.

The man grunted, bringing Jaelle back to the present. Jaelle fought to tie his arm to the table so he couldn't jerk it while Chiara moved it back into place. As she wrestled him down, his shirt moved enough for her to see the rough tattoo of a sword on the side of his neck.

Traitor to the crown.

Jaelle shuddered then tightened her grip when Chiara gave her a look. Sometimes, especially when their patients were in pain, it was easy to forget they were here because they had committed some heinous crime. Her father's tattoo had been one of a snake with fangs...venom that killed. She remembered little about her mother, but she did recall how much her mother had hated that tattoo.

The man let out a little cry even through the rag, but soon after that, the resetting was done. Chiara turned away, dusted her hands off, and took a drink from the wineskin she'd brought in with her. Her stringy copper hair stuck to her face as she shuffled past Jaelle toward the door. But before she stepped out, Chiara grabbed Jaelle by the shoulder with her good arm and pulled her close.

"Don't think I missed that wine," she hissed as the man got himself off the table with another moan. "That'll be a ham supper that you'll skip for defying me."

Jaelle yanked her shoulder away and stalked out to her garden. But just as she paused to open the back door, she heard the man speak again.

"Have you ever seen her face? I haven't seen many women as old as she is still wearing one."

"When she was very young," came her stepmother's reply. "Her father gave her the mask just after I married him. But if she's anything like her father, which I think she is, she'll not be much to look at."

"I bet she's decent, or he wouldn't have put the mask on her in the first place." The man made a clicking sound with his tongue. "Her figure's fine."

"Well," her stepmother huffed, "if you're looking for an obedient wife, she's not the one. Now get out of my house."

Jaelle didn't stay to hear any more. For while she was glad that her stepmother wouldn't allow her to go to someone like this man, she wondered how she would manage to escape her grasp when the time came to leave.

CHAPTER 4

SEHF

Kneeling in the middle of her little herb patch, Jaelle began pulling weeds with violent fury. She'd been resolute that morning that she and her sister would find a way to escape. But now a new fire burned in her soul that refused to be quenched.

If they stayed, Jaelle would work under Chiara until she, too, was middle aged and bitter, waiting for her mistress to die. Either that, or Chiara would eventually feel threatened enough and give her to the person who offered the highest bid. The marshals were supposed to stop such auctions, as they were illegal, but Chiara had the entire town wrapped around her finger. No marshal in his right mind would offend the only healer in the region.

But no. Jaelle yanked another root out of the ground. That wouldn't be her. She wouldn't let it. She refused to be the broken toy that was discarded as soon as its shine wore off the way her doll's painted face had faded from all her hugs when she was little. She was going to find a way to leave if it killed her. Because being in Terrefantome was like a long, painful death itself.

The longer she spent in the garden, however, the more regular Jaelle's breathing became, and the gentler she was with her beloved plants. There weren't many birds nearby, and the landscape surrounding their little hill, one of gray sky, swamp, and fields of mud didn't make for a particularly pleasing landscape.

But there was something soothing in weeding and cutting her herbs. Bees buzzed to and fro as they landed on the leaves and petals, and a gentle breeze made her lavender stalks wave. Their sweet, savory scents allowed her to close her eyes and pretend her father might come through the cottage's back door, muttering to himself about how he needed to fix the roof.

Two mice scampered out from beneath a large leaf, making Jaelle jump. With her jump came a flash of inspiration. Since Seth wouldn't be escorting them the way they had originally planned, she and Selina would have to hire someone to travel with them. Young women were as good as claimed the moment they tried to leave their protectors. Of course, they could draw on their wrists to make themselves look marked. But if their trick was discovered, they could be thrown in prison...with the men. And if they were caught on the road by themselves, it might not matter whether they had a protector. Chiara only held the power she did because so few healers resided in Terrefantome.

But what if two could work that grindstone? Jaelle could heal as well as her stepmother, better even. The only reason she didn't was because her stepmother was already known as the only healer around for miles, and she'd have a conniption if Jaelle tried to take that from her.

Or...maybe that time was coming to an end. Jaelle's hands worked faster as she considered possibilities. What if there was a way...There had to be a way to heal on her own, where Chiara couldn't see. If Jaelle charged less than her stepmother, she might be able to find work here and there. Not enough to make her stepmother suspicious. But maybe one or two people a day. Selina would be able to help her figure something out, she was sure. She could earn back the money Seth had taken from them and more within the year. Chiara had been getting greedy lately in raising her fees, and there were many who were unable to afford her. Jaelle could take over for the poorer people easily. She wouldn't even need that many tools. She knew where her father had put his old set in the barn.

Spurred on by this thought, Jaelle got up, dusted her hands off on her skirt, and headed to the barn. Only twenty yards from the house, it wasn't a big barn, not by farming standards. All it had space for was a cow—although they hadn't had one since theirs had been stolen the year before—a goat, six chickens, a rooster, and the old calico cat that had come to live with them last spring. Jaelle hadn't told anyone about him.

She had to use both hands to slide the door to the side. Usually, she would have done a cursory glance around the barn to make sure there weren't any ragamuffins hiding out in the loft with the hay. But today, her elation made her careless. And she regretted it the moment the door slid shut behind her and her eyes adjusted to the dark.

A handsome middle-aged woman with sharp features and a young man stood in the corner of the barn, a single lit candle between them. Or rather, the woman stood. The young man lay in the goat's pile of hay. A sheen of sweat covered his face, and his breathing was labored. Both were dressed in swaths of fabric in bright blues, purples, and oranges, and the woman wore dozens of rings, necklaces, and bracelets. A scythe hung from her hip.

"Jaelle," the woman said, "we need your help." Then she squinted and leaned in closer. "You look a lot like your father."

Jaelle just stood there, her mouth hanging open like a fish. There were two Taistille in her barn, and one of them knew her name. Whatever she had been expecting to find, it certainly hadn't been this.

"You know my name," she whispered. Then a wave of panic struck her. Her hands flew to her face.

"Don't worry. Your mask is still in place." The woman rolled her dark, beautiful eyes.

"Then how can you see my face?"

The woman gave her a hard smile. "My dear, who do you think makes those masks? It certainly isn't your *hoht* people." She spat, and Jaelle winced at the crass term. "Your father approached me when you were young and asked for a mask. In return, he gave us medical assistance." She paused and studied Jaelle. "You don't believe me, do you?"

Jaelle was frozen to the spot, still trying to grasp the fact that there were two Taistille people in her barn.

"Tell me, girl," the woman said, "how many times have the Taistille come to your village since you were born?"

Jaelle decided it would be safer to play along. "Four," she squeaked. Four awful times. The village had been ransacked, and much of it had been set on fire. Bodies of men had lain in the streets by the dozen. Her father and then Chiara had received more patients on those days than ever before.

Jaelle shook her head to clear it. "My...um, my father died three years ago."

"And it is out of respect for his memory that your house has never been touched."

Jaelle frowned, trying to sort it all out in her head. But the more she thought, the more she realized the woman most likely spoke the truth. Jaelle had always assumed their house had been spared because they lived on a little hill on the outskirts of town, but when she thought about it that way...

"Your father told me that he was training you in the arts of healing," the woman said. "So I have come to ask your help just the same as I did him."

Jaelle was reminded of the sick young man at the woman's feet. With her heart pounding in her stomach, she took a few timid steps forward, just close enough to see him better.

Dried blood caked the poorly wrapped bandage that covered his right shin. The color of the blood meant that the wound must have been several days old. Jaelle's heart fell when she realized how infected his wound must really be. Dangerous or not, he needed help. Before she had time to consider the wisdom of her actions, she was kneeling at his side.

"I'll need someone to distract my stepmother," she said as she examined his exposed skin. "She'll be suspicious if I go in for supplies." She was already calculating which supplies she would need and how much she could take from their stash without her stepmother noticing. The bandage cloths she'd rolled the week before, at least two. A bottle of wine for soaking. Several of the herbs and a mortar and pestle.

The woman smiled widely before clicking her tongue. Jaelle nearly fell over from fright when a little boy sprang from the horse stall behind her. He ran up to the woman, and after she had whispered something in his ear, he grinned and scampered off into the evening.

"My stepmother is not a kind woman," Jaelle said as she began to slowly unwrap the bloodied bandage. "If she catches him—"

"I suggest you worry about what you're going to do for my son, while I take care of your stepmother," the woman said.

Jaelle nodded and finished unwrapping the bandage. Just as she'd feared, the skin surrounding the three-inch cut was red and hot to the touch. The wound itself was unusually deep.

"How long has he had this?" she asked.

"It happened two days ago." The woman pursed her lips and frowned down at the young man. "We've tried to treat it, but none of my healers have been successful, as you can tell."

"All right." Jaelle wiped her hands on her apron, running through a list of the herbs she would need for such a wound. "Just tell me when I can go."

Not a minute later, Chiara shrieked. Jaelle opened the barn door and peeked out to see her stepmother in her nightdress, running about in the rain that must have just begun. She was slapping her hair so hard that Jaelle nearly gave them away with a laugh.

"What's wrong with her hair?" she whispered as she continued to watch in amazement.

"My grandson is particularly fond of frogs." The Taistille woman eyed Jaelle. "You should go now."

Jaelle nodded and darted through the rain into the cottage. She knelt before the supply cart and began to toss tools and herbs in her basket, along with rolled bandages, a mortar and pestle, water, and a jar filled with sap. Then she went to the garden and gathered the herbs she would need. When this was done, she could still hear Chiara's screams, so she dared to fetch a bottle of bitter wine as well before running back out to the barn.

Her skin prickled again when she knelt beside him. Though she and her neighbors were hardly on friendly terms, there was little to bring the village together like the threat of the Taistille. What if the young man didn't survive her treatment? What if he was already too far gone, and they blamed her? She worked to steady her hands as she poured some of the wine on his leg. He had ceased most of his movements and seemed to be in a state of light sleep. But as

43

soon as the wine touched him, he let out a cry. His mother muffled his mouth with a rag.

"My father was a physician," Jaelle said slowly as she walked to the nearest lantern and stuck the needle inside. "I learned by watching him. Not in a room of students."

The woman drew her eyebrows together. "Are you saying you cannot help my son?"

"No! No, I just...I wish I had seen him sooner. The wound grows worse with each day it waits to be treated." She picked up the little bucket of water and poured it over the wound, making the young man groan. Jaelle apologized and offered him a swig of the wine before pouring it over the wound once more.

What she did not tell this fierce woman as she worked was that this was her first time stitching up a gash on her own. Her father had taught her and supervised her once or twice, and she'd watched Chiara countless times when men had stumbled in at odd hours of the night after some drunken altercation at the tavern. But now her heart was beating so fast it felt like it might burst through her chest as she began to stitch.

"How did he injure it?" she asked, needing something to keep her mind off of what she was doing.

"It was raining, and one of the wagons became stuck in a muddy rut just outside Caidston. Fool boy tried to lift it out himself, though all the men told him not to. He slipped and landed on a sharp rock."

"Good." Jaelle nodded and pulled the light closer to see better.

"You're glad he fell?"

"I mean it's good that it was a rock rather than a work blade or weapon." Jaelle wiped her forehead with her sleeve. "The cut could have been far worse."

"Tell me," the woman said, her eyes glittering in the light of the lamp, "how did your father come to be branded here? He doesn't seem the kind of crass *hoht* the other kingdoms usually send our way."

It was a bold question, one that, when asked under the influence of wine, caused no small number of fights in the tavern, Selina said. But Jaelle didn't mind.

"My father was a practicing physician in a small town in Giova, where we lived with my mother while she was still alive. There was a wealthy woman who lived in that same town, and my father treated her for the loss of her voice." Jaelle pursed her lips for a minute while she studied the leg as the wine drained off. "It should have been simple. Just a few days of an herbal tea without talking. But too late, my father discovered that she hadn't simply lost her voice."

"What was it?"

"She had a tumor in her throat. My father thinks—He thought it was from all the snuff she took, but her husband didn't care. He had powerful friends, and after she died, he made sure my father was sent here."

The woman muttered something about *hohts* and their heathen bribery, and Jaelle couldn't help wondering how she had come to tell the woman so much in such a short amount of time. Even this morning, whispers of this group of Taistille had sent shivers up her spine. And yet, as she sat here, stitching up the leg of one of their young men, she conversed with his mother in a way she'd never conversed with her own stepmother.

A few minutes later, it was wrapped and nearly ready to go. Jaelle paused and looked at the young man. Now that her eyes had better adjusted to the dark of the barn and its one torch, which the woman must have brought, she could see that he was even younger than she had thought, perhaps only thirteen or fourteen years of age. She hesitated before digging in her basket one more time.

"Give this to him when he wakes up," she said, pressing the small, round cake into her hand.

The woman frowned down at it. "What kind of treatment is this?"

"Pastry," she said with a smile. "My sister got it for me, but I think he needs it more."

"What for?"

Jaelle paused. "To make him smile." She looked down at the boy's face. "It will be a while before he gets to play again."

"How old were you when you came here?" the woman asked, studying Jaelle even more.

"I was two years. I don't remember living anywhere else." She pulled out her jar of pine sap.

"That is a shame."

Jaelle looked up, surprised at the sentiment.

The woman gave a humorless chuckle and stood before stretching. "This land was created for my people. Or perhaps my people were created for this land. We are fierce and wild. But flowers like you..." She shook her head, and her voice softened. "You were not meant to be here. You see the world differently. And that is a gift."

In a moment of insanity, Jaelle cleared her throat. "Do you... would you be able to take my sister and me to the gate?"

But the woman was already shaking her head. "I wish we could, little flower. But we're forbidden by your so-called king from nearing the gates." She stood a little taller. "Of course, we could force our way there. But getting you to the gate would attract far more attention than you would have otherwise. And the moment you stepped out of our protection, you'd be snatched up just because it was us who delivered you." She gave Jaelle a small, sad smile. "I'm sorry."

"I understand." Jaelle nodded, trying to ignore the sudden stinging in her eyes, stinging that was brought about by stupid, premature hope. But before she could embarrass herself further, something made a sound outside. Jaelle rushed to finish her work, and the woman grasped her scythe, which Jaelle prayed she wouldn't decide to use while Jaelle was nearby.

"How will you get him out?" she whispered as she hurried to check his bandage once more. The poor boy had passed out and was lying on the pile of hay like someone dead.

"I'll carry him on my back."

"But surely he's too heavy!"

"I am strong." The woman came back from the door after whistling out several times into the rain.

Jaelle wanted to argue further, but instead, she began gathering her supplies. "The sap from pines is good for stopping infections. Rinse the wound with clean water three times a day and put sap on the bandage before wrapping it again. The fever should break soon." At least, she prayed it would.

In response, the woman pulled on a leather thong that hung about her neck until it snapped. Then she pressed a circle of leather into Jaelle's hand. Calloused fingers closed her own fingers over it.

"If you are ever in need of assistance, I want you to find a Taistille troop and tell them you need it sent to the sehf."

Jaelle gave a start and studied her guests with eyes anew.

"You mean..." She swallowed. "You're the Taistille *sehf*?" The most powerful and feared Taistille chief in Terrefantome was in Jaelle's barn?

The woman squatted and pulled her son's arms around her neck. Then she stood slowly, lifting him ever so gently, and walked to the barn door. Before she pushed it open, however, she looked back at Jaelle.

"You have saved my son's life. The troops may squabble, but they all know my crest and obey my orders. Send that to me, and you'll never be forgotten." Then she walked out into the night, and Jaelle was left alone.

CHAPTER 5
BLESS US

Jaelle had nearly made it to the room she shared with Selina when a voice behind her made her jump. She turned to find her stepmother holding a candle. Her eyes glittered in the light of the flame.

"Would you like to explain why some of my supplies are missing?" She stepped closer. "And where have you been all evening?"

Jaelle stiffened. "Someone needed help. And you were...preoccupied."

"Preoccupied. Oh, you mean by the gift someone left in my hair?" She held the candle higher. "Was that you, too?"

"No! I hate frogs! You know that."

Chiara smiled. "I never said it was a frog, but thank you for clearing up that little misunderstanding."

Jaelle wanted to kick herself. So much for her secret. She closed her eyes and spoke slowly. "I didn't put the frog there."

"But you know who did, and you helped them, obviously. Free of charge, I'm assuming, which means you stole money from me as well."

"They're my supplies, too! I work just as hard on them, if not harder!"

"As long as you're living under my roof—"

"It's my roof, in case you forgot!" Jaelle shouted. "I lived here

49

before you ever did! I planted that garden, and my father and I treated the people you snub!"

"You mean the ones that can't afford my care but can buy brandy? You ungrateful wretch!" Chiara's voice was rising fast. Her graying red hair stuck out in every direction, making her look like a banshee from children's stories in the flickering light of the flame. "Since your father died, do you know how hard I've worked to rise to the level of protector for you and my daughter? Do you know how difficult that is for a woman?"

"You mean so you can barter with us and our labor?"

"One daughter is hard enough to protect. I don't need you making it worse!"

Maybe it was her frustration about the confrontation with the men that emboldened Jaelle. Or perhaps the taste of compassion she'd gotten from the Taistille woman. Or maybe the way Chiara had spoken to her patient about Jaelle as if she weren't human enough to understand. Whatever it was, Jaelle still felt fear for what her stepmother could do to her, but not enough to bow in submission. Not this time. And the words were out of her mouth before she could regret those, too.

"You married him for the land, didn't you?"

"Shut up!" Chiara shrieked.

But Jaelle was too caught up in saying what she had longed to say for years to listen. "You married my father because you saw that his would be a stable income. No matter who commits crimes, everyone needs a healer. And when he died, you would be able to take over for him. And you did! But you still have one problem!"

"You're right in that," Chiara growled. "And I'm now considering pruning that problem like I should have long ago."

Jaelle's blood began to race. She was fast moving into territory she had never dared cross into.

"You wouldn't."

"I could, and the crown wouldn't care a whit. You might think you have rights here, but no matter what your fool of a father told you, you belong to me."

"Without me, you have no free labor. No one here knows how to heal or use herbs like I do. You also have a lame foot and a lame hand. Do you wish to use those on your own?" Jaelle straightened.

"Besides, Selina would never forgive you." What was wrong with her? Jaelle was shocked at the words that were still flowing from her. Where was this confidence coming from? Her success in treating the Taistille woman's son? The leather medallion hidden in her belt?

"You're right," Chiara said, jabbing a bony finger at the girls' bedroom door. "And she's the only reason I've allowed you to stay here for as long as I have." She straightened her shoulders and held the candle higher. "But cross me again, and you'll be out in the streets for anyone who wants you before you can blink. Where are you going? I'm not finished with you!"

"I'm finished with you."

"Don't you walk away from me!"

Jaelle turned and glared at her stepmother.

"Watch me."

Then she resumed her march to her bedroom, where she slammed her door shut before collapsing against it, shaking.

What had possessed her to speak to her stepmother like that? Since the day her father had married Chiara, Jaelle had wished to tell her stepmother what she really thought of her. But she had always kept her tongue before. What had brought on her explosion now? All she needed was another year before she and Selina were gone.

And yet, she hadn't been able to wait.

Tears ran down her face, and with shaking hands, she felt under the bed until she found her beloved book. Clutching it to her chest, she sobbed and curled up against the door.

"And if I catch you alone with a patient again," came Chiara's muffled shout, "I'll make sure you leave with them as well!"

SOMETIME LATER, after the candle had burned itself out, Jaelle woke up to find herself in bed. She couldn't remember actually moving to the bed, nor did she remember getting under the covers. All she could recall was her argument with Chiara.

Her questions were answered, though, when she felt cool

fingers brush the hair out of her face, and Jaelle huddled against her sister for warmth. The room they shared was the coldest in the house, and they needed another blanket for proper heat.

"You had quite a day, didn't you?" Selina's low, melodic voice broke the dark quiet of the room. "I was barely able to get in when you fell asleep in front of the door."

"I got into an argument with her." Jaelle rubbed her eyes and groaned. "What was I thinking?"

"You weren't." Still, there was a smile in Selina's words even as she spoke. Moonlight streamed through the window, and Jaelle could see Selina's hand move from brushing her hair to rear-ranging their blankets. "She was still furious when I got home, and she told me all about it." Selina chuckled. "I have to say, I'm proud of you."

Jaelle shook her head. "I was being stupid."

"You were standing up for yourself. Now, morning will come soon enough. It's time to get some sleep."

As soon as Selina said the word, Jaelle was half-conscious again, as though she had needed to be reminded of just how tired she was. Still, there was something nipping at the back of her mind, something she was supposed to tell Selina.

"I have a plan," Jaelle yawned.

"A plan for what, love?"

"To get us out of here," Jaelle said sleepily.

"As do I."

Jaelle turned to look at her sister, but Selina pushed her back down onto the thin pillow. "Sleep now, and leave it all up to me. I decided today that I'm going to get you out of this place sooner rather than later." Her voice hardened just slightly, but not enough for Jaelle to make much sense of it. "No matter what anyone says, you're leaving here, and fast." She kissed the top of Jaelle's head. "I promise."

Jaelle began to do as her sister said. Then she remembered something.

"Selina?"

"Hm?"

"I've been thinking lately…"

"About what?" Selina sounded like she was already beginning to doze off.

"The holy man that used to visit my father and me before your mother brought you here, the one that gave me the book."

"As if there were lots of holy men all over Terrefantome." Selina sounded rather smug for being so tired.

But Jaelle continued.

"He used to say that the Maker always has a purpose in everything. Even the bad things. And that he used them to somehow bless his children." She paused. "Do you...do you think that's true? That maybe he could use all this to bless us one day?"

Selina rolled over again with a huff.

"Your holy man told you that, did he?"

"More than once."

"Well, first of all, the Maker's not going to be blessing *me* with any of it because he doesn't exist. Second, see how well your holy man's philosophy worked out for *him*." Selina snorted. "Go to sleep, Jaelle. You've got me, and I've got you. And we don't need anyone or anything else. They'll just get in our way." She lifted her head off the pillow. "Imaginary or not."

Jaelle didn't say anything more after that. Instead, she put her head against her sister's shoulder and tried to fall asleep.

CHAPTER 6

ALONE

The first set of gates towered over Lucas's party, large and white as they approached it. He'd seen the gates from afar, of course, as they were nearly in sight of the palace's higher towers. But never had he come so close. He'd never had a reason to.

The gates were unusually narrow, just wide enough for two men to pass through at a time, and they were forty feet tall. Bars ran across the doors as well. Lucas didn't dare touch them, but he could just make out steel burrs that covered the bars. They looked sharp enough to pierce even the toughest old sailor's calloused hand or even leather gloves. He'd briefly wondered before how so few criminals had ever escaped Terrefantome, but now he had an idea.

The guard behind him gave him a shove to the shoulder. Lucas turned and gave the man a look, but the man only barked for him to go faster. It was all for show, of course. Lucas and the three escorts Michael had found to guide him through Terrefantome were being brought in as prisoners. It would look suspicious, the guides had told Michael, if they simply waltzed in and went about their business. There were a number of men, and even women, working for their masters, who always sat near the gates and waited for unsuspecting newcomers to arrive. Those who weren't familiar with the ways of the land and its people were easy targets, and these thieves often took much of what the newcomers brought with them to their new home. And yet, as bad as this might be, it would be even worse, Michael and Lucas were told, for someone to figure out who Lucas really was or what he was doing. The general consensus was that newcomers in were bad enough, more people to fight over the few resources the land provided. Someone from the outside who didn't have to be there might as well resign himself to a hard life, often sprinkled with suffering and pain.

As this was not the end Lucas was hoping for, he and Michael had agreed it would be best to pose as prisoners, complete with false tattoos, bindings, guards, and absolutely no communication, save the shell Arianna had given him for emergencies. Once they were through the gates, Lucas and his guides would be on their own.

Papers, false, of course, were checked at the first gate. Then again at the second gate, which was even taller than the first, and once more at the third, which was twice the height of the first, matched only by the wall that surrounded Terrefantome in its entirety. The air grew wetter and wetter as they moved through the gates, and gravel beneath their feet gleamed wet and grimy, as though they were walking on something far dirtier than dirt. Lucas made a mental note to burn these boots when he got home.

The guard at the third gate grunted as he read their charge papers, detailing their criminal pasts, then looked back up at Lucas and his companions before nodding at the final guard.

Lucas glanced at his guides as the guard moved to unlock the third gate. Brudneck, a thick man in his early fourth decade, stared ahead, a look of stone on his angled face. Harry, the man closest in height and build to Lucas, snapped quietly at Zed, their youngest member, to stop shaking and be a man.

"This is a mistake," Zed hissed back, his eyes welded to the final gate. "I never should have agreed to come back. My mum would roll over in her—"

"It's too late to think about that now." Harry scowled. "Best focus on how to get out of this place alive."

"Both of you," Lucas hissed, "that's enough."

"And you," Brudneck said, turning to Lucas, his gray eyes dark, "Don't let those well-bred manners leak out here."

Lucas gave a curt nod as they were roughly pushed into a line. Then each one, starting with Brudneck, was shoved through a strange metal contraption that turned only in one direction. And when it was his turn, Lucas caught his breath as he spilled out into the strange new land.

The sun had been shining when he'd reached the other side of the gate, low enough in the sky to set within an hour. It would be best to arrive when the crowds were thinning, Brudneck had told them, when the city dwellers were too tired to be looking at the new arrivals. But the deep yellow sky was nowhere to be found. Instead, a thick blanket of gray clouds stretched as far as Lucas could see.

His gawking was interrupted, though, when he was jostled from behind as Zed nearly landed on top of him. Brudneck gave them a look of annoyance, then after consulting quietly with Harry, nodded to the right. Lucas followed silently, though it wasn't without internal protest. He was used to leading, or at least, being in the know with those who were. Following blindly was painful, and it set him on edge. Not that he had much of a choice.

They'd only been able to contact five individuals who had left Terrefantome, and as one of them was a woman and the other was an old man, he'd been left with three guides, rather than the four Michael had wanted. But with Bartol's deadline looming, Lucas had convinced Michael to let him go with the three men willing to act as guides.

Now he just hoped they were as loyal as they'd claimed to be when they were hired. Lucas could only guess Michael's hefty sums of payment might have inflated their confidence when they were asked about their knowledge of the land.

For each of the three gates that dotted different parts of the wall, Lucas had been told, there was a city built up against it on the inside. And this particular city was larger than Lucas had expected. Many of those who had been banished, Harry said, had learned that the newcomers would need supplies, food, and a place to stay, and they were only too willing to provide all that for a price. The buildings were mostly made of mud, which had been laid on criss-crossed log frames. Though some of the buildings were impressive in height, with a few of the inns reaching five stories and a few of the other buildings sprawling out in multiple directions, there was little in the way of beauty. Many of the smaller mud huts had sloppy little gardens, but Lucas could not spot a single flower.

"There's an understanding between merchants," Harry had told Lucas on the way to the city, "that once inside the establishments...inns and such, the new customers are to be left alone. It's a way for them to ensure income of some kind on a regular basis. If there's too much crime, any potential gold will flee town." He'd pushed some of his floppy brown hair out of his eyes. "Whereas, if they feel safe in the buildings, they're more likely to stay for days or even weeks."

"And when they're not in the buildings?" Lucas had pressed.

Harry had grinned, revealing more than a few missing teeth. It wasn't pleasant. "Anyone's game."

Now, as they made their way away from the gate, which sat at the corner of the city, Lucas kept a wary watch out for those who might consider him game. He lightly felt for the knife in his belt, hidden under his coat, and he took comfort in the pressure of two more in his boots. He had his sword, of course, but he would prefer not to reveal that to everyone. At least not yet.

As they rounded a corner, darkness falling steadily around them, Lucas came to a halt. Brudneck and Harry had already stopped. When Zed joined them, the way he whimpered made Lucas wonder if he might faint.

Three men blocked their path. In the failing light, Lucas thought he was able to make out the tattoo on the first man's neck as a circle with a crooked line through it. Attempted murder. He couldn't see what the other two men wore, but he guessed they weren't unfamiliar with violence, either way.

"Do we have ourselves a group of friends?" the first one asked in a low voice.

Brudneck held up a hand. "We don't want your territory. We just want to move on through and out of the city."

Harry let out a cry and fell to the ground, holding his hand over his left eye. Lucas heard a sound to his left and ducked just as something went whizzing past his ear. Zed let out a cry, too, though Lucas couldn't actually tell if he'd been injured or was just frightened. Brudneck had already engaged with the man he'd been speaking with. Lucas couldn't tell who was winning, though, because two new men were moving at him.

He fell into a ready stance and waited for the first to throw a punch. The men were large and their hands meaty, from what he could see, but they were also slow. With almost no difficulty, Lucas knocked one to the ground. The other was faster, but as long as Lucas stayed out of his grasp, he would be fine. As they hadn't yet disappeared, they were probably recent arrivals as well.

A shout from Brudneck distracted him as he was knocking his opponent's teeth loose with a knee to the jaw. He must not have used enough force, though, for the moment he stopped to see Brudneck's opponent throw him to the ground, Lucas's man grabbed his ankle and twisted. Lucas went down, rolling until he was upright enough again to return the gesture. The man jumped back and held up a huge knife, but he was too late. Lucas had already pulled his own.

"Stop!" he barked. They all turned to stare at him as he held his blade against the man's jugular. He spoke slowly and clearly, staring down both of the men who were still conscious. "We don't want trouble. All we want to do is pass."

The big man bending over Brudneck made a sudden move with his hand. Lucas expected him to try something, however, and was faster, yanking the man he was holding in front of him. The throwing blade stuck fast in the man's shoulder, and he shouted as Lucas let him fall to the ground and gathered up a petrified Zed, pulled Harry over his shoulder, and motioned for Brudneck to lead them on. Brudneck didn't hesitate, and for the first time, Zed didn't fall behind.

They ran through twilight and into the night, until they were out of the city and into the edge of the woods. Brudneck didn't let them rest though, forcing them to use the light of the hazy moonlight pushing through the clouds. They searched until he found a low ridge beside a creek at the bottom of a hill that was full of fallen trees the perfect size to serve as seats.

"We'll sleep here tonight," Brudneck announced, tossing down his pack.

Lucas followed suit, and soon they had the smallest of fires going, just large enough to warm stones to put in their sleeping sacks.

Harry came to his senses not long after they made camp, and when he was told what had happened, seemed rather put out that he'd missed the entire fight. Once he'd recovered, they sat around the fire, chewing on the biscuits and dried meat the palace kitchen had sent. Lucas had a million questions to ask about what he'd seen in the city, but he dared not speak until Brudneck broke the silence.

"That was impressive back there," he said in low voice, glancing at Lucas. "Before I saw you fight, I honestly wondered at the sanity of your brother."

"What do you mean?" Lucas asked.

"No offense, but for most men of your rank, being sent into a place like this would be a death sentence."

Lucas gave him a wry smile. "Years of war will teach you a few tricks." Then he paused. "Do you think they'll follow us?"

Harry shrugged as he unwrapped a second biscuit. "Who knows? Most stay in their territory so no one else claims it. But every once in a while, they stray if they think the reward will be good enough. Zed, what's wrong with you? Why do you look like a ghoul is haunting you?"

Zed shook his head at his untouched meat. "I should never have done this."

Brudneck turned and frowned at him. "You act as though you haven't been here a day in your life."

"It's been a while," Zed snapped.

"How long?" Harry pressed. "And on that thought, how old are you?"

Zed pressed his lips into a thin line as he reached up to worry the mustache he'd grown in an effort to blend in. It looked more like a caterpillar than anything else, but Lucas waited for his answer. Why was the man always so terrified?

"I'm twenty years," Zed said, glaring at the fire. "And I haven't been here in twelve."

Harry choked on his food, and it was a moment before he could speak. When he did, his voice was pitched high, and he kept having to stop to cough.

"You mean...you haven't been here since...you were eight?"

"No wonder you're useless," Brudneck muttered, shaking his head.

Lucas refrained from commenting, but deep down, he was groaning as well. He was rather sure that if Zed had divulged that little detail, Michael wouldn't have allowed him to go.

"I'm not useless," the young man muttered at his food. Then he turned to Lucas. "Besides, that reminds me, I meant to ask you something."

"Yes?" Lucas kept his face neutral.

"If you're going to pay Bartol, where's your money?" His thin face went white. "You didn't drop it back there, did you? Because if you dropped it, and those thugs find it, when Bartol finds us—"

"There's no need to panic," Lucas said, the way he might talk to his horse when it was frightened. "It's my job to pay him, and it's yours to get me there and back."

"That's right." Brudneck stood and pulled a few of the stones away from the fire and dropped them down his sleeping sack. "Another lesson of Terrefantome, in case you weren't paying attention the first time, mind your own business. Doing anything else will get you killed."

Soon, they decided to sleep. Lucas took the first watch, then after midnight, Harry replaced him. Lucas felt guilty as he got in his sleep sack. He didn't trust the men like he did his own sailors at home, and he had a sudden ache for their company. Or even more, his brother's. He purposefully ignored the third ache, which smelled like perfume and had eyes of blue and hair of gold.

Still, wish as he might for a familiar face that he could trust, he had to sleep sometime during this venture, as it would be at least two weeks long, and they had no longer than four until the deadline expired. He might as well do his best to sleep as much as he could in the shortest amount of time. He sensed they had a long journey ahead of them, and as he dozed off, he prayed that the Maker would grant them safety and time. Because if he failed, everything would be lost.

LUCAS STRETCHED in his sleep sack, already regretting that he would have to leave the warmth of the blankets. The ground here was cold and soggy, but the sleep sack had been made of some of the finest, supplest leather in the land, specifically for situations like this. And he'd slept better than he'd expected for his first night in this strange, new place. As soon as he opened his eyes to the gray light surrounding him, however, his heart nearly stopped.

"Brudneck?" he called in a low voice, slowly getting to his feet. "Harry? Zed?" But no answers came. Not only did he not get an answer, all signs of his companions were gone, too. The sleep sacks and even the circle of stones they'd used for the fire was gone. When Lucas dug into the ground, he was able, much to his relief, to at least feel the warmth in the sand from the fire that had been there. They couldn't have left him too long ago if the ground was that warm.

But after searching for hours, Lucas, it seemed, was alone in the most dangerous land in the western realm. That his guides had abandoned him, he was rather certain. They'd probably had enough after their brawl. And if they'd gone when he guessed they had, based on the dying fire, they would have already made it back to the gate by now and used their emergency crest papers to gain back their freedom.

Lucas put his hands on his head and closed his eyes. Then he took long, deep breaths as it dawned on him that he, alone, would need to pay Bartol the debt. Because if he didn't, his land was going to war again. And this time, he wasn't sure they'd win.

CHAPTER 7

COLOR OF HONEY

The morning after their argument, Jaelle had to try for ten minutes before she could force herself out of bed. All she could think about was how awful the day would be, and how every time she and Chiara were forced to talk, it would be like dancing with a pit viper. Still, she had no choice but to eventually get out of bed. Taking care not to wake her sister, she washed her face and brushed her hair. As she made her way out to the kitchen, however, she relaxed slightly when she heard a man's voice in the entryway. If they had a patient, Chiara would be too busy to punish Jaelle. At least, not immediately. Jaelle fled silently to the kitchen to pour herself a cup of tea as she waited for Chiara to call her.

But as she stood in the kitchen, she began to realize that the conversation, of which she was picking up bits and pieces, didn't sound like it was about any injury or illness. Their visitor didn't sound like he was in pain, either, or even as though he might have an upset stomach. Instead, his tone sounded far too intrigued to have anything to do with Chiara's line of work. Jaelle pressed herself up against the wall beside the doorway so she could hear.

"...has a mask," her stepmother was saying. "I don't know why she's so determined to keep it on. You'll have to do something to fix that because she's never listened to me when I told her to take it off."

Jaelle nearly dropped her cup.

"I'm sure it won't be a problem," the man said. Jaelle didn't recognize the voice. There were three men to every woman in Terrefantome, so newcomers weren't ever much of a surprise. But this...

"How many others are applying?" the man said, uncertainty in his voice. Jaelle could hear them getting to their feet. She knew she should move, but she couldn't.

"I have several gentlemen lined up," Chiara said, sounding as though she'd stumbled upon a great treasure.

"And when will you decide who gets her?" the man asked.

"If it's you," Chiara said, her words dripping with honey, "I'll make sure you know."

"The new marshal won't like it if he finds out." The man sounded nervous. "It's easy enough to turn the old one's head, but this new one says the king is trying to make us more like—"

"If he knows what's good for his expectant wife," Chiara said in a flat voice, "he'll turn his head as well."

Jaelle still stayed at the wall, but this time, it was for support, rather than secrecy.

After Chiara saw the man out and came to the kitchen to pour a cup of tea for herself, she said nothing, just smiled. Only after she had added milk did she say in a soft voice, "Without me, you are nothing. Make sure to remember that the next time you feel the need to be willful. All I have to do is sneeze, and you'll be out with the worst man I can find." Then she floated out of the room, leaving Jaelle feeling as though she were gasping for air. Her desire for her tea dissipated, and it was all she could do to stumble back to her room, chest tight as she slammed the door behind her and sank to the ground against it.

"For the love of the sun, what's going on?" Selina moaned from the bed. When Jaelle didn't answer, Selina flopped over and squinted at Jaelle through tired eyes. "Could you be any louder?"

"She wants to sell me," Jaelle whispered, still sitting against the door, as though that would keep her stepmother out.

"Wait...what?" Selina grimaced and rubbed her face. When she was sitting up in bed and looking slightly less like she would pass out again at any moment, Jaelle told her of Chiara's meeting that morning.

"She's going to get rid of me," Jaelle said, pressing her palms into the floor until her wrists hurt. "I pushed her too far, and she's done."

But instead of acting terrified, Selina only rolled her eyes then flipped back over to face the wall, pulling the covers up to her neck once more.

"Nonsense," she yawned. "My mother can't do what she does without you, particularly with her bad hand, and she knows that. She's just trying to scare you."

"Well, it's working," Jaelle said, somehow getting off the floor, despite her shaky knees, and walking back to the bed. "She's interviewing men."

Selina growled and sat up again, glaring at Jaelle through red, tired eyes. "Listen to me. She is not going to sell you. And even if she were thinking about it, she'd need a lot longer than a week, considering she'd want the most money out of the deal that she could possibly glean."

Jaelle stuck her tongue out. "Well, that makes me feel so *much* better."

"Just be patient." Selina took Jaelle by the shoulders. "A few weeks. That's all you need to last."

Jaelle frowned. "Why that long?"

Selina studied her. "Do you trust me?"

"Of course."

"Then," Selina said with a sad smile, "if you can last a few weeks, you'll be just fine. You'll be more than fine." She quirked an eyebrow. "Agreed?"

Jaelle stared at Selina a long minute before slowly nodding.

"Very well."

WAITING WAS HARDER than Jaelle had anticipated. Word had gotten out that the healer was taking applications and offers from men who might want her stepdaughter. And even if Chiara didn't mean to take anyone up on the offer, as Selina insisted, Jaelle wore dread like a cloak every morning when she awoke to find her stepmother with a new man to interview. On the second day, she found the butcher who had glared and snapped back in the market, as well as the tailor, and two potato farmers, one of which had a boil right below his bottom lip that made Jaelle want to gag every time she looked at it. The third day was no better, with men from ages seventeen to sixty-two. On the fourth day, one of the men assured Chiara, with Jaelle in the room, that he was a man from a fruitful line. The fact that he had eleven children already should prove that.

Jaelle nearly used the sehf's leather crest that night. Anything to get out of *that*.

And so the pattern continued. Many of the men began to make second and third calls, annoyed that Chiara was dragging the process out so long, but Jaelle got the distinct feeling her step-mother liked all the fuss. But there was little she could do. Selina never said another word about her promise, and Jaelle knew better than to press, particularly as Selina began to come home even later than usual.

Two weeks after Selina's promise, Jaelle thought she might lose her mind and even walked a ways into the forest, looking for signs of the Taistille. She didn't see anyone and scurried home before she was there for any length of time, but she promised herself she would try again on the morrow. The next day, however, she awoke to find Selina already at the table for the morning meal. Thankfully, her stepmother was nowhere to be seen.

"You're up early," Jaelle said as she buttered a piece of bread. "I didn't even hear you come in last night."

"That's because I didn't." Selina rubbed her temples and leaned her head against the back of the chair. "I got home five minutes ago."

"Let me make you some tea," Jaelle said, going to the water bucket. She frowned, however, when she reached it. "That's odd."

"What?"

Jaelle picked up the bucket and examined it. "I filled this yesterday. How in the world could it be empty?"

"Perfect. Just what I need." Selina buried her face in her hands.

Two seconds later, she sat up straight. "Can you get some more now?"

Jaelle began to say yes, then paused. "But I thought you told me never to leave the house alone again."

But Selina was already shaking her head, her eyes closed as she slumped against the table. "I don't want you going into the city. The well is just up the road. You should be fine."

Something in Jaelle's stomach warned her that this wasn't a good idea.

"Selina—"

"Jaelle, just get me the blasted water!" Selina shrieked.

Jaelle hesitated, torn between telling her sister to be nice and demanding an explanation. But as Selina began to look paler by the second, Jaelle snatched the bucket and ran out the door, wondering which herbal tea might best help Selina when she got back. And hopefully, make her nicer.

If she hadn't been reeling from Selina's sharp words, Jaelle might have enjoyed the walk. The path to the outer well was lined with an unusual number of little flowers, some with colors rarely seen in the area. Pink, purple, and yellow blossoms bobbed in the slight breeze, bright against the brown background that covered fields and led into the distant forests. The air was moist, as usual, but comfortably warm without being hot. Jaelle paused at the foot of the hill to the well and closed her eyes. Breathing slowly through her nose, she let the scent of nature and unpolluted air fill her lungs and imagined the air healing her hurting heart from the inside out.

"You there."

Jaelle opened her eyes to see an old woman crouched by the well at the top of the hill. Jaelle glanced around. "Me?"

"Is there anyone else in this barren wasteland? Yes, you. How about you get what you came for and bring me a drink while you're at it."

Jaelle blinked at the old woman, but the woman just stared at her expectantly.

"Um, very well." Jaelle began the trek up the hill. She was pleasing everyone else. She might as well please one more person while she was at it.

The old woman was even uglier up close. That she was a Tais-tille was obvious. Bright orange and purple fabric had been wrapped around her head and body, and bangles of gold dangled from her wrists. Several tinkling earrings stuck out from one ear, while the other only had a single hoop. Her skin was a deep shade of brown that would have been lovely if it hadn't been for the strange, fearsome tattoos of menacing creatures up and down her arms. She watched Jaelle with eyes the same shade of green as those of Jaelle's barn cat.

"Well," she put her hands on her hips when Jaelle arrived at the top. "It's a relief I haven't died of old age yet. Are you going to get me that water or not?"

Jaelle briefly fantasized about filling the bucket and pouring it on the rude woman's head. Her hair was greasy and looked as though she hadn't washed it in years. Instead, she put the bucket on the rope and began to lower it into the well.

"You're rather old to be unmarried yet, aren't you? And to still wear your mask?"

Jaelle froze before her panic subsided again.

"My father thought that if men couldn't see what I looked like, they would be less likely to take me, for fear I might be disagreeable."

The woman snorted. "That's always the reason. What I mean is that most girls wear it while they're young and their parents don't want them to fall prey at an early age. But most women your age have long ago removed it for their husbands." She winked. "Or to *find* one. And catch themselves a ride to the other side of the wall."

Jaelle grimaced. Apparently, this woman hadn't spent much time looking at the selection of local men. Then again, Jaelle was nearly past the point of caring. Maybe it would be better if someone would just take her. Then Selina could at least move on with her life, and Chiara wouldn't get any sort of payment.

Instead of taking Jaelle's hint, the woman only tilted her head and shuffled closer, so close, in fact, that Jaelle could smell the tobacco on her breath and clothes. Then the woman touched a tendril of Jaelle's hair.

"The girl was right," she muttered, seemingly to herself. "There is something different about you."

Jaelle tried to give her a false smile, but she was unable, watching the woman out of the corner of her eye as she began to pull the bucket back up. The water was heavy, and it took all her strength to get it to the top.

The woman shrugged then let out a strange laugh as Jaelle drew it to the top. Eager to be done with the whole ridiculous ordeal, she held out the bucket, and the woman took a long sip before wiping her mouth.

"Well," she said, "I suppose I've been paid to gift you, not make decisions."

Jaelle had taken back the bucket and was leaning it on the edge of the well wall, but at this exclamation, she nearly dropped it.

She'd been paid to *gift* Jaelle? What did that even mean?

Before Jaelle could ask, however, the woman closed her eyes and began to mutter incoherently as she picked up a handful of gravel.

"Madame?" Jaelle asked, taking a half-step back.

The woman's eyes flew open as her mutterings ended, and she threw the gravel at Jaelle. Jaelle cried out in surprise as dozens of pebbles hit her skin. Wherever they touched, her skin briefly burned. Jaelle looked up to tell the woman that she was thoroughly annoyed and had half a mind to tell the village constable, as he greatly disliked the Taistille, but when she did, the woman was gone.

"What—" As she spoke, something hard and cool touched her lip. Jaelle reached up, and to her amazement, a round purple gem the size of a pea rolled into her hand. "No," she breathed. But as she did, she felt yet another stone fall from her lips. This one was larger, the size of her thumb, and it was the exact color of honey.

Bucket forgotten, Jaelle took off down the hill.

CHAPTER 8
GOODBYE, SISTER

J aelle nearly fell several times as she ran home. Her muscles, unused to running long distances, cried out for her to stop, but she ignored them. By the time she reached the cottage, she could barely put one foot in front of the other. Panting, she made it into the house, only to realize that neither Selina nor Chiara was home. This was a great blessing, as Jaelle was still spewing diamonds whenever she spoke. But Jaelle didn't stop looking until she'd spotted her sister sitting on the bank of a nearby creek, her legs dangling off the edge and over the water.

Jaelle called her name several times on the way over, but Selina didn't turn. Finally, only after Jaelle had climbed down the embankment and seated herself on one of the larger rocks right beside the creek, did Selina even acknowledge her with a short nod.

Though the creek wasn't deep, the embankment that surrounded the creek was, and it was possible to sit down inside and stick one's toes in the water without being visible from above. The natural comforts of the day, however, no longer captivated Jaelle.

"You did this, didn't you?"

Selina just stared into the water as it bubbled.

For a long time, neither said anything, partially because Jaelle wasn't sure what to say, and partially because she wasn't sure how many jewels she could fit into her pockets if they continued to come. She didn't want to lose any and make vagabonds or wandering gentlemen suspicious. Or Chiara. Chiara would be the worst.

"Selina—" Out tumbled a diamond the color of blood.

Selina held up her hand, her face red and puffy, like she'd been crying. But for once, Jaelle didn't care.

"Selina, what have you done?" As if being a young unmarried woman in Terrefantome wasn't enough, now she was producing what were considered to be the most valuable forms of currency and the best weapons in the land. Jaelle folded her arms and sat straighter. "Selina, I am going to hound you and hound you," she said, diamonds pouring from her mouth like a thin waterfall, "and I'm not going to let you rest until—"

"Gifts come at a cost."

"Gifts?" Jaelle echoed. Two blue stones, a green stone, and six little red stones clinked into her hand. She pocketed them and continued. "What *gifts*? And why?"

Selina still refused to look at her. "Because I hired her."

"You...?" Two white stones. But before Jaelle could examine them, she saw something else out of the corner of her eyes and in her shock, stumbled backward and fell off her rock. She missed hitting her head by inches, and her back hurt, but those were the least of her concerns as she watched twin snakes slither out of her sister's mouth.

"Selina, what..." she shrieked, but Selina just looked at her.

"I know," she said when the snakes had finished their escape.

Jaelle watched in horror as a slimy toad poked its way between her sister's lips and then plopped onto her lap.

"You..." Jaelle stared up at her. "Selina, what did you do?" she whispered.

Soon it was agreed that Jaelle would sit perched on a very tall boulder six feet away while she listened to Selina tell her story. Their seating arrangement was Selina's idea, but after watching two black adders make their way out of Selina's mouth, which also made Selina's speech very difficult to understand, Jaelle was forced to admit that she did indeed need to back up, if only for her safety.

"Balbina is a Taistille witch," Selina began, watching two toads make their way down her clothes.

"You hate the Taistille."

"I hate what the Taistille do. But we all have our uses from time to time. Anyhow, when you told me what Mother was threatening you with, I realized she was never going to let you go. She lets me go my own way, as long as I contribute. But you're too useful. You know her trade, and her bad hand and stiff leg would make it impossible for her to work without you." She paused. "My mother is concocting a fear in you now that she can leverage for the rest of her life."

Jaelle's heart fell as she listened. She'd known all of this, of course, but hearing it from Selina only made it more real.

"So as soon as I realized how miserable she was determined to make you, I knew my time was limited."

Jaelle was too horrified to say anything. So Selina went on.

"I found Balbina. Balbina doesn't travel with any of the Taistille troops nearby, so she was rather difficult to locate."

"Why?"

"Why what?" Selina asked, this time producing a rattlesnake.

Jaelle swallowed. "Why doesn't she travel with the others?"

Selina didn't even blink. "They say she's too dangerous."

"Well, that's a surprise," Jaelle muttered.

"Will you just let me finish?" Selina rolled her eyes, and Jaelle nodded, so she continued. "When I told her I wanted a way for you to buy your freedom, she became curious."

"How much money did you give her?"

Selina gave Jaelle a funny look. "None." Then her jaw went taut, and she looked up at the sky.

"Well, how did you pay her? The Taistille never work for less than a steep price."

"It doesn't matter," Selina said quietly. Three red and blue frogs hopped down her dress to the water.

"Yes it does!" Jaelle put her hand over her mouth, nearly choking herself in the process as two of the smaller gems tried to roll back down her throat. She had to wait for a moment before trying again. "Masks are one thing," she rasped. "But Taistille witches use dark—"

"You think I don't know that?" Selina snapped, and two of her snakes hissed. Then she sighed. "You know that I lived in Maricanta's capital city before Mother and I moved here, correct?"

Jaelle froze as Selina paused to allow a large rat snake out. Only when it had made its way down Selina's leg, did Jaelle remember to nod.

"Our queen, Drina, was—and to my knowledge still is—greedy. She loves wealth and glory and beauty. And as she has two sons, I paid a few bribes to have a message delivered to her."

Jaelle paused. "Wait, you wrote to a *queen*? And how in the blazes did you get a message over the wall?"

Before she could answer, Jaelle's stomach growled, and for the first time, Selina seemed to notice the hour of the day. She looked around at the gray sky and gave a little start. "What time is it?" she asked, somewhat breathlessly.

"The clock tolled the tenth hour a few minutes ago." Jaelle paused. "Why?"

Selina turned and shook her head. "Look, we don't have much time, so you need to listen fast."

"But—"

"She'll be coming by soon to fetch you, so you need to pay attention."

Panic fought with anger as Jaelle stared at her sister.

"Why?" She tried to keep her voice from breaking as a few warty toads hopped out of her sister's mouth. "Why would you do this?" Tears began to stream down her face. This was ten times, a hundred times worse than what Chiara had planned to do. "You've made a deal with darkness," she whispered. "Don't you understand that this is more than snakes or jewels or money?" Jaelle leaned forward. "We can find another way to escape, but not one that will cost you everything!"

Selina gave her a sad smile. "You've always been so good to me, even when my mother did everything in her power to break you."

"But you've been good to me, too. You're not like her!"

"Maybe I wasn't at one point. But I've given far too much of myself to this place now to live unaffected on the other side of the wall. I've done...things that wouldn't make you proud. You, however," she wiped away a tear. "You have always belonged to another place." Selina paused, her ear cocked. "Mother is calling for me." Then she gave a dark chuckle. "If nothing else, I shouldn't have trouble with men from now on."

"No. No!" Jaelle shook her head emphatically. "We're going to find a way to get you out of this!" She racked her mind for some way...any way to pierce the darkness her sister had involved them in. "The other side!" She hopped up and moved closer to her sister. "I've heard there are people who can break this kind of curse! I've heard stories in the village! There...there's a king." What was his name? "Evergone. Everand. Everard! That's it. We'll find a way to get to the other side of the wall, and we'll find him! He destroys things like this. I've heard enough stories from people from all over that mention him."

Selina hopped off her rock and walked toward Jaelle.

"And that," she said, a little garden snake wiggling its way out of her nose, "is where you're wrong." She glanced at the road again. "The queen is coming to fetch you any minute. She's going to take you back to Maricanta."

"I'm not going to Maricanta without you."

"I've already drawn up some guardianship papers myself and signed Mother's name, so if the queen mentions those, pretend they're part of our usual traditions here."

Jaelle gaped. "Guardianship papers? What does that even mean?"

"Nothing, really. They're just papers I've written myself stating that Mother has relinquished guardianship of you and that you'll be traveling under the queen's protection with the intention of marrying Lucas. But they're important because they'll make the queen think Mother has given you up legally, and they'll make the royal betrothal papers faster to draw up in Maricantan courts."

"Selina, who is Lucas? Now you're talking nonsense."

Selina rolled her eyes.

"Shut up and listen. You're going to get married, and you're going to get away from this place forever." Her mouth quirked slightly, despite the tears in her eyes. "Just don't fall for him too hard. He's still a man, and even on the other side of the wall, men do as they please."

Before Jaelle could respond, Selina held a wet rag over Jaelle's face. Jaelle began to cough and sputter. She recognized the faint scent of cotton musk. She broke free of her sister's grasp and tried to run to the river to wash it off. But she'd only succeeded in taking three staggering steps when Selina caught her again and wrapped her in a tight embrace.

"Let me go." Jaelle fought weakly, barely able to keep her eyes open. "Don't put me to sleep. We can fix this." But already her words were slurring, and her legs buckled beneath her.

"Goodbye, sister," Selina whispered just before Jaelle fell asleep.

CHAPTER 9

EVERARD

Jaelle woke with a start and caught herself just before she fell off the bench. The bumping beneath her didn't stop, however. Instead, the bench threw her in the air again, and this time, she landed on the floor.

"You certainly aren't an easy one to wake, are you?"

Jaelle looked around in a daze to see a stately woman dressed in rich purple staring at her. They appeared to be in a coach of some sort. Brown trees passed outside the windows, and the sky was just as gray as ever. Which meant they were also most likely still in Terrefantome. As her focus cleared, however, Jaelle also realized that the gray was the gray of morning.

"How..." Jaelle whispered, looking around. As she did, a pearl-sized emerald fell from her lips. The woman's brown eyes widened and followed the jewel as it rolled toward the door. She looked as though she very much wanted to chase it, but after a moment, leaned back and refocused on Jaelle.

"How long have I been asleep?" Jaelle mumbled.

"A whole night, believe it or not." She pursed her lips together and her brow creased as she studied Jaelle's entire person. "Well, you're in slightly better shape than Arianna was. The mask is a bit off-putting, but your sister told me all about that. And at least you can walk and talk." Her face brightened, however, as the emerald came to a stop at the edge of her shoe. "I suppose you'll do."

Jaelle stared at her. Who on earth was Arianna, and why couldn't the poor thing walk or talk?

But the woman just held out her hand and smiled. "I'm Queen Drina of Maricanta." Then she huffed and waved. "And no need to stay silent. I know all about your little trick. Your sister told me all about it when she wrote to send the guardianship papers. Your secret is safe with me!" She beamed and brushed back a lock of brown hair.

"Guardianship papers?" Jaelle asked, her head still ridiculously foggy. The title of queen sounded familiar, but she didn't know why.

Queen Drina's smile grew as a ruby fell onto Jaelle's lap. "For the betrothal," she said, her eyes not leaving the ruby. "Apparently, in this...place," she waved a hand at the window, "I needed the legal permission to take you." She held up a parchment sealed with green wax. Then she peered at Jaelle's face more closely. "How long have you been wearing that thing?"

But Jaelle was too busy trying to clear her head to answer. As soon as the woman had mentioned the sham legal permission, memories came flooding back. The Taistille. Her curse. Selina's curse. Selina's plan to get her out of Terrefantome. Jaelle shook her head. She was fast developing a splitting headache.

Even more concerning than her headache, however, was the sudden panic that shook her when she realized what she had left at home. A quick, desperate search around the carriage, however, had her breathing a sigh of relief when she found a black satchel at her feet. Selina hadn't forgotten. Inside were some clean undergarments, Jaelle's second dress, a second pair of stockings, a few bread rolls, and Jaelle's beloved book. Jaelle hugged the bag to her chest and took her time breathing slowly to calm her racing heart.

Queen Drina seemed not to have noticed Jaelle's panic, though. Instead, she opened her mouth, then closed it. "Not that it really matters," she said.

What were they talking about again?

"What's important," the queen continued, "is that you're here now, and you're on your way to wed a prince! Isn't that exciting?"

So that was Selina's game. She must have snuck Jaelle out while she was still unconscious. Jaelle's stomach tightened. Chiara would never forgive Selina for stealing her assistant, though the snakes might make her hesitant to do anything too reckless. Jaelle could hope.

Also, this queen from Maricanta seemed to have very little understanding of how marriages worked in Terrefantome. Selina must have allowed her to believe whatever she wished, and in the process, made the queen Jaelle's protector.

Jaelle studied the queen as she pulled out a little mirror and examined parts of her face. She was a handsome woman, really. With a strong, angled face and large, dark eyes. She had fewer lines on her face than most women of her age, though Jaelle had to guess at that as well. She had probably been quite thin at one point, though now her opulent gown was slightly strained at its seams. And with her hair pulled up, which had a little gray in it, she looked slightly imposing. She also, however, looked very unfit to be Jaelle's protector, or anyone's protector, for that matter. Particularly as she patted splotches of white powder all over her nose and forehead, seeming completely oblivious to the world she was dabbling in.

This might turn out very badly.

Then something she said finally dawned on Jaelle.

"Wait..." Jaelle held up a hand. "Did you say I'm going to marry a *prince*?"

"Oh, yes!" The woman bent and picked up a sapphire that had rolled over to her side of the carriage. "I'll keep this for you," she said with an overly sweet smile before tucking it in her reticule. "That way you don't lose it."

"So we're going to Maricanta?"

"Oh, yes. Well, eventually. First, we're going to surprise my son and present him his bride!"

"And where is he?" Jaelle could already feel her heart picking up speed. Selina must have been confident enough that the youngest Maricantan prince wasn't a monster, otherwise she wouldn't have betrothed Jaelle to him. But...married? Jaelle shivered. She hadn't the first idea how to be a wife. Let alone a princess.

"Oh, at that town, the one at the gate...I can't remember its name." The queen pulled a map from her reticule and unfolded it, frowning thoughtfully as she studied it. Hoping she didn't mind the intrusion of space, Jaelle cautiously went to sit beside her so she could see too, though she had no idea what any of the little marks meant.

"We're somewhere here," the queen said, pointing to the line on the map that ran through a little patch of trees. "And we're going here." She pointed to a dot. The dot was beside a drawing of a gate.

They were going to the gate. Jaelle's first reaction was to panic. She couldn't leave Selina behind. Especially not after she'd just entrenched herself in darkness.

And yet...

"You're a queen," Jaelle began slowly.

"Yes." Queen Drina nodded and smiled.

Jaelle took a shaky breath. "Do you know King Everard?"

At this, Queen Drina made a face. "Unfortunately, I do. The man is a bit of a bore, I must tell you. Always suspecting trouble. And his wife is polite but a bit self-righteous, if you ask me."

Jaelle nearly let out a scream of joy. If they could get to the other side of the gate, Jaelle would plead with whomever she had to to meet this King Everard. Then she would beg him to help her save Selina. Then she and Selina could begin their lives on the other side of the wall. Together.

"Oh, his name is Lucas, by the way." Queen Drina jarred Jaelle from her thoughts.

"I'm sorry, what was that?"

"Your betrothed? His name is Lucas, and he's twenty-one years. He's a younger prince, mind you. Not in line for the throne. But still a catch, if I do say so myself." She nodded and folded the map again. "Anyhow, he's at one of the inns in the town by the gate, and if he's not now, he will be sometime again in the next few weeks. It's the last place he'll stay before coming home." She shrugged. "We can just wait for him there until then."

"You mean you don't know where he is?" Jaelle sat straight up. Was this woman really that daft?

"It doesn't matter." Drina sniffed. "We're going to go find him." Then she sighed happily. "I was so surprised when your sister's letter was delivered to the palace that I hardly believed it at first. A girl who could speak jewels? But the night after reading the letter, I decided I must try. After all, such miracles have happened before. Now," she added with a delicate snort, "Michael and Lucas will have to take back all those dreadful things they said."

"Michael?"

"Oh, my older son. Very organized and often dull, but I suppose he's done a good enough job for the kingdom."

Jaelle was glad the woman couldn't see her face. Until very recently, she had doubted there could be anyone more self-centered than her stepmother. But now she was having second thoughts. Still, at least for the moment, Drina seemed more congenial than Chiara had ever been, if not more than slightly obtuse.

Jaelle peeked through the window. The guards that walked on either side of the carriage wore no uniforms.

"I'm aware that I know very little of your customs," she said, no longer caring about the jewels that spilled into her lap, "but aren't soldiers supposed to wear uniforms?" She was rather sure her father had told her of Giova's military on more than one occasion.

"Oh, those aren't my guards. Well, they are, but they're not my palace guards. I hired these ones after crossing through the gate." Queen Drina giggled as though she'd done something very clever. "My sons think I'm completely incapable of caring for myself or others. So to show them better, I hired men from the village near our palace. Then I simply switched and found new ones when I got here." She smirked. "Just like this carriage. I rented it, too. The gate guards didn't even know who I was! I just told them I was with the man in front of me!"

Then she sobered slightly. "Not that it will matter in a few hours. My son will take care of us from there. He's on some sort of mission or something. Some nonsense my eldest son sent him on. Either way, he's quite good at all that fighting stuff, so we'll be more than safe." She stopped powdering her face and looked at Jaelle. "What's wrong?"

Jaelle, who had just bitten into one of the bread rolls Selina had packed for her, had choked on it at Drina's words, and was now coughing up the remnants of her bite. How had this woman run a household, let alone a country, without running it into the ground?

"Queen Drina—" she croaked when she could speak again.

"Drina, dear," the queen said while scooping up some rubies Jaelle had dropped on the bench. "We're going to be family, so you must call me Drina."

"Drina," Jaelle said in a low voice, "with all due respect, I don't think you realize just how dangerous my country is."

"Oh," Drina waved a hand at her and made a face, "now you sound just like my sons."

Jaelle took this as a compliment. Perhaps her sons were why Maricanta hadn't collapsed completely. If they made it to the gate in one piece, it would be a miracle. As it was, she was shocked they hadn't yet been boarded and robbed.

"You...you didn't tell them about all your plans, did you?" Jaelle asked in a lower voice. "These guards, I mean." Please, please say no.

"Not all of it." Drina rolled her eyes. "I'm not stupid. If my son says he's on a secret mission, I'm not about to tell them all about what he's up to."

"That's good," Jaelle said slowly, not wanting to offend the woman and get kicked out along the road. "But what about me?"

Drina looked at her with large eyes. "Why are you so worried, my dear? Haven't we made it this far safely?"

"Because," Jaelle said, exasperation seeping into her voice, "in Terrefantome, it's nothing for a man to take a woman and keep her for no reason except his own pleasure! Surely you can find another way to contact your son after we make it through the gate. Or we can wait for him." She paused. She needed to convince Drina to return to Maricanta. Immediately. But how? Then an idea came to her. "If I'm going to meet my betrothed..."

"Lucas," Drina offered with a condescending smile.

"Lucas." Jaelle nodded. This was ludicrous. "If I'm to be introduced to Lucas, shouldn't I bathe and have cleaner clothes first? Perhaps this would be better done back at the palace?"

"Half the time Lucas comes to supper drenched and rumpled from the sea. He'll survive."

So much for that attempt. The woman's stiff dress and

perfectly shined shoes had given Jaelle hope that such a request would appeal to the queen's vanity, but apparently, the pride her sons had injured was to be put first.

Jaelle reached into her belt and touched the leather medallion just inside her clothes. She could use it. Surely there would be Taistille not too far from the border city. After all, it wasn't unusual for Taistille to disguise themselves and sneak into towns for supplies or to scope one out for a ransacking. She could find one and request that they help her cross the gate, or at least hold everyone else off while she attempted to get through herself. Then she remembered the sehf's words about how Taistille avoided the gates, and she sighed.

She lay one arm on the window and rested her chin on it as she tried to imagine this prince that she was about to be thrust upon. That he wouldn't want to marry her, she was certain. At least, not for the right reasons. Still...Jaelle had heard that men on the other side of the wall were different from most of those in Terrefantome. Her father was a testament to that truth, and she'd known several men throughout her childhood who were rough but had their own strange sort of moral code. But, if she was being honest with herself, who would want a lanky, ignorant girl from Terrefantome who lived in a mask? Even if he could look past his mother's hasty actions, wouldn't he want someone beautiful? Surely no prince, one who could have any woman he wanted, would want a peasant girl without a glimpse of her face.

She could remove her mask, of course. He might be more likely to keep her if he thought she was beautiful. But there was no guarantee that she would be beautiful or to his taste. Removing her mask on a gamble also would be breaking her promise. And that was a promise she wasn't about to break.

But then, what kind of man, particularly a prince, went into Terrefantome by himself? And why was he there? What could have been so important that it was worth putting himself in such danger?

What kind of man could fall in love with a poor, faceless stranger?

She shook her head. None of this mattered. All that mattered was whether or not he would take her to the other side of the gate so she could find King Everard. And for the first time in her life, even if her presence was an inconvenience, she could now pay whomever she needed whatever they wanted to help her, thanks to Selina's ill-fated attempt at generosity.

As long as they didn't get greedy. She shuddered.

Besides, what did she know of love? Only what her father had told her of her mother. Her real mother. Having a husband must be different on the other side of the wall. The other girls her age had done nothing but scheme since they reached adolescence to get out of Terrefantome, and marriage was usually part of that deal. But their marriages were never for love, only for what they could bring the participants. Marriage in Terrefantome, she'd been told, was rarely wonderful. It was simply another way to survive.

But she couldn't help wondering once again, might this one, this prince from Maricanta, be different? She hoped he would. Otherwise, this journey was doomed from the start.

CHAPTER 10

LOOKING

Two hours later, they reached the city. Instead of taking the carriage to the front of the inn Drina had directed them to, the hired men drove the carriage around the back of the inn, which Jaelle could already tell was larger than the inn above Selina's tavern at home. As little as Jaelle trusted the men Drina had hired, she was thankful for such foresight on their part. The carriage was bound to draw too much attention if they stayed in public. Jaelle had only seen a few carriages in her lifetime, and one of them had belonged to a former king, who had since been replaced.

The carriage lurched to a stop, nearly throwing Jaelle from her seat. One of their hired men came back and looked through the window, far too close to Jaelle's face for comfort, but he didn't seem to notice the way she drew back. Or didn't care.

"All right, madame," he told Drina. "We'll let you out here, then we'll go put the carriage away." He seemed polite enough, but as he was talking, Jaelle felt her heart skip a beat when he looked at her lap, and his eyes nearly fell out of his head. There lay all the jewels she'd dropped while speaking, and Jaelle suddenly wished she'd given them all to Drina to hide in her little pouch.

But Drina didn't seem to notice the pause.

"Good man." She held out her hand until he seemed to realize what she wanted and opened the door. With exaggerated movements, he helped the queen down first. Then he reached up for Jaelle, but, thinking fast, Jaelle flashed him a weak smile before dumping the contents of her lap into his outstretched hand and scurrying down the carriage steps herself. As she did, she nearly stumbled into Drina. Drat. Her stupid legs didn't want to work, thanks to Selina's sleeping herb.

Whenever Jaelle did finally save Selina, she was going to give her sister a good dose of sleeping herbs. Then Selina could see how much she liked being a rag doll.

Glad to be free of the carriage, though, Jaelle unsteadily followed Drina around the side of the inn and to the front. And there, she gasped.

Dozens of men and almost as many women walked the main street in front of the inn. There were horses, donkeys, chickens, and even several dogs running about and barking at everything that looked their way. Countless shops and buildings lined the street, and men, women, and children moved in and out of them at regular intervals.

Carts rolled noisily up the streets, which weren't mud like at home, but were covered by large, flat stones. Strangest of all, however, was the visible line of clouds that hung over the wall of the city. They stretched, gray as ever, over the city. That in itself wasn't odd. The sky was always gray. Jaelle couldn't remember a day when the sun had shone directly on her land. But what made her breathing hitch was that beyond the clouds was the color blue. It was even more wonderful than in her mother's paintings.

The only thing that could have pulled Jaelle's attention from that perfect, piercing blue, was the gate beneath it. Jaelle sucked in air when she finally saw the impossibly tall gate for herself. How many times had she wondered how it would feel to be so close to freedom, to the world that the holy man and her father had painted for her over the years? Uniformed guards stood on both sides, and the glares they gave passersby seemed to keep the area around the gate clear. Not that glares would deter Jaelle. She would crawl through if they wanted her to.

"Come, Giselle," Drina said, tugging on Jaelle's arm. "You need to meet your future husband. You're just going to love him!"

Jaelle resisted the urge to roll her eyes and correct the queen and followed her instead. She would have to take care not to speak until they were hidden again, she realized as she made her way down the path. The last thing she needed was for half the city to see her speaking gems.

Drina pushed the thick wooden door open as if she owned the place. The room, four times the size of her front room at home, was filled, nearly every square inch of it, by dirty men. Some threw darts in a corner, and a few seemed deeply engaged in a conversation by a window. But the vast majority quieted upon their entry and simply watched them from tables, stools, and whatever else they were sitting on or leaning up against.

Coming here was a mistake. She could see it in the bright interest reflected in the men's eyes as they watched the two women make their way to the bar.

"I'm looking for Prince Lucas," Drina said to the tavern keep.

The tavern keep chewed slowly, most likely tobacco, and looked at her as though she'd lost her mind.

Drina tried again. More loudly. "I'm looking for my son, Prince Lucas!" she called above the low din.

The tavern keep, a thin man with a white mustache and bushy white eyebrows, leaned toward her and spat whatever he was chewing on the floor. "We don't have any princes here! At least not by that name." He looked her up and down, a scowl forming on his face. "I don't want trouble. And that's exactly what you're going to bring if you keep walking around, hollering like this."

Drina huffed and muttered something about a buffoon.

"What's that?" He raised his bushy white eyebrows.

"I said what about a young man of about twenty-one years? He's got black curly hair and hazel eyes. And he would be a new customer."

For a moment, Jaelle was sure he would kick them out. But finally, he nodded slowly. "Got a young man named Michael who looks like that." He pointed at a dark set of wooden stairs in the corner. "Up on the second floor, third door on the right." His eyes shifted briefly to the crowd behind her. "You'd best get up there now before any real trouble starts."

Drina looked as though she wanted to argue, but Jaelle grabbed her by the hand and pulled her to the stairs instead. She nearly turned to thank the man, but stopped, remembering at the last minute to keep her mouth closed.

Protector or no protector, half of Terrefantome would try to claim her if they knew what she could do.

Drina wasn't a particularly large woman. In fact, in her prime, she had probably been quite thin. But now she seemed rather unaccustomed to physical activity, for by the time they reached the top, she was out of breath.

"I should have known to ask for Michael," she panted as she climbed the steps.

Jaelle raised her eyebrows.

"Oh, it's Michael and Lucas's signal." She rolled her eyes. "If one ever has to keep his identity hidden, he'll use his brother's first name and some made up title or other. That way the other knows who it is when he comes looking."

Jaelle wished Drina had remembered that before they'd arrived at the inn. Then they might have avoided alerting the entire city to the prince's whereabouts. But they were here now, and Jaelle was closer to the gate than she'd ever been before. Her pulse quickened as they stopped in front of the third door and Drina knocked.

"Oh, *Michael*, it's your mother!" She turned and gave Jaelle a self-satisfied grin. "I've got someone I want you to meet."

As Jaelle tried to recall if Drina's voice had been that loud in the carriage, the door jerked open and a young man stared at them, his mouth falling open.

Jaelle had been expecting someone reasonably good looking. He was a prince after all, most likely with people to shave, dress, and otherwise groom him, so his appearance would be neat at the very least. What she hadn't anticipated, however, was how very attractive he really was, even without all the princely details.

Though he wore simple brown, nondescript clothing beneath a long black coat, it was impossible not to notice his broad shoulders or the muscles in his neck. Wide hazel eyes looked out from a face with strong angles and a square jaw covered in stubble. His hair was short, but even so, its curls looked black and silky, and she had the foolish urge to touch them. Overall, his was a very nice face, really.

"Hello, *Michael*," the queen said with a smug smile.

But in the split second it took for Jaelle to be pleased by his appearance, he seemed to feel the opposite about theirs. He grabbed them both by the arms and dragged them inside so hard Drina fell onto the bed, and Jaelle landed on the floor. Her inner hope for a gentle man withered as she sat up and glowered at him, but he seemed too busy frantically bolting the door to notice. When he turned around, he looked as though he were struggling for words.

"Mother...What...What are you...How did you find me?" He gaped down at Jaelle. "And who is this?"

"Oh, don't be such a fuddy-duddy." Drina sat up on the bed and brushed herself off with a scowl. "Be a good boy and give your mother a proper greeting."

"Mother! This is supposed to be *secret*. Only Michael, Arianna, and a few of my men know where I am." He ran his hand through his hair and began to pace. "How did *you* know where I was?"

Drina shook her head. "Son, it's not as though the queen doesn't know where important papers are kept. I knew you and Michael were up to something. It didn't take very much looking to find the plans in his desk." She raised an eyebrow. "Really, I thought you would know me better by now."

Prince Lucas pinched the bridge of his nose and closed his eyes. "You are no longer the queen. You are the queen *mother*. That means," he opened his eyes and glared at her, "that secrets need to stay just that. Secrets."

So that's what this was all about. Jaelle could see it all now. Drina's sons, who seemed to at least have enough common sense to do whatever they were doing in the dark, had offended their silly mother. And now, Drina was out to prove them wrong, putting both her own life and Lucas's in the balance. Jaelle cringed. She was putting her hopes of finding an answer for Selina right in the middle of royal family drama. Terrific.

"And you still haven't told me who this is." He gestured at Jaelle, who had picked herself up off the floor. Drina's eyes widened, and she clapped her hands like a little girl.

"Oh! This is why I came here, Lucas! She just happened to be in the same country I knew you were going to be in. So I thought to myself, why not make it a party?"

Lucas closed his eyes and spoke slowly. "But who is she?" He opened his eyes again and frowned at Jaelle. "And why can't I see your face?"

As much as the man annoyed her, Jaelle couldn't blame him for his frustration with Drina.

"That's what I've been trying to tell you!" Drina stood and went over to Jaelle and put her hands on Jaelle's shoulders. "Lucas, I would like for you to meet your betrothed. This is Jaelle, and I will be planning your wedding as soon as we all get back to the palace. There," she beamed, "isn't it exciting?"

Prince Lucas looked as though he might fall over.

"I thought you'd be excited," Drina said with a pout.

"Oh, you mean the way Michael was supposed to be excited about Princess Ines?" Lucas spat out.

"But this is different!"

"How so? You've never spotted a girl for us that didn't have some sort of boon in it for you as well."

At this, Drina looked at the floor and shuffled her feet.

Prince Lucas nodded. "Ah, so I'm right. Tell me then, Mother, what about this girl makes you want me to marry her?" When Drina didn't respond, he pressed again. "Mother?"

As he waited for her response, Jaelle turned and looked longingly out the window at the gate across the street. It really wasn't that far. Surely she could run without being accosted for the whole four minutes it would take to get from this room, down the stairs, out the door, across the street, and to the gate. She would have to use her invisibility, which she greatly detested. But if it meant freedom, it would be worth it.

Drina finally mumbled something unintelligible.

If Prince Lucas's eyes had been wide before, they looked as though they might fall out of his head now. "Excuse me?"

Drina looked at the ceiling. "When she speaks, she produces gems with her mouth." She looked back at her son. "There, are you happy?"

Silence filled the room like smoke, until it was nearly impossible to breathe. Finally, Prince Lucas put one hand on his waist. The other, he used to point.

"All right, this is how this is going to work." He pointed to his mother. "*You* are going to take *this* poor girl," he pointed to Jaelle, "back to her family. You will not try to take advantage of her in any way, and when you are done, you will have your guards take you straight home." He glared, his eyes surprisingly red. "Am I understood?"

"About that," Drina cleared her throat, "I don't have palace guards, per se."

"Why not? Who brought you?"

"I might have hired some nice young men so no one from the palace would know where I am."

Prince Lucas looked as though he might throw something through the window, and Jaelle had heard enough. She had hoped this family might be able to get her across the gate, but from the looks of things, they could barely sit in the same room together. Jaelle closed her eyes and let the ground ripple beneath her. Hopefully, she still *could* become invisible, and Selina's witch hadn't taken that from her. For there was a good chance the curse would prevent her from using her invisibility, thanks to her gems. For even if a gem was merely touching someone's clothing, invisibility became impossible. And here she was producing them.

But to her delight, when she looked down again, her hands had turned the expected pale blue tint, and so had her feet. As soon as she knew she'd disappeared completely, she darted for the door, threw open the bolt, and dashed downstairs.

Her invisibility wouldn't shield her from those who had been in Terrefantome the longest, for they could see her blue, wispy form as well as she could. But at least the newest arrivals couldn't see her. As she pushed her way through the tavern and out onto the street, she ignored the curious looks of those who could see her. And though she was nearly run over by two carts and a donkey as she crossed the street, she finally made it to the gate. She let herself reappear and ran up to the nearest guard she could find.

He wore the same bluish green uniform as the other guards standing at the gate, and his hair was cropped short to his ears. A long sword hung at his side, and Jaelle spotted several smaller knives and daggers hidden around his person as well. She clasped her hands together and approached him.

"Please, sir," she called above the chaos of the street behind her, "Let me through! I need to see King Everard." As she spoke, gems forced their way out of her mouth. Blast. She'd forgotten about that. But she was too close now to stop, so she turned her head so he could see that her neck was free of marks, hoping against hope that he'd have compassion. "My father was sent here, but I'm an innocent."

When she first approached, the guard had only frowned, but now, his eyes bulged as gem after gem dripped from her lips. He obviously wasn't listening, so she took a step closer.

"*Please!* I need to get to the other side! I need to find—"

Before she could finish, two thin, grimy hands wrapped themselves around her waist and spun her around. She found herself face to face with a skinny woman a head taller than she was. Her stringy hair hung in her eyes, and her clothes were full of holes.

"You've got Taistille magic." She jerked Jaelle closer, so Jaelle could smell her breath. "And I want some."

"I...I was cursed!" Jaelle gasped, trying to wrench herself from the woman's grasp. "My sister—" Jaelle looked back at the inn, as though doing so might bring help. But the woman grabbed Jaelle's right wrist and glanced at it for a second before pressing it against her side and taking control of Jaelle's left arm as well. She looked to be in her early fifth decade but was surprisingly strong for her age.

"She's not my protector!" She tried to plead with the gate guards to help her, but not one moved a muscle. "I beg of you—"

"Also looks like you've got no protector, darlin'."

"I do! She's in that hotel—" Jaelle tried to point, but the women kept her arms plastered to her side and shook her head.

"You've still got a mask, which means no man has claimed you for his own." Her grin widened, revealing a mouthful of yellow, rotting teeth. "But don't worry," she whispered gleefully as she began to drag Jaelle down the street. "I'll make sure no man harms you. And you are going to make sure I never go hungry again."

CHAPTER 11

DISCONCERTING

"W hat just happened?" Drina stared at the open door. "Where did she go?"

"That's what I've been trying to tell you!" Lucas fumed. "This place is dangerous. The people *literally* disappear."

"They what? Wait, where are you going?"

Lucas spun around and jabbed a finger at his mother while he slipped another knife into his belt. "*I* am going to get her. *You* are staying here."

"But Lucas..." His mother went white as she looked back and forth between him and the door, "if it's a dangerous—"

"Yes, it is dangerous. Because you have no idea what they do to women here." Lucas paused, his hand on the door. "I mean it. As soon as I'm gone, you bolt this door, and you don't open it for anyone, even me." Then without waiting for her response, Lucas shut the door and locked it before throwing the key in his boot and sprinting downstairs.

He had to pause once outside the inn to search. It only took him seconds to locate the scuffle happening just inside the gate between the girl, whose visibility flickered on and off, and a tall skinny woman. Just as Drina had said would happen, a pile of gems lay at their feet, and the more the girl tried to get away, the tighter the woman seemed to hold her.

Lucas froze for one brief second to weigh his options. That he was even in this position was ridiculous. This mission was already difficult enough without his mother barging in and dragging some poor girl into it. He wasn't even sure if he could trust this stranger, and now he was being forced to put his entire plan in jeopardy to save her. Part of him wanted very badly to march his mother to the gate, hand her to the guards, and let his brother deal with her. But great measures had been taken to ensure his anonymity, and alerting the gate guards to his true identity would put his entire mission in jeopardy.

Besides, his mother was the reason the girl was here. He couldn't just abandon her.

With a grimace, Lucas charged the woman as she began to drag Jaelle down the street, a parade of onlookers following, Jaelle's visibility continuing to flicker as if she was trying to hold it but failing. He had his sword drawn beneath his coat and was only feet away when the woman disappeared. A second later, Lucas received a sickening kick to the gut.

He put his arms up to defend himself, but it did little good. No matter how fast he turned or how ready his stance, the woman delivered blow after blow to his legs, stomach, and face. Lucas tried to move randomly, but he continued to get pummeled. The woman was quickly succeeding in knocking him silly.

Just when he was beginning to see double and considering throwing off his disguise and ordering the guards to help, the woman reappeared. Lucas looked up to see Jaelle with her hand on the woman's collar. This served only to confuse him more, until he caught a flash of what looked like a white diamond in her hand as it slipped from her fingers into the woman's dress.

So gems did break their invisibility. Well, everyone else's, at least. Jaelle didn't seem to be affected by it, or she hadn't back at the inn. With the woman visible again, Lucas was quickly able to knock her unconscious. Then he looked at the girl who stood behind her.

"Can we at least go back to talk?" he panted. From what he'd seen, scuffles and brawls were common here. Even so, people were beginning to stare, and he was very close to losing his cover.

She looked long and hard at the gate once more.

"I promise," he said in a softer voice, "I'll do whatever I can to help. But I need you to come with me now."

She looked at the ground and nodded, so he held out a hand and gestured toward the inn. She didn't take his hand, but she did follow, at least. As they walked, he couldn't help letting loose an incredulous chuckle. When it came to women, he and his brother seemed to have a knack for stumbling upon those with very few words.

His humor disappeared, however, when someone screamed that there was a pile of diamonds on the ground. It was all he could do to keep from breaking into a run as they left the scene that was fast becoming a frenzy.

Lucas couldn't leave this place soon enough.

THEY MADE their way back up to the room without being stopped, but Lucas didn't feel any safer until they were in the room with the door locked.

"Is she well?"

"Huh?" He looked up to see Jaelle staring at his mother, who was stretched out on the bed and snoring like a bear. He went up and examined her. Concern briefly coursed through him until he noticed the little white line of powder on her upper lip. Rolling his eyes, he turned away from her in disgust.

"She'll be fine."

"Are you sure?" A little white gem hit the ground as Jaelle came and bent over Drina, seeming to study every inch of Lucas's mother's body, though he couldn't tell for sure.

He'd seen several of the masks since he'd arrived, but he'd never had the chance to study one closely. Usually, they seemed to be on girls younger than Jaelle, girls who, from their dress and shape, were slightly too young to marry. Now that he looked at it up close, it was clear power of some sort had created the object.

The silhouette of her face was somewhat distinct whenever he glanced at it out of the corner of his eye. But when he turned to look at her head-on, her face looked as though it was made of water. There were no defining characteristics that he could see. Not eye color or the shape of her mouth or even the color of her skin. It faded just in front of her ears, at her chin, and below her hairline on her forehead. The white and blue shadows that faded in and out were also like water ripples, never staying still, even when you stared right at them.

And the whole thing was more than slightly disconcerting.

He shook himself awake to answer her question.

"Whenever she gets overwhelmed about something, she takes this awful white powder called Dormen—"

"Dormendanto," she finished, nodding to herself.

"Yes," he said, studying the girl anew. "How'd you know that?"

"I'm a healer," she said, turning her head toward him. A sapphire landed on the floor with a thud. Then she huffed. "It's a fool's powder. Muddles your senses and thinking for hours after taking it."

A healer. Well, this one had some sort of use, unlike the other girls his mother had thrust at him so far. Not that he was about to force this poor thing to marry him because his mother had gotten dreams of grandeur. Despite Lorenzo's words, he was still holding out for Vittoria. As soon as he was done with this nightmare, he was going to show her father exactly how determined and brazenly honest he really could be. Not to mention, this girl was an absolute stranger from the most dangerous land in the realm.

"What?" she asked, taking a step back when she seemed to notice him staring.

"I'm sorry," he said. "I'm just not used to..." He waved his hand around his face. "This."

"Oh. My mask." She nodded and leaned against the wall, sliding down until she was on the floor.

"Look," he said, scratching the back of his neck, "are you hungry?"

She nodded slowly. She looked hungry enough. Though she was slightly taller than average, at least for the women he knew, she looked rather underfed, and that bothered him.

"If you stay here, I'll go downstairs and get us something to eat. Then I'll bring it back up, and you and I can get to know one another properly." He nodded at his mother. "Without interference. How does that sound?"

She nodded again, so he shut the door softly and went downstairs to talk to the tavern keep. And as soon as he was holding a less than appetizing plate of various sorts of what he guessed to be meat and vegetables and dry bread, Lucas went back upstairs and tried to prepare himself for what was going to be a decidedly awkward and possibly dangerous conversation.

After he'd locked the door behind him once again, he turned and found her standing at the window, staring across the busy street at the gate once again, her shoulders slightly hunched. Had she been properly fed, she would probably have been able to put up a better fight at the gate. Lean muscles were visible where her sleeves ended halfway down her forearm, and during the struggle with the woman, her dress had flared enough for Lucas to get a good look at a well formed calf on one of her legs.

Vittoria wouldn't like him noticing such things.

He glanced down at the gate as well to see a full-fledged fight going on over what he guessed to be the jewels she had dropped. The soldiers would most likely have to call for reinforcements if the fight grew any closer to the gate. As it was, twelve men and several women were still throwing kicks and punches as they dove to the ground and wrestled about in the dirt.

Stay invisible, Michael had said. Thanks to his mother, he was off to a terrific start.

"It's probably not best to stand where they can see you." Lucas reached to draw the ratty brown curtains. "Soon they'll start looking for the source."

She reluctantly nodded, sat on the floor, and began to pick at the plate he set down beside her.

Annoyance warred with pity. Her foolish bolting might have compromised his entire mission. Any attention drawn to himself was an invitation for someone to realize he couldn't disappear. It wouldn't be hard for them to then discover and steal the gold he carried for his brother. His honor wouldn't allow him to sit and watch someone take the girl. But he also had an obligation to fulfill for his brother and the kingdom, and letting some strange girl get involved was probably most unwise.

Sometimes his honor could be a great pain in the rear end.

"So," he plopped down across from her and poured them both a mug of odd-smelling cider, "would you like to tell me why you were trying to get into my country?" Why did she have to wear that mask? It made everything she said subject to suspicion. And yet, the diplomatic lessons his brother had given him over the years forced him to stay his tongue. At least for now.

She looked down at the bread she'd taken from the plate and picked at the seeds on top.

"My father was a physician in Giova. When I was a baby, he was accused and convicted of malpractice when a woman died after he treated her. Rather than face death, he moved our family here." She shrugged. "A few years later, my mother died." She paused and rearranged her skirt so the gems would plink softly onto the fabric rather than the wooden floor. Then she took a bite of her bread but chewed slowly without seeming to enjoy it. "As I grew, he trained me in the way of healing. It was always his dream that I would leave Terrefantome the moment I was old enough."

"So he sent you away?"

"No, he kept me with him. But after he died when I was fourteen, my stepmother insisted my stepsister and I earn our keep."

Lucas frowned as he bit down into a sour apple. "Even her own daughter? How old was she?"

"Selina is definitely my stepmother's favorite, but not so much a favorite that she doesn't have to do any work. Chiara found work for her at the tavern."

This bothered Lucas more than he allowed to show. He liked visiting the tavern as much as the next man whenever his ship came to a new port. But he never drank enough to be unaware of what he was doing...or what the other men were doing. And if he ever became a father, he would see to it that his daughters never saw so much as a peek inside. He shuddered. Then another terrible thought came to him.

"You didn't work in the tavern, too, did you?"

"No. My father had trained me in his profession, so Chiara kept me home to tend the herbs and assist her. Besides, they would never let an *ascunz* work at a tavern."

"A what?"

"*Ascunz* is a Taistille word. It means 'hidden'. Taistille are feared much by the exiled, but they respect courage, and some very brave...or very foolish parents will seek them out to purchase a mask like mine. If the Taistille don't kill them then and there, in exchange for gold or silver or services, they'll make a mask with the power of our land. The parents will then give the masks to their daughters in an attempt to protect them."

"Why would it protect you?" Lucas asked.

"It prevents others from seeing through the mask directly, so one who might be tempted to take a girl in the absence of her protector might think twice first."

"Why would they do that?"

"Because they're not guaranteed she's pretty or that she'll ever even choose to remove the mask. And common law here states a man can only keep one woman as a companion at a time, or others can pillage what he claims as his."

Lucas stared at her, for the first time in his life, at a loss for words.

"Anyhow," she shrugged again and turned her face down. "Tavern keeps like pretty girls, and since I'm an *ascunz*, I could never find work in one. Not that I would ever want to." She shivered.

Lucas handed her the mug of cider he'd poured, which she took and drank deeply from. It was so strange watching her eat and drink through the mask. It was like the food disappeared as soon as she put it close to where her mouth should be. He wasn't sure if he'd ever get used to it.

When she was done, she wiped her mouth delicately on the edge of her sleeve and continued.

"It wasn't so bad, though, while I had a way out. Or thought..." She drew in a long breath. "But the plans my sister and I made to escape failed. And my sister got desperate."

"What did she do?"

"She..." her voice faltered.

Lucas found himself wishing that he could see her face. If he didn't focus directly on her, he could make out little details, like what she was doing with her mouth, or the fact that she had almond-shaped eyes. But every time he looked directly at her to study her more, those details were lost again, looking like nothing more than a little pond.

"I don't know about your land," she said quietly, "but here, there is a dark power even most of the Taistille do not touch."

"I know of it." Lucas shuddered as he recalled the darkness he'd been unfortunate enough to witness when it took some of the merpeople. "In the rest of the realm, we call it Sorthileige."

"Sorthileige." She said it slowly, as if tasting it, then took a deep breath. "Like I said, even the Taistille don't usually harness such darkness. The masks use the power of the land, and that's all. But there are a few who use something darker, and my sister sought one out."

Lucas felt his heart drop into his chest. He rubbed his chin, which was now covered in stubble. "Is that how you got your..." He waved at the pile of gems in Jaelle's lap. "This gift?"

She snorted.

"If you can call it that." She turned to face him directly, and he guessed she was looking him in the eyes. He tried to look back, but the mask made it difficult to focus. Where was he supposed to keep his eyes?

"I promise," she said, putting her food down. "I knew nothing of your mother's plans. After arranging to get me this..." she indicated to the impressive pile of gems in her lap, "my sister apparently granted some favors to those who frequent her tavern. They helped her contact your mother." Jaelle paused, and her voice dropped. "She and my stepmother are from Maricanta. She mentioned how much the queen...the queen mother likes jewels."

Lucas wanted very badly to curse. As always, his mother was muddling everything.

"I swear, though," she said, holding up her hands, "I had nothing to do with this. My sister put me to sleep, and I woke up in your mother's hired carriage. I never meant to take advantage of you. And I don't expect you to marry me," she added quickly. "I just had hoped that you would be able to help, and when you started arguing, I was afraid you would send me back to my stepmother, and I would have to start all over again."

In spite of his misgivings, Lucas leaned forward. "Start what?"

Jaelle took another deep breath and looked back down at the

jewels. "In order to get me this gift, my sister had to give up something of her own, and I'm afraid as a result, evil will visit her more than once for what she's done." She shook her head at the jewels. "This...this wasn't created by anything good."

Something inside him, though he couldn't tell what, desired to know more. Maybe it was the way her voice shook when she spoke of the darkness, or how her thin fingers trembled as she worried the hem of her faded purple dress. Whether or not his mother had truly stumbled upon this girl by chance, there was something different about her. Either that, or she was a very, very good actor. Trying desperately to see past her mask, Lucas leaned toward her. "What is it that you want, Jaelle?" he whispered.

"Take me with you."

Lucas had been about to wake his mother, but when she spoke the words, he froze.

"What?"

She leveled her chin and sat up straight, and he could hear her take a deep breath as though she had practiced for this moment. When she spoke, her voice only shook a little.

"I want to seek the help of King Everard to free my sister. And once we're free, I never want to come back to Terrefantome ever again."

"No." He didn't even have to think about that answer.

"I mean it." She straightened her shoulders. "I don't know what you're doing here, but you need a guide." She leaned forward. "Terrefantome is a deadly place for those of us who have lived here our entire lives. For someone unfamiliar like you..." She shook her head. "You won't make it out alive. Take me with you, and I'll help you finish whatever it is you're doing."

For one fleeting moment, Lucas wondered if taking her would really be such a bad idea. She certainly knew this world better than he did. She could also create gems with words, enough gems that he wouldn't even have to delve into his bag of dirty sea gems. Also, he was beginning to grow more and more curious about this stranger who knew of King Everard and smelled of lemongrass.

He stood and began to pace. Months of planning, and only two and a half weeks were left before Bartol's date came and went.

"Why are you here?"

"What?" Lucas looked down to see Jaelle's face turned up toward him.

"Your mother said your mission was secret."

He gave her a dry smile. "If I told you, it wouldn't be secret now, would it?"

She seemed to study him for a moment, though it was impossible to tell without seeing her eyes.

"The guards don't know you're here, do they?" she finally said.

"My brother feared that their knowledge would have them act differently toward me," Lucas said as he began sorting the bags to see how much he could actually carry. "That would have put me in even more danger."

"And now you're placing yourself in more danger again to get us across the street to the gate." It wasn't a question she was asking, but a statement.

"Unfortunately, yes," he said. Then he sighed. "But that's not your fault. None of this is." He cast a look of frustration at the sleeping body behind him.

As if she could hear them, Drina let out a snore from the bed. Lucas rolled his eyes.

"If you haven't noticed already, she greatly overestimates her ability to control things, and unfortunately, my brother and I have to clean up after her." The words tasted bitter. "I think, however, that this is possibly one of the worst things she's ever done." He looked up at Jaelle and tried to pretend he could see her eyes. "Not that it makes everything better, but...I'm sorry. And once I get back, I'll do everything in my power to help you help your sister."

"Which means you don't want to take me with you," she said, squaring her shoulders.

He ran a hand down his face.

"Here's what we're going to do. I'm going to escort you both across the street. I won't talk to the guards. You and my mother will do that. Have her demand to see my brother. My mother should take care of everything, but if they don't recognize her, show this to the guards."

Lucas felt slightly sick as he pulled the little square of parchment from his boot.

"What is it?" she asked, taking the paper.

"That's a secret sign for the guards. It's not the royal crest, but they'll know what it means. Anyone with that image belongs to the crown, and all of my men know it. We only use it in the most dire circumstances." And this was possibly the direst of circumstances Lucas had ever found himself in. The fate of his kingdom was in his hands, and his mother had come along for the ride.

To his surprise, though, Jaelle stood, letting the pile of gems spill out of her lap.

"I don't know what you think you know about my land," she said, her voice decidedly harder. "But I'm going to tell you now that unless you have some sort of guide, you will not make it to wherever you're trying to go. There are a hundred ways you could die simply walking down the street." She pointed to the window, each word growing crisper and in volume.

He crossed his own arms, standing taller as well, which made her about three inches shorter than him. "So I've been told."

"Where are your guards?" She jutted her chin out. "Or your guide? Do you have any of those?"

He worked his jaw for a moment. "I did."

"What happened to them?"

He huffed. "They ran off." They'd run off, and he'd been forced to return to their starting point to try to find a guide that wouldn't rob or kill him. And a week and a half later, he was still unsuccessful and starting to run out of money.

"You need me," she said fervently. "I can take you wherever you need to go. In return, you can protect me, and when we get done, you'll take me to meet King Everard."

Lucas stared at her, not sure if he was more impressed or angry. "I will try to help you escape, but there is no way you're going with me on this mission."

"And why not?"

He leaned down slightly. "Because I know what they do to women here, and having two women to protect, one being my *mother* of all people," he pointed back at his mother's sprawled form, "will make it ten times more dangerous than if I were by myself."

"Being by yourself will do you no good if you're wandering in circles." He couldn't be sure, but he was rather convinced by the tone of her voice that she was smirking. "Especially when the Taistille find you."

"And I suppose you have protection from them?" There, let her talk her way out of that one. Unfortunately, this only seemed to heighten her excitement.

"Actually, I do." Now he was sure she was grinning. "So, Prince. What will it be?"

What had just happened? She'd gone from a poor, frightened girl to a predator of her own sort in a matter of minutes. And where did that leave him?

"I'm sorry." He spread his arms akimbo. "I just can't in good conscience take two women into the heart of evil, knowing that if something happens to either one of you, I'll need to choose my country over you. And why are you so determined to go with me? Why can't you just wait with my mother?"

"Because if you're dead, there's no one to take me to Everard. And I also think you're wrong." She set her arms like his.

Lucas was about to retort that while the men in her country might not care about honor, he did. But a shout in the street interrupted him. They went to the window and peeked through.

A man stood outside their hotel, staring up at the windows and pointing at them, one at a time. Several others stood behind him, and still others were joining them. Even from where they stood, he could hear talk of diamonds.

"I think they've found us," Jaelle said, suddenly sounding breathless.

Before he could reply, a bang sounded downstairs, followed by several shouts.

"In the inn!" a deep voice shouted from below. "She has to be here!"

CHAPTER 12
RUN

Lucas hauled his mother into a sitting position.

"Time to wake up," he muttered as he reached into her reticule and yanked out a handful of pepper, which he blew in her face. Her eyes flew open, and she began to cough and gag as Lucas pulled her to her feet and pushed her toward the window.

"She hates pepper," he said to Jaelle as he leaned his still coughing mother against the girl. "My brother and I began sneaking pepper into her reticule when we realized she was putting herself to sleep. That way we'd have something to wake her with no matter where we were. All right, Mother, up you go."

He heaved his mother, who moaned piteously, up onto the little table beneath the window. Once he'd opened the window, he stuck one leg out and pulled her up with him.

"What are we doing?" his mother mumbled as she rolled her head over lazily toward the light. Then her eyes opened, and she let out a shriek, clinging to him as one of her legs dangled over the edge of the building.

"Mother! You're going to let them all know where we are!"

"Are you trying to kill us all?" Her fingernails dug into his skin.

The pounding of many feet sounded on the stairs.

"Do you think you can make it?" Lucas leaned back so Jaelle could see.

Jaelle took a quick look down. "I think so."

"Good. Because we don't have a choice." Lucas climbed the rest of the way through and out onto the flat roof outside the window before reaching back to help his groggy mother, who uttered threats as he pulled and Jaelle pushed. Once his mother was through the window, Jaelle started as well. Behind her, there was pounding on the door.

"Open up! We know she's in there!" someone yelled.

"You can't keep her to yourself!" another voice called.

Jaelle made it out just as the door burst open. Lucas led his mother while Jaelle took her other hand and followed him across the roof. Running was difficult, as the roof tiles were uneven and haphazardly placed, and pulling his mother along behind him made it even harder. Jaelle might have done well had it not been for his mother, who continued to moan and plead for them to walk as the entire group stumbled along toward the lowest overhang.

As they went, Lucas's mind raced. They needed to get across the street. But when he glanced at the gate, there were more people there than before.

"Can we get across without being noticed?" Lucas asked Jaelle as he pulled his mother behind him.

She shook her head. "They'll probably be there for hours. Whenever new wealth comes into a city, everyone wants some."

Well, that complicated things.

They came to the far edge of the roof. Lucas made sure Jaelle had a good grasp on his mother, then he jumped to the ground before turning back to the women.

"Lucas, I can't!" His mother drew back. "It's too far!"

"Mother, you have to!" he snapped, cringing as she used his real name. "They're coming!"

As he spoke, men filled the street just south of them. Lucas itched to pull his bow and fit an arrow to bring them down before they spotted his little party, but there were too many.

"Mother, now!" Lucas hissed instead.

Without waiting, Jaelle shoved his mother toward him. His mother shrieked as she fell, but Lucas didn't have time to encourage her because Jaelle was coming after her. He barely caught his mother, who nearly knocked him over. Thankfully,

Jaelle jumped lithely on her own, landing gracefully on her own two feet.

Then they were turning to run again. They came to a halt, though, as they came to the end of the alley and reached the street. They seemed to be nearing the edge of the city, but just as Jaelle began to call out that they were on the wrong side of the city, a wave of men, along with a few women, appeared coming from the next street over, all shouting when they spotted Lucas and the women. Lucas whirled back around and pulled them into the crowd going the other direction.

"Duck," he hissed at the women over the noise of the crowd. "Don't let them see you!"

"But the gate is in the other direction!" Jaelle cried.

"What's going on?" his mother sobbed. "Why are they chasing us?"

"Why do you think?" Lucas asked, exasperated.

"Run!" Jaelle began to pull them along again.

Lucas glanced back just in time to see a very large man with a circular scar on his face disappear behind them. Seconds later, he received a sharp strike to the chin that made him stumble back several feet. His mother screamed. Before the invisible man could hit him again, however, he reappeared. And to Lucas's surprise, Jaelle was riding on his back. As he tried to shake her off, he turned just enough that Lucas saw her drop several jewels down the back of his shirt. This gave Lucas the chance to regain his balance and land a sturdy kick to the man's large gut. Jaelle slid off his back, and Lucas followed up with two punches to the face. As soon as the man was stumbling, Lucas grabbed his mother's hand again and tried to drag them further into the crowd. They would use the crowd as a cover and double back to the path.

Before they had gone ten steps, however, Jaelle shrieked and yanked them all in another direction. Lucas looked back as they ran. He saw nothing, but he could hear the pounding of feet following them, kicking up dust like a herd of ghost horses. In theory, he'd known this could happen before he'd come to Terrefantome. But here in the middle of it, the whole sensation of being chased by invisible opponents was more unnerving than he could say.

And so their pursuit continued, Jaelle taking the lead, zigging and zagging and yanking Lucas and his mother along until they were all breathing raggedly. Lucas eventually lost track of the route which they'd taken, and it was all he could do to keep his mother moving, following Jaelle's lead. After two more fights with invisible opponents, always only surviving when Jaelle jumped in and put diamonds down their backs, Lucas was nearly convinced he would most likely be brutally murdered here in some back alley. But finally, the edge of town appeared. And beyond that, the forest.

"Lucas!"

Lucas turned to see his mother fall to her knees. Her dress was covered in mud and her hair was falling out of its pins. "I can't go on! I can't do it!" she gasped. Lucas glanced back to see two of their pursuers spot them from halfway down the street. Jaelle had managed to give them a lead, but now the men grinned, pointed, and faded into nothing.

Lucas looked at Jaelle. "What do we do?" As he spoke, he bent to pick his mother up, but he knew no escape could last long if he was carrying his mother the entire time. Though she wasn't as stout as many of the women her age, she was no Jaelle, either.

Jaelle froze for one full second, looking back and forth between the forest and the men who were quickly gaining on them. Then she held her hands up, and for the first time, began catching the gems in her hands as she spoke.

"Take her into the forest!" she called, gems dripping blatantly from her lips. "I'll find you!"

"I'm not leaving you!" Lucas's muscles screamed in protest as he hoisted his mother onto his shoulder, but Jaelle shook her head.

"You don't have a choice. If they catch you, she'll be taken and held for ransom. And they won't hold her nicely. Now go!"

Lucas hesitated for one moment longer. Shame ate him alive for leaving the girl behind, but he knew she was right. His mother was obviously rich, and she wouldn't hold up for a minute when questioned about her origins or his mission. With nausea rolling in his stomach, he began to race for the forest. As he turned once more, he saw her toss her hands in the air. And down came a shower of gems.

"Look, everyone!" she shouted to the passersby on the road. "Diamonds!"

The crowd became a living, moving thing as it surged toward her.

Don't let her be harmed, Lucas prayed as he fought to escape the road and run for the trees. The going was torturously slow, though. Even through the grass, the mud grabbed for his boots, squelching each time he yanked his boots free of it, and he tripped on the weeds, the extra weight in his arms sending him stumbling again and again.

A lifetime later, when they were just inside the forest, he leaned his mother against a tree and turned back toward the road. Before he could move, though, she gripped his leg.

"You're not going to leave me?" she whispered, her eyes half shut as she gasped for air, as though she'd been carrying him.

"If it hadn't been for your greed and pride, that girl wouldn't have had to risk her life to save you. So yes, I'm going after her."

He charged back toward the road, the crowd in a frenzy as they dove and fought for the jewels. Men and even a few women disappeared and reappeared so fast the crowd looked like a clump of spirits. He searched frantically for her. She wasn't short, but there were many men in the crowd, and it would be easy for a girl of her weight to be knocked to the ground and crushed by someone larger.

"Jaelle!" he shouted as he reached the edges of the throng. "Jaelle, where are you?"

But she was nowhere to be found. Other masked faces appeared, but none with black silky hair and an olive complexion. His heart threatened to stop as he breathed harder and faster, panic beating down the self-control he usually prided himself on. But just as he began to despair, something invisible slammed into him, nearly knocking him over.

Relief washed over him as she reappeared. Her limbs trembled, and from the way she leaned against him, he knew she would collapse if he let go. He slipped one arm under her knees and the other behind her back before turning and running into the forest again.

CHAPTER 13
FAR MORE DANGEROUS

When Jaelle opened her eyes again, it was dusk. And immediately, alarm bells, like the one that rang when the town had a fire, went off in Jaelle's head. A man was touching her. Not just touching her. She was in his arms.

Jaelle let out a cry so loud that the man carrying her startled and nearly dropped her. She took the opportunity to free herself and scrambled away. She was still too weak to go far, though, so she leaned against a tree, panting as she watched him carefully.

"It's all right," he said softly, holding his arms out in front of him. "I'm not going to hurt you."

At the sound of his voice, Jaelle's mind was jolted back to the mob she'd almost been engulfed in. She'd thought she could throw the diamonds and get away, but the people had been faster than she'd expected. The last thing she remembered was not being able to breathe as she made one last effort to escape the pile of violence that had erupted over her gems. And landing right in Prince Lucas's arms.

And with Prince Lucas's name, everything else returned as well. She also noticed Drina leaning back against a large tree not far from where they stood. She appeared to be dozing.

"I'm..." Jaelle tried to catch her breath as she slowly straightened. "I'm sorry. I just...I didn't expect you to carry me." As she spoke, more gems fell from her mouth, and she was reminded again of the disaster they'd just escaped. "I have to find a way to stop this."

"I only wanted to get you away from the mob." He paused, then his eyes lit up. "I have an idea."

He darted over to his mother's bag and began rifling through it.

"What are you doing?" Drina snipped.

"I don't usually make it a habit to go through women's bags," he said without looking up, "but my mother got us into this mess, so she's going to get us out. There." He held up a long scarf and nodded to himself. "She doesn't go anywhere without extra clothes of some sort."

"I can hear you, son."

The prince ignored her and held his prize out. It was a scarf, muted red, nearly dark enough to be brown, and when fully shook out, it was nearly wide enough to have been a skirt. Hopefully it was strong fabric as well.

"I apologize," he said, taking a step toward her and holding the scarf in front of him. "But I need to try something."

"I can do it." She reached for the scarf, understanding his purpose. But after trying unsuccessfully several times to tie it snugly around the back of her head, Jaelle was forced to admit defeat.

"I'm afraid I can't tie it," she said, unable to keep the apprehension out of her voice. The last thing she wanted to do was encourage this man to touch her. He seemed decent enough, far more than any man she was currently acquainted with. But he was a man. And Jaelle knew better.

She gave a small start when his fingers brushed hers as they took the scarf. But to his credit, he kept his eyes on his work, and when he spoke, his voice was soft.

"Bithiah, our head housekeeper, is from the south." He continued to arrange the scarf around her head and shoulders, though his skin didn't touch hers again. "Whenever the sun became too harsh for her taste, she would wrap herself like this to keep from burning."

"Burning?"

Prince Lucas paused.

"I suppose you wouldn't know it here, but in other places, if you stay in the sun too long, your skin gets pink or even red, and it stings and itches later if you don't cover it properly."

"Oh."

He stepped back to examine his work. "It's not as fashionable as when Bithiah does it, but the folds should catch the jewels," he said. "It only has to hold until you get to the other side of the wall."

"The wall?" Jaelle said. Then she gave a sharp laugh. "We're not going back to the wall."

"We are," Lucas said. But before he could argue further, a shout sounded in the distance.

"I see tracks! They went this way!"

They didn't wait to hear any more. Lucas slung his mother's bag across his chest and pulled her to her feet. Jaelle hurried along behind them.

And so they ran deeper and deeper into the forest. Every time she thought they might rest, they heard more voices. So they pushed on.

Thankfully, the moon must have been shining on the other side of the clouds, because the night wasn't quite as dark as usual, providing enough light for them to continue their trek even after the sun set.

Eventually, the voices called out less and less, but Lucas continued to push them deeper. Maybe he wasn't quite as simple in the head as Jaelle had first thought. His boots were nearly silent as he trod the forest floor, even in the dim light from above. And unlike many men Jaelle had seen in her years, he didn't seem to feel the need to fill the night with idle chatter. Instead, he stayed alert, turning his head at every sound.

The queen mother, on the other hand, was inconsolable about the entire escapade, sobbing about how she couldn't go on and about how she'd never seen so much savagery in her life, but Lucas was able to silence her eventually with threats of leaving her behind for those savages to find. At this threat, she turned so white Jaelle was worried she might pass out. But she did at least stop her blubbering. When she'd fallen far enough behind that they could whisper without being heard, Jaelle drew a little closer.

"You're not actually going to leave her," she whispered, casting a glance behind them.

Prince Lucas followed her gaze. "Pitiful, isn't it?" He rolled his eyes as Drina let out yet another moan. "My brother and I have begged her to take up some sort of physical activity during the day, something to get her off her couch or away from her mirror. But she insists that it's undignified for a queen to cover herself with sweat for no purpose." He glanced back again as Drina muttered to herself, trying to pull her gown free of a bramble bush. "Maybe she'll listen a little better after this."

"But you're not going to leave her?" Jaelle pressed.

"Of course not. She's my mother." His mouth turned up slightly. "Just don't tell her that, or we'll never get to wherever it is we're going." He stopped and looked around. "Speaking of which... where are we going?"

Jaelle looked around, too. For a long time, she'd given no thought to the castle or the gate. In their first haste, all they'd wanted to do was escape their pursuers. But it had been a long time since they'd heard any shouts behind them.

"The city is that way. And my house is northeast of the city." She pointed to their left.

He hesitated so long she wasn't sure he'd speak. But finally, he asked, "And Bartol's castle?"

That was an odd request indeed, and possibly slightly disturbing. And yet, she tried not to let him see her surprise.

"The castle is east of my house. Since we're too far from the main highway, we would need to go up and around, north and east." She gestured at the road which they had been following from a distance. "This is the best road on which to do that."

"And how long do you think that will take us?" He started walking again, and she fell into step beside him. But not too close. It was bad enough that she'd collapsed in his arms in the city. She'd have to work doubly hard to make sure he didn't think that kind of touching was going to happen again.

"Probably two weeks," she said, trying to gather her senses.

He grimaced. "That's close."

"Close to what?"

"Oh, the king's deadline." He paused to help her over a small brook. She ignored his outstretched hand and jumped over it herself. He said nothing but gave the slightest shake of his head as he looked back at his mother, who was now carrying half her skirts in her arms as she made her way through the mud from which they'd just come.

What was he hiding? Why was he so determined to reach the one place in the land he should be trying to avoid? Everyone knew better than to gain the attention of the crown. There were rumors, of course, that this king was more progressive, and that he wasn't as harsh as some of his predecessors. But that didn't mean one should waltz into his arms. Anyone who did that was a fool. And yet, this prince clearly wasn't a fool.

But if not a fool, what was he?

A sensation deep inside warned Jaelle that this was a far more dangerous quest than she was giving it credit for. But Selina was worth it.

"So," she said breathlessly. "Where are we going?"

He looked at her long and hard before his shoulders dropped, and he shook his head at the ground.

"Since the mob seems determined to follow us, and I'm already pushing the date as it is...I suppose you're taking me to the castle."

TRUE DARKNESS FELL SOON after that. And though Drina often moaned and murmured to herself as they made their way slowly through the dark, the prince remained quiet, and Jaelle was glad. Even with the mask, Selina had told her on more than one occasion that she was a terrible liar and easy to see through. Her voice trembled whenever she was uncomfortable, and she had a tendency to shrink back inside herself whenever she was scared. And Jaelle couldn't risk letting the prince see how his touch had unnerved her. Even now, since her head had cleared, she could recall exactly how it felt when she'd collapsed against him before she'd passed out. His chest had been warm, and his arms were thicker than she'd first thought.

Of course, all this might be expected, considering that Jaelle had never purposefully come into contact with any man other than her father or her patients to came to her for healing. There had been situations over the years like the one Selina had saved her from, where advances from other men had been unwanted. Thankfully, Jaelle had always managed to slip out of those. But she knew better than to let a man touch her.

And yet...the moment she'd fallen into his arms, Jaelle had felt safe.

Right now, she couldn't afford to feel safe.

"How did you do it?"

"Huh?" Jaelle looked up to find the prince staring at her again.

"How did you know your plan would work?" the prince asked. "Back with the mob."

"I didn't." She shrugged. "We can't stay invisible for very long. It's exhausting, like running at full-speed, even if we're standing still. I figured if I gave them something to run for, they'd tire themselves out to get there." She stepped carefully over a fallen tree. "I relied on their greed, and it didn't let me down."

"But if jewels ruin their invisibility," Lucas argued, "why would anyone here want them?"

"Well, to begin with, new arrivals generally dislike feeling disadvantaged, so they like to keep jewels on them in case they're attacked." She bit her lip. "More than that, though, the crown gets most of its gold that way."

His head snapped up. "How so?"

"By hiring desperate new exiles to collect dues."

"Like taxes?"

She pursed her lips. "They call it that, but really, they just take what they want. And not only that, but the threat of it also keeps everyone subservient to the crown."

Lucas thought for a moment. "Why would they hire new arrivals?"

"Because once you've been here long enough, you realize everyone else is fighting to survive, too. And most decide to abide by a sort of unwritten code to leave their neighbors alone. But the new arrivals have no allegiances, so most don't object to theft. The diamonds simply ensure they can see their victims." She paused and listened until she was sure she heard it. "Come on," she waved to the left. "There's water nearby."

Prince Lucas stared down into the water before lifting some to wash his face. As he did, the moon lit the clouds with a glow that allowed her to study him once more.

The angles of his face, while defined, weren't harsh. His curly hair was thick and silky, and she had the ridiculous urge to run her hands through it, just to see what it felt like. Most distracting of all, however, were his eyes. They were hazel, with more brown than anything else, but just enough green and gold to make her look twice.

Not that she hadn't seen men with hazel eyes before, she chided herself as she stepped carefully over a crooked fallen tree. Maybe it was his code of honor that made him so attractive. So few men had one here. She didn't trust him, of course. Selina made that mistake with Seth, and Jaelle knew better than to give everything to a man the way her sister had nearly done. But still, there was something...relieving about knowing this one was at least unlikely to mug her in her sleep.

She hoped.

If men don't want you, Jaelle, they want something from you. How often had Selina uttered those words? No, it was far better that she still wore her mask, and even better that she and the prince weren't actually getting married. If she was stupid enough to believe men like that existed, she would end up more than a little disappointed. She and Selina were finished with being disappointed by men. After this was all over, and when Selina was free from her curse, they would buy a house and live their lives as the sisters they'd always dreamed of being. Happy. Together. Without her stepmother or men or anyone else who could hurt them. Maybe they'd get an ill-tempered dog, too, just for good measure.

"Let's stop here."

Jaelle was yanked from her daydreams by the prince, who stood over a small brook. Gently, he lowered his mother onto a fallen log. In low, gentle tones, he knelt beside her and pulled a cup from his pack, which he dipped into the water and brought up to her mouth for her to drink. Jaelle watched as discreetly as she could from her perch on a smaller rock as he continued to speak in soothing tones to his mother. Jaelle couldn't hear what she said, but whatever it was, it brought Lucas to pull a second cloak from his pack and wrap it tightly around her.

If any man could make her change her mind about men, though, it might be this one. As awful as Drina could be with her whining and scheming, her son's love for her was evident in the way he cared for her. Drina was obviously exhausted. She seemed barely able to sit up on her own, and though that was her fault completely, Jaelle could relate. Her feet ached, and her head spun with hunger. The meal the prince had brought her seemed like days ago, rather than hours. She squinted up at the hazy sky. It had to be near the tenth hour, if not later. They'd been walking for hours, fear of being discovered driving them on.

After drinking her fill from the brook, she curled her knees up to her chest. The water wasn't sweet, but at least it smelled and tasted clean. Wrapping her cloak about her to ward off the wet cold settling over the forest, she pulled out one of the rolls her sister had packed. Selina had probably expected them to be long gone from Terrefantome by now. Still, this was better than nothing.

"Here."

Jaelle turned to see the prince holding out an apple.

"I picked up a few of these from the market this morning." He looked up and swept the thicket with his eyes. "It's not much, but these should hold us until I can figure something out tomorrow."

"I need to relieve myself," Drina announced a little too loudly. Lucas's eyes went slightly wide with horror until Drina scowled. "I'm not asking you to come with me. I can take myself to the bathroom."

"Mother," the prince rubbed his face. "You've never been to the bathroom in the forest before."

"I can go with her," Jaelle said. She started to get to her feet, but Drina only waved her down.

"I'm a big girl! I can relieve myself, thank you!" She lifted her skirts and slowly made her way to a thicker patch of bushes at the edge of the thicket while Jaelle and the prince exchanged a glance. Well, she looked at him. He looked at her, but her expression would be hidden from his eyes.

"We'll keep a good ear out for her," Lucas finally said softly. "She'll make an even bigger scene if we try to force her."

"How is she going to hold up?" Jaelle asked just as softly.

He shook his head. "I don't know. Honestly, I'm going to be impressed if we can keep her going at the rate we've been walking." He stopped and sat on the rock beside Jaelle's and pulled his coat tightly around himself. "Look, about earlier. When I went back for you." He paused. "Why did it frighten you so?"

Jaelle stiffened.

"I..." She took a deep breath, not daring to even hint that she had liked it. "I prefer not to be touched." If there was one rule Selina had pounded into her time and time again, it was that she must never, ever let a man have power over her. And power, Selina often cautioned, began with the kindest of touches.

"Even when someone's saving your life?" He raised his eyebrows, which annoyed her for some reason.

"Ever, if I can help it." Before she could finish her retort, though, someone screamed. Jaelle and the prince both jumped to their feet.

"Mother?" the prince called.

His answer was another scream, and this time, Jaelle recognized it, too. They both grabbed their bags, and the prince took off with Jaelle close on his heels. When they exited the thicket, though, they came to a halt. Drina was nowhere in sight. The scream came again, and Jaelle saw movement behind the trees.

"There!" She pointed, and they were off again.

They skidded to a stop at the edge of a small cliff that jutted out over a large pond. The pond itself was strange. It moved like its water was being disturbed from beneath, sloshing in every direction, as opposed to being perfectly still, and its surface was nearly white. Drina lay several feet from the pond with one leg tucked under her body and one leg stretched out toward the water. Jaelle followed on Lucas's heels as he ran down the embankment.

Jaelle was nearly to them when Drina's ankle caught her eye, and Jaelle let out a small scream herself.

White worms covered Drina's ankle and foot, which were already dripping with blood. And they weren't just crawling on her skin. They were trying to burrow in it.

The prince's jaw slackened as he fell at her side. But Drina only screamed louder and pointed with a shaking hand out at the water. Jaelle threw her hand over her mouth as she realized that the worms on Drina's ankle weren't the only ones.

The water was also full of worms. It was so full that they crawled on top of one another, writhing and wriggling as the water moved around them. The entire pond was teeming with the worms. And as they watched, the worms began to clump together into something like a giant arm. Then the arm lunged at Drina.

CHAPTER 14
MILA

Lucas and Jaelle grabbed his mother's arms and tried to drag her away, but the worms continued to pile onto one another. The clump fell on her leg, joining those already there, and latched on. His mother shrieked again as it began to pull her back toward the pond. Jaelle and Lucas fought, but the worms were too strong. Lucas's heart thundered in his ears as all three of them were hauled closer and closer to the writhing mass, his mind searching frantically for any way of escape.

As the mass of worms pulled, his own feet, as well as Jaelle's, were dragged to the pond. But just before their feet were consumed as well, the air lit up orange. Audible squeals went up from the pond as flames quickly covered the entire surface of the water. The arm released his mother and retreated back to the water.

"I told you little buggers to leave folks alone!"

Lucas looked up to find a stubby old woman on the other side of the pond. She held a torch and what looked like an oil jar. She tossed the jar's contents out onto the pond's surface and then touched it with the torch, shouting some sing-songy rhyme. And as the surface of the pond and the worms went up in flames, she threw her head back and laughed. Only after two or three minutes of this behavior did she seem to remember Lucas's party and immediately stopped dancing in place.

"Come on! Come on!" she called with a welcoming smile, waving them toward her. "We've got to get that poison out if you want her to live!"

Lucas looked at Jaelle and subtly shook his head.

"She needs help!" Jaelle hissed.

"We don't know who this woman is." He looked again at his mother, who was turning paler by the second. "What if she kills her?" He and Michael had thought they'd planned for every scenario. They'd spent hours poring over the few maps they had and arguing over what weapons he should bring and when he should leave. Apparently, they'd missed the scenario where his mother snuck out of the kingdom to find him an accursed fiancee and then was eaten by worms. Then he remembered.

"You're supposed to be a healer. You can do it!"

"She's not going to make it at this rate if we don't do something!" Jaelle indicated his mother then the pond. "And I can't help her like this...not out here! I don't even know what these things are. I can't heal her from something I didn't know existed until now!"

"Well," the woman called over her shoulder. "Are you coming or not?"

Lucas glared at Jaelle for another long moment before he picked his mother up and began walking toward the woman, Jaelle on his heels.

The woman whistled to herself while they walked, as though Lucas weren't carrying a dying woman in his arms and a pond of worms wasn't on fire behind her. He wanted to grab her by the collar and hurry her along, but he kept his arms around his mother instead. After moving up another little hill, they came to a ramshackle cottage that blended in with the trees. The woman ushered them inside with the joviality of someone who had just come upon old friends in time for tea, rather than happening upon a stranger who was looking more dead than alive by the minute.

The cottage looked far sturdier inside than it did from the outside. Thick wooden beams crossed one another evenly to frame the ceiling. A large fireplace was roaring with a pot large enough to hold Jaelle sitting over it. The smell of sage and a few other flavors Lucas didn't recognize wafted out. The cottage itself was oddly shaped, as there seemed to be three sections. The main area, which they had walked into, was filled by a giant wooden table, seven wooden chairs, the hearth, and a miniature dresser, and it was about the size of Michael's study at home.

What was strangest, though, were the enormous piles of objects that were stacked on every flat surface and even some surfaces that weren't. Hats, pots, shoes, tools, axes, plates, cups, bolts of fabric, and even books were piled high everywhere he looked. And as if that weren't enough, more furniture of every shape and size was crowded into the room, making it look far smaller than it would have if it were properly furnished.

The woman hummed to herself as she cleared the table then indicated for Lucas to lay Drina down on it. Lucas laid his mother down, and Jaelle was immediately at her side, dumping the contents of her bag out on the table. A large book, several little jars, a few bread rolls, and various articles of clothing spilled out. Lucas hadn't noticed the book earlier, but before he could ask about it, Jaelle grabbed everything but the jars and shoved it back in the bag.

"I have several salves here if you think they'll help—"

"Pine sap, huh?"

Jaelle jumped as the woman bent over her shoulder, studying the little jars. She took one from Jaelle before dropping it back on the table with a sharp crack. Jaelle snatched up the jar and examined it as the woman shook her head.

"Not bad," the woman said, "but it won't help her this time." Then the woman grabbed a whalebone pipe from the nearest chair and stuck it between her teeth as she moved over to a miniature dresser in the corner and began to rummage through the bottom drawer. Finally, she held up a small clay jar and smiled. "Here it is."

She moved back to the table and shoved Jaelle's goods out of the way, nearly knocking several off as the girl tried desperately to catch them.

"Here." The woman held her clay jar out for Jaelle, who sniffed it cautiously. Lucas kept his hands at his mother's side in case he needed to scoop her back up and run outside again. Still, he prayed the woman was telling the truth. His mother's breaths were getting more and more shallow by the minute, and even if they did escape, he wouldn't have the slightest idea of what to do with her once they were free of their captor.

"Lemon?" Jaelle asked as the woman took her jar back. Lucas could see the tiniest movement of the scarf covering her mouth as the jewel landed inside, and he was grateful she'd thought to put it back on after their last stop. Of course, he also hoped she didn't talk too much and need to empty it, either.

"Aye. But not just lemon!" The woman paused, seeming to notice the scarf, too. She stared at it for a moment, her eyes far too curious for Lucas's taste. Thankfully, she finally shrugged and went back to what she was doing. "Also timmeroot." She held up one of the weeds Lucas had seen all over the forest's groundcover. "It's why the worms like the water. Our soil is acidic, so they stay in the pond. I found that when I first arrived here and got stuck near that pit like all the other poor souls who fall in. Only thing I had on me was a little waterskin of lemon juice I brought for cooking. So I poured it on them. Then I used the timmeroot to dry the wound, as I had nothing else within reach. And they all..." she paused to drip droplets of lemon juice on the worms that were still stuck to his mother's ankle. "Fell away."

Sure enough, with each drop, the worms writhed. Lucas had to hold back the violent need to gag as they made their way out of his mother's foot, a few of them up to an inch long, rather than the little white dots he'd assumed them to be. His mother began to scream and twist back and forth.

"Hold her still!" the woman called as she pulled out a sharp little tool and began trying to pull the remaining worms out with it.

Jaelle rolled up one of the shirts that had fallen from her bag and stuck it in his mother's mouth, then she held Drina's head and whispered gently as his mother continued to whimper.

Lucas felt more useless than he ever had in his life. He should be helping Jaelle. He should be helping his mother. After training with King Everard, living on the seas, battling pirates, and surviving a war, he'd seen about every wound imaginable. But worms that burrowed into skin?

Even he had limits.

Though it seemed like it took forever, the woman eventually

pulled all the worms out and threw them in the fire. Then she tossed Jaelle a handful of weeds and told Jaelle to bandage the little holes the worms had left in his mother's skin, putting the weeds against the holes under the bandage.

"Will it scar?" his mother, who had seemed to regain her senses, asked tearfully.

"Some." The woman nodded, seeming oblivious to his mother's look of horror. "But the timmeroot will heal nearly any kind of wound. I never saw it before coming here. Works so good I wish I could sell it elsewhere."

"What is timmeroot?" Lucas asked.

The woman began to put away her things. "That blue-ish green grass that grows everywhere outside. It's all over the kingdom."

"What do you mean I'm going to scar?" his mother cried. "I can't be deformed! I'm the—"

"Where did you learn about healing?" Jaelle asked quickly as Lucas sent his mother a scathing look.

"I was an apothecary," the woman said as she bustled around and gathered food and bowls from all over the kitchen. She paused to pull down the collar of her dress so they could see her small, blue tattoo. "See that? I was convicted of attempted murder." She grinned, as though this were quite humorous.

"What for?" Lucas asked. Jaelle made a sharp sound, but the woman didn't seem to care.

"There was a fellow that fancied me something fierce. I thought it was fun at first, but when he wouldn't stop leaving me flowers and writing me love poems, I decided to gift him a salve to grow out his hair."

"You can do that?" Lucas asked incredulously.

The woman, who was rather short, threw her head back and laughed so hard her graying curls bounced. "Isn't this one a man through and through? No, dear, there isn't such a thing. But I told him there was, and when he woke up the next morning, his head was so red and swollen he could barely see." She sighed happily to herself as she stirred whatever was in the pot.

Lucas gave Jaelle a long glance, and though he couldn't see her features, he was rather sure she looked as horrified as he felt. What had they gotten themselves into?

"Come, it's time for supper," the woman said, waving her ladle in the air before serving up four bowls of stew. "Well, don't all just stand there looking at each other. Let's eat! Here, dear," she shoved Lucas toward his mother. "Get her off the table so we can use it." She chuckled to herself as she pulled a pile of spoons off another chair. "As if I'm going to eat around that woman's hip or foot."

Lucas did as she said, lifting his mother off the table and setting her down gently on the bench, but he was still heavily considering grabbing his mother and Jaelle and making a break for it when the woman, who was already digging into her stew, shook her head.

"I know what you're thinking." She broke several large chunks off a round loaf of bread. "You won't want to leave now. The worms are worst at night. They'll be crawling all over the ground until the light comes again. Your mum here was lucky. She fell in before they all went out to feed the way they're doing now."

"You mean," Jaelle's voice shook slightly, and her fingers twitched. "They're out there right now?"

"Mm-hm. You can hear them squealing if you listen closely enough." And the woman put her hand to her ear. And sure enough, when Lucas went to the window by the door, he could hear the faint high-pitched sounds coming through the dirty glass. The little pond still glowed orange as the flames licked up the last of the oil on the water.

"See?" she said, waving him back. "Come eat. I don't get visitors as often as I'd like. Tell me about yourselves." She took a long swig from a clay mug beside her bowl. Milk dribbled down her chin, but she didn't stop until she'd emptied it.

Slowly, he and Jaelle turned and sat at the table with her. Lucas looked at Jaelle, who gave him the smallest of shrugs. Then she picked up the bread and began nibbling. Lucas did the same. The woman had broken their bread from the same piece as her own, so it was unlikely to be poisoned or drugged. He wasn't taking a single sip from the stew, though, until their host did.

"Name's Mila."

"Pardon me?" Jaelle asked, her bread halfway to her mouth.

"My name. It's Mila." The woman pointed at herself. "And I know you're Lucas. I heard your mother crying for you earlier." She pointed at Jaelle. "And you two are?"

Jaelle hesitated slightly. "Jaelle."

Lucas was relieved when she didn't give her surname, but before he could relax, Mila was looking at Drina, her dark eyes a little too bright with interest.

"And you?"

"Angelica," Lucas said quickly as he wrapped his arm around his mother. Thankfully, she was still too dazed from the worm fiasco to contradict him for using her second name. It was bad enough this woman already knew his first name. He'd let his hair grow a little longer than usual and was wearing nondescript clothes, but it still wouldn't be hard for people to figure out who he was. Maricanta was small, and Lucas and his brother were often out with the people. The last thing he needed was for his mother to give enough information for Mila to figure out who they really were.

"So you live alone?" Jaelle asked in a voice that was slightly too loud. Lucas could have danced with her for such a rescue that pointed delightfully away from his mother and their identities.

"I do." She poked a finger in Lucas's direction and gave him a wry grin. "And don't you go thinking you're going to lay claim to me." She sat straighter and smoothed her dress. "I'm not an easy one to woo, mind you." Her eyes twinkled. "But you can try."

The bite of bread he'd been chewing hadn't been so bad, but suddenly, he had the urge to gag it all up.

"Besides," Mila added with an even bigger smile, "this one must be enough for you. Or would be, if she'd remove the mask."

Jaelle stopped chewing as Mila stood on her bench and climbed onto the table. Then she crawled over it on all fours until she was only inches from Jaelle's mask, studying her intently.

"Oh," Lucas said, scrambling for words, "I'm not her protector. I...uh, I don't keep women. Not like that at least."

He'd meant only to reassure the woman that he intended Jaelle no harm. But by the quick breath Jaelle sucked in and the dark look Mila gave him, he knew he'd said the wrong thing.

"Don't ever," Mila's voice deepened dangerously, all hints of the impish smile gone from her face, "let anyone hear you say that." She crawled back to her seat, where she sat and began swishing around the contents of her bowl with her spoon. "Ridiculous boy," she muttered to herself, "putting the girl in danger like that. It's like he wants to get rid of her."

Lucas wanted very much to look at Jaelle again, but he couldn't raise his head to do so. Shame burned his cheeks as he realized why the women's reactions had been so strong.

Dolt.

Thankfully, this woman, odd as she was, didn't seem the type to want Jaelle taken, at least not based on the way she was still muttering to herself. But from the way Jaelle was sitting, too still, as though she'd turned to stone, he knew he'd broken whatever trust they'd managed to build that evening. If there had been another man with them, he could have easily put her in great danger.

"Well," Mila finally said as she finished her stew, "if she's not yours now, she won't be with you for very long." That gleaming curiosity returned to her eyes as she looked back and forth between Jaelle and Lucas. "Where are you traveling to anyway? Must be trying to avoid something if you're as far back as I am." She leaned forward and gave Jaelle a half-smile. "And hiding something if you're wearing a cover over your mask."

Jaelle said nothing, but her hand trembled as it clutched her spoon. After several seconds of silence, Lucas could stand it no longer.

"We've just become betrothed," he said, hoping Jaelle wouldn't punish him for it later. Technically, they were engaged, thanks to his mother, though Lucas wasn't bound by law to follow through with the marriage, as his mother did not have the crown.

Mila studied him for a moment with those sharp eyes before letting out a laugh. "Think they have the time for betrothals here." She stood and shook her head as she picked up her bowl and put it beside a bucket of water. "They're in for a big surprise the first time some bloke lays eyes on this one, they are." She shook her head again as she came to gather their bowls as well. "You'll be staying on then tonight."

"We couldn't impose," Jaelle said in a small voice, but Mila only shook her head harder. She shook her head a lot, even when no one had spoken.

"Like I said, worms will be out until just before sunrise. If you'd been out another half hour, you'd all be dead by now."

"Are the worms in all the forest?" Lucas asked, praying very much that they weren't.

"Just here. Well, this is the only pit of them I've seen." Mila shrugged. "Not that I've done much exploring. Found this old shack abandoned the day I arrived and haven't looked back since."

Lucas couldn't help wondering if the house had really been empty when Mila arrived, but he decided it was better not to ask.

"It's getting late." Mila stood and stretched, her short curls seeming to stick out in every direction. "I suppose you'll want the far bed." She nodded at the bed in the corner of the room. "These two," she waved at Jaelle and his mother, "can have the bigger one. And no, Lucas, you don't get the big one just because you're a man."

"I would never—" Lucas began, but Mila continued.

"Sleep tonight. I'll feed you in the morning, then you can be on your way. I have some extra food stored up for now and then, but I can't go feeding you endlessly now, you hear?" She chuckled and turned away. "Course they hear. I'm standing right next to them talking. They're hiding something, but they're not deaf." Then she waved at the corner without turning. "Blankets are in the basket by the fire. Help yourselves." She left through the door on the other side of the table, and Lucas could hear the lock turn after it shut.

CHAPTER 15
WHAT IT IS

P rince Lucas," Jaelle said softly.

"Huh?" Lucas turned, then saw what she was talking about. His mother had fallen asleep with her face in her bread on the table. Lucas sighed, shook his head, and stood to pick her up again.

"It was a long day," Jaelle said, her voice still low.

"Please, call me Lucas." He scratched his head and looked at his mother again. "Carriage thieves, chased by a mob, nearly eaten by worms." Lucas let out a humorless laugh. "Honestly, I think the thought of having a visible scar might be the thing that does her in." He stopped and peered down at the bed. It looked clean enough, but how could he tell?

Jaelle leaned down and sniffed the blanket cover.

"Lavender," she said, surprise tinging her voice.

"Is that unusual here?" he asked.

"Well, yes. But I grow it at home. If she was an apothecary, I suppose she would know how to grow it." She shrugged. "Seems clean enough to me."

That was all he needed. Lucas's arms were beginning to feel quite strained, so he lowered his mother onto the bed. They could make their decisions when he wasn't about to fall over.

"Do you think it's safe?" Jaelle asked, her voice nearly inaudible.

Lucas went to the front window and peered through it. The glass was dirty, but even through the grime, he could see the way the ground wriggled and shone in the thin moonlight.

"I don't think we have a choice," he said, turning away from the window.

"You don't trust her, do you?"

"Of course not." He grabbed a few more of the blankets from a big basket by the fire and sniffed. These smelled like lavender as well. "But considering she's the one who locked her bedroom door, we might as well try to get some rest." Well, he didn't plan to do much sleeping. But at least he could lie horizontally, and his feet greatly appreciated that.

Jaelle tucked the blankets up around his mother, who was already snoring, and then plopped down on the bed beside her. She still clutched her bag to her chest and stayed upright instead of lying down.

As frustrating as his unexpected guest could be, Lucas couldn't help feeling his heart swell a little at the sight of her looking after his mother. Any human who had seen Drina at her worst and could still treat her like this had to have some extra measure of grace from the Maker.

The feelings of appreciation quickly moved into a feeling of aching emptiness, however, as his thoughts of one young woman turned to another. Vittoria had always been unusually good with his mother, too. Of course, their favorite pastime had been going to the market together to peruse the stalls and carts. But after everything the war had put them through, Lucas had thought they deserved some time to be happy. And anyone who could put up with his mother deserved extra happiness.

Of course, try as he might, he wasn't sure he could imagine Vittoria holding his mother down as someone extracted worms from her foot. But then, he hadn't done so well with that part, either.

Too tired to dwell on such thoughts, he nearly groaned as he sank down into his bed. His whole body cried out for respite. He hadn't slept well in days, and this would be no exception. From his feet to his neck, he ached. But he couldn't sleep. Not here, and especially not with the way their host had continued to fixate on

Jaelle. Even when he closed his eyes, he saw her sharp little eyes following the young woman's every move. What could she want with her anyway? Of course, recalling the evening brought back the shame of his misstep. Unable to rest for his guilt, Lucas finally opened his eyes to glance over at her. She was still sitting up.

"I'm sorry for tonight," he said quietly.

At first, he thought she might have dozed off. She continued to face the fireplace, which was now burning low, and she stayed still for a long time. As he studied her, though, he realized that he could make out her face's silhouette when she wasn't looking directly at him. And what he found was surprisingly pleasing.

She had the smaller, less prominent nose of the people of the east, but her jaw, cheekbones, and chin were decidedly western, high and well-defined. Those lines began to blur, however, when she looked down and shrugged.

"You're a man. It is what it is."

"Here, how about this?" Lucas forced himself into a sitting position. "I'll take first watch tonight. You can sleep, and maybe we can switch later."

"No thank you."

"I really don't mind—"

"I said no thank you!"

Lucas paused, the sharpness of her words taking him by surprise.

"You still don't trust me."

"Have you given me a reason to?" she snapped.

Well, for one, he hadn't laid claim to her. But the threshold for common decency in Jaelle's world wasn't anything Lucas wanted to stoop to.

"I guess I haven't." He ran a hand down his face. His eyes felt like they might fall out of his head from exhaustion. This might be a very long night. He had to distract himself if he was going to stay awake longer than five minutes.

"So if you don't trust me, are there any men you trust back home?"

"I'm engaged to you, aren't I?" She turned to look at him this time, and though he couldn't see her face, the sarcasm in her voice was thick.

"May I remind you that it was my mother and your sister who got you into this mess." He held his hands up. "I am completely innocent in that scheme, I swear."

"I know."

He waited for her to go on, but instead, she just hung her head. His plan, however, was working. Curiosity was quickly fueling him the way his sleep should have been.

"In truth, though," he said in a softer voice, "did you have any men you trusted? Not that I would blame you for not having any." He shuddered. "Not after being here myself."

"That I trusted? Two. That didn't betray me?" She let out a shaky breath. "One. And he was killed when I was twelve."

"I'm sorry." He paused. "You must miss your father very much."

"I never said it was my father."

Sadness settled over Lucas as that sank in. He'd simply assumed her father had been the faithful one. After all, what more were fathers for than to be there? His own father had died when he was young, but in the few short years they'd shared, he'd never doubted for a minute that he was cherished or that his father would put him and his siblings first. This girl must have been wronged horribly. No wonder she'd reacted so strongly to his slip earlier that evening.

"Who was it?" he asked gently.

"Does it matter?"

He sat up and turned toward her. "It does." He tried to focus his gaze on where her eyes would be if he could see them clearly. Someone ought to try. She deserved that, if nothing else.

At first he was sure she would ignore him, or better yet, tell him to shut up. He deserved it. But several minutes after he asked, just as he was shaking himself awake again, she spoke.

"He was a holy man."

Lucas was immediately more awake. "A holy man? Here?"

"We don't have many. But every once in a while, a foolish one will decide he's going to save souls and wander Terrefantome until someone kills him." She drew in a deep breath then let it out. "My father wasn't religious, but he enjoyed intellectual discussions.

And as the holy man was also from Giova, he would stop at our house and stay whenever he made his rounds."

"How long did you know him?" Lucas asked.

"A long time. He started coming even before my mother died." Her voice softened slightly. "Every time he came, he would stay for several days. In the mornings, he'd rise early and stand in the town square, calling for people to repent and believe in the Maker." She shrugged. "Whenever he wasn't in the square, he was back at our house fixing roof leaks or patching holes in the barn. He was actually quite handy with tools."

Lucas wasn't sure, but in the low flicker of the firelight, for a moment, he could have sworn he'd seen her smile.

"He told me all sorts of stories about other kingdoms and the adventures he'd been on. I know much of what I do about the world because of him." She paused again, and when she spoke, her voice wavered. "He even told my father once that he'd take me and my mother back to our own country if we wanted to stay with my mother's family. My mother was sick, and my father was sure it was from the air, since it's always wet here."

"What did your father say?"

"He said no." She pulled hard at the faded decorative button on one of the blankets. "He said we were a family, and we weren't going anywhere without him."

Something inside Lucas hardened. Coward. The man had brought his wife and child with him to this horrible place, then refused to let them leave. Guilty or not, he'd punished them for the crime he was accused of committing.

"So the holy man kept coming," she said, "even after my mother died. For ten years he came. Then one day, when I was twelve, he was beat senseless while on his way to our house. His attackers stole everything he had but his copy of the Holy Writ."

"What happened?"

"My father found him that way the next morning. He brought him back, but there was nothing we could do." She swallowed. "He died the next day."

"I'm sorry." It was such a trite thing to say. But really, what else was there? Then he remembered something. "Is that book in your bag—"

"Yes."

"Do you read it often?" He turned to better see her.

"I don't think that's really your business," she sniffed, and he took the hint.

They didn't talk again after that. Instead, he sat wishing he could see her face better. It was disconcerting to talk to someone without being able to see her face. Then it struck him, and he nearly laughed out loud, more for the irony than the humor. Michael had been able to see Arianna, but as she was mute, they couldn't speak. Now he was stuck with a girl who could speak, but was next to invisible.

Not that Lucas was planning on marrying this poor girl. After his guides abandoned him, he'd gone back to the city to try to find a new guide. During the brief times he'd spent in bed, when he wasn't searching, he'd come up with a million ways to ask again for Lorenzo's blessing for Vittoria's hand. If he closed his eyes now, he could see her golden hair, shining like the sand on the beach in the sunlight. How many times had he gone to bed, imagining what it would be like to have a family and grow old with her?

A sound broke him from his musings, and he opened his eyes to see that in spite of her resolution, Jaelle had collapsed into a little heap on the bed, all curled up and breathing deeply, and he couldn't help smiling. He would nail his eyes open if he had to tonight. *Let her sleep soundly,* he prayed as he watched her thin shoulders rise and fall with each breath. She may not want to rely on him, but he would show her that she could. Ridiculous betrothal or not, she deserved one man she could trust. *Let me see her the way Michael heard Ari,* he prayed. *Let her know that she...*

That she what? What was she to him? Not his betrothed. Not really. He didn't know her last name, let alone what she was really like. Then it came to him as she mumbled softly in her sleep.

Let her know that I can be a friend.

CHAPTER 16
DEAD OF NIGHT

Jaelle didn't mean to fall asleep, but the moment her eyes flew open, she knew she must have slipped into a slumber sometime after telling the prince about the holy man. Why had she told him that? And what was it that had awakened her now? She blinked into the darkness.

The moonlight was about as bright as it got in Terrefantome. Not blinding, the way her father had once said moonlight could be in other kingdoms, but it was bright enough, its light pushing through the clouds enough that one could see the world outside through the window.

The fire had weakened to merely burning embers. Drina was still snoring quietly beside her. When she looked at Lucas, however, she realized that something must have really awakened her, for though he was lying on his bed, he was facing their host's door behind her, and his eyes were wide open. His body was rigid, tightly wound and ready to spring.

Then Jaelle heard the shuffling of feet. As she watched, the figure of their hostess made its way across the room. Jaelle glanced at Lucas again, who gave her the subtlest of head shakes. So she remained perfectly still. She wanted nothing more, though, than to leap up and run straight out the door.

The old woman's breathing became audible as she drew closer

to Jaelle's bed, and Jaelle braced herself, mentally preparing to explode from her place.

The expected sound of sudden movement didn't come, though. Instead, Jaelle heard the sound of rustling and the familiar flutter of pages where she must have dropped her bag beside her when she'd fallen asleep. She cracked her eyes open just enough to see the old woman rifling through her things, cringing when her beloved book hit the floor. The old woman muttered something about rubbish and then continued going through Jaelle's underthings.

As she searched, Jaelle had a flash of insight. So this was how Mila had come to possess so many objects. She must rescue people from the worms and then invite them inside. After feeding them and giving them a good night's rest, she claimed her plunder.

But what did she do with her guests when she was done with them?

Jaelle's heart nearly failed completely when a very large knife in the woman's right hand caught the light from the window and threw it around the room. But another look at Lucas had him shaking his head again. She was tempted to leap out of harm's way anyhow. But then, that would leave Drina completely exposed and at the mercy of their host. She would have to find another plan.

After she was done pawing through Jaelle's bag, Mila turned to Jaelle. And before Jaelle could blink, Lucas had sprung from his bed and was on their host in a second. Jaelle flipped around to see Mila raise the knife, but Lucas had her by the wrist before she could bring it down. Jaelle leapt up and grabbed Drina by the shoulders. Yanking her out of bed, she deposited the protesting woman on the floor by the door before turning back at Lucas.

He and Mila struggled for the weapon. He should have won the fight quickly, as Mila was half his size and quite old. But Mila reached down under the mattress and pulled a second knife, which she began to wave at him as well. Jaelle darted back to where Lucas was quickly being forced into a corner as Mila came at him, stumbling over a pot and struggling to stand.

"Think you're a match for Mila, do you? Foolish boy didn't even know to keep his girl safe!"

Jaelle looked around for something with which to distract the woman. Then she spotted the green rug beneath her feet. She reached down with both hands and yanked.

Mila fell forward with a sharp cry, and for a moment, Jaelle feared she'd fallen on Lucas with the knife. But just as she was about to run over to check, Lucas leapt up.

"Go!" he yelled.

Jaelle ran back to her bag and started to stuff her things inside.

"We don't have time for that!" Lucas cried as Mila got to her feet again.

But Jaelle couldn't leave the book lying on the ground. She snatched it up and held it to her chest, looking up just in time to see Mila coming after her. She narrowly missed the knife again as she rolled. Mila let out a shriek as Lucas grabbed his mother, who was also screaming, and turned for the door.

Rather than bothering to unlock the front door, he rammed into it with his shoulder. The wood, which must have been quite old, gave way on the first try, cracking loudly as the door crashed to the ground.

"Lucas!" Drina sobbed, "I can't—"

Lucas swept up his mother as Mila chased them down, and he and Jaelle darted back toward the hill from which they'd come. Worms squished beneath their feet as they raced into the night, high-pitched squeals filling the air. But they didn't slow as footsteps pounded behind them.

They lost speed quickly, as Lucas couldn't keep up while he carried his mother. She didn't help him either, screaming and clinging to him as her legs flailed in the air. Just as they got to the bottom of the hill, not far from where Drina had first fallen, Lucas tripped, and Drina tumbled down. The worms weren't as thick here, but as soon as Drina was on the ground, little white bodies began to inch their way toward her.

Mila still clutched one of the knives as she ran for them, her curls sticking out in every direction and her mouth open wide, yelling as she charged.

Lucas struggled to get Drina back on her feet. But just as he was finally able to get her to stand, Mila reached them. She grabbed at Jaelle's scarf.

"Come back, dear, and stay with me! I'll protect you more than this ungrateful imp will! Stay with him, and you'll all end up dead soon enough!"

Jaelle leaned back, but Mila pulled until the scarf dumped its contents. Dozens of shining gems sparkled in the weak moonlight, and Mila and Jaelle both stopped, seeming frozen in time. Just as Mila looked up at Jaelle, a new, wicked grin on her face, Lucas planted a solid kick to the woman's side. Then he grabbed Jaelle's hand and ran. And for the first time in her life, Jaelle was thankful for the dark of the forest in the dead of night.

CHAPTER 17
VITTORIA

They walked for several more hours, far beyond the worms and until the moonlight began to fade and the gray of day began to take its place. Drina continued to whimper as they walked, eventually cajoling her son into carrying her again. Jaelle couldn't help feeling annoyed at this. The woman certainly hadn't spent much time looking at her son. He was clearly exhausted, as evidenced by the deep, dark bags beneath his eyes and his steps less sure than they had been before. Finally, as dawn came, Jaelle pulled everyone to a stop.

"You need to sleep." She faced Lucas and put her hands on her hips.

He shook his head and rubbed his eyes. "I'm fine." But even as he said it, his words slurred into a yawn. "But you're going to have to walk again, Mother. My arms are about to fall off."

"No, you're not fine." Jaelle looked around until she found a few relatively flat boulders. She started to reach for his hand, then thought better of it, pointing to the boulders instead. "Over there. Your mother can rest as well."

Drina mumbled to herself as she followed, picking her way over the underbrush, and Jaelle caught something to the effect of, *it's about time.*

"I'll take watch," Jaelle said, crouching in front of the boulder on which he sat. "You sleep."

He shook his head. "You only slept for an hour last night, maybe two. I need to—"

"You need to rest." Jaelle emphasized every word. "If you want to do whatever it is you're here for, you're not going to do it by going without sleep for the next week and a half. You'll start getting sick by tonight, and you'll begin to lose your sanity in a few days." She looked down at his clothes. "It's going to be warm and wet today. You should take off your coat so you don't overheat—"

"No!"

She must have jumped at the sharpness in his voice because he sighed and rubbed his eyes. "I'm fine, thank you," he said in a more subdued tone. "I'll sleep. But the coat stays on."

Jaelle nodded and backed up a few steps until she stumbled into a log beside the rock where Drina was preening herself in a little pool of water beside the boulder she'd claimed.

"Oh, don't take offense at him, dear." Drina waved her hand lazily at her son as his breathing deepened. "He's been a bear since Lady Vittoria's father turned him down."

Jaelle looked at her. "Turned him down?"

"Oh, yes. You see," she paused to give Jaelle a sickly sweet smile, "Michael, my eldest, took after his father. All business and no fun. But Lucas here is a lot more like I was." She smiled, as though this were a good thing. Inside, Jaelle gagged. So far, she'd seen nothing in Lucas that was similar to his mother aside from her coloring. He had her nose, too. But as she was a handsome woman, this wasn't necessarily a bad thing.

"You should have seen him when he was little." Drina chuckled as she pulled her long, dark hair down and began to braid it. "He would practice his flirting in the mirror. During his first official ball, he danced with every single girl in the room twice, even the ones who were several years older than him. At the end of the night, they were all sure he was going to propose to them the very next day."

"How old was he?" Jaelle watched the prince as he slept. Selina had warned her of such rakes, and despite his undeniable bravery, she wasn't sure she liked this side of him.

"Thirteen. And dashing as the day I met his father, only his father was twenty and six the day I met him, mind you." She sighed and stared up into the trees as though they were full of green leaves and beautiful blossoms, rather than skeleton-like branches the color of bone. "Lucas had his first sweetheart when he was seven, and he kept a string of them through adolescence. One for every week of the year, we used to laugh."

For some reason, Jaelle didn't think it was very funny.

"Is…" She paused. "Is he still like that?"

"Well, he's an accomplished flirt, if that's what you mean. But he has begun to pare down the beauties on his arm. Particularly since the war. Those were…unpleasant days. Not as many balls and parties as I should have liked." She sniffed. "He grew a lot less fun when Michael asked him to head the navy. I was quite put out with Michael for that, you know. But Michael insisted. He claimed we'd lost too many men and needed…Oh, what were his words? A sword in every man's hand, even after the war. And Lucas was all too delighted to do as he asked." Drina stuck her bottom lip out in an absurd pout. "We actually thought he was going to be married by now. He still enjoyed his ladies, mind you, but after the war, he found only one he seemed to esteem over the others."

"Lady Vittoria."

Drina nodded, leaning back over the pond to examine herself. One would think she'd have learned a little caution after her last experience with a pond.

"Lady Vittoria was honestly the most perfect fit I could see for him. I'd somewhat counted on the match. Lucas liked his fun, and Vittoria was one of the few girls who could keep up. In only a few months, he had us all convinced they would be wed before the year was out."

"What does she look like?" Jaelle asked. She couldn't say why, but she was morbidly curious.

"Oh, she's absolutely breathtaking. Blond curls the size of your fist. Lips as red as rubies, eyes like cornflower, frame tall and willowy." She gave Jaelle a smirk. "Almost as thin as I was when I came out. A swan among ducks if I ever saw one."

"What happened?" Jaelle nearly allowed herself a laugh. If she had truly been Lucas's betrothed, she couldn't imagine enjoying such a conversation from the very woman who had set them up.

"Oh, Lucas sought her hand from her father. But her father said that Lucas was...Oh, I didn't even understand it, to be honest." She scoffed. "He hasn't been the same since. All he ever pays attention to now are those absurd ships." Then she brightened. "But all that is behind us now with you here. And don't mind him. He may pout, but your marriage shall work out splendidly. I just know it."

"And how do you know that?" Jaelle couldn't resist giving her a slight tease.

Drina's self-satisfied smile disappeared, and her eyes widened as Jaelle pulled her scarf forward and let the diamonds fall to the ground.

"It wouldn't have anything to do with these, would it?"

"No! Of course not." Drina laughed nervously. "All done for your happiness, I assure you."

Jaelle was disinclined to believe the woman, but she refrained from saying so as Drina rested. If the woman was silly enough to have come here, she would hardly be of the mind to admit that her son's happiness wasn't her chief end.

Drina stretched and curled up on the rock. "Don't mind me. Since we're here, I'll just sleep a little as well." She opened one brown eye and waved for Jaelle to get down. "You should, too, dear. I can't see your face, but I can only suppose you're starting to look peaked."

Jaelle forced a smile. "Thank you, but I think I'll sit here and enjoy the sun." It was a weak excuse, as weak as the sunlight filtering through the gray clouds above. But Jaelle needed to keep watch. And if she was honest, she didn't really think she could sleep anyhow. The faster they were done with this suicidal trek, wherever it was leading, the better. She would get her sister back, King Everard would cure her, and they would start their life far from the royal family and its drama.

And maybe she would find a man who wasn't in love with a blue-eyed blonde.

CHAPTER 18
MANKA

Lucas's stomach grumbled as they walked up a gentle knoll. Mila's meal had been only the night before, but he felt as though he hadn't eaten in days. Jaelle had offered to share the rolls her sister had put in her bag, but Lucas had recommended they save them until they were truly desperate. His mother, however, oblivious to such threats, had greedily gobbled up two of the rolls, and her continued whining that had begun again within the last hours had made him suspicious that she wanted the third and fourth, too.

After waking up, the rest of the morning had been rather uneventful. The few hours sleep had truly done him good, and he'd been more than grateful that Jaelle, true to her word, had kept watch over them after all. As much as his instincts told him to distrust the girl, he knew he was quickly coming to rely on her and would need to do so more as this journey continued. She seemed to be married to the idea that the king of Destin could really help her sister. Hopefully, that would fire her to be faithful through the end.

Unfortunately, Jaelle was warming to him far more slowly than he was to her. The few times he attempted to draw her out with conversation, her returns were vague and bare of details, and as soon as she'd answered him completely, she would clam right back up again. And when Jaelle wasn't talking, his mother was.

His musings were cut short, though, when they came to the top of the knoll to find the land on the other side cracked open. It was as if a giant had come and snapped the earth in half. The chasm was narrow, running in a straight line perpendicular to their path, but it was also deep and black enough that Lucas couldn't see its floor.

He had been walking slightly ahead of the party, but now he threw out his arm to steady his mother. She stumbled into him a little, and probably would have fallen had he not stopped her.

"Lucas, what in the—" Then she saw the chasm. "What is that?" she shrieked, throwing her arms around him and clinging to him the way his little niece, Lucy, did when she'd had a nightmare.

But Lucy was eight. And his mother was not.

"A *manka*," Jaelle said. "I don't remember seeing any of these around here the last time I came through with my father. It must be new."

"What is a manka?" Drina's voice trembled.

"It's a piece of the land that shakes violently until it splits open." Jaelle got down on her knees and leaned carefully toward the edge. "This one is longer than most. And I can't see its depth."

"Which means we'll have to go over it." Lucas grabbed a fallen branch and started testing the ground closer to the opening. "I'll cross first. Then I'll help you over one at a time."

He led them to the place where the hole was most narrow, which was only a few yards away, and began poking it with his branch. The outcrop gave way the moment he touched it.

He would have to jump and then find a safe place for the women to cross, as their legs weren't as long as his. He had the feeling that Jaelle would probably be willing to jump if asked, but he wasn't certain she would make it. And the idea of his mother jumping on her own was laughable.

"Jaelle," he said when he'd found sure footing, "can you help my mother take a running start?"

"A what?" his mother cried.

Before he could explain, though, the ground began to shake again, and the layer of soil closest to where they stood crumbled into the hole. Without waiting for the chasm to grow any wider, Lucas grabbed his mother by the waist and tossed her onto the other side. Then, without waiting to hear her shouts of indignation, he turned to Jaelle to do the same.

As though it were in a race with him, though, the ground shook once more, and the chasm widened yet again.

"What will we do?" Jaelle called above the noise, but Lucas didn't answer.

He'd managed to reach a vine from one of the larger trees on the hill behind him. Once he had a good grip on it, he would grab Jaelle, and they would both jump together. If he could get both of them across the hole, they could roll down the hill before the ground quaked any more.

Another violent shudder rocked the earth, and Lucas knew it was now or never. He reached out and wrapped his arm around Jaelle's waist.

Jaelle hadn't been looking at him when he tried to pull her in. Instead, she'd been watching the chasm itself. But the second he touched her, she recoiled. Her ankle caught on a root, and she stumbled toward the chasm. Lucas watched in horror as the earth beneath her groaned, and the ledge she'd fallen on crumbled.

"Jaelle!" Lucas shouted as he watched her disappear into the dark. He lay down on his stomach, having to hold his breath when a puff of dust came up out of the hole, and tried to adjust his eyes to the dark, praying the whole time that she wasn't dead.

"Jaelle?" He called her name several times, each one making his heart fall lower in his chest, until after the fifth call, a familiar voice came up.

"I'm here." Her voice sounded faint, but he closed his eyes in relief. Then he opened them again to try to see if there was a way up or down.

Once his eyes had adjusted, he could see that rather than a new hole, Jaelle had fallen in what likely had been a cavern. He could see the bare hint of a silver ribbon running through the bottom, probably a stream, and he could just make out different levels of land attached to the walls like shelves. Not close enough for him to reach her at the bottom, but if only he had a rope...

"Hold on!" he called down. "I'll be back."

Fear alone had squeezed his chest before, but now another emotion began to pump his blood fast and heat his face as well.

"Stay right there," he barked at his mother as he ran, took his boots off, and prepared to climb the tree behind them. "And don't you dare move until I come back." Once he was up in the branches, he searched until he found the top of the thick vine he'd just been holding. It wasn't as long as he would have liked, but it was thick enough and would be better than nothing. Then he found a second that was only slightly thinner, so he cut that one, too. Scrambling back down the tree, he tied the second vine to one of the boulders just outside the lip of the chasm and left it there, dangling over the edge. Then he tied the other to his waist, and using the vine that he'd attached to the boulder, he let himself down into the chasm.

Thankfully, as he descended, the shaking seemed to stop. Once he'd lowered himself onto the first shelf near the top of the hole, he waited briefly for his eyes to adjust again. When they did, he saw that he had been right. There were numerous steps naturally carved into the rock. They would make descending much easier than if he'd tried to go straight down. He should have been relieved, but with each step, as he relived the moment over and over again in his head, his chest tightened, and his frustration grew. By the time he reached the bottom, he felt like he was ready to explode.

"What was that?" he demanded as he made his way over to where she was standing. Then he paused and looked down. The ground was strangely soft. Now that he thought of it, she should have been killed by such a fall. It was at least a thirty foot drop from the top.

"It's not as if I fell on purpose!" She put her hands on her hips, but her voice shook. "And I told you, I don't like being touched."

He gaped at her. "What did you *think* I was going to do?"

"You don't grab women in Terrefantome!"

"Well, forgive me." He gave a mock bow. "I'll take that into consideration the next time I'm trying to save you. Looks like you're doing a bang up job down here on your own."

She said nothing, but he could guess from the way her jaw lifted that she was glaring. "Come on," he said, taking a step toward her and reaching for her arm, "Let me lead you back up."

Her flinch was so discreet he nearly missed it, particularly as they still had very little light. And yet, it was there.

"Are you..." He squinted at her in the dark. "Are you really afraid I'll hurt you?"

"No."

He turned to face her directly but this time made no move toward her.

"I'm being honest, Jaelle." He paused. "Are you afraid of me?"

"No." She answered, again, too quickly.

He shook his head and took a deep breath. "What brought this on?"

She stared at the ground and turned her body toward the light, rather than to him.

"Look." He put his hands over his eyes then ran them through his hair. "I don't—"

"Hands are different."

"What?" He dropped his hands to his sides again and blinked at her, cursing the wretched mask silently. Arguing would be a lot easier if he could see her face.

"I didn't know you were going to try to grab me like that." She stared at the ground. "I only did what I've always done."

Lucas cursed under his breath. Then he took a deep breath.

"Jaelle," he said, forcing his voice to remain calm. "I only wanted to get us to safety."

"I know that," she blurted. "I just don't like being taken by surprise."

Lucas pinched the bridge of his nose. They had a mission to complete, and he was in no mood to stand in a dark cave arguing with a girl who clearly had problems he was not able to fix. "What then," he forced himself to speak slowly, "can I do to get you to trust me so that the next time I have to save your life you don't end up falling over a cliff?"

"You can tell me where we're going." She reached up and moved the scarf to let her diamonds fall into the soft ground beneath them.

"Would that change your mind?"

"No," she retorted, "but I would love to know whether or not I'm walking into a death trap!"

"Why can't you just trust me?" He was shouting now. "What in my conduct has indicated I ought to be treated as a villain?"

"If there's anything my sister taught me," Jaelle fired back, "it was to never let a man have all the power without making him give some back!"

Lucas was about to embark on a tangent about her hypocrisy when her eyes widened, and she pointed at something behind him.

"What is it?" he snapped.

"That shadow," she whispered. "On the wall. It's not a shadow at all."

"What do you mean?" Lucas groaned.

"I just saw it move."

Lucas turned to see what she was pointing at. Sure enough, the dark spot beneath one of the walls was no longer a shadow. Instead, it moved down the wall until it had covered several of the stalagmites, turning them from a pale white to an inky black. The hair on Lucas's arms stood on end.

"It just moved toward us," he whispered back, taking a step away from the wall and toward Jaelle. "Didn't it?"

"Is that..."

"Sorthileige?" An icy shiver moved up his back. "It sure looks like it." For once, Jaelle didn't seem to notice that he had moved closer to her. Instead, they both watched as the dripping from the stalactite above stopped.

The place Lucas had stepped seemed even softer than before, but his foot hit something hard as well. Without thinking, he looked down. Only then did he realize that the ground on which they walked was not sand after all, but clothes. And animal skins. And bones.

"Lucas," Jaelle hissed, pulling his attention up once more.

This time, where the water droplets had been falling from the stalactites, a single drop of thick, shiny black liquid rose from each of the three stalagmites and floated up into the air, where they hovered. Lucas got the distinct feeling that he was being watched.

As he stared, he was yanked back in time to the day his brother had nearly killed him. There had been a shine in Michael's eyes and a darkness to his smile that Lucas had never seen before as his older brother had stood over him, gloating as Lucas's blood dripped from his knife. And now Lucas was looking that darkness in the eye.

"Jaelle," he said in a low voice.

"Yes?" Her voice was even quieter.

"I'm going to take your hand," he reached back slowly, "and we're going to run."

For once, she listened. They both broke into a sprint.

"Jump!" he yelled as they came to the place where the shadow had left a trail of darkness during its travel from the wall to the stalagmites. She jumped, and then they were making their way up the shelves.

He could see why she'd had trouble seeing the ledges from the bottom. Looking up into the distant light was blinding when contrasted with the dark, wet walls that surrounded them.

On the fourth ledge up, Lucas began to feel hopeful. Until he looked back to see the shadow following them. It slid up the walls and ledges behind them as though gravity had no hold.

"Faster!" Jaelle screamed.

Still, several of the ledges were too tall, and he had to pull her up with the vine.

By the time they reached the top, Lucas felt like his legs might fall off. But when they fell gasping into the sun, he was sure they'd made it. One glance back at the hole, however, told him they weren't safe yet. The shadow was crawling up the vine, withering it as it moved, inch by inch, toward the top. Jaelle ran to the boulder around which the vine was tied and tried to pry it loose, but Lucas pulled her away.

"Don't touch it!"

"We have to get rid of it!"

"I know." He whipped the bow off his shoulder and fitted an arrow.

"You're going to attack it with arrows?" she screamed.

He exhaled and loosed a prayer and the arrow. Just as the shadow made its way to the top, his arrow sliced through the thick, green vine, severing it completely. Both the vine and shadow fell back down the hole.

The world began to quake once more, this quaking harder than any they'd endured so far. Lucas didn't even attempt to stand until the shaking was done. When he finally did sit up, he was amazed to discover that the earth had been pushed back together, the hole was gone, and the path had been restored. He and Jaelle looked at one another, unable to answer his mother, who was still moaning about the indecency of it all.

"What just happened?" he panted as his heart refused to slow. "What was that?"

"The land..." She gasped, sounding just as out of breath as he was. "I told you the land is cursed. It's not so bad in some places, but in others..." She shook her head. "Sometimes the land is worse than the people."

"It eats people." Lucas continued to stare at the place where the ground had opened. A slight crack no wider than his thumb was all that remained. "Why does the ground eat people?" He looked at her again. "Have you seen this before?"

"No. But I've heard of it."

He shivered. He'd listened to Michael's stories of the darkness in the ocean that Arianna was ever responsible for repressing. But never before had he been so close to it or known evil could be so visceral that he could feel it in his bones.

They spent a long time sitting that way. Finally, he pushed himself to his feet.

"My mission," he said, "is to repay to the king a debt my grandfather borrowed when my kingdom was impoverished and at war." He swallowed. "If I fail, your king is going to break down the gates and loose all of Terrefantome on my kingdom. And every man, woman, and child will be in more danger than they knew was possible before this day." He extended his hand to her. "And I need your help to do it."

She kept her face turned up toward him for several long seconds before slowly putting her hand in his and letting him pull her to her feet.

"And it might be worth considering," he said in a softer voice before turning back to the path, "that your sister might know a good many things about Terrefantome. But she might be wrong sometimes as well." And with that, he rejoined his mother, leaving Jaelle in silence behind him.

CHAPTER 19

THANK YOU

J aelle's conscience ate at her for the next two days as they made their way uneventfully. She and Lucas said little, and he didn't bring up her stubbornness or the chasm situation again. For that she was grateful. In truth, she felt deeply mortified over her initial response to his touch, because she truly did get the feeling that Lucas would be the last person to take advantage of her, particularly in a life and death situation. A lifetime of mistrust wasn't something to be overcome easily, though, and when he'd reached for her, her body had acted the way it might on the street if a stranger had come up behind her.

Thoughts of her overreaction aside, however, even worse was that in her head and heart, she felt as though the world was out of sync. And it wasn't just because she was traveling with strangers through a part of her country that she'd never been in before as she spoke diamonds into existence.

No, it had something to do with Lucas and his nagging suggestion that niggled at her mind every time she closed her eyes to sleep.

But she might be wrong sometimes as well.

Selina wasn't wrong. She'd spent too much time around men. The stories of the men at the tavern and their habits and words and excessive selfishness that Selina had shared had never ceased to amaze Jaelle, though Selina had seemed resigned to the fact that such was the world. And she'd spent years ensuring Jaelle had a perfect understanding of this truth as well. Men looked out for their own selves. Even her father, as much as she had loved him, had proved her sister right in his refusal to send Jaelle and her mother back to his relatives, and then in his marriage to Chiara and his refusals to listen to Jaelle's pleas not to wed the awful woman. The only man Jaelle had ever found this maxim to be questionable in was the holy man before he died. Such was to be expected, though, she supposed, of a man who had time only for his god.

But now Lucas was part of her world. And she really didn't have the slightest idea of what to do with him. He didn't fit into any of the neat little boxes Selina had painted for her of the male sex, the weak or the tyrannical. Instead, he, if she was honest, had done everything possible to honor her.

None of it made sense.

Her greatest relief, as she tried silently to work out the dissonance in her head, was the distraction of entertaining Drina. Or rather, of keeping Drina on a short leash so Lucas could focus on keeping them all alive. Because if she didn't, Lucas's mother might not make it after all.

"Really," Drina wheedled as they made their way up yet another hill, "I don't understand why we can't stop somewhere and buy a horse." She stopped and glanced at Jaelle. "We have more than enough wealth. We have more wealth than anyone could ask for."

"Mother, we've been over this."

"And what do we do? We bury it in the ground. Every few hours we stop just so she can bury ten thousand gold pieces worth of diamonds in the dirt."

"Mother, we're not using—"

"Yes, I know. You've told me! I'm not deaf."

"Will you stop going on about it then?" he roared. "I've been carrying you at least three times a day! What more do you want?"

"Lucas," Jaelle hissed, holding her finger up to her mouth. In truth, she sympathized with him. But his voice carried farther than Drina's, and he was going to get them killed.

He gave her an annoyed look, then rolled his eyes before stomping ahead.

"Then you can walk next to her," he muttered.

Jaelle nearly laughed. As grumpy as he was, she couldn't blame him. At least Drina didn't have a thousand embarrassing stories to share about *her*.

As he walked ahead of them, Jaelle realized the sun was at its zenith, and Lucas was still wearing his black coat.

"Why don't you take your coat off?" she asked as she puffed, trying to keep up with his long strides. "It's only going to get hotter." Too late did she realize she'd broken her self-imposed rule about only speaking to him when necessary in order to avoid further complication. But his attachment to the coat really was odd.

He just shook his head. "No thank you."

Jaelle shook her head, too. She was about to let it go, but Drina called, "Ignore him, Jaelle. He's just being bizarre as always." She came huffing up behind them. "Just like he was with Lady Vittoria." She clicked her tongue. "If you ask me, Lucas, you weren't attentive *enough*, and her father's a fool."

Lucas's resolute expression turned to one of horror. "What do you know of my correspondence with Lorenzo, Mother?"

Drina shrugged and fanned herself with a large, broken leaf she'd found on the ground. "I read her letter."

If Lucas was red earlier, he was nearly purple now.

"You did what?"

"Well, I supposed it was her father's letter, and since Lorenzo and your father were friends—"

"That's it!" Lucas threw his mother's pack on the ground. "Mother, I have had it. From now on, you are forbidden from talking."

"I'm what?" Drina scowled.

"You heard me. You're not allowed to talk any more. Not about food, not about friends. Not even about the family. And that includes me."

"Whyever not?"

Lucas bent until he was eye-to-eye with his mother, his hazel eyes flashing. "Because you make everything worse." He pointed back in the direction from which they'd come. "I don't know what you think you're doing here, but whatever it is, it's ruining everything."

"I'm doing nothing of the kind!" Drina protested, but Lucas's frown only deepened.

"Do you know what happens if I don't successfully pay the king back what Grandfather borrowed?"

For the first time, Drina looked a little uncomfortable.

Lucas continued. "The king of this charming land will start a war. And if you thought the war with the merpeople was bad, this one would be ten times worse." He picked up the pack again and put it on indignantly. "Our people will not only be poor and destitute, but they'll be pulled from their homes and murdered in their beds. Their little ones will cry out, and no one will be there to help them because my military isn't recovered enough yet to thoroughly protect the kingdom. I will die, and you and Jaelle will probably be sold to strangers as spoils of war to enjoy as they see fit." He glared down at his mother. "Do you understand now? We cannot go to war. We will not survive another war. And if I fail now, our kingdom as we know it will die."

Drina's lip quivered. Instead of looking thoroughly cowed, she looked like she was going to cry.

Jaelle took the opportunity to come up beside him before they could take the argument any further. She'd been waiting to talk with him, hoping Drina would sleep sometime without overhearing, but now seemed as good a time as ever, before their argument alerted the entire forest to their whereabouts.

"I'm sorry," she said softly as he held back a branch for her.

He blinked at her. "For what?"

"It's..." She took a big breath before her courage failed her. "It's not that I don't want to trust you."

He waited until his mother had passed, and they were a little way ahead of her again.

"I know it must be difficult to trust a stranger," he finally said, but his voice was stiff, and she wondered if she detected a faint hint of hurt.

"Lucas." She stopped walking.

He stopped as well.

"This is all I've ever known," she said, hoping...willing him to understand the chaos that had been eating her up from the inside. "But my sister spent her childhood on the outside. And when she came, she became the protection I lost when my father died. Doesn't it make sense at least that I would struggle to trust a man I've only just met? Particularly one," she added, "who wants to venture into the darkest part of my world without telling me why?"

He opened his mouth to answer, but several shouts captured their attention. Darting behind the nearest knoll, they peeked over the top to find the source.

Jaelle saw it first. She tugged on Lucas's sleeve and pointed through the trees in the direction their path led.

A road crossed through the forest, perpendicular to the one they were following, and a crowd of at least thirty surrounded something. A few men, women, and children darted this way and that, running back up and down the road with random objects in their hands. But most of the crowd was angry and focused on something in its center.

Lucas waved his mother over to them, and for once, she listened. They all lay against the hill.

"We'll stay here," Lucas whispered, "until they're gone."

"Hey!" a man from the other side shouted. "Out there. In the forest! Come here!"

Jaelle looked at Lucas, but he was staring into the forest, one hand on his sword, the other on his bow, which was slung across his chest. Before he could respond, four men appeared, two on each side of their little knoll.

Jaelle's heart nearly stopped. They should have run when they had the chance. Now the men had seen them, and with Drina, there was no way they could outstrip any pursuers in the forest.

"Get up," one of the men said as he brandished a club. When they hesitated, he fixed his eyes on Jaelle. "The marshal's not angry. He only has a few questions." Lucas glanced at her, and she sighed and nodded slightly. There was no escaping now.

As they made their way down the hill, she could see that the crowd surrounded an overturned carriage. A man and woman stood in the center of the group, the woman sobbing and the man ordering everyone else to back off.

"Which one's the marshal?" Lucas whispered.

"See the one in the red and brown?" she murmured. "The one telling everyone to stay away?"

"Hello, there." The marshal turned to them as they approached, a pleasant smile on his whiskered face. "Who do we have here?" He looked appreciatively at Drina. Drina colored and smiled, and Jaelle rolled her eyes. Foolish woman. Getting noticed here should be the last thing she wanted.

"We're breaking no rules, sir," Lucas said, holding his hands out. "I assure you."

"And I'm sure you're telling the truth." The whiskered man said with a pleasant smile. "But as we're already here, I was hoping perhaps you'd seen something of this accident."

Unlike Drina, Jaelle did her best to avoid their notice. So instead of trying to attract his attention, she kept her face turned toward the accident. The carriage was not a fancy one, but definitely large enough to have been hired. Whoever the criminal was, he or she must have brought enough money to rent such a sizeable vehicle. The woman who was crying was dressed in clothes nicer than the vast majority of those in Terrefantome would ever set eyes on. But from the way she was weeping, Jaelle could see that her neck was free of any marks, and she got the sick feeling that this poor woman's horrible introduction to her new life, however her move to Terrefantome had come about, was about to get even worse.

"We only just arrived," Lucas said. "We hid only because we heard many voices."

The marshal nodded. "I'm sure. Particularly with a wife and mother in tow." But even as he spoke, he frowned. "But why the mask?"

Lucas remained silent on the matter, only nodding respectfully. But instead of letting the matter drop, the man caught Jaelle's right wrist and examined it. Her blood ran cold.

"Not married, then." He eyed her with a new curiosity.

"Betrothed," Lucas said quickly.

"Marshal!" a fat man on the other side of the carriage barked. "Are you going to tell us what to do with this or not?"

The marshal reached out and grabbed one of the skinny boys who was about to make off with a painted clay jar, snatched it from his hands, and gave the boy a scowl and a good shake before letting go.

"Mind your manners," he growled at the boy. "I said nothing was to be touched, and that goes for you street urchins as well." Then he turned back to the man. "Of course. Now, as this woman is now unprotected—"

"She's a widow, sir!" One of the older women called out. "Not some young girl without a mind for the world. And her husband only died here an hour ago!"

"Rightly so, madame," the marshal said. "But as she is new to the land, she'll need someone to help her find her place."

"Couldn't we just send her back to the gate?" The objector's husband asked. "Her husband was the reason she was here. Why keep her here to eat up more resources when we could just send her back?"

"She won't make it as far as the next town over," the fat man sneered. "We might as well give her a protector." His bulbous eyes grew even wider. "You could marry her off here and now!"

"He can marry people?" Lucas whispered, his nearly inaudible words still sounding horrified.

Jaelle nodded. "So he can give a woman protection on the spot." She shuddered. "He even carries the tools needed to mark her as well."

"Tools?" Lucas whispered.

"Who here would be willing to take responsibility for this woman?" the marshal asked, interrupting Lucas's thoughts. Several men raised their hands, much to Jaelle's chagrin, while a few others called out with the first man that she should be brought back to the gate to go free. Voices rose, and the likelihood of a fight became palpable.

Jaelle jumped when she felt a slight pressure on her hand. But when she turned, it was Lucas. He'd taken his mother's hand as well. He nodded at the marshal, who was now trying to calm the frenzy that was beginning to take the crowd.

Jaelle nodded, but they'd only taken a few steps backward toward the forest when the marshal turned back to them.

"Hold on!" The marshal jogged up to them and fixed a hard stare on Lucas. "What exactly are your intentions with this girl?"

Lucas stepped slightly in front of Jaelle so he and the marshal were face-to-face. Jaelle prayed this wouldn't lead to a fight. Because if the mob saw a new citizen fighting with a marshal, as little as most of them liked the marshals, they wouldn't for a second hesitate to defend their law man.

"We were just betrothed less than a week ago," Lucas said firmly. To Jaelle's great relief, there was no hint of uncertainty in his voice this time.

"Betrothed." The man raised his eyebrows, and a smile played on his lips. "You are quite new here, aren't you?" He chuckled slightly. "I could marry you now, and all of this would be solved."

"Marshal!" the fat man yelled again, but this time, the marshal ignored him.

Jaelle thought fast. They couldn't get married now. Especially not when he was in love with another woman, or when she had a million plans that he wasn't a part of.

"I want my sister to be there!" she blurted.

The marshal looked at her again.

"And how far away is your sister?"

"She lives with my stepmother several days north of here." Jaelle did her best to remain calm.

The man stared at her for a long time. She knew he couldn't see through the mask, but it was unnerving to have him stare so long. Finally, he let out a gusty breath and rubbed his eyes.

"I may be a marshal, but I'm also a father." He ran his hand over his balding head. "And I don't know where your father is to let you run about with your betrothed—"

"He's dead," Jaelle said. "Which is why I need to stay with my betrothed."

"Fair as that may be," he continued, "you need to remove the mask."

"Why?" Lucas asked.

The man looked at him in surprise. "You really are new here. Look, son, that mask is a dead giveaway that she's unclaimed.

And without even a mark on her wrist, she's as good as someone else's. It would be different if her father were with her, but..." He huffed. "I'll let you go free this time. Lucky for you, the king is pressing us to make our laws more modern in those aspects, or rather, more like other kingdoms'." His eyes darkened. "But few people around here care what the king says. And few marshals for that matter."

Lucas nodded. "Noted. And thank you."

"You're letting them go, too?" someone called, but Lucas didn't wait to hear what else was said, for as soon as the words were out of the marshal's mouth, he had Jaelle and Drina by the wrists and was dragging them across the road and into the forest once again. No one followed them, much to Jaelle's relief, but her heart couldn't seem to keep a steady rhythm as they continued to stumble through the underbrush at breakneck speed.

Even Drina stayed unusually quiet for a while. But after half an hour, she begged to stop at a creek so she could soak her feet. Lucas, uncharacteristically quiet as well, let her stop without a word.

As he stood, scanning the forest in the direction from which they'd come, Jaelle went up to him. She couldn't look him in the eye as she spoke, for it was far too humiliating. How pathetic he must think her to have to rely on others so heavily for her welfare.

"Thank you," she said, playing with the end of her braid, "for saying that."

"Hey." Rough fingers gently took her chin and turned her face up to his. "We're in this together. We made an agreement, and I'm not backing out."

Her breath hitched slightly at his touch, but, she realized, it wasn't an unpleasant sensation. For a long moment, he studied her, as though trying again to see through her mask. And she studied him back unabashed.

"Oh." His gaze fell to his hand, and he yanked it back. "Sorry." Then he laughed nervously. "Habit, I suppose."

But for the first time, Jaelle's smile didn't feel forced. "It's all right."

He gave her a funny grin that turned into a grimace. "I hate to ask this," he said, "but is there any way you could take that thing off?" He nodded at her face, and immediately, her hand went up to her mask.

It would be safer, of course, to travel without it. Married women didn't wear masks. A mask meant protection and innocence. If she removed hers, she wouldn't be questioned nearly as much, and they wouldn't constantly be checking her wrist. But it would also mean stripping herself of her last vestige of power.

"I'm sorry," she whispered. "I can't." She couldn't bring herself to look at him, and when he didn't respond, she knew she'd gone too far. He was angry, and she knew it. Such a reaction would be understandable. The attention she would draw by continuing with a mask and without a mark would put them all in greater danger.

But instead of shouting or fuming or even ignoring her completely, she felt the hand again, lifting her chin to look at him once more. And to her even greater surprise, he was wearing a kind smile.

"Then we'll just have to be more careful."

"You're...not angry?"

He chuckled. "I'm not saying this is going to be easy. And I won't pretend to understand." His smile faded softly, and he stared once more into her eyes, though how, she didn't know. "But if it means that much to you, we'll just have to find another way."

Though he couldn't see her, Jaelle smiled back. "Thank you."

CHAPTER 20

HUMAN

Five days. They'd been walking for five days, and Lucas was about to lose his mind. In front of him was a wasteland, and behind him was...his mother.

Brown seemed to be the only color in Terrefantome. Even the leaves on the trees were a dull green, which was odd, considering it rained often. The mud and his mother's poor choice in footwear severely hampered their progress. They must have doubled the time it should have taken to cross the scattered rocky outcroppings, fallen trees, and lots of underbrush. And dragging his mother through it all was like pulling teeth.

Thankfully, they hadn't met anyone else since the overturned wagon, so his mother's constant complaining was unlikely to be heard by anyone but them. Still, as the days dragged on, he grew more and more restless. They were just over a week from the deadline, and they seemed to go more slowly by the day.

What about this assignment hadn't his mother ruined?

Lucas cast a sideways glance at Jaelle. She'd been quiet since the day they met, but after the wagon incident, she'd seemed more silent than ever. She would answer when asked a direct question, but she rarely offered any other information. And yet, though he couldn't see her eyes, he got the distinct feeling that she was watching him more than ever. And he didn't know what to make of it.

Not that he'd been a ray of sunshine, either. His mother seemed to make it her goal to keep him in a sour mood, and the constant quiet drove his thoughts far too often to his beloved.

What was she doing right now? How had she taken her father's refusal? He hadn't spent enough time with her yet to be sure of what her temper would be when she heard that she could no longer be the object of her prince. Had she shed tears over the loss of what could have been?

She'd sobbed the day she'd received news that her cat had died. She'd been at the palace with her mother that day. Drina had invited them over for tea, and Lucas had been home between voyages. They'd known one another for years, of course, as her father was part of Michael's court. But when the missive arrived, silent tears had begun to course down her cheeks. And in that moment, he had the distinct need to comfort her, to protect her from whatever it was that had made her cry. That had been the catapult for their first long walk through the market. She spent the time talking about her dear little cat, and he listened in raptures, certain she was the sweetest creature he'd ever met. In an effort to get her to smile, he bought her a pretty little hat she admired, and the way she blushed and smiled at him through wet lashes had melted whatever was left of his heart.

He'd also bought them each a piece of honeycomb to chew on as they walked. Unfortunately, he hadn't considered the practicality of giving a honeycomb to a woman in a delicate dress. But instead of crying out in dismay when a glop of honey landed on her skirts, she'd only laughed and tried to smear it on his face. He'd realized that day, without a doubt, that he needed someone with a sense of adventure, rather than one of the delicate flowers his mother so often shoved at him. Someone who could laugh at a glob of honey rather than cry. He'd known then and there that he needed Vittoria.

Only now, she wasn't to be his. Where did that leave him?

Lucas shook his head. If he didn't get some real conversation going soon, he just might go mad. But his mother was the last person with whom to have a sensical conversation, and Jaelle refused to give him more than one or two word answers to his questions. Still, her answers had grown softer and less bristly than they had been before. Maybe he could goad some sort of emotion from her if he chose the right angle.

"Jaelle," he said, clearing his throat as he stopped to help his mother over a log. "How does one find all the answers?"

She turned her head toward him, and though he couldn't see her face, there was surprise in her voice. "Find all the answers?"

Lucas smiled. He'd been exceptionally good at needling his sister when they were small. He could move her from a good mood to a muttering mess in two minutes flat without even touching her. And as touching Jaelle was off the table, he would just have to employ his power of words.

"You're just so...put together," he said, holding another branch back so the women could pass through. "There has to be something that—"

"That what?" Her reply was indignant.

"I don't know. Makes you a little less perfect."

"I am not perfect." She walked slightly faster. "You should know that after the *manka*."

He shrugged. "Everyone's allowed their mishaps. You're a healer. You have the patience of a heavenly being with my mother—"

"What?" Drina cried from behind them, but Lucas ignored her.

"You have all these plans to escape this awful place, including," he gave her a wry smile and arched an eyebrow, "somehow convincing me to make a deal with you, so you could lead me into the depths of this mud hole. I don't know. I just don't see how you qualify as an actual human."

He could hear her start to say something then stop several times.

"You could change my mind," he said coyly.

Her chin rose slightly higher. "And how would I do that?"

"I'll ask you questions. Answer me honestly, and you might convince me that you're at least half human."

She kicked a rock out of the way harder than was necessary. "You'd like that, wouldn't you?"

"Yes. Yes, I would." He grinned then paused. What questions should he ask her? Which ones would she answer? He was rather sure he couldn't push too hard, but she did seem to have a slightly competitive edge. Maybe he could work around that. But first, he would warm her up.

"What's your favorite food?"

"Lemonade with mint."

"That's not a food."

She turned to him, and in the light of a weak sunbeam, he nearly imagined that she was scowling at him.

"So you're going to be choosey now with my answers?" She tossed her hair. "I could refuse to answer any more."

He squinted at the trees. "Do you even grow lemons here? Or have sugar, for that matter?"

"No," she paused. "But the holy man once brought a few lemons with him when he came back from visiting outside the wall."

"He was allowed to leave?"

"Holy men and guards are the only ones allowed to come and go at will. Anyhow, my father had managed to buy some sugar from a newcomer at the market." She pulled an acorn from a tree and tossed it into the woods. "It was the best thing I've ever tasted."

Lucas hadn't expected such an answer, and it was half a minute more before he could pretend to be unaffected. When they got out of this horrible place, assignment or no assignment from his brother, he was going to make sure Bithiah had a chance to stuff Jaelle full of sweets to her heart's content.

"All right, fine." He pretended to scoff. "Have your sour water. What about pets? Have you ever had one of those?"

"No. But when I do, I'll get a dog, and I'll name him Eatem."

"Eatem?"

He could hear the smile in her voice this time. "Yes. So he can do just that to anyone I don't like."

Lucas stared at her for a minute before letting out a laugh. "Fair enough. What about—"

"It's my turn now."

He huffed. But really, it was only fair. Also, it was nice to finally have her carrying on a real conversation. "Fine. What do you want to know?"

"What's Vittoria's favorite food?"

He began to speak but stopped. "I...I don't know." How did he not know that?

"Very well, then. What about her deepest desire?"

"I don't follow."

"What does she want to do with her life?" Jaelle reached out and plucked a dying flower from the grass on the side of the path, then she rubbed it between her fingers and sniffed at it. "What are her dreams? What mark does she want to leave on the world?"

Once again, Lucas found himself stumped. Not that he would own such. "She wants a new kitten."

"Mmm. What about her favorite color?"

"Blue."

"It's pink," his mother puffed. "She told me at the market. Can we slow down a bit?"

"What did she think of her father's refusal to your request for his blessing?" Jaelle continued.

Lucas opened his mouth, but again, no words came. He'd been denying it to himself for months, but now that Jaelle asked, he could only answer faintly, "She didn't."

Jaelle came to a stop and turned to face him. "Didn't what?"

He stared up at the eternal gray of the sky. "She didn't write to tell me what she thought." When he looked back down, she was nodding slowly.

"Just as I thought."

He faced her as well, folding his arms over his chest. "What is?"

"I don't think you're in love with Vittoria."

For once, Lucas found himself speechless. "Excuse me?"

"You don't know anything about her." She leaned slightly closer. "I think you're in love with the *idea* of Vittoria, rather than Vittoria herself."

His mouth fell open, and he could almost feel her laughing at him. He knew Vittoria. He knew that she hated dogs. Her favorite sweet was...obviously honey. And she wanted a son and a daughter, though she said an extra boy might not be so terrible, so as to preserve the line of her future husband.

"Well," he sputtered as she turned and began to walk again. "For someone who isn't in love, how do you know so much about it?"

"I don't. But I know what love *isn't*. I also know that men on both sides of the wall can be guilty of betrayal where love ought to reign the most."

"How so?"

"Before my sister came here," she said, as if discussing the price of radishes, "her father was the betrayer."

"What did he do?" Lucas asked uneasily. Did he want to know?

"Nothing. He did absolutely nothing." Her hands balled at her sides, but only for an instant before she flexed them and seemed to find her calm again. "Then, when she was here, she betrothed herself to a man who, like us, wanted to leave Terrefantome."

"What happened?"

She took in a deep breath. "My stepmother found out, and as I can only assume she threatened to tell his father, they decided to make a deal." She straightened her shoulders. "It's expensive to travel the main road. If you're not in a large group or don't have some sort of special protective status, you have to hire guards like your mother did when she came to fetch me. So he took all the money we'd saved together, all three of us, and found someone new. They fled, and my stepmother made sure we never attempted anything like that again."

Her voice hardened at the end, and Lucas was struck by the desire to know just what her stepmother had done to prevent them from running. He was also struck by how angry such a story made him on her behalf. What kind of woman was her stepmother that she would contrive to keep her daughters in such a place?

"We need to stop!" Drina let out a moan and collapsed on a boulder. "I can't go on."

"All right," Lucas said, stooping to help her up onto the rock. "Let's see what it is this time..." His words trailed off when Jaelle took off his mother's shoe.

Throughout the journey, Jaelle had been stuffing his mother's slippers with soft cloths and a salve, which she said would prevent the shoe from rubbing her skin too badly. But now the slipper itself had been worn through, and his mother's feet were covered in blisters, several of them bloody. Regret compounded his self-loathing. Five days of walking for the woman who didn't like to walk from the palace to the beach. Of course his mother would be suffering. Because he needed another reason to feel guilty.

"We'll need to get her new shoes," Jaelle said, looking up at him while still holding the shoe. "Or better yet, a donkey. She can't keep walking like this."

He flexed his jaw. "Do you think paying a merchant will be safe?" He'd spent most of his spare coins to pay for his room at the inn while he searched for another guide. But using the diamonds would be dangerous, to say the least.

Jaelle let out a long, slow breath. "I don't know how else we'll be able to go on." She stood and looked in the direction they were going. "There should be a village with a sizeable market about a day from here. My father used to venture there for medicinal supplies. If we stick to the outer stalls instead of going farther in, we should be able to avoid most of the attention. And whoever we pay isn't going to want anyone else to see what we give him, so he'll probably be quiet about the whole transaction. We'll just need to make sure we're discreet in our payment."

Lucas nodded and bent to pick up his mother, who was crying softly. "Come on, Mother," he said, more gently than he had in a long time. "Let's get you a ride."

THAT EVENING, when they stopped to make camp, Lucas noticed Jaelle wincing as she rubbed one of her heels as well.

"How are your feet?" He nodded at her worn boots as he built a small fire. Drina was already snoring on a blanket on the little place he'd cleared for her on the ground.

Jaelle sighed. "I'm fine."

"No, you've been limping for the last few miles." He moved from the fire pit he'd dug to kneel at her side. Doing so was painful, as his back ached immensely, but he ignored it as he looked at her boot.

Jaelle sighed again and slowly removed her boot. Sure enough, there were red welts on her heels and toes.

"I guess I'm not used to walking quite this much, either," she laughed nervously.

He reached out to turn her foot so he could see it better, but before he could touch her, she jerked back. He held his hands up and fell back a step.

"I'm sorry," he said. "I wasn't thinking. I just—"

"No, it's my fault." Jaelle put her boot back on and hugged herself. "Habit, I suppose." She turned, and briefly, he thought he saw the ghost of a sad smile through the mask. "Sorry."

"If you don't mind me asking," he said, pulling out the remains of the berry cakes Jaelle had mashed together that morning, "how long have you been wearing the mask?"

Jaelle took her cake and turned it slowly in her hands. "I was nearly thirteen."

"Did your father give it to you?"

She nodded. "He did. Said he didn't want men following me around, since I was starting to look like a woman."

"And you said you can't take it off?" Why did he so desperately want to see her face?

"I'm the only one who can remove it. But once it's off, I can't put it back on."

"What are you waiting for?" He stoked the fire, daring another glance in her direction. "You're what, eighteen?"

"Nineteen," she said, straightening, a touch of indignation in her voice. Then she slumped slightly again. "The day Seth betrayed my sister, I made a promise to myself that the only man I will ever take this off for is the man who I know loves me more than life." She laughed without humor. "But at the rate it's taking me to leave this place, that's never going to happen."

He slowly eased himself onto the log next to her so she wouldn't startle. "You mean, you're willing to hide forever rather than take the chance that someone might think you're worthy of looking at?"

She stared at him. Or at least, he assumed so, as her face was less than a foot from his. When she spoke, her voice was faint.

"I'm keeping a part of myself sacred. The only part I truly have the power to keep in this world."

"I understand that." He frowned. "But what about—"

"Hello?"

Before he could finish his question, a man's voice called out in the twilight. Lucas leapt to his feet and grasped the hilt of his sword. Jaelle's shape dissolved quickly into the strange blue nothingness. It wasn't unexpected, but it was still slightly unnerving.

A man stepped through the trees five seconds later. He was holding a lantern, and his eyes were on them. "Thank goodness," he muttered before turning. "You can come out now," he called behind him. "There are only three."

CHAPTER 21

TOGETHER

U pon the stranger's announcement that there were three of them, Jaelle became visible once again. He didn't attack, though, at least, not immediately. Instead, he only held out a cautioning hand and shook his head.

"We mean you no harm, I promise." As he spoke, two more figures came up behind him and peered out of the trees, the smallest on horseback. Jaelle's heart, which had been thundering in her throat, finally slowed when she saw that they were a woman, probably in her fourth decade, and a girl whom Jaelle assumed to be their daughter. The girl was a bit younger than herself, probably fifteen or sixteen, and she looked a great deal like the man, with hair so blond it was nearly white. Now that Jaelle thought about it, his accent wasn't one she'd ever heard before. And that was saying a lot, as Terrefantome received criminals from all over the western realm.

"Can we help you?" Lucas asked, his hand beneath his coat where Jaelle knew he wore his sword. His words were polite but held a thinly veiled warning.

"We mean," the man said as the woman came to stand beside him, "to head into Piata tomorrow. And we were hoping to perhaps join forces while in the city."

"Piata?" Lucas echoed.

The woman nodded. "The town just north of here."

"The town is dangerous," the man said. "Last time we were there, our daughter was almost taken. But it's the only place nearby that sells horse feed, and we're in desperate need." He looked at the fire. "Would you mind if we joined you? We have some corn cakes we could share."

Lucas looked down at Jaelle with questioning eyes, and Jaelle hesitated. Joining forces was common in Terrefantome. Larger groups often meant more power and safety. But when comrades turned their backs on those who trusted them, it was easy to lose everything. Still, she did recall her father being rather nervous every time they'd ventured into this particular city. He'd even tied her waist with a rope and then tied himself to the other end, in case someone tried to snatch her. And as this man already had his own wife and daughter, they would naturally be slightly less inclined to do the damage that many of the young, unattached men were capable of. And after days of forest roots, berries, and rabbits, her stomach gurgled. The corn cakes sounded like a feast.

She couldn't speak, as she had to reattach her scarf. But once it was safely on again, she gave Lucas a small nod.

He turned back to their visitors.

"Thank you then. Your presence is welcome." He indicated for them to sit.

"Oh," the man held out a hand to keep his family back. "I apologize, but before we do, what mark do you carry?"

Jaelle had a moment of panic until Lucas pulled down his shirt. There, emblazoned on his neck, was the symbol for military desertion. Hopefully, it wasn't permanent.

"And yours?" Lucas asked.

The man pulled his shirt collar down as well to reveal the symbol for thievery. At least it wasn't a violent crime.

"My name is Gerhard Fischer, and this is my wife, Ingrid, and my daughter, Frieda."

"Are you from Vasksam?" Lucas asked.

The man nodded. "I was in the service of an earl." He grimaced. "Made the mistake of thinking I could borrow some of his gold."

Some was probably an understatement. Being thrown into Terrefantome for thievery was rather rare and usually only reserved for the worst of thieves. But then, Jaelle couldn't help remembering her own father's unfair exile.

Gerhard sighed and looked around. "Had I known my punishment would be a shadow of this, I would have turned tail and never eyed a piece of gold again." His gaze fell on his daughter. "Coming here, we had no idea our child would be in danger every waking moment. Now I've spent three years begging the Maker every night to give us some reprieve. But my wife here won't leave without me."

"Don't know where we'd go," Ingrid said, flipping aside a blond curl. "My family disowned us as much as yours did."

Frieda remained silent as she stared into the fire, and Jaelle's heart went out to her. What it must have been like to come of age in a land such as this, without sunshine or kindness. Away from every promising marriage match she might have entertained as she grew closer to being of age? Jaelle might have grown up in Terrefantome, but at least it wasn't a shock the way it must have been for this girl.

The way it must have been for Selina.

"Do you live near here?" Lucas asked, accepting the corn cakes the woman offered.

"About a day's walk." Gerhard pointed south. "We often tarry around this area to find others with situations similar to ours." He gestured to Jaelle and Drina. "Not everyone is a brute in Terrefantome." He took a bite of his corn cake. "Now, what about you?"

"Seems dangerous to be riding with your girl unclaimed," Ingrid said, examining Jaelle's mask. The food in Jaelle's mouth went dry.

"We're engaged." Lucas gestured to his mother who was still asleep. "That's my mother. We need to get her some new shoes tomorrow and some sort of beast for her to ride. She can't keep up with all the walking."

Oh, Lucas was good. Jaelle couldn't help being impressed by his ability to gloss over the topic of their engagement and focus on his mother. The fewer questions, the better. Unfortunately, Ingrid didn't seem to care about Drina or her riding situation.

"Engaged or not, you'll need to do something about that," she waved her corn cake at Jaelle's face. "I don't know how long you've been here, but those masks announce to the world that you've got a bud ready to blossom. Most foolish practice if I ever saw one."

"It's only until we're mar—" Lucas began, but Ingrid cut him off.

"Then get married quick. Because as long as you go parading her around like that, especially in places like Piata, you're just asking for someone to knife you and take both your girl and your mother."

Jaelle could barely swallow her food. The woman was right. Not only was her mask an enticement...a challenge for some, but with Drina being a handsome woman herself, the temptation might be more than a horde of criminals could bear. And if the prince of Maricanta was killed and his mission failed, his whole kingdom would suffer. And Lucas would be dead because of her.

"I'm going to get some firewood," Jaelle squeaked as she stumbled out into the night. But before she'd gone ten steps, heavier steps ran up behind her.

It was Lucas. He stood there, one hand half stretched out, looking quite unsure of himself.

"Jaelle..." He pulled his hand back. "What's wrong?"

But Jaelle just shook her head, trying to keep her tears at bay. "You'll need to go into town without me."

"And why would I do that?"

Jaelle pointed back at the camp. "She's right. As long as I'm wearing this mask, I'm a danger to you and your mother." She pressed her hands to her sides and flexed them, willing her voice not to tremble so precariously.

Lucas just watched, his face unreadable in the distant, flickering firelight.

"I..." Jaelle took a deep breath. "I wish I could do what she's suggesting. I really do! But I...I just can't." She started to pace as her breathing sped until panic threatened to make her chest explode. Hot, angry tears began to fall, heightening her frustration. Of all the things. If there was a god in this world like the holy man had claimed, why would he put her in this situation? Why would he threaten to take away the one source of power she had over herself?

Strong hands reached out and took her by the shoulders. Lucas turned her to face him, and when he did, her breath caught in her throat.

His eyes were wide as he searched her mask, and there was none of the resentment that there should have been given their situation.

"We'll find another way," he said, leaning toward her until their faces were only inches apart. "I told you I'm not going to ask you to remove your mask. And I plan on keeping my word."

She shouldn't believe him. A week together wasn't long enough to truly know someone, not the way she should if she was going to trust him. And yet, the panic quickly evaporated, and in its place, something new sprouted in her chest. It was warm and felt oddly like what she imagined sunlight to be.

"How?" she whispered.

He gave her a half-smile. "I've seen the Maker do more than you can imagine." He leaned even closer, the warmth of his whispers making Jaelle's heart trip over itself as she realized just how near they were. "I'm not going to ask you to compromise yourself. And I'm not going to leave you alone in the forest. We're going to do this together, just like we agreed."

She nodded, not trusting herself to speak. He held out his hand, and she took it without thinking. As he led her back to the campsite, she was startled to find herself wishing briefly that he wouldn't let go. She hadn't been touched like that since...well, since her mother had died. The sensation of his calloused hand enclosed around hers gave her a feeling of security.

Which was dangerous.

And yet, as they entered the campsite, an inexplicable peace settled over her. He sat down on the log beside her and began making conversation with their guests once again, letting go of her hand to reach for another corn cake. But Jaelle heard none of it. All she could think about was his touch and how this journey was becoming far more complicated than she'd bargained for.

CHAPTER 22

GONE

Lucas was grateful for their companions the next day as they took up their journey on the real road. Their hosts had offered to let Drina ride on the horse with Frieda until they reached their destination, which put him in a better mood than he'd been all week. The feeling of walking on level ground was also a relief to his feet, but the eyes of those who passed them were far more disturbing than the comfort was worth. Every person they passed felt like a threat.

Ingrid had made several changes to their party before leaving the campsite, and though Lucas had been annoyed at first, he was now grateful they were traveling with others who were more experienced than they. To begin with, Ingrid had removed Jaelle's scarf.

Lucas nearly had a heart attack until he saw that the scarf was empty.

"I don't know what this is for," Ingrid had announced as she removed it. "But it cannot be worn."

"Why not?" Lucas asked uneasily, inexpressibly grateful that Jaelle must have dumped her diamonds that morning before everyone else woke up.

"Enough to cultivate curiosity." Ingrid pursed her lips. "She's already got a mask. Why does she need another?" Ingrid had shaken her head, answering herself, as was her habit. "It must go."

It was decided his mother would wear the scarf over her head and shoulders. It would help cover her fine gown.

Still, even without the scarf, the looks their party received from passersby kept Lucas from feeling at ease. Far too often, their gazes rested on Frieda and Jaelle, and Lucas could see why Frieda's parents didn't wish to go into the market alone.

They could see the village long before they arrived, as the land in these parts was flat. The forest grew on the left side of the road, while potato fields grew to their right.

"I didn't know there were this many farms here," Lucas leaned down and whispered to Jaelle.

Jaelle looked at the farms they were passing by, but without her scarf, all she could do was nod.

The trees at the edge of the forest seemed slightly less muted than the woods they'd passed through the night before. The colors filled Lucas with a bit of hope, as did the little diamonds in his pocket. Not that he wanted them there. But Jaelle had secretly passed them to him that morning when their guests weren't looking. If everything went as planned, they would soon have new shoes for both the women and a donkey for Drina, and they could make their way to their destination at twice the speed they'd been going. By Jaelle's estimation, that was just under a week away, which would even leave them a few days to spare.

Please let us make it, he prayed for the hundredth time that day.

Jaelle was quiet as she walked, but Lucas was glad to note that she seemed to be more relaxed than the night before. She carried herself confidently this morning, her arms swinging slightly at her sides. She really was a pretty girl, so far as he could see. Still underfed, of course, but if that were remedied, she would have a strong build. Not at all heavy, but sturdy. Guilt ate at him for not being able to fix that, at least yet. As soon as he got her back to the palace, Bithiah would set to fattening her up a bit. He smiled to himself as he imagined his old servant scolding them all for keeping her so thin.

Then it hit him. He'd made a deal to bring her back with him so he could introduce her to the Fortiers. But now that he thought about it, a part of him really did want to bring her back, if for no other reason than to show her that the world really could be a wonderful place. He wanted her to know what it felt like not to be afraid. What had possessed him to touch her the night before, he still couldn't say. But her skin had been soft, and the moment he'd touched her, her trembling had ceased. He couldn't necessarily say why this pleased him so much, but it had.

And, he realized, he wanted to do it again. But what did that mean?

It meant he needed to get back to Vittoria. Lucas shook his head and tried to focus on the road ahead of him, rather than the girl at his side.

Thankfully, they came to the town's edge before he could dwell on the topic too much. He needed to focus if they were all to get in and out safely.

Frieda had been instructed to kick her horse into a run at the first sign of trouble, and Drina, who had slept off and on all morning, had been instructed to hang on. Lucas had given her very specific instructions that morning, in private, to keep her mouth shut. She'd been affronted at the time, but at least she was doing as he asked. Lucas reached out and caught Jaelle's hand in his. She turned and looked up at him.

"I want you by my side the entire time. Not more than an arm's length away," he whispered while staring down a fat man who was looking at Jaelle with far too much curiosity.

She nodded, and he straightened, but he couldn't help feeling a little satisfied that she hadn't pulled away.

The town was large, but even as they entered, Lucas could see that it was still quite impoverished. Cottages, little more than shacks, lined the streets. Mud was everywhere. On the houses, on the animals, even on the children as they ran about in the uncobbled streets. The road they traveled, however, was busy, making Lucas pull Jaelle even closer to him. Out of the corner of his eye, he could see Gerhard doing the same with his wife. Frieda and Drina rode between them.

Lucas allowed Gerhard and his family to attend to their errands first, as he could use the time to familiarize himself with the market. It was indeed busy, even more so than the road traffic had indicated. But unlike the bustling markets at home, these stalls had little that was new to offer. Most of their wares—clothing, horse gear, weapons, even baubles—were dirtied or cracked. He could only guess that this was because everything new that came into the country had to come from those who were newly exiled. Before Lucas had left, Michael mentioned that the crops grew so poorly it was difficult to supply the growing demand.

On compulsion, Lucas leaned over and whispered in Jaelle's ear, "Wait until you see a real market when all of this is done." He didn't expect a reply, as they'd agreed it would be best for her not to talk and produce more gems, but to his surprise, she gave his hand a slight squeeze. And for some reason, that made him happy.

They finally stopped at the feed store, one of the few log buildings in the market. Gerhard did his business, and Lucas stayed out with the women and the animals, glaring down anyone who looked too closely. After that, Ingrid said they needed a new dress for her daughter. This errand was also accomplished quickly, as the gowns were secondhand and there were only two that would even have fit Frieda.

Then it was Lucas's turn. Gerhard pointed them in the direction of a stall that had several skinny animals inside of it. While the old, half-broken mule would have hardly been Lucas's first choice, the man selling it was more than happy to trade the poor beast for a few diamonds. Then Gerhard guided them toward another stall that was closer to the middle of the market but still on the outskirts.

Lucas would have liked to skip this part of the visit. People were pressed all about them, and he nearly lost his grip on Jaelle's hand twice as they tried to follow their guide over to the final stall. But they couldn't do without shoes, so he trudged silently along behind.

Ramshackle would have been too good a word to properly describe the stall. But Lucas kept his mouth shut when he saw the few shelves of boots lining the stall behind the skinny man that greeted them. Lucas quickly found a pair for his mother after showing the man her slipper, and for once, she didn't protest. Then he turned back to the man.

"I need a pair that will fit her." He gestured to Jaelle. "But I don't know if her current pair is really the right size."

The man came out and measured Jaelle's current shoes with a

notched stick. Then he went back into the stall and searched another pile of boots in the corner before finding a pair that was decidedly dirty.

"Do you have anything a little newer?" Lucas asked.

The man frowned until Lucas cast a careful glance around and leaned forward. Pulling the raisin-sized gems from his pocket, he gestured for the man to be quiet.

"How about one of these?"

The man's eyes nearly fell out of his head as Lucas opened his hand halfway, and he dove back into the pile with renewed gusto. Finally, he produced a pair that looked far better than the first.

Lucas turned to where Jaelle was seated on a roughly hewn bench behind him.

"If you don't mind..." he said quietly, gesturing to her leg.

She watched him for a long minute, and he couldn't help praying that she would say yes, that she would trust him. Then, much to his delight, she slowly held out her leg.

Gently, so as not to frighten her, he took her leg in his hand and pulled off the boot. He tried not to think about how warm and soft her skin was and instead tried to focus on the redness of her foot when he removed the shoe.

After he'd taken it off, he placed the new one on her foot. The sole was worn but not nearly as badly as hers.

"How does that feel?" he asked. As a bit of weak sun briefly parted the clouds, he thought he could see a small smile spread across her face. And it was stunning.

Lucas felt as though he were rooted to the spot when Gerhard cleared his throat. Remembering himself and where they were, Lucas quickly replaced the boot on her other foot as well. Then he turned to the man in the stall and held out Jaelle's old boots and the three little gems.

"I want four," the man said flatly.

Lucas gaped. "You nearly tripped over yourself for the one! You can't possibly want more."

But the man nodded, his jowls flopping as he moved his head. "You heard me. I want four. That was one of my best pairs."

"Three is what I have." Lucas glared at the man. "And if you don't take it, I guess I'll just have to take them somewhere else."

"Lucas!"

Lucas turned to see a man trying to drag Jaelle toward the outskirts of the market. A second man was facing Gerhard, who was begging for him to let her go. Lucas's heart sank when he recognized the circular scar on the first man's cheek. He'd been one of those to chase Lucas's little party out of town at the city gate. All that running, and they'd still been followed.

"Please!" Gerhard cried. "She's taken. Her betrothed is here."

"Another word from you," the large man growled, "and I'll take your girl while I'm at it."

Lucas abandoned the diamonds and ran after Jaelle.

"Get the women out of here!" He called over his shoulder to Gerhard as he chased the man. Lucas had hoped not to draw his sword while in Terrefantome. Not that he doubted his skills, as he'd been trained by King Everard himself. But fighting alongside his men or even against a single worthy opponent, such as his brother, was one thing. Fighting invisible foes alone in enemy territory was another matter entirely, especially with Jaelle's life hanging in the balance.

Sure enough, the moment he jumped the broken fence, something hard slammed into his temple. Then his stomach. Then his knee. Lucas did his best to fight back, but fighting one invisible opponent was nearly impossible, much less two. What concerned him even more than his pain, however, was that Jaelle hadn't put a diamond in the man's clothing. What had he done to her to keep her from helping the way she had in the past? Then he spotted her body in the grass only a few feet away. She wasn't moving.

Lucas looked around desperately for some of the diamonds Jaelle must have loosed with her shriek. Several kicks to the ribs later, he found them and threw them into the air. It wasn't a good toss, but he thanked the Maker when one of the men reappeared. Lucas grabbed the visible man's ankle and twisted it, sending him sprawling. Then he rolled over, anticipating the second man's kick. His intuition was rewarded as the second opponent reappeared as he fell.

But when he looked up to find Jaelle, she was gone. A desperate search revealed that she'd been thrown upon a mule and was being led by an invisible leader toward the eastern woods' edge.

Anger made Lucas shake nearly as much as his pain did as he grabbed an arrow from his quiver and fitted it in his bow. He took aim at the mule as it entered the forest. His first mark missed. Before he could loose his second, a sweep to his legs knocked him flat on his back, and his vision spun.

CHAPTER 23
RIGHT ATTACHED

If Jaelle had doubted her trust for Lucas earlier, that doubt was long gone as her new captor pulled her at a quick pace through the fields. Where she had jerked away from the young prince before, now she would do just about anything to have him holding her instead of this stranger.

She did her best to look for any weakness to exploit. At first she tried spooking the animal she rode so he would run away. But the man just pulled her off the beast's back with a cheerful admonishment and dragged her along beside him.

"Won't do you much good, love," he said in a sing-song voice as they left the main path and turned onto an older one that led into the forest, the road itself nearly overgrown with weeds. "My youngest son needs a girl, and you'll do right fine. So just rest your bonny self so you're able to eat supper when we stop." He paused, and his smile widened. "Daft lucky it was that those two big 'uns weren't right able to keep you for themselves. Now you won't have to go with the likes of them, and my son'll have a wife."

Jaelle only redoubled her efforts when he said this. All her life, she'd been afraid of being taken. And now it had happened. Just when she'd been on the cusp of keeping up her side of the bargain and gaining her freedom for life, along with the chance to help Selina, she'd allowed herself to get sloppy. One moment, she'd been wondering at the way Lucas's warm fingers felt on her calves as he'd helped her with her boots. The next, she'd been dragged away in the thick of the crowd. And now this was it. She was going to live out the rest of her miserable days in this colorless, ugly world. Every ridiculous hope she'd recently dreamed up for herself about finding a life of her own one day would be dashed. And Selina's fate would most likely be worse. For as many dangers presented themselves to unclaimed maidens, the people of Terrefantome were far less friendly to anyone touched by Taistille magic.

She trembled as she bounced along behind her captor, his powerful steps dragging her no matter how hard she dug her heels in. But even resisting in such a small way eventually was too much. An hour after he'd taken her, she simply let him drag her until they came to a small campsite in the woods. Several logs had already been dragged over to the fire pit, and a few odds and ends, such as pots and pans and a roll of cloth hung from a dead tree. Sitting close to the ashes were a three-horned goat and a duck.

"Make yourself comfortable," he said, waving at one of the logs. "Only, before yous go trying to run out on me, know that Lippit here is a good runner, and he'll have you on your face before you can get ten yards out." The man chuckled to himself as he ran a hand over his graying mustache. "Best for your backside's sake if you just stays here and does as you're told." He started a little fire in the pit. "My last two wives thought they'd make haste while I was sleeping, but theys didn't know Lippit here was so quick. Figured I might as well tell you bout him before you put him to the test."

Last two wives? How many wives had the man had? And where were they now? Jaelle settled herself on the log farthest from the man and hugged her middle as the goat gave her a sneer. But she wasn't so frightened she couldn't stick her tongue back out at him. If only he could see it.

"Now that we're all settled like," the man said, putting a few strips of meat on one of the pans and holding it over the fire, "tell old Jake a bit abouts yourself."

Jaelle only glared at him.

"I see," Jake said after a long stretch of silence. "Well," he reached down to adjust his meat strips, "seeing as I got plans for

you, it's fine with me if you're a mute. And if your face's covered."
He leaned forward, his blue eyes so light they were nearly opaque.
"You'll be my son's problem tomorrow." He pointed east. "Left 'im
back that ways to tend the animals. Got a lot of bad stuff up our
ways, we do. It's why Lippet here has three horns. Spent too much
time out at the back pool at the edge of our property and drank
from it every day." He shrugged and sniffed, her lack of response
obviously posing no threat to his conversation. "We thinks about
moving every so often, but we gots the house and farm. Been in
our family for three generations. Can't think of where we'd go if we
left it."

Jaelle stared at him. Was he mad? Not only had this man not
committed a crime, at least, not one that had exiled him, but
neither had his father. In fact, his own son was still with him. And
they lived near a poisoned water source. Who in his right mind
would stay when he was four generations removed from the orig-
inal exiled member?

But then, as she watched him dig into the hunk of meat he'd
pulled from his pack, not bothering with any sort of social or
personal etiquette, she realized there wasn't much about this man
to suggest he was in his right mind at all.

"My son can deal with your mask." He looked at her out of the
corner of his eye as he chewed on the skin of the meat. "He has a
right temper, mind you. Had a wife before, but she wasn't hardy
enough. Died after only giving him three babes. Now, I'm a right
soft old chap, but he's got a bit more of his mother in him. Best do
as your told, and you'll learn to be content soon enough."

Jaelle felt as though she'd been frozen to her seat. It wasn't bad
enough that an old, stinking brute had yanked her away from the
life she'd been living. No, now she was going to be expected to be a
wife to his son and a mother to three of his grandchildren on a
poisoned farm. And hope to avoid his anger while she was at it. A
little part of her heart seemed to shrivel up and die as she glanced
angrily up toward the sky and the god Lucas and the holy man
liked to speak of. What good god allowed this?

The man stood up and came to sit beside her. Jaelle was
tempted to flee, but she saw Lippit giving her another mean look.
What would she do if this man touched her? Her heart pounded

heavily as the distinct scents of onion and body odor wafted toward her. Could she really stand to live like this?

No. No, she would rather die.

But instead of caressing her face or giving her some other unwanted amorous gesture, the man pinched her on the arm. She let out a little cry at the pain.

"There you are. I just wanted to make sure you had a…"

Before she could process the odd behavior, his eyes went wide as several diamonds tumbled down into her lap.

"Well," he finally said in a soft voice, picking up one of the jewels. "It appears we might not need that drafty old house after all." He stared at the jewel for a long time, but eventually, he turned his eyes back toward her. And on his face grew the meanest smile she'd ever seen on a man. "I'm so glad we crossed paths." He reached up and touched her face. But somehow, the same closeness she'd delighted in with Lucas the night before now held the tension of a rattlesnake as it coiled to strike. "I think the whole family will be right attached to you."

He began to lean in, but before he could reach her, he leapt up.

"Who's there?" Two knives were suddenly in his hands as he searched the forest, which was fast becoming dark.

Something whizzed through the air, and the man cried out as one of his knives was knocked from his hand with a clank. A second later, the other knife followed. And when she heard the voice that called back, Jaelle felt as though the Maker himself had kissed her ears.

"Let the girl go, and I'll do the same with you." Lucas appeared as he neared them, bow in his hands and a third arrow nocked.

"The one that speaks diamonds?" The man chortled. "I think I'll be keeping her." He reached back. "Lippet, attack!"

The goat charged Lucas, who swung his bow down toward the animal.

"Lucas!" Jaelle screamed his name as the man reached under the log and pulled out a crossbow. But as he raised it, an arrow stuck fast in his heart. He slumped to the ground, nearly knocking Jaelle over as he fell.

Jaelle stumbled backwards to find Lucas at her side. On his face was a look of seething hatred, one she hadn't seen on him before, and it sent chills down her spine, though for what reason, she couldn't say.

"Are you all right?" Lucas asked, not moving his eyes from the man as he rolled him over with his foot. Sure enough, the man's eyes were blank, and he'd ceased to breathe.

Jaelle's voice fled her as she stared at the body, and she began to tremble. At first, it was simply a little shudder. But soon she was shaking so hard that her breath moved in and out too fast, and the world seemed like it was slightly tilted to the side. Only when Lucas had sat her down and gathered her in his arms was she able to make a sound. Wretched sobs racked her body as she leaned into him. Gone were her worries about his intentions or the way he might read her actions. She was too tired to fight anymore. She needed someone to lean on.

He smoothed her hair with his hand over and over again, talking to her in low, gentle tones as he rubbed small circles on her back. She couldn't hear what he was saying through her crying, but she clung to his shirt even harder and buried her face in it. She would probably regret it later. They both might. But for now, she needed him.

"I thought you wouldn't come," she gasped between tears. "And when he said he was giving me to his son—"

"What did he do?"

Lucas pulled back from her, much to her chagrin. His face was hard, and she could feel his body tense, even as he studied her. Once again, she was reminded that this man could indeed be dangerous. But this time, she didn't mind.

"Jaelle," his voice was like a stone. "Did he hurt you?"

She licked her dry lips and shook her head. "No. I mean, not yet. It's more...what he had planned for me." She told him of the man's plans for her. As she spoke, she could feel his grip on her tighten. And against her better judgment, for one long moment, she wished she could stay in his embrace forever.

Eventually, they lapsed into silence. He stopped rubbing her back, but he didn't push her away, and she drank in the way it felt to be close to someone. The only person she'd been close to after her father's death had been Selina. But, she now admitted to herself, even her big sister's hugs had never comforted her like this. In Lucas's arms, she could close her eyes and let him watch over her and the horizon. For once, she didn't have to be strong. Selina had always sworn nothing like this existed. It was too good to be true. And yet, she was beginning to find doubts even in her sister's earnest warnings.

"I hate to say this," he finally said in a low voice, "but we need to get going."

Without moving, Jaelle opened her eyes to glance at the forest around them. This forest was far thicker than that which they'd traveled through with his mother.

With an inward sigh, she stood, too. She stopped, though, when she heard a noise from the other side of the campfire.

"What about him?" She pointed at the mule which was tied to a tree. But as she spoke, the beast snorted and laid its ears back, pawing at the ground.

"Probably better to leave him be," Lucas said. "I really don't want to do any more chasing tonight if I can help it."

Jaelle nodded and let him turn her in the right direction. Then a new thought hit her, and with it, guilt.

"Where's your mother?" she asked. If he'd left her in the town to track down Jaelle, Drina wouldn't have lasted an hour on her own.

"She's still with Gerhard and his family. Gerhard was taking all the women back out to the western woods last I saw." He turned to go, but first, he held out his hand. Jaelle accepted it gladly.

"I'm sorry you had to leave her to find me," she said as he lifted a small lantern from the man's belongings. After lighting it, they headed back out into the woods. She would feel terribly guilty if something happened to Drina, frustrating as the woman could be. If there was any woman least suited to life in Terrefantome, it was her.

"While I won't deny that I'll be much happier when she's with us again, I do think the Maker sent us Gerhard's family for a reason," Lucas said. "If I had to leave her with someone, I'm at least grateful it was with the kind of family that's least likely to do something dastardly." He glanced back at her. "You know, not everyone in this world is out to get us."

"Still," Jaelle mumbled as they stepped carefully over a brook, "if something happened to her, it would be my fault."

Lucas whirled around and gave her a fierce look. "Now see here, Jaelle." His voice was rough, and the fire in his eyes took her by surprise. "I'll have none of that now. You keep thinking I'm going to either leave you or use you for my own devices. But know that for some reason, the Maker has put you in my trust. And as long as I'm breathing, I'm not about to let something happen to you. Or my mother. Understand?"

"But why?" Jaelle stopped walking.

"Why what?"

"I just...I need to know why you're so intent on doing what's right when nearly every man I've ever known does what he wants instead. Surely that would be easier for you."

His hazel eyes seemed to search hers for a long time, though she knew he couldn't see them. When he spoke again, his voice was surprisingly gentle.

"It would be easier. But maybe that's not the purpose."

Jaelle thought hard on these words for the rest of their walk. An hour and a half later, they made it to Gerhard's little camp, which he'd made just at the edge of the eastern woods.

"Thought you could use a slightly shorter walk," he said when Lucas and Jaelle stumbled upon them.

Lucas thanked him deeply before giving Jaelle something to eat and then sending her to bed. His instructions usually would have annoyed her to no end, except now all she wanted to do was sleep and dream of how she'd felt when he'd held her in his arms.

CHAPTER 24

NORIO

Morning came far too soon. Jaelle couldn't remember her dreams when Frieda woke her, but she did have the delicious sensation of knowing they'd been good. She couldn't remember the last time she'd slept so well, either.

"Where are you headed?" Gerhard asked as they all shared bread and fruit from Ingrid's basket.

"North," Lucas said, sending Jaelle a quick look. "Then west."

"The capital." Gerhard didn't bother to hide his surprise or his dismay. He looked back at Jaelle and Drina. "Surely not with them."

"I'm afraid we have to," Lucas said grimly. "It's a delicate matter."

"I see." Gerhard rubbed his neck then ran a hand through his straw-colored hair. "I don't mean to pry," he said slowly. "But I can't help getting the feeling that you all," he pointed to their little group, "aren't exactly here like the rest of us."

Jaelle's heart beat a little faster, but Lucas was smooth, as always, as he gave a little laugh. "We're definitely not your average travelers, though I'm rather sure I can credit most of that to my mother."

Gerhard looked at Drina for a long moment before throwing his head back in laughter. Drina looked slightly affronted, but she said nothing, thankfully, and the subject was dropped until they were all packed up and ready to say their final goodbyes.

"I can see I can't dissuade you from your destination," Gerhard said to Lucas. "But at least take heed when I warn you that the Taistille troops are moving again."

"Yes," Ingrid said, taking her husband's arm. "This was our last trip into town until they leave." She shivered. "Some aren't as bad as others. But word's come recently that they've been pillaging something worse than usual. Burnt three towns to the ground recently, and slaughtered nearly all the men along with them." She jerked her chin toward the north. "I hear they're headed to Norio."

Jaelle's feet became rooted to the ground, but Lucas didn't seem to notice.

"You'll want to make sure you're sheltered every night once you pass the beach," Gerhard added, no sign of a smile on his face. "Don't want to be caught out alone if they pass by."

Lucas studied the Fischer family for a long moment before taking a deep breath.

"I...I can't tell you what the nature of our journey is," he said softly, giving Jaelle a meaningful glance. "But I can tell you that you've done my family a great service. Perhaps...would there be a way for me to find you again? Say, after this infernal trek is over? I would like to repay you somehow if we survive all this."

Gerhard and Ingrid shared a long look, but before either of them answered, Frieda spoke from her perch on the horse. "You can find us north of town." She pointed at a small field nearby. When Lucas looked confused, she only smiled. "Papa likes to go south first so few guess where we're from."

Gerhard laughed. "Well, there you go, I suppose. We've got a garden behind the house and a barn so ugly it hardly deserves the name."

They parted ways after that, and Jaelle, despite her natural suspicions, found herself wishing otherwise. It would have been nice to have the others with them, if not for Gerhard's easy laugh and Ingrid's corn cakes, to let Lucas have another man to share watch with so he didn't always look so tired.

They had five days left in their walk, if everything went as planned, thanks to Drina's new mule. They would pass within viewing distance of the ocean as they moved north around the thickest part of the forest, then they would head east. A knot began to tighten in Jaelle's stomach, though, as they began to pass through potato fields, and she realized just how far north they'd already come.

"Have you ever seen the Taistille?"

"What?" Jaelle was roused from her musings to find Lucas looking at her expectantly. His dark curls were still ruffled slightly from sleep, and he was walking with a bounce in his step that she hadn't seen before.

"Have you seen Taistille?"

"I have." Her hand went to the leather medallion she kept tucked in her belt. "But I'd prefer not to repeat the experience."

"Are they as fierce as everyone makes them out to be?"

"Oh, they are. I mean, the ones I met were kinder to me... because of aid my father used to give them. But that was only one troop." She shivered as she recalled what that same troop had done to their town.

"Do you think we'll meet with some on the way?"

"Unfortunately," Jaelle said, kicking a rock out of her way, "if they're going to Norio, we're headed right for them."

Lucas stopped, Drina's mule coming to a halt beside him. "You're sure?"

"Yes." Jaelle took a deep breath. "Because Norio is my home."

Drina, who had been rather sullen all morning, sniffed. "I could have told you that, son, if you'd bothered to ask me."

Lucas ignored her. "You mean, we're going through your old village?"

Jaelle nodded.

He looked around, but there was nothing for miles but potato fields. "Surely, there has to be another road."

"No." Jaelle took a deep breath and began walking again. "The only road that leads to the castle in these parts passes through Norio. And Gerhard was right. We'll want to find shelter. Only..." She frowned, remembering again what the inn had looked like the last time the Taistille had come, blackened and smoking. "We won't want to stay in the village itself."

"Why not?" Lucas asked.

"They have a particular fondness for burning Norio to its foundations each time they visit."

Lucas shook his head and muttered something beneath his breath. "Where do you suggest we stay then?" he asked.

Before she answered, Jaelle weighed the risks. True, she had the medallion. And she hadn't doubted the sehf's good intentions in giving it to her. But she highly doubted most Taistille troops would stop to listen to her or even give her time to pull out such a gift and show it to them. Most were known for the speed at which they killed and destroyed. Gambling with their likelihood to listen wasn't something Jaelle was in the mood to try. And the fields were out of the questions, too. Travelers had horror stories of what the Taistille had done to the men in their camps when they were discovered out in the open. So she squeezed her eyes shut and sighed.

"I know a place where we can go. The Taistille won't touch us there." She opened her eyes and tried to focus on the path. "But you'll have to do exactly as I say."

"I understand that," Lucas said, giving her a slight frown. "But I want to know what you're talking about first."

Jaelle fingered the medallion again. "We'll be staying with my stepmother."

LUCAS GAPED at her for a long moment before shaking his head. "Absolutely not."

"We have no choice. If we stay in the town, they're likely to torch our beds in the middle of the night. But they leave my father's land alone because of the healing services he gave them back when he was alive."

"But she was cruel to you!" Lucas was glaring at her. "And you know she'll be no different the moment we step through her door. Probably even more than she was before you left."

"Not if we buy her off." Jaelle loosened the scarf she'd donned again that morning and dumped the gems inside. "We can tell her that you've come with the bride price."

Lucas frowned. "Is that even a real tradition here?"

"No. But she's greedy enough I think she'll accept it without asking too many questions. We'll all go to bed early, and then we'll leave at dawn the next morning." She nodded, as if to convince herself. It would work. It had to.

Then it dawned on her, and she felt herself growing excited.

"We can also find my sister and bring her with us!" Jaelle clapped with joy as her greatest fears seemed to slide off her shoulders. "And when we're done, we can go straight to King Everard instead of coming back to find her!" It was perfect. Maybe the Maker did care about them after all.

He scratched his head. "I don't know—"

"Lucas, there is no other way. If you want to get to the king, we'll have to pass through Norio. It's as simple as that. We might as well get her now rather than having to come back to find her when we're done." When he didn't answer, she turned to find him staring at her. "What?"

"Nothing." He gave her a slight smile. "You just keep taking me by surprise."

Jaelle was suddenly glad he couldn't see her face, as her cheeks were burning pleasantly at his praise. And she couldn't help being reminded again of the night before.

Still, here in the daylight, the rush of emotions she'd been through seemed a bit ridiculous. She'd been so quick to let him hold her, and she'd even hungered for his embrace once it was gone. Those desires, strong as they had been, must have been merely emotions born of fear, she told herself. Anyone would want to be held after being kidnapped.

Still, she couldn't deny that she had come to trust him. And that she wanted to trust him. Was there, a little voice inside wondered, a sliver of possibility that her attachment might even go beyond trust? That maybe this sham of a betrothal might be more than a sham after all?

A few hours later, which was far too much mulling time for Jaelle's taste, they crested a hill. All thoughts of worry and fear were cast away, and Jaelle's breath fled her as she made out the sparkle of waves in the distance. There was the ocean, stretching as far as the eye could see.

Terrefantome had very little of its own beach, only a few miles. And those miles, everyone knew, were guarded heavily by the other kingdoms, though she knew not how. Many desperate men had lost their lives in those waves. Even the children knew the stories of bodies washed up on the beach—their faces and limbs discolored and contorted in monstrous forms. She couldn't see any bodies from where they walked on the low bluffs now, though, and she also found she couldn't imagine any. Not where everything looked beautiful and clean.

"See that?"

They'd stopped walking, and Lucas's breath was on her ear. She shivered slightly as she realized just how close he was. He'd taken her shoulder with his left hand and was pointing with his right out at the water.

"See what?" she asked breathlessly.

"Out there. There are two ships on the horizon. They look like blue shadows from here. That one's the *Spada* and the other one is the *Scudo*."

"What are they doing?" Jaelle squinted at the horizon, trying to make out more details than just the blue blobs in the distance.

"They're waiting for me."

She turned. "For you? But why?"

He grinned. "I'm the admiral of my brother's entire navy." He pulled a leather thong from inside his shirt. Hanging from it was a small but lovely swirled shell. "When I'm done with this mission, I'm supposed to try to make it back to the gate and lose my disguise for the guards to let me through. But if I can't make it all the way there, I can throw this shell into the water."

"What will it do there?" She frowned at the little shell in confusion. Many stories of power she'd heard from her father and the holy man, but none involving shells.

A bemused smile played on his face as he held the shell out, watching her masked face once again.

"My brother's wife is the queen of the merfolk. Well, queen is understating her position. She's really the Sea Crown."

Jaelle didn't know what any of that meant, but the idea of Lucas knowing a mermaid was fascinating, and her title sounded incredibly important.

"Anyhow," he said, looking back down at the shell, "as soon as this shell touches the water, they'll hear the song of protection she's placed inside of it. Then they'll know to come get me and bring me out to my ships, so I can sail safely home."

Jaelle turned to study him with new eyes. She'd known he was important to his kingdom. Such a mission could only warrant that, particularly when the man making it was the king's brother. But until now, she hadn't realized what kind of power the man beside her must truly wield. Lucas wasn't just some bothersome errand boy like she'd treated him as early in their trek. He was the king's chosen hand. An entire nation depended on him, and with good reason. For the first time, in the weak sunlight, she noticed some of the scars on his face. And without thinking, she reached up to touch them.

"You seem rather young to have so many scars," she whispered.

"Should I be worried?" He grinned, though she thought she noted a slight hint of insecurity in his voice. "Do they take away from my rugged good looks?"

She slapped his arm, then marveled at how relaxed and familiar she'd grown around him. "You know they don't, or you wouldn't be so cavalier about it."

"If you two are done," Drina called from her mule, "I'm ready to move on."

"Coming, Mother," Lucas called back. And again, as they made their way back to his indignant mother, Jaelle marveled at how he made her feel like he could see her. How long had it been since she'd truly been seen?

They never ventured to the beach, only walked close enough to see it. Doing so would have added hours to their walk. But Jaelle couldn't help staring hungrily at the foamy waves as they curled in on themselves and crashed against the shore for hours without fail. How had she lived this close to the beach all her life and never seen it?

"What do you want, Jaelle?" Lucas called several hours later. Drina had fallen asleep on the mule, and after tying her carefully to her mount, they had continued.

"I'd like a piece of ham," Jaelle answered with a dry smile. "And a big cup of mint lemonade."

Lucas laughed. "I mean if you were to pretend that your sister is safe and sound, and you weren't in Terrefantome, what would you ask for in all the world?"

The first answer on Jaelle's tongue was *you*. But as that would be highly embarrassing for both of them, particularly considering his recent attempt at a betrothal, she thought instead for a long moment.

"A box of paints," she finally said. "And a few brushes and canvases, too."

"Really?" He widened his eyes and stared at the clouds for a moment, nodding slowly to himself. Then he turned back to her. "Why?"

Jaelle stopped and began to search her bag. Lucas joined her, mule still in hand. Eventually, she produced a frayed, slightly torn little picture. It had a sunset over the ocean and a ship moving into the fading orange and yellow light.

"It's beautiful," he said, studying it for a moment then handing it back.

"My mother painted this," she said, smiling down at the little picture before returning it carefully to her bag. "She tried to teach me when I was young, but she died before I was old enough to learn much, and my father refused to buy any more paints after that. Too expensive and hard to get, he said." She shook her head. "He was probably right. But since then, I've always wanted to put the colors of the world on a canvas." She felt her smile fade as she looked again at the sea. Far out over the water, so far she wondered if she was imagining it, she saw what might be blue sky. Direct beams of sun must be hitting the water, though, because the water glittered until Jaelle's eyes hurt from looking at it.

"But I've never had a canvas," she said, shaking her head and resuming their walk. "And no colors to put on it, even if I did. That picture is the closest thing I've ever gotten to beauty." She swallowed hard. "And it's foolish to want anything more." She tossed a handful of gems over the edge of the cliff. The closer they drew to Norio, the more she was reminded that she was living in a dream. This was merely a means to an end...for both of them. And it was ridiculous to expect anything else. She glanced at the snoring woman on the mule. Especially if it had been brought about by *her*.

"What do you mean?"

Jaelle looked at Lucas, who was giving her a funny stare. She picked up a small stick and used it to tap the road with each step.

"In this land, beauty is a commodity. It's bought and traded and stolen, but it doesn't bloom." She shook her head. "Nothing blooms here. At least, not on its own."

"Nothing?" he asked.

She held out her arms to the brown and gray world around them. "Do you see any beauty here?"

For a long moment, he didn't give her an answer, only studied her with a look so intense that it made her want to turn away. Then, to her surprise, he stopped again and came so close that his proximity threatened to buckle her knees and send her over the edge of the bluff they were standing on.

"I can't see details through the mask," he said hesitantly. "But sometimes...sometimes I think I can make out the shape of your eyes."

"My eyes?" she echoed.

He nodded. "They're shaped like almonds. And," he touched her jaw, "I can tell your face is shaped like a heart." He smiled, and Jaelle couldn't have moved from the spot if she'd wanted to. Then he took a step back and gave her a funny tilt of his head. "Sometimes you have to search for beauty. But that doesn't mean it's not there." He started to walk again, but the thoughtful expression didn't leave his face. "The Maker puts all sorts of beauty in the world," he said, pausing slightly as he stole a glance at her. "And I think he put it here, too."

They resumed their walk, but it was nearly an hour before anyone spoke again. Eventually, however, Lucas cleared his throat. "When we're all done with this, how about I take you on a ship one day?"

"I'd love that," Jaelle laughed, not believing what she was saying.

He grinned. "Just stick with me, and you'll get your sunset. I promise."

Jaelle lapsed into silence. What was he saying? Did he really mean he wanted to see her one day, even after their business deal was concluded? Jaelle didn't know, but whatever his promise meant, it made her happy.

CHAPTER 25

JUST A BOAT RIDE

Lucas had to keep himself from staring as they walked along the bluffs. Jaelle's long, shiny black hair whipped behind her in the wind, and he wished again that he could see her face as she laughed.

He also couldn't help wondering at the rash offer he'd made her, to bring her out in one of his ships when all of this was done. Not that he regretted it. Far from it, as she'd sounded more excited about the possibility than he'd heard her yet. But it did make him wonder at his own motivations. What exactly was he making these promises for? He'd asked the Maker to let her trust him, but no matter how he stretched it, taking a girl on a boat at sunset seemed slightly beyond trying to gain her confidence.

It was the colors, he decided, that had possessed him to talk so. With each day, he couldn't help wondering if he'd ever remember what color looked like again. But the way she'd sounded, staring out at the ocean...If he had the power to make her world a little brighter, why wouldn't he? After all, he wasn't Vittoria's. Not anymore. And it was just a boat ride. It wasn't as if he'd asked her to remove her mask or to actually marry him.

Although, now that he thought about it, whatever man eventually stepped into those shoes would deserve nothing less than a lashing if he didn't treat her right. Lucas's grip on the mule's reins tightened as emotions from the night before assaulted him again. The panic he'd felt as he'd watched the man drag her away was like nothing he'd ever felt before, not even when he'd thought he was going to die in the middle of the ocean. The entire time he'd followed their trail had been spent praying and imagining all the horrific abuses she might be suffering. Briefly, so briefly, he'd forgotten his mission in Terrefantome. All he could think about was saving the girl.

"Let's make camp here," Jaelle called from the front of their little party. The path had grown too narrow to all walk together, so Jaelle had taken the lead.

"Are you sure?" He surveyed the landscape. "We still have daylight. We could make a few more miles before dark."

But Jaelle pushed her hair out of her face and shook her head. When she spoke, the joy in her voice was gone. "We're safer out here. Only the desperate come to the beach, and even that's unusual." She wrapped her arms around herself and shivered slightly as she looked to the east. "Tomorrow we'll make it to Norio. That'll give us more than enough excitement for one day."

A week ago, Lucas would have protested and pushed them farther. But there was something in her voice that bade him listen, so without complaining, he pulled the mule off the road to the spot Jaelle was standing on. It didn't take him long to start a fire and pull out the little bag of supplies Ingrid had forced upon them as they'd said goodbye.

"Jaelle," he said as he cooked the corn cakes on a piece of plank wood, "how many here are like them, the Fischers?"

Jaelle's head moved up, as though she were looking at him. He could almost imagine big brown eyes behind the mask, but only for a second.

"What do you mean, *like them*?"

"I mean...I guess I mean people like your father. People who were sent here but don't belong."

She waited so long to answer that he nearly gave up, but finally, she sighed.

"I don't know. People like us...we often try to stay hidden. Especially those with daughters. There are a lot who are the children or grandchildren of those who were exiled here. And some of us get out but..." She shook her head and smoothed her dress down. "Not enough."

"Mother," Lucas called to his mother, who sat glaring daggers at the fire, "have the kingdoms ever tried to do something about this place?"

Drina gave him a look that was far from pleased. "What on earth could you do with this place?"

Lucas pulled out a piece of flint and began sharpening one of his knives. "I don't know. I just...something about this feels wrong to me."

"I suppose we should just let them all into our kingdom then," Drina snapped, wrapping herself more tightly in Lucas's blanket. "Let all the criminals out."

"That's not what I'm saying, and you know it." Lucas scowled at her, but he got the distinct feeling of being watched. Sure enough, Jaelle's head was turned directly toward him.

Please let me see her eyes, he found himself praying. *Just once.* If only he could see her eyes, he was sure he'd remember them forever. Because right now, he couldn't help hoping that whatever she was looking at in him was something worth seeing. For even though he couldn't see her face, he could see the tilt of her head. Vittoria had never looked at him like that.

"What is it?" he whispered.

"Nothing," she whispered back. "You're just...different from what I first thought."

Her words stayed with him that night as he sat, staring into the embers of the fire while the two women slept. Was he gaining the approval of the woman who didn't trust men? And if so, why was he so desperate to do so?

"As usual," he murmured, casting a wry glance at his mother, "you've managed to muddle everything again."

"ALL RIGHT, MOTHER," Lucas said as they neared the town. "I need you to do one thing for me from here on out."

Drina gave him a scowl from her mule, looking very much like the indignant queen she'd been born to be. "Only one?"

"I need you to talk as little as possible. And this time, I mean it. Absolutely nothing is to come from your lips unless you're in the process of dying."

She gaped at him. "You're not serious."

He shook his head as he moved her mule slightly to the right so as not to be in the middle of the road. "Why wouldn't I be?" Did every road here have to be made of mud that squelched and sucked at the bottom of his boots?

Drina crossed her arms. "I have spent the last day and a half giving you the cold shoulder, and you didn't even notice?"

Lucas gave Jaelle a sly grin. "Did you hear that? My mother was angry with us. And here I was, thinking she was simply giving us a holiday."

"Why...you are one of the most disrespectful, ungrateful—"

"Just spit it out, Mother. You know you'll feel better when you've gotten it off your chest."

"You left me with those...those strangers!" Drina's chin quivered.

Lucas frowned. "Where?"

"Back at that awful town! When Jaelle was taken! You just took off after her and left me!" Tears were streaming down her face now, and Lucas could tell a complete meltdown was on the way.

"Mother," he said, lowering his voice and eyeing the passersby, "this isn't the time or place."

"One week with this little tramp, and you've already—"

"That's it." Lucas got as close as possible to his mother, who was still on the mule. He glared up at her. "I am sick and tired," he hissed through his teeth, "of your attitudes and high airs!"

"But I'm—"

"Yes, Mother, you! *You* are the one who schemed and connived to get information that wasn't yours in order to find a girl who could feed your greed, all so you could prove a point to the sons who are still trying to clean up a mess you helped make."

She glared at him, eyes red and shiny, but none of her theatrics could move him. Not after the words he'd just heard. He glanced back at Jaelle, who was turned toward the town. She didn't appear to be listening, but there was no way she could have missed his mother's cruel words.

"Then," he continued, "you came to this god-forsaken land and put that girl's life in danger, my life, and the fate of our entire kingdom!"

"But—"

"Now," he glowered, "if you had been the one taken by some villain who dragged you out to take everything that was yours, you can bet your biggest jewels that I would have been going after you. But admit it. *You* were the one who put her in danger. *You* were the one who put your own son in danger." For some reason, the corners of his eyes stung, but he just glared through the tears as she stared fish-mouthed at him. "Never once," he said, his voice warbling in an odd way, "did you apologize or even admit that what you did was wrong. You just keep on moving through life like it's your jewel box that you can overturn on a whim, and everyone else is expected to pick up the pieces."

A soft hand took hold of his wrist.

"Lucas," Jaelle said softly, but Lucas wasn't done. Hot tears ran down his cheeks as he stared up at his mother.

"I never told you this," he said through clenched teeth, "but after you pushed Michael into trusting Arianna's aunt, she took control of his body and mind."

Drina's mouth was still open, but the look on her face was... Well, he didn't want to interpret that look. All he could think about was making her feel the consequences of all she'd done. Because he couldn't keep carrying it around with him anymore.

"Once he was under her siren song," Lucas continued, unable to stop the tears, "she told him to take a knife and gut me in the stomach. And if it hadn't been for Arianna, he would have killed me."

"We need to get off the road," Jaelle said softly, glancing around again.

Lucas pulled up his shirt and pointed at the ugly raised web of scars on his chest. Drina's eyes grew round as walnuts, and she let out a little cry.

"You know that baby son you like to talk about holding and crooning to when he was little? You say you loved him. But your greed and your incessant meddling did *that* to him. And if that's how you love people, I don't want any part of it."

He let go of his shirt and pulled the mule back to the road with slightly more force than necessary.

What had just happened? How had twenty-one years of tension and frustration just boiled over? In the middle of a dirt road in a kingdom of horrors, at that. He could hear Drina crying softly behind him. For once, she wasn't using the dramatic wailing she often employed at will to get what she wanted. But he didn't care. He was an admiral. He was a soldier. And he was on a mission. It was inappropriate to let his mother get him riled up, particularly when the success of their mission relied on secrecy and shadows.

Still...it hurt.

Fingers wound their way into his hand as they approached the village gates. Lucas didn't look at the girl next to him, but he held onto her hand for dear life. Somehow, Jaelle had become a pillar for him. Of course...it was all a business arrangement. And an act. The men glaring at them from the sentry points of the village made that act all the more necessary, particularly with Jaelle's mask. And yet...maybe he could go along with the act and pretend for now that it was real. Because he needed a hand in his, someone to keep him grounded until he moved beyond the turmoil inside. And since his mother obviously wasn't interested in such gestures, this stranger would have to do instead.

"Back now, are you, Jaelle?"

Lucas turned to see a middle-aged man leering at them from outside a ramshackle building at the edge of the village. He patted his middle. "Tryin' to get with this one's child, too, eh?" He snickered through a dirty mustache. "Little stunt didn't seem to keep the last one, though, did it?"

Jaelle's face was turned to the ground, and she gripped Lucas's fingers so hard it hurt, her gait picking up speed.

"She's back!" Another woman, this one rather plump and disheveled, stuck her head out the window of a two-story building to their right. "They not let you through the gate, eh?" Her smile wasn't a kind one, and Lucas pushed them faster yet again. He couldn't see Jaelle's face, of course, but if Lucas had been a betting man, he could almost swear he heard her crying.

"Are you all right?" he leaned down and whispered in her ear as they neared the edge of the town. He tried not to sound too serious, but he couldn't help the questions that sprang to mind. Get with this one's child...too?

Other much less chivalrous comments were made as they hurried toward the end of the street. Not that he understood many of them. But whatever they were speaking of wasn't something Jaelle seemed to be able to brush aside, and an uneasy feeling stirred within him as he contemplated the possibilities.

Had she been with child before? If so, he shouldn't be surprised by such a revelation, particularly not in this world of darkness. There were a hundred possible explanations, but he couldn't help being bothered by the possibility that perhaps...just perhaps she'd lied to him.

But what was it to him? He and Jaelle had known each other less than two weeks. What was it to him if she had hidden truth like this? It wasn't his business. Still...why did it bother him so much? It wasn't as if she was his real intended.

"Turn here," she said tearfully, shaking her head instead of answering.

He knew women well enough not to push the issue, but he promised himself silently that this would not be the last they spoke of it.

They left the highway and made their way up a dirt path that led to a house on the hill. A small barn, though it had more in common with a shed than most barns Lucas had seen, lay about twenty feet to the left of the house, which was surrounded by farm fields on all sides, the forest flanking it in the distance. The house was long, with at least three visible windows made of clear glass, glass that was probably in better shape than that in many of the houses in Maricanta. The house itself was made of brick, and its roof appeared to be sturdy.

"Are you sure about this?" he asked in a low voice as she raised her hand to the door.

She paused slightly, her hand inches from the door. "In

earnest? No." She cleared her throat and straightened her shoulders. "But as usual, I don't think we have a choice." And with that,
she knocked on the door.

CHAPTER 26

NOTHING SPECIAL

A woman who looked distinctly Maricantan, tall and thin with gently tanned skin and dark, curly hair, opened the door. Her dress was simple but far nicer than most clothes Lucas had seen in Terrefantome, including Jaelle's. When she saw Jaelle, her mouth fell open and then scrunched up into a scowl.

"You," she spat.

Lucas stepped forward. "Madame, I hope we're not imposing, but my betrothed said this would be a good place to stay."

"Your betrothed?" The woman sneered until she had studied him for a moment. Then she gasped and threw her hands over her mouth. "You're...you're the—"

"Yes," Lucas said, glancing around, hoping no one had followed them or was snooping nearby. His heart sank as he realized she definitely must be one of the outcasts of his own land. A shiver ran across his shoulders. Maricanta didn't exile lightly. She must have done something truly horrific to have been sent here.

"And you're the queen!" The woman was now looking at Drina, who looked more pacified than she had all day.

"Queen mother," Lucas said softly. "But yes."

"But..." The woman gawked. "Why are you here?"

"My mother," Lucas said, forcing a smile as he wrapped his arm around his mother's shoulder, "was contacted by your other

239

daughter, Selina. She promised us Jaelle would be the perfect addition to our family. And as I was without a princess, we thought we would come to see about her offer."

"But why?" The woman looked as though they'd suggested she drink sour pond water. Then she seemed to remember herself. "Of course, come in." She shook her head slightly, as though to clear it, and hurried them all in. Then with a furtive glance out the large wooden door, she bolted it shut.

The house was far more comfortable inside than it had appeared from the outside. Although, if, as Jaelle had said, this woman was the only healer for miles, Lucas could easily imagine her getting the finest of belongings from those who were losing their health.

The front room was unusual as well as fine. After walking straight in, there was a very large table with leather straps of varying shapes and sizes on each side. Then there were what looked like several bedrooms beyond that room and to the right. To the left lay a kitchen.

Jaelle turned in a slow circle, a crease on her brow. "Chiara," she called in a low voice, "where's Selina?" Lucas hoped that she would remember her goal of silence while here. If her stepmother was as clever as Jaelle had said, they would be in for an interesting evening.

"I hope you're all hungry." The woman ignored Jaelle's question. Instead, she ushered them toward the kitchen, which had a large hearth and a large table and four chairs. She had stood straight enough at the door, but now she walked with an obvious limp. And if Lucas looked carefully enough, one of her hands was curled in like a claw. "I just had this pork cut up yesterday," she said, pointing to a slab of meat on the table.

"Where's Selina?" Jaelle asked again, slightly louder this time as their host bid them sit.

Chiara's eyes narrowed as she set out plates for her guests.

"She didn't tell me. Left a short note saying she couldn't live this way anymore, along with a few pouches of money, and then she was gone." Chiara sniffed. "Would you like ham, my queen?"

Lucas watched Jaelle as she absorbed this, wishing, as always, that he could see what she was feeling. Before he could make any discreet inquiries, though, Chiara drew his attention again.

"But let's not talk of my sorrows." She gave Lucas a smile that made his skin crawl. "Your Highness. While I'm gloriously happy, of course, to see my youngest so well matched, I have to admit," she took a sip from her mug, "I'm a bit confused as to why you're all back here if you claimed her already?"

"I was hoping to say goodbye to Selina one more time," Jaelle said before Lucas could think up an excuse.

The saccharine smile melted from Chiara's thin face as she turned to Jaelle. "Really? That's intriguing, considering she disappeared the same day you did." There was a bite in the woman's words, and Lucas watched with dismay as Jaelle seemed to fold into herself. Chiara turned to give him that sickeningly sweet smile again, but Lucas couldn't bring himself to mirror it. Instead, he spoke.

"From what Jaelle has told me, you'll be suffering more financially now, as I've taken her from you. I hope you'll allow us to compensate you for your losses." His words were polite enough, but he made sure his eyes didn't break contact with hers. "A bride price, perhaps?"

Chiara sat a little straighter. "A bride price? Oh, I couldn't." But her tone as she looked back at Jaelle said otherwise.

"It won't be any trouble," Lucas said. Why did his voice sound so strained?

"Well," Chiara paused, returning her gaze to him. "I suppose it is tradition in some lands." Her smile widened. "Yes, that will be very kind of you."

"What sort of crime did you commit to be sent here?"

Lucas gaped at his mother, who was looking expectantly at their hostess. He tried to bump her leg under the table with his, but Chiara was already laughing.

"Oh, that. Well, we were sent here, what, about six years ago, Jaelle?"

Jaelle said nothing.

"I am a healer, as I'm sure you know. Unfortunately, I made a mistake with some poultices once while I was tired, and it had unfortunate consequences." She shrugged then gave Drina a sad smile. "I...I had heard a rumor, though, of forgiveness being offered in Maricanta?" She turned her eyes on Lucas.

"I will have to speak with my brother," Lucas said, forcing a polite nod. "I am simply the humble younger brother who does the king's bidding." And thank goodness for that. Lucas had no desire to rule, specifically because of situations like this. Although, he didn't think it would be rising above his position if he were to tell this woman now that she was going to stay here for the rest of her miserable life. That probably wouldn't help them with the sleeping situation, though.

"I see." Chiara's smile grew brittle, and she turned to Jaelle. "Tell me, darling, why are you wearing that scarf tied around your head? You look a bit like a Taistille yourself."

"I thought it best," Lucas jumped in again, meeting Jaelle's eyes, "that she not flaunt her...fine features, as not all are hidden." Well, her lower jaw and the bottom of her chin were visible, so there was some truth to that.

"Well, it's probably for the best." Chiara gathered their plates from the table with a few loud clinks. "She's not much to look at," she called over her shoulder as she moved to a large bucket of water. "I met her just before her father gave her the mask. I'm not sure why he bothered to hide her in the first place."

His face grew hot, and Lucas opened his mouth, ready to give the woman a few words about beauty herself when something gently squeezed his hand. He looked at Jaelle, who gave him the slightest of head shakes. He frowned at her, but snapped his mouth shut again. She was right. Angering this woman would get them, at best, a bed under the stars. At worst, she could report them to the local marshal. But that didn't mean he had to like it.

"Really, I'm curious as to what you see in her," Chiara continued. "I mean, I don't know what Selina promised you when she contacted you, but this little chit here barely knows how to work for her bread."

Even Drina looked shocked. Chiara poured herself a glass of wine, and this time, she didn't offer any to her guests.

"To be candid," Chiara continued, "you could have any woman of your choice, Your Highness. Ladies who are cool and refined and intelligent. Instead, you choose a mud rat from the country of exile. She can't read. She can't write. You can't even see her face, which, like I said, is nothing special to look at." She leaned forward and ran a hand along Jaelle's cheek. "I can't even begin to dream of what Selina used to lure you here for her."

For a moment, Lucas was sure she was going to make a grab for the scarf. Then it would all be over, and he would have some very hard decisions to make. But thank the Maker, she only went back to leaning against the window as Jaelle cowered down in her seat, hunched and small. Seeing her like that made Lucas burn on the inside.

No wonder the girl trusted no one. To be abused this way for the last six years of her life would make anyone a hollow version of their former selves. And even worse would be the feeling of abandonment when one's father allowed such maltreatment. In that second, Lucas found himself wanting to do nothing more than scoop Jaelle up in his arms and run back to the beach, throwing her to the mermaids to take her away from this horrible place forever.

Instead, he pushed his chair back and went to stand behind his mother.

"Is there somewhere I can let my mother rest? She's had a long day of riding."

Chiara, who was now busy lighting herself a pipe, didn't even look up. Instead, she waved a lazy hand at Jaelle.

"Show them to your old room. Then go weed out your garden. It's about overrun with weeds. I can't get a healthy herb to save my life."

Jaelle nodded and stood before heading toward the back of the house. Lucas and Drina followed. For once, Drina didn't put up a fight or even pout as he left her tucked into the little bed in the corner. She truly did look tired.

"Is there somewhere we can talk?" he whispered to Jaelle as they closed the door on his mother.

She nodded. "Follow me."

CHAPTER 27
WHAT YOU WANTED

J aelle was glad Lucas couldn't see her face as he followed her out to the herb garden. Her cheeks burned from Chiara's words, shame sliding down her body. She felt exposed, like someone had stripped her naked and laid her out for the world to see. Only, Lucas had been the one to see, or hear, rather, all of Chiara's words. And now he knew everything she wasn't.

"Where's your stepmother?" he asked in a low voice as they went out the back door.

"Probably smoking her pipe in her room. She often complains about headaches this time of day." Jaelle wrinkled her nose. "I think it's all the wine she drinks, but what do I know?"

Lucas didn't answer, but she could feel him studying her as she began the task of pulling up weeds. Suddenly, she was glad for something to do. Obeying Chiara would have been far more distasteful had she not already been longing to revisit her beloved garden once more. Anything to get out of that house. Away from the memories and the gradual understanding of just how imprisoned she had truly been these last six years. Away from the shock of realizing that not only would she need to get help for Selina, but now she would have to find Selina as well.

And anything to escape her stepmother, Jaelle thought as she buried her hands in the dirt and relished the feeling. To her surprise, though, she wasn't the only one getting dirty, for Lucas got down on his knees as well and began pulling up weeds with her.

"Chiara's right about one thing," she said as she yanked a handful of dandelions up from around her beloved lavender.

"What would that be?"

Jaelle forced her voice to sound light. "Your mother probably couldn't have found a less suitable partner to be your princess." She let out a breathy laugh. But when she looked up at him, he wasn't laughing.

"Why would you say that?" he asked, no hint of a smile on his face.

"You heard her." A lump formed in her throat. "I'm not refined or elegant. I don't understand high society. I can't read..." She wanted to go on, but a sob lodged itself in her throat. Before she could figure out what to do with it, his strong hand was holding her face, forcing her to look up at him.

"Is that why you didn't want to talk about your book?" he asked, his voice nearly inaudible.

She nodded, the tears running freely now. "I needed your help, and I was sure that if you knew I couldn't read, you wouldn't—"

His fingers pressed against her lips as he gazed, searching, at her face. "My life has been saved more times than I can count by sailors who can't read a word. But like you, they have courage. And they study the world around them." He gave her a half-grin. "They often seem to know the world better than many scholars because they take the time to look."

Jaelle didn't know what to say to that. Her heart was racing, and her skin felt funny, warm and tingly as his fingers left her mouth. She tried to think of something to say, but her head was too crammed full of feelings and emotions. Thankfully, he thought of something for her.

"Why didn't your father teach you to read?"

Jaelle pursed her lips. "He was going to. I was little and don't remember much from when my mother was alive, but I do remember that they had plans for me. They wanted to educate me as much as they knew how. Father didn't want to send us away when I was little, but they were sure I could easily leave and make a life for myself alone when I was older." How did she remember these things? Vague recollections of conversations between her parents, fuzzy memories of her mother's smile. "But after Mother died, he changed."

"How so?"

"He swore he would teach me to read, but he never did. Every time I asked, he said we'd start *soon*. Never now. Always soon." She rubbed her eyes with the backs of her wrists. "And the holy man was never there long enough, or he would have tried."

Lucas's jaw was tight, and he watched her for a measured moment. But finally, he shook his head slightly.

"So," he leaned back on his haunches and surveyed the house. "I take it he built this?"

"Yes. I was born in Giova, but we came here when I was two years. We stayed in an inn at first, and then with another family with children the same age. But it wasn't very long before we were able to afford our own house, as there were no other healers nearby."

He studied her. "Do you miss him?"

Jaelle sighed, her hands pausing in their work. The little garden was looking much better than it had five minutes ago, but that wasn't saying much.

"I used to."

"What changed?"

She frowned as she went back to pulling. "He married my step-mother when I was thirteen. She'd just been banished here, and I think he was so delighted to find another intellectual that he hardly paused to consider the wisdom. My mother had been dead for years, so it wasn't an unusual thing to remarry once he'd found a woman who seemed to be a good fit. He wanted a woman to help raise me, and in this world, if you find someone here you can tolerate, you usually marry them before someone else does." She shuddered.

His brow furrowed slightly. "How did Chiara treat you when he was alive?"

"Well," Jaelle chuckled, "I certainly wasn't her favorite. And Selina didn't like me much either when they first arrived. But Chiara didn't treat me the way she does now. And she wouldn't have dared sending either of us to work in the tavern while he was alive. I can guarantee you that."

"What did he die of?" Lucas asked.

"According to my stepmother, a weak constitution." Jaelle shook her head at the sky. "But I wouldn't be surprised if she killed him herself."

Lucas raised his eyebrows.

"She'd gotten everything she wanted," Jaelle shrugged. "A warm house and a place of prestige, as people were quickly learning that she was a healer as well. It wouldn't have been too hard for her to poison him off after."

"You think she poisoned him." Lucas's eyes were dark, and once again, Jaelle was glad he was a friend rather than a foe. "Why that particular method of death?"

"Because," Jaelle said, yanking at a particularly stubborn weed that was nearly as tall as her hip. "Four years later, she poisoned me."

Lucas looked like he might fall over. "Excuse me?"

"Those things they were saying in the village today." Jaelle's throat constricted as she recalled the look of surprise that had crossed his face as her old neighbors had called out their taunts and jeers. "I think I told you that two years ago, Selina was engaged to a man named Seth."

Lucas pursed his lips. "I don't like him already."

Jaelle couldn't help laughing a little.

"I had known him since childhood, and Selina met him not long after she arrived. He was also the child of a criminal, so all three of us were technically free to leave. And as he was less...He wasn't a gentleman, not as you royals would be concerned. But he did protect us from the worst of the men in town. He was known for being territorial, so many saw him as our keeper even though he and Selina weren't married."

She shrugged. "It seemed the perfect way of escape. They would marry, so we would be safe while we traveled under his protection, and I would come with them." She tossed another weed into the growing pile. "We saved for two years, all three of us, scrimping every coin we came across that our parents wouldn't notice. That way we could hire guards to take us to the gate." She let bitterness color her voice. "And then two months before we had enough coins saved up, it all fell apart."

"Did he refuse to claim you?" Lucas asked, his voice oddly petulant.

"Not exactly." Jaelle sat back and stared at her garden morosely. "My stepmother found out that we were going to run. We didn't realize this until it was too late, of course. I got so sick I couldn't leave my bed for three months. I was so delirious, in fact, that I didn't even know it had been three months until I had a moment of clarity one day and saw Chiara putting the root of a dangerous weed in my food. When Selina came home that evening, I asked her how long I'd been sick. When she told me, the first thing I realized was that we had missed the date we were supposed to escape."

Jaelle buried her hand in the soil and squeezed, anger she'd long tried to push away filling the air like the stench of a skunk. "As soon as I told Selina what had happened, she nursed me back to some sort of health, enough to leave my bed at least. But when I asked what Seth had thought of the wait, she told me that he'd broken it off." Jaelle's throat grew thick as she relived one of the worst days of her life.

"I was still far from recovered, but as soon as I could, I stumbled into town to look for Seth. I wanted to explain that Selina wasn't to blame, and that Chiara had been making me sick. He hadn't listened to Selina, but I thought perhaps he would see how sick I looked and believe me."

"Did you find him?" Lucas's voice was tight.

"Oh, yes, I did. I also found his new wife. She was even pregnant already." Jaelle let out a laugh that sounded more like a snarl. "Gate guards are more sympathetic to families with children, so they'd decided to make their chance as good as it could get."

"He didn't even try to wait for you or your sister?"

"He didn't have to." Jaelle looked down at her dirty hands. "My stepmother had told everyone I was suffering from morning sickness. And that it was a demon's child at that." She shuddered.

"A demon?" He'd quit pulling weeds long ago and was staring at her as though she were growing a daisy right out of her head.

"A Taistille man. It wasn't true, of course, as I hadn't so much as talked to a Taistille of my own accord. But she told them all that I carried his child, and the rumor spread all over town." She shrugged. "So Seth immediately made new plans, as he knew Selina would never leave me. Not in that condition."

Lucas muttered a word Jaelle knew better than to repeat in company, but for some reason, it made her feel better.

"And not only did he find himself a new family," she added, her confidence bolstered, "he used all the money we'd saved between us to make the trip. 'Just remember that you made escape for my child possible,' he said when I confronted him about it. 'All your hard work didn't go to waste.'" She threw up her hands, feeling nearly as helpless as she had when it had happened. "So there we were, back where we started. No money, no prospects, and I was in even more danger because I was seen as 'loose', thanks to my step-mother's rumors. Even after the pregnancy turned out to be nothing."

"Which is why your sister turned to Sorthileige," he said.

Jaelle nodded and looked up at the sky. Sometimes, if she tried hard enough, she could imagine the sky being the color of peach, just like her mother had painted in her picture. Lucas had seen that peach-colored sky reflecting onto a peach-colored sea. It was little wonder he stared at the water the way she'd seen some men stare at women that weren't their wives.

Would she ever have a man look at her the way Lucas looked at the ocean? Such longing conceived within her soul a stupidly bold question, one that, to her horror, was rising to her lips.

"Are you in love with Vittoria?"

Almost immediately, she regretted it. Such a personal question was rude and was sure to make him feel awkward. She'd teased him about it earlier, of course. But that had been back before she knew so much. Before she knew him. Before he'd touched her face and held her tightly in his arms. And yet...for some reason, she needed to know the answer.

He turned back to her. His face and neck were slightly red. For some reason, the emotional reaction made her feel sick. And yet, as they were merely business partners, she forced a giggle.

"Look who made who blush first." That wasn't true. He'd made her blush plenty. Not that she was about to admit that.

He let out a weak laugh as he looked down at a dandelion he'd plucked. "Yes, I suppose you did." Then his smile faded, and he let out a sigh. "I'm afraid it doesn't matter how I feel. She'll never marry without her father's blessing, which is perfectly appropriate and respectable.

"I don't know that it matters. I'm beginning to think I'll never be the man her father seems to think I'm supposed to be." He picked up a discarded dandelion and began to pluck its petals.

That didn't answer her question, which filled her with even more dread. But to cover her foolish disappointment, she chose to sympathize, though it killed her to do so. "I don't understand how any man could object to a gentleman prince asking for their daughter's hand," she said lightly as she began apportioning the soil evenly throughout the little plot.

He dropped the dandelion stem and searched through the weed pile to find another. "My adolescent years were not easy ones. My grandfather sowed dozens of seeds of unrest among our enemies and our allies. My sister-in-law's scheming aunt caused the death of my father, my sister, and her husband, as well as dozens of others, and it set off a war between our people. And I was always caught in the middle."

Jaelle could only watch him, hanging on his every word.

"I had always been my mother's baby," he said, a strange smile on his lips, "and I was quite good at it. No one could get a smile from even the harshest courtiers like I could with my antics." He let out a deep breath. "After my nieces were orphaned and my sister and father were gone, I realized the job of making others happy was mine more than ever."

"Why?" Jaelle asked.

He shrugged with one shoulder. "A bloody five-year war... Someone had to remind them how to smile. And so I began to excel in just that. Whatever someone needed in that instant I became. To my brother, I was a sea captain. To my nieces I was a playmate. To my mother I was charming and silly, reminding her of the little boy she'd once doted on." He paused. "To the woman I pursued, the doting admirer."

"That doesn't seem so bad," Jaelle said cautiously, "being for others what they needed."

"Yes, well," he stretched his neck and shoulders, "it's bad when you allow that part of you to become you."

"What about Vittoria?"

"What about her?"

"Well," Jaelle said slowly, "not that I know much about courtship as you would have it, but did she ever ask you what you wanted?"

Lucas looked at her blankly, as though this thought had never occurred to him.

"Though," Jaelle added quickly, "I guess it wouldn't be so much a matter of what you wanted, but what you thought. Surely...surely someone would have *listened* to what you had to say." And though Jaelle was indeed ignorant on the matters of courtship and love, she couldn't find it in her heart to pity a woman who never thought to ask her prospective husband about his own thoughts and wishes. Not to puff up his ego but for the sake of hearing the heart of the person with whom she was about to share her life.

Lucas stared at her for a long time. This time, there was no smile, and his eyes looked sad.

"That's a question I suppose we'll never know the answer to."

There was a slight tremor in Jaelle's stomach as she looked at him, but she tried to brush it away. Before she could think of anything to say, however, he took a deep breath and stood. Then he held his hand out to her.

She accepted, not sure what she thought of his admission... whether she was pleased or dissatisfied.

"But enough of this talk." He smiled, though it didn't touch his eyes. "I have a proposition for you."

She turned her nose up like a haughty horse, though she was really dying to know what he was talking about. "I'm already neck-deep in my first deal with you. What makes you think I'm going to want another?"

He poked her in the side, which made her giggle like a little girl. "Would you stop talking? I'm not done. Now look." He took her hands again and forced her to face him, which made her feel all gooey and giddy inside. His face grew more serious. "I was think-ing. How about I teach you to read?"

Her breath caught in her throat. "You mean it? But..." she stuttered. "We'll be done in less than a fortnight. Surely that's not enough time."

"Actually," he said slowly, "I was thinking that after we help your sister, you might stay on at the palace a bit longer. Until you get on your feet, at least, with a place to live and all."

"But—"

"You've done my kingdom a bigger service than I can express. After this, you deserve all the relaxation you could possibly desire. Consider it a gift of thanks, I suppose."

Jaelle wasn't sure how she felt about this. Of course, Lucas teaching her to read would be a dream come true. But when she remembered that this was all just a deal...it dulled the shine a bit, if she were honest. When she was brave enough to look back at his face, though, he was once again looking to the west, where the vestiges of sunlight were fast disappearing.

"Are you thinking of your ships?" she asked.

"Yes," he said, turning his burning gaze back to her. "And no."

"Why do you keep doing that?" Once again, she felt like she had no more air in her lungs.

"Doing what?"

"Trying to see me."

He tilted his head thoughtfully. "I don't know." He gave her a sad smile. "But I really want to see you."

"What if I'm not beautiful?" He'd heard Chiara's declarations of her beauty at the supper table.

"The Maker shaped you, didn't he?"

"I don't know," she breathed. "I can't read to find out."

At this, his grin widened. "Well, we'll just have to fix that, then, won't we?"

CHAPTER 28

MOVING ON

J aelle vaguely recalled climbing into her little bed, but she didn't realize she'd fallen asleep until she was awakened by a muffled whimper. For a few long seconds, she was paralyzed with fear that it had all been a dream, and she was waking up in the room she always woke up in, the same room she would awaken in for the rest of her life. But then she rolled over and saw that Selina wasn't beside her, and the whimper sounded again, a bit louder this time.

Her conversation with Lucas from the night before came flooding back, and with it, the realization that Selina shouldn't have been beside her. Drina should have. And Drina was gone.

Jaelle pulled her shoes on and silently made her way to the door. It was slightly ajar. Peeking out, she could see into the hall, but she could only hear Drina and her stepmother. Neither sounded happy. Darting into the hall, she peered around the corner.

In the light of the main hearth, Drina was strapped, head, wrists, and ankles, to the patient table. Chiara was standing before her, her little tool pouch laid out beside her. She was holding a scalpel.

"I don't know what you want!" Drina sobbed. "My son won't tell me!"

"I found a pile of gems in my stepdaughter's garden," Chiara snapped, and Jaelle wanted to kick herself for not burying the diamonds deeper. "Now I want to know why my stepdaughter is suddenly swimming in riches and betrothed to a *prince* at the same time my other daughter went missing." She tapped the back of the scalpel against her chin. "I also find it interesting that Selina went through the trouble of sneaking a letter through the wall to get you here. I may not live in Maricanta any longer, but I know enough about you to know that *you* wouldn't come here unless there was something in it to benefit you."

"I promise," Drina seemed on the verge of hysterics, "I've told you all I know!"

Chiara opened her mouth as if to say something, but then she closed it again and stared for a moment at her scalpel. Jaelle was torn between staying with Drina and darting down to find Lucas. It would only take her a few moments to get to the cellar. But Chiara could work quickly. In spite of her stiff and withered hand, Jaelle had seen her perform enough surgeries with her good hand to know that even half a minute could mean life or death for Drina.

Then Chiara smiled. That was never good.

"I also know that you're a woman of beauty." She ran the backside of the scalpel down the edge of Drina's face. "But beauty's hard to come by, particularly here. And once you lose it," she paused to brush the knife back and forth across Drina's mouth, "you'll never find it again. Will you?"

Drina began to sob, and Jaelle looked around for something... anything to distract Chiara with. The only thing close enough was the little cart of herbs and supplies.

"Now," Chiara said, returning the knife to the other side of Drina's face, "I'll ask you again, what did my daughter tell you?" As she spoke, Drina saw Jaelle, and her eyes widened. Chiara followed her gaze, and Jaelle wanted to melt.

"Jaelle," Chiara said, her tone conversational. "Why don't you put back that bottle of yarrow root and come join us."

Jaelle didn't move. She'd just managed to grab one little bottle to throw across into the kitchen to create a diversion, but that obviously wasn't going to work now. When she didn't move immediately, though, Chiara slid the scalpel up to the spot where Jaelle knew Drina's main neck artery to be. Drina let out a squeak, and Jaelle felt herself stand and walk stiffly to the place Chiara was indicating.

Because Chiara *would* kill Drina. Jaelle had no doubt about that.

"Maybe you can tell me where your sister is," she said, pressing the knife slightly harder into Drina's neck. "Since this one doesn't seem inclined to talk."

"I told her I don't know!" Drina sobbed. "Just tell her so we can leave."

Jaelle thought fast. She didn't want to speak in front of Chiara. Not without her scarf, which she had foolishly left in the bedroom. There was no telling to what lengths her stepmother might go to get Jaelle back permanently if she knew what she could do. Then not only would Jaelle's fate be sealed, but also that of all Michael's kingdom. They'd counted on Chiara's greed to let them stay for a price, but it seemed like that bet had paid them back poorly.

"I'm waiting." Chiara twisted the knife, and Drina let out a shriek as a small drop of blood rolled down her neck. Jaelle felt as though her own insides were being torn open, as she watched Lucas's mother suffer. If only she could face her stepmother alone. But she was too far away to take Chiara by surprise, and with the knife to Drina's neck, she'd be dead before Jaelle could reach her.

"And before you get an idea to scream for that prince of yours," Chiara cooed, "you should know that he'll be sleeping soundly for a while."

Jaelle's heart nearly stopped. What had she done to Lucas?

Chiara pulled a chair out with her foot. "In fact, why don't you sit? Since it seems as if we'll be a little while."

Jaelle nearly disobeyed and turned tail to look for Lucas, but one look at Drina, and she did as she was told.

"I don't know if my stepdaughter told you, Your Highness," Chiara said, smiling at Jaelle, "but my hand isn't as useless as you might think. I don't do surgery with it, but it can hold a knife quite well. In fact," As she spoke, she took another scalpel in her curled, claw-like hand and this time, held it to Jaelle's face. "You're ugly enough, my dear, that anything I do to you would only be helping. Not that anyone would be able to see my work, thanks to your devotion to that mask." She tilted her head. "I might as well have a little fun."

Jaelle's breath came in and out faster as the knife traced her face. Was she going to die? A single bad turn and the knife could end her life. It could also give her a reason to never remove the mask at all. Would she be able to take Chiara by surprise if she grabbed her? Or was that still a risk to Drina?

This time, it was Drina's turn to gape. "You would do that to your own daughter?"

"She's not my daughter, but I absolutely will carve both of your faces out if you don't tell me what I want to know!" Chiara ended in a shout. "Now where is Selina?" She removed her hand from Drina's neck, dropped the scalpel, and brought it across Jaelle's face. Hard. Then she yanked Jaelle forward by her clothes until their faces were inches apart.

"You may think you're being brave, you worthless girl. But if you're waiting for your prince to come rescue you, you should know he won't be waking up for a while. So you might as well content yourself with me."

At this renewed mention of her threat to Lucas, something in Jaelle snapped. She sprang forward, knocking Chiara backward. Chiara hit the back of her head on the floor with a sharp crack. The scalpel flew out of Chiara's hand and rolled across the floor. Instead of going unconscious, as Jaelle had hoped, however, Chiara wrapped a leg around Jaelle's ankle and tripped her. Then, as Jaelle scrambled to get the scalpel that had rolled to the wall, Chiara kicked her in the ribs. Surprisingly fast for having a bad hand and a bad foot, Chiara rolled over to Jaelle, and Jaelle let out a cry as Chiara grabbed and twisted her wrist.

For a moment, the world stood still as a single green gem fell from her mouth and hit the hardwood floor. Chiara's eyes went as wide as the gem, and she looked back at Jaelle. "The diamonds are from you," she whispered. Then her eyes went flat. "What does this have to do with Selina?"

Out of the corner of her eye, Jaelle could see the knife where it still lay on the floor. Chiara seemed to see it as well, though, for in the next second, they were both scrambling for it. Unfortunately, as Chiara had been grabbing Jaelle's wrist, she reached it first.

Snatching it up, she turned on Jaelle, a new shine in her eyes as she grinned. "Let's see how many more of those we can get from you, shall we?"

Jaelle rolled, but she was at the far end of the room by now, and hit the corner hard. She looked up to see Chiara raising the scalpel above her head. But just before she brought the knife down, a chair flew through the air and knocked her to the ground. In a second, Lucas was at Jaelle's side, crouching over her as they watched Chiara's body where it lay under the chair. But when she failed to move, even after Lucas removed the chair, Jaelle let out a sigh of relief.

"She's unconscious," Lucas said, rubbing his face. Then he blinked several times. "Are you both safe?"

"No!" Drina shrieked. "She cut me!" She glared at Jaelle, tears beginning to run down her face again. "She cut me because you wouldn't tell her what she wanted to know!"

"I know." Jaelle closed her eyes and put her head in her hands, suddenly feeling weak. "I'm sorry."

"Did it ever occur to you, Mother," Lucas asked as he freed his mother from her bonds, "that Jaelle was protecting more than just herself?" His voice was quiet, far different from how it had been that morning on the road. And yet, after he'd spoken, Drina looked as if she'd been slapped.

"What about you?" Jaelle asked after clearing her throat.

"What about me?"

"She drugged your drink." Jaelle took his face in her hands and examined his eyes for the signs of insobriety that often came as a result of the kinds of drugs her stepmother used. The motion was all done as a healer, of course, and without the slightest bit of flirtation. But she would be lying to herself, even in the stress of the moment, if she said that touching him so intimately didn't bring her a good deal of foolish happiness.

"I know she did," he said with a wry smile. "I could taste it the moment I put it to my lips. Why do you think I drank next to nothing at dinner?"

She frowned. "Then why do you look so tired?"

"Probably because I'd just managed to fall asleep when I heard the sound of wrestling on the boards above my head." He scowled, looking down at the unconscious woman. "Well, what do we do with her?"

"She knows about the diamonds," Jaelle said, wishing again that she hadn't cried out. "Which means, when she comes to, she'll do whatever she can to get me back." It would put their entire mission in danger.

"Jaelle," Lucas said.

Jaelle dragged her eyes from the body to look up at him. His eyes had an ancient look to them.

"What?" she asked.

"You know this woman. You know what she's willing to do. So tell me what *I* need to do to keep you safe, and I'll do it."

Warmth for his dedication and regret for the decision they had to make hit her in dual waves. He looked so sincere, as if her safety might be more than a matter of honor to him.

Did she dare hope it was?

Jaelle shook herself and tried to focus. "We're not going to kill her."

Lucas raised his eyebrows. "What do you suggest we do with her then? Tie her up and leave her alone?"

"No." Jaelle turned and marched to the supply cart. "Someone will need healing, then they'll show up and set her free. She'll tell the nearest marshal she can find that you've taken me from her, and we'll have all the marshals breathing down our necks."

"Then what are we going to do?" He frowned.

She turned around, arms full of jars, bottles, and a mortar and pestle. "You're going to do nothing." She looked back down at the woman she'd once hoped to call Mother. "This is mine." She settled down beside her stepmother and began sorting the bottles and pouring herbs into the mortar and grinding them with the pestle. As she was nearly done, though, Lucas reached out and put his hand on hers, stopping her work.

"Before you do this," he said in a quiet voice, "just remember that revenge isn't justice." Then he gave her a sad smile. "Take it from someone who knows the price of death all too well."

She put one of her hands on his and squeezed. "This isn't revenge." If only he could see her reassuring smile. "This is my way of making sure that she's not going to hurt me or my sister ever again." She wasn't able to prevent her captor from following them and endangering all they were working for. But she was here now, and she could make sure Chiara couldn't touch any of them ever again.

As always, Lucas studied her with that strange intensity, as though he could see through her mask. She didn't know what he saw, or thought he saw, but finally, he nodded and let go of her hands. "Very well."

She went back to mixing.

"And Jaelle?"

She looked up.

He gave her a tired but sincere smile. "Thank you."

Her throat was suddenly too thick to speak, so she just nodded and went back to her work. Soon, the concoction was ready, and Jaelle rolled it into a dry ball.

Chiara's eyelids began to flutter just as Jaelle finished, but that was fine with Jaelle. Actually, it was more than fine.

"All those lies you told me," she said, staring into her step-mother's unfocused eyes, "I knew they weren't true when I was young. And I'm starting to remember that now."

Chiara moaned.

"I could kill you, and the threat you pose to us would completely justify it. But because I'm not like you, I'm going to leave you alive. And you're going to live in this miserable land for the rest of your life, wondering what happened to the girls you used and bartered for your own gain. But *I* will be moving on."

And with that, Jaelle pressed the ball of herbs into Chiara's mouth. Chiara coughed and sputtered as the herbs slid down her throat, but Jaelle didn't stay to watch. Instead, she was gathering her things to leave. And as she walked away from the house on the hill for the last time, she didn't look back.

CHAPTER 29
BECAUSE

They found Jaelle's father's old cart in the barn, and Lucas hooked it up to the mule, allowing Drina to sleep as they slipped away in the night. And as Lucas urged Drina's mule on with comforting words and mild threats, Jaelle wished it were appropriate to walk closer to him. He seemed unaffected by the dark of night, but she'd never gone walking in the dark hours of morning, particularly not when the Taistille were said to be close by.

The Taistille. In their haste to escape her stepmother, they were running right into the woods, which were rife with the dangerous tribe. Jaelle was nearly nauseous as she considered all the things the fearsome people might do to them before she could show anyone the sehf's gift.

Adding to her foreboding thoughts, the wet chill seemed to get under her clothes and made her shiver. The forest was thick here, and little of the gray light from the clouds got through to the ground. Just enough to see the path on which they were traveling. And even that sometimes disappeared when the clouds grew too thick.

"So."

If she'd been tired before, Jaelle wasn't now, as Lucas's voice jolted her from her reverie in the solemn silence of the night.

"What exactly did that little ball of leaves do to her?"

Jaelle paused to move a large branch out of the road so the mule, which Lucas was leading, wouldn't trip over it. "She'll forget everything that's happened to her for the last few days. It will be as if we were never there."

Lucas didn't answer, and Jaelle wondered if he disapproved of what she'd done. When he finally did speak, though, his voice was surprisingly warm.

"I'm proud of you."

Jaelle's face heated, and she smiled slightly as she realized just how good he was at making her blush. Not that she would admit that to him.

"I feel strangely free. Even after your mother found me, I felt as though I had ropes still binding me back to that house. As long as I thought Selina was there, I knew I'd have to go back. But now that she's gone..." She shrugged. "There's nothing that will ever call me back to that place again."

"How does it feel to be free?"

She huffed.

He chuckled slightly. "That doesn't sound good."

"No, I'm happy. It's just..." How did she express the mix of emotions that were flying through her like bats in the night, the greatest of which was guilt? "I've been so focused on reaching the castle that I've nearly forgotten my sister." She rubbed her face. "Chasing my own freedom has made me neglect hers."

When Lucas spoke again, there was a frown in his voice. "But you've taken on this entire venture for her."

"I have. But I could have been faster or smarter or more motivated to finish. Meanwhile, she's been cursed in such a way I can only imagine her living alone and afraid in her situation. And the closer I get to life on the other side, the less I seem to think about her."

They didn't speak for a while, and Jaelle nearly drowned in her guilt, wondering what her sister was doing at that very moment. Was she cold or hungry? Had some man taken her, or worse, hurt her because of her curse? Jaelle's insides curled at the thought of losing her sister. And behind all the guilt was another voice that was growing increasingly louder in the silence of the night.

How would she find Selina when all was said and done? Even if the Fortiers agreed to help her, how would she get Selina to them if she had no idea where to find her?

"You're wrong, you know."

Jaelle looked up again and smiled in spite of herself. "You seem to think I'm wrong about a lot."

He leaned over and elbowed her in the side, and she laughed.

"You're wrong that it's an either-or situation."

"I'm still lost."

Lucas sighed. "You seem to think that either you have to be happy for your own freedom, or you have to be miserable for the sake of your sister." He looked up, and even in the weak moonlight, she found his eyes boring into hers. "You can rejoice in your liberation while mourning your sister." He gave her a half-smile. "The world isn't as black and white as you think."

Jaelle bit her lip as she held onto his gaze. Oh, how she wished he were right.

"Speaking of which," he paused, "have you thought about what you're going to do when all of this is over?"

Once again, Jaelle's heart stumbled. Even now, as they walked in one of the world's most dangerous places, she was enjoying herself. But he was right. This adventure would soon come to an end. Lucas would no longer be obligated to talk to her every day. He would go back to trying to win Vittoria's hand. His mother could enjoy the comforts of the castle. And hopefully, she and Selina would be free of their wretched curses.

Why did that bother her so much? If she had Selina, everyone else would simply be a gift.

"I...I was thinking of finding a house by the sea. Somewhere I could learn to paint sunsets."

"How would you earn a living?"

"My father said healers will always have a job. I suppose if we weren't too far away from civilization, I could always come to town to heal." She kicked a rock. "At least, that's what I would like to do. But Selina's not so sure."

"And why is that?"

Jaelle paused to slip the diamonds from her scarf and throw them into a little pond as they passed, which set off a chorus of croaks from the frogs she'd disturbed.

"My sister...Selina doesn't think it's quite wise to choose a place quickly. She would prefer us to travel before we choose a location to settle."

"Well," Lucas said, "how far does she want you to go?"

"I don't know. But when I asked her what should happen if I...if one of us found someone we might wish to marry," Jaelle felt her face flush, "she got flustered."

"That doesn't seem fair. Denying you happiness because she wants to move about?"

"It's not her fault," Jaelle said quickly. "While my father had several key failings, he wasn't a bad man. And I had the holy man as well, so I grew up with some sort of trust in men." Jaelle sighed. "But Selina never had even that. I just wish she would give one the chance to show her otherwise."

"Do you want to travel?" Lucas asked quietly.

Jaelle thought for a moment. "I do wish to travel. If I'm honest, I want to go all over the world. I want to try everything new."

"But?" he asked, seeming to notice the hesitancy in her voice.

"But," she said warily, "I'd like to have some sort of home, someplace to always come back to. I don't want to travel because we have no other choice. I want to travel because it *is* my choice."

"What does your sister think of this?"

"She thinks that I'm very sweet. And that I'm also very naive."

Lucas was quiet for a moment.

Were the crickets always so loud at night?

He cleared his throat.

"The palace has the best view of sunsets you'll ever see."

"Oh," was all she could think to say.

"Well," he said after another long moment, "what about it?"

"What about what?" she echoed faintly.

"Moving to the palace when we're done here."

Jaelle longed to speak, but her mouth felt as if she'd just swallowed a ball of mud. Forming an answer felt impossible for a long moment as thoughts rattled around in her head. "I...I thought this was a business arrangement."

"Oh, it is," he said a little too quickly. "But I don't see why you couldn't take a few months and get settled first. You know, acclimated to the world outside the wall. Ari would love to have a friend at the palace that's *not* my mother, and we could really use a second healer. Actually," his voice brightened, "I'd love to have one for my men, too. Each ship has a few men trained to treat emergency wounds, but it would be a huge help to have someone in the harbor who actually knew what she was doing. And...I don't know. Just because it's a business agreement doesn't mean we couldn't be friends after."

For some reason, Jaelle's skin felt hot, and she wanted nothing more than to crawl under a rug. What was wrong with her? She should be overjoyed. A prince had just offered her both employment and a home until she was settled on her own. Selina would never have to work another day in her life if she didn't want to. Or she could find something she loved to do as well. Jaelle could never have even dreamed up such an opportunity three weeks ago. But there was that word...

Friends.

Jaelle knew better. She'd known from the start that their betrothal was a sham. And it wasn't as though she was ready to marry anyone at the moment. Far from it. She needed time to explore the world and to see who she really could be in a world of sunlight and color. And yet...Jaelle wasn't sure if after this journey, she would be able to work and live near him forever. For even if he didn't get Vittoria, which he seemed set on doing, she was sure one day he would find the perfect woman. And watching him fall in love and marry someone would not only do cruel things to the knots that were already in her stomach, it would also mean the death of even their friendship. Jaelle wasn't familiar with the etiquette of the socialites Selina had once told her about, but she knew enough to know that no woman would want to share her husband's time with another female.

Besides, when all this was done, she would just be another commoner with no diamonds to spare. And he would still be a prince.

A low sound blared through the forest, its resonance so loud it nearly knocked Jaelle off her feet. Several more echoed the call, this time from all around them. Lucas grabbed Jaelle around the waist and tossed her in the cart beside his mother. Then he drew his sword, his head whipping frantically from side to side. But no matter where they looked, the sounds continued to blast through the darkness.

"Go invisible!" he whispered to her as dozens of bodies began to emerge from all sides of the forest.

"It won't work!" she hissed back.

"Why?"

Jaelle reached into her belt and pulled out her leather medallion. "Because these aren't outsiders. They're Taistille."

CHAPTER 30

THE ONE THING

L ucas's heart sank as he watched more than twenty torches light the forest around them. Men dressed in sashes and billowy pants and tunics of bright colors surrounded them, short-swords in hand. Lucas was a formidable swordsman, but, as with the village, he wouldn't be able to defend himself and two women from this many foes.

Please, he prayed, as he and the Taistille made and held eye-contact, *don't let me lose them. For their sake, keep us safe.*

One of the men, probably in his late third or early fourth decade, stepped forward and began calling out in a language Lucas had never heard before. Several of the younger men handed their torches off and began to advance upon Lucas and the women, who were now at the center of the Taistille circle. One began to loose the mule, and another set eyes on the women. Three of them stalked toward him.

He could take three easily. King Everard had trained him to fend off as many as five at once. But these men weren't likely to watch their brothers go down. Their eyes were too sharp, too focused. Briefly, thoughts of what they might do to Jaelle and his mother sped through Lucas's mind, prompting him to send up another volley of prayers.

"We mean no one harm," Lucas called as they began to advance. "We only mean to pass through the forest."

This only seemed to bring them faster, which was why he was shocked when Jaelle's cry was received so differently.

"Stop!"

Everyone, even the Taistille leader, paused to look at her. She was holding up a thick circle of leather about the size of her fist with some sort of crest stamped upon it. Then, to Lucas's horror, she removed her scarf. Diamonds came tumbling down, and even worse, she continued to speak.

"Your sehf bestowed this on me!" she shouted. "She said if I were ever in need, to give this to the first Taistille troop I saw, and you would deliver it to her!"

No one moved for a long moment. But after the elder warriors exchanged a round of wary glances, one of them stalked forward and snatched the medallion from Jaelle's hands. He squinted at it and turned it over again before gesturing to some of the younger men, who jogged up to him. They spoke for a moment in hushed tones in a language Lucas didn't recognize, and Lucas wished he could understand what the man had said to them as four of the young men took off, each in a different direction.

As they obeyed, the man did something that couldn't have surprised Lucas more. With the toe of his boot, he buried the diamonds that Jaelle had let loose in the dirt, careful not to actually touch any of them. Then he waved the others on, but he remained by Jaelle and Lucas's sides as the other members of the circle spread out. More lights began to flicker on as lanterns and more torches were lit. And rather than a Taistille army, the light revealed all sorts of wooden vehicles.

The vehicles themselves looked like large wooden rooms with windows, and each of the wooden rooms sat on a wooden platform which was balanced on four large wheels. As horses and mules were tied to trees near most of them, he could only assume they pulled the contraptions, an explanation which would have justified the rumors that the Taistille traveled far more than they stayed in one place. In just a few minutes, Lucas found himself in the middle of what felt like a Taistille village. From where they stood on the road, he counted at least fifteen of the big vehicles. Many of them were painted in the brightest hues of yellow, orange, blue, purple, green, and red that Lucas had seen since arriving in

Terrefantome. At the sound of a cry in the foreign tongue, women began to come down the steps, seeming to resume what Lucas and Jaelle must have interrupted. Children peeked out from behind the doors and their mothers' skirts, and the smells of cooking filled the air as fires were built and coffee was put on. Did these people usually have a meal in the middle of the night?

Only then did Lucas realize that they'd spent much of the night walking after Chiara's episode, and it was really nearly morning.

The head Taistille pointed at them and spoke again in that other language. This time, Lucas, Jaelle, and a now shrieking Drina were taken from the cart and seated back to back on the ground. Their hands were bound, and then they were all bound to each other. Lucas tried to quiet his mother, but she continued to cry and carry on as one of the Taistille women walked up, studied her for a moment, and removed her jewelry.

Usually, Lucas was immune to her tantrums. But when he finally deciphered what she was talking about through all the sobs and wails, he understood.

"Please," he called to the man in charge who was now watching something else. "You can keep the other jewelry. But please give her back the blue one. My late father gave that to her just before he died." He felt foolish as he spoke. They obviously spoke another language. Still, though, they'd understood enough when Jaelle cried out to them about her leather circle. They should be able to understand him. Hopefully.

"You shut up," the man said, rolling his eyes.

"But my mother—" Lucas tried again.

"Will wait until the sehf arrives. Then we will hear what she has to say about the matter. And you," he glared at Lucas's mother, "if you utter one more word, I'll gag you so you don't have to struggle with the temptation."

"Mother," Lucas hissed, "he means it. Please, for once, just listen!"

His mother sputtered about the indecency of it all until the man produced a long, thin cloth and wrapped it around his wrist, never looking away. Finally, much to Lucas's relief, after his mother had been silent for a minute or two, he stalked away.

As soon as the man was gone, Lucas did his best to look at

Jaelle over his right shoulder. "Would you like to explain what that was all about?"

"I healed the sehf's son earlier this year. As payment, she gave me that medallion and told me that if I ever had Taistille trouble, to show them her crest."

"What's a sehf?" Lucas asked.

This time, Jaelle's voice dropped, and she sounded slightly like she was shaking. "The head of all Taistille in Terrefantome. She's ruthless and powerful, and every Taistille, no matter the troop, bows to her wishes."

"It would have been nice to know that earlier," he muttered, imagining what it might have been like to get a ride with the Taistille from the start. Particularly if they were as indebted to her as the sehf's actions would suggest.

"They're quite dangerous," Jaelle whispered back, "and I had no way of knowing if they would believe me or not." He felt her shiver. "They could just as easily have slit our throats, and no one but our families would have felt our absence. I didn't want to take that chance until we had no other choice." She paused. "But...in case we don't get out of this," she drew a shuddering breath, "I'm sorry."

They lapsed into silence as several Taistille gave them cold looks. Hours passed slowly, marked only by the sluggish brightening of the sky. Eventually, Lucas felt both his mother and Jaelle's heads roll against his shoulders. His back ached with the strain of keeping them both upright, but he couldn't help reflecting with satisfaction on how Jaelle had changed in the short time they'd been together. In just over a week, she'd gone from flinching at even the thought of touching him to trusting him with her sleep.

The feeling, he realized as he watched the camp begin to come to life around him, was bittersweet. The Maker had answered his prayer about letting her trust him. It was an odd feeling, knowing he'd earned her confidence. Neither Vittoria nor any of the other court girls had ever hesitated to trust him. Rather the opposite, they'd often thrown themselves at him and other men of high standing with the blatant intent of being seen and desired. He'd never had to do anything to gain their attention. Jaelle, though...

Her trust was far more precious than any he'd ever been given before.

He closed his eyes. *Don't make me betray her now.*

JUST AS THE smells of food filled the camp and made Lucas's stomach grumble, and as each family gathered around a small fire to eat together, horns sounded again. He tried to sit higher as a second Taistille troop joined the first. This second group was over twice the size of the first. And among the arriving vans, there was one van that was far richer in its colors and covered in twice the decorations as the others. It was also lacking the everyday tools the others had hanging from their walls and roofs, such as buckets, cooking pans, or bundles of firewood. Instead, it was ornately painted with wavy lines, stripes, and a variety of flourishes.

This particular van came to a stop beside Lucas's group. The back doors opened, and a handsome woman of notable height and strength walked out and climbed down the folding steps that one of their guards hurried to open for her. She wore wide, baggy trousers like the men, but like the women, her long, dark hair was swept up in a thin blue scarf. She stopped in front of Lucas and kicked his foot.

"Well, where is it?"

He stared up at her. "I'm sorry, but I—"

She huffed and looked up at the man who had been ordering everyone else around thus far. "You said she had my medallion. Where is it?"

The man said something to her in the other language. When he was done, she rolled her eyes and moved over to Jaelle, who was still asleep. "What about this one?"

The man produced the leather circle, and the woman frowned at it for a moment before leaning down to see Jaelle's face better. This struck Lucas as odd, considering Jaelle still wore her mask. The mask didn't seem to make any difference, though, for as soon as she'd examined Jaelle, the woman's eyes grew wide. She whirled around and threw the leather medallion back at the man before launching into a flurry of words Lucas couldn't understand but could guess the meaning of.

He was proved right a few minutes later when their little party had their bonds untied, and Jaelle and his mother were looking around groggily.

"This woman," the woman declared in a loud voice, taking Jaelle's hand in hers, "saved the life of my son. Just as we honored her father's home after he saved my own husband's life and tended to our kind, so we shall honor Jaelle."

"What about these ones?" One of the women nodded at Lucas and his mother. Lucas put his hands on his mother's shoulders, bracing himself for the fight that might possibly be his last.

"Please!" Jaelle cried out, pulling her hand from the woman's and running to his side. Then she surprised him by slipping her arm through his. "They're with me!"

"So," the woman said, her dark eyes sparkling and the corner of her mouth turned up, "you have taken a husband, I see."

"No," Jaelle stuttered, leaning slightly into Lucas. "It's...I'm afraid it's complicated."

"Well, then." The woman gave Lucas a dry smile. "I can see you're new to this land, so let me tell you how our little world here moves. I am Esmeralda, sehf, or as *you* might say, queen of the Taistille. My fathers and mothers were the royals of this land long before your royal *hoht* came and began to dump your undesirables here before walling us in. As long as you do what I say when I say it, you shall be protected by and from our people. But dare to cross me," her eyes sparkled even more, as though such a threat delighted her, "and you will rue the day you ever set eyes on Jaelle."

"I am grateful for your protection and your care for Jaelle," Lucas said before his mother could introduce herself as a queen as well. But to his surprise, she didn't even seem to want to speak. She only stared morosely at the goings-on around her. Well, as long as events had taken a turn for the better, he chose to take his chances. "Would there be a way for my mother to rest? She's quite tired from our journey. And..." He hesitated briefly under the sehf's scrutiny. "I was hoping she might have back the necklace my late father gave her before he died."

"You all look as though you could use some rest," Esmeralda said. She turned and waved to a girl who looked to be about thirteen. "Show Jaelle and her guest to my second van. And get back the jewelry, as well as the oaf who took it before I got here." The girl nodded and gestured for Jaelle to follow. Lucas shot Jaelle a grateful smile as she took his mother from him and let her lean on her shoulder as they followed the girl.

Esmeralda looked at Lucas. "You shall have different quarters."

"Of course." Lucas inclined his head.

"But first," she said, "I wish to speak with you."

Lucas blinked at her, and an uneasy feeling turned in his stomach. But as he wasn't in the position to refuse, he bowed his head again.

Before they could go, though, Jaelle ran up to them once more.

"I'm sorry to interrupt," she said breathlessly. "But I was hoping...Would you be able to break my curse?" As she spoke, diamonds fell from her mouth in a soft waterfall to the ground.

Esmeralda's eyes softened, and she took Jaelle's face in one of her hands.

"I'm sorry, flower. But to undo the witch's magic would take far greater power than we have here."

Jaelle nodded, but Lucas's heart twisted as she whispered her farewell and made her way back to where she'd left Drina and their guide. Lucas wanted to go after Jaelle, but Esmeralda began to walk in the opposite direction, so he had no choice but to follow.

"I will not hide my curiosity," she said as they made their way between family camps. "I wish to know how Jaelle has come into your care."

Lucas took a moment to answer, knowing that one small slip could have the entire camp turned against them again. But these people had become a safe haven for now, it seemed.

And he could only assume from their reactions to Jaelle's jewels that they had no desire for Jaelle's "witch" diamonds, as someone had called them. Still, he didn't know these people. If they knew what *he* carried and who it was for, there was a very good chance that they might decide to take a cut for themselves. And that would be the very best scenario.

"My mother came into contact with Jaelle's sister," he said slowly, "and they agreed that we might be a good match."

"Honest," Esmeralda said, giving him a sly smile, "but vague." Lucas must have looked surprised, because she chuckled. "Jaelle does not know it, but her father rendered my people more healing services than he let on. In return, I have made it my business to know Jaelle's comings and goings since she was a small girl." She gave him a sideways glance. "I also know that there have been rumors of the younger Maricantan prince and his mother running about Terrefantome."

Lucas slowly took a deep breath, praying she wouldn't see just how disheartening this news was to him. After all that work, they'd been recognized.

"And they are accompanied," she said with a slight frown, "by a girl who speaks out diamonds. And I would like you to tell me why." This time, she turned and faced him straight on. They were by themselves now, out of the camp and away from most prying eyes and ears. Not that it mattered, though. Either way, there seemed little left to lose.

"My grandfather," he said, staring out at the little river, "was not a wise man." And with that, he told her everything. How his brother, in desperation, had sent him to save their kingdom from an invasion of criminals when his best men had failed. How his guides had disappeared, and his mother had become entangled with Jaelle and her family. How they'd chosen to continue the appearance of a betrothal to keep Jaelle safe.

After he finished, the sehf seated herself on the ground and sat for a long time, staring at the opposing riverbank. As she sat, Lucas looked around. Was it just his gratefulness at being alive, or were the leaves on the trees here really green? And were those...apple blossoms?

Finally, just as the overcast sky moved to a shade near white, she drew in a deep breath. "You are right. Your grandfather was a fool. And if I'm to be honest, I'm not greatly impressed with your brother either."

"My brother is a good king." Lucas frowned. "We both agreed there was no other—"

"I did not say he was wrong." She turned and looked at him.

"Only that I hope he knew what he was sending his little brother into." Her brow creased slightly. "One does not go into Terrefantome without bearing some mark on his way out. Like mold, it ruins even the whitest of things."

"Once I knew of the situation, I told him I was going whether he sent me or not."

She smiled slightly. "You remind me much of my sister. She was brave and foolhardy, too." Her eyes tightened slightly before she returned to staring at the river. "But you are both different from your grandfather for sure. If you survive this venture, you will be a credit to your kingdom. But there is one matter in which I must counsel you to do otherwise."

Lucas suddenly felt like a small boy again, as Bithiah scolded him for sneaking figs from the kitchen. "And what would that be?"

"You are trying to protect Jaelle. But the law of the land does not protect betrothals. There are not enough women here to sate the men. The one law this self-crowned king insists on enforcing through the marshals is the allowance of one woman to each man. Now, this does not include blood family members, so your mother has a better chance of winning an argument before the marshal, should someone try to claim her." She turned and looked at Lucas, obsidian eyes boring into his. "But if you truly want to protect Jaelle, you will need to marry her here and now before you take another step toward that malefactor. Then she can remove her mask, and you will at least have a chance of getting her returned to you, should another man take an interest in her. No married woman wears a mask."

Lucas's heart stopped. *No,* he pleaded with the Maker. *Not that.*

"Surely," he said, his breath coming a little too fast and making him dizzy. "Surely there must be some way she can leave it on. This was simply a business deal," he continued, tripping on his own words. "She has no desire to marry me, and I'm...not ready for marriage myself."

Still, she shook her head.

"I'm sorry, but this is the only way Jaelle will be truly safe." She nodded back at the camp. "We can protect you for now. My people have many troops who will come as soon as the summons is sent. But the king, particularly in places like this that are nearer to the place he calls *his* castle, often sends out his lap dogs to plunder us. If they do not see the marriage mark on her, they will take her under the guise that we abducted her first." Her voice hardened. "Particularly after they find out about the diamonds."

"You don't understand," he said, his voice sounding oddly tinny. "She has made herself a vow to only remove the mask for the man who loves her more than life. I can't ask her to break her vow. It's all she has." Some voice in his mind wondered how this strange, strong woman could so quickly have become such a trusted source of authority. But then, Lucas was out of options. And, he realized, he was tired of secrets.

Her eyes softened, and a sad smile touched her face.

"Then I suggest you learn how to be that man."

With that, she stood and dusted her trousers off. She began to walk back to the camp, leaving Lucas feeling as though the world were crumbling beneath him. But before she had gone too far, she turned one more time.

"Jaelle has saved the life of my young son, and for such, by Taistille law, I owe her my own life in return. We will call in more troops to make sure our numbers are strong, and a wedding can be celebrated first thing in the morning. That will still allow you to finish your mission several days early."

Lucas felt like the earth was about to open up and swallow him whole. He was going to get married. Provided Jaelle agreed, of course. But this decision he'd agonized over before sending Vittoria's father the letter...It was being made for him.

"Do..." He licked his suddenly dry lips. "Do you have rings I might borrow and then return after the ceremony?" If nothing else, Jaelle at least deserved a temporary ring. It wasn't like he could give her anything else she deserved for having the most joyous day of her life stolen away from her.

"People in Terrefantome do not use jewelry to mark our spouses. We receive tattoos." Esmeralda pulled up her sleeve to show him a small tattoo of an elk. "And do not worry about having a holy man. One of our own left the land as a young man and returned to us." She rolled her eyes, but a small smile played on her lips. "The fool trained to be a holy man and then insisted on returning. He'll be delighted if you wish to uphold a few traditions from your world."

Twenty minutes later, Lucas lowered himself onto the sleeping blankets their hosts had provided. He was assigned to sleep on the outside of the camp, along with the other unmarried men without families. The others were all gone now, their blankets rolled up and stowed away, but Lucas was fine with that. He groaned slightly as he stretched, his muscles tight from the tension that never seemed to go away. And yet, spent and weary as he was, he had a hard time falling asleep knowing he was going to ask Jaelle to do the one thing he'd sworn never to ask of her.

CHAPTER 31

SLIP AWAY

Lucas awoke several hours later. Had he not known the chore awaiting him, he would have counted himself refreshed and strengthened. It had been the first time since coming to Terrefantome in which he'd slept without having to keep some sort of watch. But now he lay staring up at the gray holes between the trees, listening to the treacherously happy songs of the birds as he contemplated how and when to tell Jaelle what he and the sehf had planned. Or how to even grasp it himself, for that matter. How did he tell her that her hopes of creating her own life were coming to an end when he was still suffering the realization that his own life was veering far off the course it should have taken?

Lucas had always expected to be married someday. He'd always pictured it happening in the Su Palace's chapel, where the stained glass threw rainbows of color on its guests as though bathing them in the blessings of the creator of that rainbow. He'd be surrounded by family and friends. His brother would stand in for his father, and Bithiah would cry. Vittoria would be in some sort of lovely gown covered in lace and ribbon and beads and gems and all the things that made her happy. Her golden hair, gleaming nearly white in the sunshine, would be in ringlets that framed her face and set off her big blue eyes. She would smile demurely at him from beneath her veil, but there would be a spark of vivacity in her eyes that promised so much more.

It would mark the beginning of a momentous journey into the rest of his life. Then they would embark on their honeymoon on his favorite navy vessel, loaned by his brother, of course, and they would travel to some distant land. They might even make it down so far as Hedjet to enjoy sun and sand, and he'd saved enough of his own personal allowance to ensure she could purchase as many frivolities and baubles at their markets as her heart desired.

But that would never be. Vittoria would never be his, and instead he was trading all his aspirations for a simple ceremony in the middle of a cursed kingdom to a girl he barely knew. It felt like a cheap imitation of what should have been. And yet, this poor substitute of a ceremony would be just as binding as the real event ever was. He could try to convince himself all day that it was just an act. Deep down, though, he knew better. Michael would have cuffed him for trying to pretend otherwise. And rightly so.

Someone had left a plate of food near his head. It was a larger meal than any he'd had since coming to Terrefantome. Thick strips of salty bacon, buttered hunks of bread the size of his fist, and even a few slices of apple. He sat up and chewed slowly, watching Jaelle play with a group of small children in the center of the camp near the main fire where several women seemed to be smoking an entire pig.

Instead of thick, golden curls, his new wife would have shiny, straight, black locks. For a while, at least, they would be unable to discuss his favorite books, as she would be unable to read them. She would probably need as much help as his brother's wife had in court, or rather, even more. At least Arianna had been born into royalty, even if they were merfolk. Jaelle had never set foot in anything as grand as a village regent's office, to his knowledge. To go from peasant to princess would undoubtedly be shocking and most likely painful, as she would be subjected, no matter how hard he tried to shield her, to the gossip that was sure to sprout not only in his court but in all the other western courts as well. She would be forced to choose between begging her sister to stay in Maricanta, as he couldn't abandon his duties, or bidding her farewell.

No, Jaelle was about as far from Vittoria as one could be. And

Lucas couldn't decide how he felt about that. He needed to marry Jaelle, for her sake and his. And he would be the first to admit that Jaelle was someone he wanted very much to know better. But did he want to marry her?

Did she ever ask you what you wanted?

Jaelle's question from the evening before jarred him slightly as it rose again in his mind. What had prompted her to ask that? He was fairly certain that if he searched far enough back toward the beginning of his courtship of Vittoria, several months before, he would recall some deep conversation in which he and Vittoria discussed their greatest desires. Or at least, Vittoria's desires. While he might not know her greatest aspirations, he *did* know that she was terrified of the ocean, a problem he had unsuccessfully tried to rectify, and he knew that she liked to write poetry in her spare time. She'd hesitantly told him once that she might be willing to travel with him sometimes, as long as she knew their destination was a civil one and that she could properly pack her bags.

Now that he thought of it, though, he couldn't recall a single instance in which she had ever asked him the same questions. Come to think of it, in the last letter she'd written him, she'd spelled his second name wrong.

Lucas was tempted to be incensed as it became painfully obvious that his beloved had put forth so little effort to get to know him. But before he could be too angry, he remembered the series of questions Jaelle had leveled at him the week before, questions about Vittoria that Lucas hadn't come close to answering. And it dawned on him, much to his humiliation, that whether or not he harbored the character flaw Lorenzo had pointed out, Lucas and Vittoria were perhaps not nearly as perfectly prepared to marry as he'd once dreamed they were.

And then there was Jaelle. It was fun to see her so carefree, running and giggling as she and the children danced in circles. Her laugh was bright and tinkling, like the sound of her gems as they tumbled against each other. And now that the Taistille knew her secret, she went without the scarf, which the children celebrated with much glee, diving and running after each stone she let loose. Unlike their elders, they were greedy little things, obviously scheming up ways to make her talk and sing more to produce more diamonds. But if she noticed, she played along, not seeming to mind at all.

At one time, he'd had his entire life planned out with Vittoria. She would likely age well, as her mother was still renowned as a beauty, and she was quite skilled at the game of politics. They'd often enjoyed tossing banter back and forth, and the women in her family were well-known for giving birth to at least four children each, something the court would smile upon for sure.

But now as he watched her, Lucas wondered what a life would look like with Jaelle. He doubted she would have much use for politics, and half the court at home would be scandalized if they knew the manner in which she'd grown up. And yet, there was something in the way that she continued to meet her challenges head-on that was undeniably attractive. Every time she was knocked down, she got back up again and continued her run toward freedom. Her sense of humor was drier than Vittoria's had been, but he rather liked her snark. He had no doubt that if he ever asked her to come with him on one of his ships, she would be there in an instant. Joining the court life would be hard, but with all she'd survived here, he was rather sure she could survive anywhere. And there was an appeal to having a partner to join in his escapades, rather than just someone to write to back at home.

Of course, there was the possibility she might say no. If he was honest with himself, he was far from the ideal husband. His foolish flirting aside, he was gone more than he was home, chasing pirates or attending diplomatic meetings between kingdoms. His hands were stained with more blood than she knew, and whoever he married would have to be strong enough to help him bear that burden, knowing that not only would he forever carry his stains from the past, but also that duty would most likely require him to take many lives in the future as well.

Was it fair to tie her to that kind of burden for the rest of her life? To wed her to the court's charming flirt? Of course, he'd never taken it as far as his younger cousin, Nicholas, did, but Michael had always warned him it would one day get him in trouble. And really, even if Jaelle was able to see past the lighthearted fool he'd created as a facade for himself, the one that kept others happy by keeping his worries to himself, would she want the man behind the mask?

Could they learn to be happy?

Not that it mattered. As Esmeralda had said, they didn't have much of a choice. Still, though Lucas might not be the ideal mate, surely life with him would be preferable to the kind she'd almost faced with her kidnapper. Or worse. There was always someone worse.

He hoped.

"You're awake." Jaelle waved goodbye to the children, peeling a few of the little ones off her legs and shooing them away before she sat beside his sleeping mat. She sounded like she was smiling. Again, he wished he could see her face. It was probably a little flushed as she caught her breath and tucked her dark, smooth hair out of her face. Then he felt guilty for such a wish. It was likely to come true far too soon.

"I..." he began. But as she sat there staring at him, or at least, he assumed so, as she kept her face angled toward him, he knew he couldn't do it here so close to everyone else. She deserved to at least have her heart broken with a touch of privacy. "Where's my mother?" he asked instead.

"She's still sleeping." Jaelle accepted the apple slice he offered her. "Why?"

"Jaelle..." he stammered again. "There's something we need to talk about." He stood and brushed the crumbs from his lap. "Walk with me?"

But before she could answer, an older boy, probably thirteen years of age, ran up to them, breathing heavily.

"The sehf wishes for you to come," he told Jaelle. "One of our old women fell, and the sehf wishes for you to examine her."

Jaelle looked at Lucas.

"Go," Lucas said, forcing a smile. "We can talk when you get back."

"Won't be time for that," the boy said. "Sehf wants everyone to prepare for the *Nisipivis*."

"What's that?" Jaelle asked.

The boy's eyes brightened. "You'll like it. We all eat honeyed meat while we watch the *Nisipivis* and the elders tell the stories."

Lucas was about to respond that this didn't really answer Jaelle's question, but Jaelle quickly said, "It sounds wonderful." She turned back to Lucas. "I'm really sorry. Might...might we talk tonight?"

Lucas nodded then watched as the boy led her away. And all the courage he'd somehow gathered began to slip away like the diamonds she so often tossed into the night.

CHAPTER 32
NISIPIVIS

Lucas had been seated with the other unmarried men, but he could see Jaelle and his mother across the clearing, where his mother clutched Jaelle's hand. He wasn't sure what had brought on this docile streak, as she'd hardly said a word all day, but he prayed it would last. Then, when they got home and away from everyone who wanted them dead, she could be as obnoxious as she pleased, and he'd be free to sail far away in his ships and leave her to Michael for a while. Five or six years' absence ought to even things out.

Someone shoved a piece of meat in his hands, and only then did he remember the honeyed meat the boy had been so excited about. Taking a bite, he had to admit that it was a delicacy fit for the Fortiers' table at the Fortress in Destin. Crunchy from the dried honey, which coated the outside of the smoked slab, and tender and pungent on the inside. He quickly finished his piece and was handed a second.

The camp had grown even larger since the sehf's arrival, and from what Lucas gathered, at least two more troops had joined the two already there. There were probably at least eight or nine dozen seated around the fire now. More vans, as their vehicles were called, had squeezed into the forest that morning, many from the different troops running to greet each other and exclaim over how much the children had grown since they'd last met.

Inside the camp itself, a large circular space had been cleared between the trees. Even the weeds and pinecones had been removed, leaving nothing but a pit of clean sand.

Though the darkness was falling, Lucas had yet to ascertain what a *Nisipivis* was. Most of the people he'd questioned had either given him a description like that of the boy, or they had mischievously grinned and simply said he would have to see it for himself.

As the boy had predicted, Lucas had gotten no time with Jaelle, which made him more and more nervous, as the ceremony was apparently being planned for the next morning. The poor girl at least needed time to adjust to what was being asked of her. And though he would never compel her to say yes, after the marshal's warning and her abduction, he didn't see how she could choose not to marry him. They were close to meeting the king, but then they had to travel all the way back to the gate. And losing her again wasn't a chance he wanted to take.

The chatter ceased as Esmeralda swept grandly into the circle of sand and looked around her with maternal adoration.

"Children," she said, her low voice smooth and commanding. "I am glad so many of you have returned. For though it was an unexpected event that has drawn us together, I fear we draw together far too little these days. So we shall take every opportunity to greet one another in the name of the Maker and to strengthen our bonds once more."

Lucas gave a small start at the mention of the Maker. It seemed strange that the fiendish marauders should cling to his god. And yet, here they were doing just that. As if reading his mind, the sehf gave him a small grin before speaking again.

"Very soon, our holy man will speak. But before he does, I wish to remind you of the reason we hold our *Nisipivis* as often as we can." She gestured to a small girl sitting at the edge of the circle, not far from Jaelle. The little girl ran forward, and the sehf hoisted her up on her hip.

"Ignorance is but a generation away. If we do not teach our children to remember the wisdom that has been handed down to us over hundreds of years, we will lose it forever." She gestured to the holy man. "Now," she said, "I present our holy man, who will bestow on us the remnant of the gift which has been ours since the day this land was given to us." Her voice softened slightly. "May it be restored to us one day."

"Four hundred years ago," the holy man said, his hands hidden in his robes, "this land belonged to the Taistille. We were proud and strong, but more powerful than the strength of our hands was our gift from the Maker," he looked down at the ground, "which was given in our land." He began making circles with his hands over the sand, and as he did, keeping his eyes fixed on the ground, he continued to speak.

"We build no homes, for they were built for us."

Lucas's mouth fell open as the sand beneath the man's feet began to glow a faint purple. Then, like stringed puppets, two arms of sand leapt up and followed every motion of the holy man's hands. With expert precision and grace, the holy man continued swirling his hands. And as the arms of sand wove in and out of one another, at their base, a miniature house began to take shape. Each turn of the arm added another layer until it was complete. When it was finished, it no longer looked like sand, but a house made of stone.

"We drank without digging wells."

The front row of children scrambled backward as a hole began to take shape in the ground beside the house. Just as the house had taken the appearance of stone, so did the wall that built itself around the well.

"Even our appearance could be altered."

For the first time since arriving in Terrefantome, Lucas realized as he watched the holy man disappear that the man was not becoming invisible, but rather, the sand was covering his body, grain by grain, changing to match the color of the world around him, until he was hidden from sight completely.

"We wandered where we wished." The holy man reappeared. "And we never lacked. Everything we could desire was here." His voice hardened slightly. "Then came the criminals."

Despite knowing how the story ended, Lucas's heart pounded as he leaned forward, probably as eager to hear as all the small children seated in the front.

"A band of criminals had defied the king of Lingea, and after they had plundered travelers along the highways, the Lingean king chased them into our lands." The holy man's brow puckered. "Unfortunately, our sehf did not understand his desire to find the villains, and did not allow him to continue his pursuit. The criminals remained here long enough to realize that they could use the land as well. And seven years later, they reemerged from hiding and went out into the world to wreak havoc, causing ten times the pain and suffering they had the first time."

The man began to move his hands again, and a collective gasp went up from the crowd as likenesses of men and beasts began to move along with his tale.

"And their secret was not safe with them. Soon, many of the continent's criminals were descending upon our land, and the Taistille were overrun. And to make matters worse, so busy were our people with trying to expel the evil from our land that they did not realize they were being walled in on every side."

How did they not know? Lucas wondered with a small bit of disgust. Scoundrels or no scoundrels, how did an entire people not notice that a giant wall was being erected around their people?

"Our people," the holy man turned to look at Lucas, "did not leave. No one traveled nor was there bargaining for foreign goods. We were sufficient on our own. But by the time we realized what our neighbors wished to do, they had walls erected, and soldiers where the walls weren't yet ready." And with those words, he let the miniature wall and the sandmen surrounding it crumble, the sand falling back to the earth once more.

A deep, soulful sorrow filled Lucas, along with guilt. Maricanta didn't exile many people. He'd only seen three people exiled in his life, and the more he thought about it, the more he had the vague recollection of watching Selina's mother in his grandfather's court, where she'd been tried for capital murder. Still, for so long, these people had been suffering. And each addition was another piece of darkness for them.

"We used our gift to cloak ourselves from the outsiders, and we fought. There were many deaths on their side. But with the help of the Fortiers and other gifted individuals..." He raised his eyes to Lucas once more, "even the merpeople helped, and with such strength, they were able to overpower us. We were given the chance to leave, of course, but we knew we could not abandon our gift from the Maker. So we stayed, prisoners of our own gift, moving from place to place in a land now so tainted by evil that it refuses to obey even our commands as it used to."

"And we have been working to reclaim it since."

Everyone turned to see Esmeralda, who had seated herself on a stool at the edge of the crowd.

"You think us cruel." Esmeralda fixed her gaze on Jaelle. Her words weren't accusing or angry but more a statement of fact. Then she turned to Lucas. "But if Maricanta were invaded, how long would you fight for her freedom? How many would you kill to see your brother rightfully on the throne once more?"

Lucas couldn't answer. Not with children present. Because the Maker knew he would slay far too many than he was comfortable stating aloud.

Esmeralda looked back at the holy man, and a slight smile suddenly played on her mouth. "Though our holy man does not agree with all we do—"

"Pillaging is different from defending," the holy man said with an impertinent bow. Bold words to someone as powerful as the sehf, particularly with an audience, but she only gave him a slight smile.

"It isn't when you own it."

"And killing the men?" the holy man challenged.

"We don't touch anyone who doesn't touch us."

Lucas suddenly got the feeling that their strange argument was more for him than anyone else. As though they wished him to know why they acted and what their intent was in it all. And though he took more of the holy man's view than Esmeralda's, he was beginning to at least understand the Taistille. And, he guessed, that's exactly what they wanted from the visiting prince.

Well, if it was for his sake that they were arguing in public, for he could think of no other reason to allow such insubordination, then he was entitled to a question.

"Is that," he called out, "the reason for the..." What had Jaelle called the strange earthquake? Unable to remember, he shook his head. "It is the cause of all this darkness?"

Esmeralda regarded him with a somewhat amused expression. "So you realized it's dark, did you?"

Her teasing didn't intimidate him. "The earthquake with a gaping hole and Sorthileige inside. The poisoned water." He paused and shuddered at the memory of the burrowing worms. "The Taistille witches who choose to lay curses under the guise of gifts."

Esmeralda's eyes tightened slightly, but he continued.

"Where does it come from?"

"The evil," the holy man said, coming toward him, "has polluted our land through and through. And I'm afraid," he said, his eyes flickering to Esmeralda, "that it cannot contain such darkness for much longer."

"There are, however," Esmeralda added, "beams of light the Maker allows to shine in even to us." She held her hands out and gestured up at the trees. "Take this sacred spot, for example. We have no poison water here because it is where we come and worship the Maker. Instead, we have apple blossoms, and though the land is not what it was, it is closest. Because here, we are close to the Maker." She nodded at Jaelle across the circle. "Why does Jaelle's garden grow so well? The Maker can bring beauty from darkness. But our hearts must first be made willing, and our actions must follow." She tilted her head as though he were the only one in the circle. "I can't claim perfection or anything near it, but I can promise you that an obedient heart and obedient hands never earned the Maker's wrath."

The holy man said something at that point, and Esmeralda moved her attention back to him, but Lucas didn't hear any more because he was too deep in thought.

Lorenzo had faulted Lucas with pleasing others at the cost of who he had been made to be. Lucas said what others wanted to hear at the cost of the truth. He gave those around him what they wanted instead of what they needed. And though Lucas was fast losing his surety that whatever he'd had with Vittoria had been love, he was beginning to see the rich truth of what his father's friend had said. And he knew his time to act upon such knowledge was at hand.

Jaelle wasn't ready for marriage. She'd nearly said as much

herself. He also knew she didn't wish to take off her mask. But she needed to be safe, and she needed the marriage mark to remain so. And though he was positive she wouldn't be happy to hear his offer, Lucas knew without a doubt in his heart that he needed to give her that chance.

He just hoped she didn't choose to be angry with him forever for asking from her the one thing he said he wouldn't.

I'm doing my best to act in obedience, Lucas prayed silently as the stories continued on. *But when I take this leap, please don't let me fall.*

CHAPTER 33
DON'T FOR A SECOND...

When the performance was done, everyone stood and began to mingle. Before he lost his nerve, Lucas made his way toward Jaelle and his mother. He just prayed Jaelle didn't see him trembling.

"We still need to talk," she said as soon as she saw him. He nodded, relieved she hadn't forgotten or cried off on him.

"Help me put your mother to bed," Jaelle said, helping his weary mother up. "Then we will."

Lucas shook his head and lifted his mother in his arms.

"After this," he said, "would you please dispose of her powder?"

Jaelle gave a delicate snort. "Already done. I tossed it into the bushes the moment I realized she'd taken it again."

When his mother was finally tucked into bed, Jaelle appeared at the borrowed van's door. Lucas held his hand out to her.

"Walk with me?"

She hesitated slightly, but to his relief, she finally accepted and descended the steps to walk beside him.

As they walked, Lucas panicked inside. He'd always imagined proposing in some breathtaking, dashing manner he could look back on with satisfaction for the rest of his life and tell his grandchildren that *that* was how he'd won their grandmother's hand.

Asking a frightened young woman to marry him so no one would try to kidnap her was not quite the romantic scheme he'd been hoping for.

When they reached the river, the same place he'd sat with Esmeralda earlier that morning, he stopped and turned her to face him. Light from the distant bonfire, which now roared at the center of the sand pit, cast shadows on her face, and again, Lucas was struck by the feeling of nearly seeing her. But there was no time for that now. Taking both her hands in his, he suddenly prayed that his own incompetence wouldn't frighten her off and put them all in harm's way.

"I don't know how to say this..." His voice trailed off as his mind went blank. *You need to marry me, or we'll all die?* Oh yes. That was worthy of a lady's swoon. So instead, he chose the truth. "I spoke with Esmeralda this morning."

Jaelle nodded slowly. "And?"

Lucas swallowed. "She says that if we want to finish this journey alive and together," he swallowed again, trying to unstick the lump inside his throat, "you and I need to get married." He fixed his eyes on the ground. "Tomorrow."

Jaelle didn't move for a long time. There was no crying or even protesting. She didn't even make those soft sobbing sounds. Instead, she slowly withdrew her hands from his and went to sit by the river.

"It might not be so bad," he said, attempting a smile as he followed her. "You're a load smarter than I am, but it would give you lots of time for learning to read. And I'd still make sure you were able to practice healing."

"But you're in love with Vittoria," she said softly.

He rubbed his neck. "Eh, well, I'm not sure I'll ever know what I felt for Vittoria." He paused. "But I swear, I'll be faithful."

She slowly drew in a deep breath and then turned around to face him where he was standing behind her. "Do you *want* to marry me?"

He chuckled. "I don't think we get a choice in the matter." How many times would this excuse serve as their reason for taking yet another stupid risk on this trip?

She exhaled slowly.

"I see."

They stayed that way for a long time as the sounds of the camp began to fade.

Finally, he couldn't take it any longer. "I'm sorry," he said, wanting to sit beside her but unable to do so. "I truly am. But...if this is what we have to do to get you out of Terrefantome unharmed, I swear I will be respectful and bow to your every wish to the best of my abilities." An awful thought came to him. He didn't want to say it. Everything in him rebelled against the thought, and yet, he realized that when she didn't interrupt him, he was still talking.

"And if you wish for it, I'm sure we could be granted an annulment once we return to Maricanta. The holy man would surely approve once he heard the circumstances in which we were found and the...delicacy with which we handled the situation. And my mother's here, so it's not as if we've been unchaperoned." Michael and Arianna would definitely not approve, but Lucas decided to keep that to himself, particularly when Jaelle continued on in silence. But eventually, she did respond.

"If I want to?" she repeated.

"The ceremony would involve words only." He hurried to sit at her side. "Well, that and the mark—"

"The mark." She let out a somewhat strangled laugh. "Well, if we're going to say the vows, we might as well have the marks, too."

"So," Lucas bit the inside of his cheek until it hurt. "You're going to do it?"

"I suppose I am," came her faint reply.

Lucas wasn't sure whether he wanted to rejoice or mourn most. Then an awful, icy realization hit him.

"Oh," he said, wanting to pummel himself as he did. "Esmeralda says after the ceremony, you'll need to remove the mask as—"

"Lucas!"

Lucas startled as Jaelle flipped around to face him once more. He couldn't see her glare, but he could feel it.

"You need to know this now," she said in a low, menacing voice. "I will marry you if it keeps everyone happy and safe. I will wear your mark for the rest of my life, and I will do everything you ask of me when we're back in your country. But don't for a

301

second think I'm going to take off this mask until I'm good and ready!"

Lucas stared, unable to form any coherent words as she flipped away from him again and hugged her knees to her chest. But even after he finally turned away to give their news to the sehf, he could still hear her sobbing as he went.

CHAPTER 34

WHAT IF

S uch lovely hair," the woman standing behind Jaelle murmured as she brushed it out. "I've never seen any so dark and silky." She paused, probably waiting for Jaelle to respond and tell her which of her parents was from the east. But Jaelle wasn't able to focus on small talk that morning. She hadn't been able to focus on anything since her conversation with Lucas the day before. Not the borrowed dress Esmeralda had ordered hemmed and tailored for her, nor the borrowed shoes she'd been bidden to try on. The holy man had spent over an hour with her and Lucas the night before, discussing the ceremony, a blend of Taistille flair and the holy religion, and she'd somehow managed to convince them she knew what she was doing.

Perhaps she should have done a poorer job. Then she might not be standing here in a dramatic indigo gown with tiny beaded shoes on her feet, a simple wreath of white flowers draped across her forehead, and covered in the perfumes of the forest.

Maybe, then, her heart wouldn't feel like it had broken quite so badly.

She wasn't heartbroken because he'd asked her to marry him. For though she'd balked at the thought of marrying a complete stranger two weeks ago, her last few days with Lucas had opened her eyes to a world she'd never known existed. In spite of her best attempts at caution, she'd begun to wonder what it might be like to venture through life not only with Selina at her side...but Lucas as well.

What had cut her to the heart was the apology in his proposal and the reluctance in his countenance as he'd asked. The twist of the knife had been his ardent promise that he was sure they could get the marriage annulled.

And then he'd had the audacity to suggest she remove her mask.

"Are you sure you won't remove the mask?"

Jaelle turned to tell whoever it was to leave her alone, but when she saw Drina, followed by Esmeralda, she kept her temper to herself.

"I'm sure," she said in a low voice.

"But I'm sure you would be so lovely if you would only just take—" Drina began, but Esmeralda cut in.

"Perhaps I can have a moment alone with her." She nodded to two of the attendants she'd assigned to Jaelle for preparations, and they ushered a protesting Drina out of the van. Esmeralda came and seated herself on the covered bench and began to fluff out the flowers on Jaelle's head.

"I understand this wedding is not pleasing to you," she said softly.

"I'm not sure what you mean."

"You're crying." Esmeralda continued to fix the flowers, but in the mirror, she studied Jaelle's face. "He hasn't hurt you or mistreated you in any way, has he?"

"Oh. Oh, no. He's been utterly chivalrous." Too much so.

Esmeralda frowned. "I do not understand. You have come from a world of darkness, but you're to be wed to a man from the world of light. And a prince, at that. You'll have everything you ever wanted."

"I..." Jaelle drew in a shaky breath. "I suppose I'm angry with myself."

Esmeralda's eyebrows went up. "Angry?"

Jaelle nodded miserably. "For hoping."

"Hope is not something most people here could even wish for. What were you hoping for beyond all that's being given to you?"

"I'd hoped..." Her voice caught in her throat. "I wanted him to want me." Stinging tears threatened to fall, and she pinched herself in an effort to keep them at bay.

"What makes you think he doesn't want you?" Esmeralda asked.

"He's honorable." Jaelle shrugged. "I know he's doing this to protect me. And in his attempt to protect my honor, he's willing to sully his." Annulled or not, it was impossible to predict whether or not such a mark on the royal family would be taken lightly.

Esmeralda chuckled.

"Honor hardly seems a reason a man wouldn't love a woman."

"You should have heard him. Over and over again, he apologized. He even guessed we would be allowed to get it annulled once we were back in his country." Jaelle turned to face Esmeralda. "If he had simply asked me, I would have said yes with all my heart. I would have removed the mask and..." She drew in a shaky breath and straightened her shoulders. "But I can't give him all of me. Not when I know he doesn't want all of me."

Understanding lit Esmeralda's bright eyes, and she nodded once. Then she took a soft cloth from the little table beside the bench and began wiping Jaelle's tears away.

"Couldn't it also be possible," she asked softly, "that Lucas doesn't yet know what he wants?"

Esmeralda's words echoed in Jaelle's mind as the sehf finished arranging her hair and then escorted her out of the van and back to the sandy clearing they'd gathered around the night before. There, Jaelle waited at the edge of the crowd. When everyone was seated, the holy man nodded, and she did as they'd practiced and walked out to the large, flat stone that had been dragged out to the center of the clearing. Then she climbed up on the rock, curled her legs up beneath her, and waited.

As a single horn rang out a high, soulful sound, the hair on the back of her neck stood up. The melody was enchanting, haunting and hopeful at the same time. Then another wave of sorrow washed over her. For the first time since she was a little girl, she felt pretty. Though she still wasn't highly interested in the rouge or lip color Selina had often mourned not getting to dress her up with, the wreath of soft, white petals on her forehead made her feel close to the princess she would never be, and the smooth swaths of thin, airy fabric that draped itself over her legs felt more like she imagined ocean foam might, should she ever get to touch it. For one moment, she felt real and free, like she might be worthy of the love she knew wasn't hers.

A fiddle joined the horn, and Jaelle couldn't bring herself to look up as he entered the clearing. She continued to look down at the dress as he walked the two ceremonial circles around her, growing slightly closer with each step. When he extended his hand, though, she could no longer keep her gaze on the ground. She forced herself to follow tradition and looked up. But when she met his eyes, she found she couldn't look away.

Someone had given him new clothes, and for once, he wasn't even in that ratty coat he refused to let go. Instead, he wore black trousers with a loose, ruffled shirt that was tucked in, enhancing his muscled arms, shoulders, and torso even more than usual. His jaw, which was clean shaven for the first time since she'd met him, was angled and strong. And his hand was open to her.

If only it was all real.

In spite of his misgivings from the day before, Lucas grasped her hand tightly when she slid it into his. She stood as she'd been instructed and walked in a slow circle, their hands still clasped, before he turned and led her slowly toward the holy man.

"In heart and soul, body and mind," the holy man began, "this son of the Maker has asked his beloved to join him in his journey through this world. Have you not, my son?" He turned to Lucas.

Lucas's hazel eyes never left hers. "I have."

The holy man turned to Jaelle. "And how, daughter, do you answer his call?"

Jaelle had to search for a moment before she could find her voice. "I will follow."

This was all just a dream. It had to be, Jaelle chided herself as the holy man neared the end of his homily. A beautiful, heart-breaking dream. The words were flowing, poetic and final in their nature, and Jaelle wished with all her heart that it were real. She wanted it to be real. She wanted to love him.

But as the holy man pronounced them man and wife, she knew it was all just a lie.

And yet, when Lucas cupped her face in his hand and gently

tipped her head back, the feel of his lips meeting and moving against hers was more real than anything Jaelle had ever felt. Against her better judgment, she leaned in and inhaled deeply, wishing she could drink deeply of his kiss forever, sure that if she could, she would never be thirsty again.

His fingers dug slightly deeper into her hair, and he moved his other hand to her waist where, warm and strong, he set aflame a new kind of yearning she'd never known before. His mouth was warm and hungry, and she leaned in closer for more.

But, just as with all their games of pretend, the kiss couldn't last forever. His eyes were large and a little too bright as he slowly pulled back. The crowd cheered, and music erupted on all sides, but neither she nor Lucas seemed to be capable of pulling their eyes away from one other.

All too soon, they were ushered by the holy man back to the flat rock, where someone had placed several long, thin sticks with what looked like different shades of ink on the ends. Jaelle's heart slightly sped for an entirely new reason when she saw the tattooing materials. Annulment or not, this would be a part of her that Lucas carried with him until death. And Lucas with her.

"In this part of the ceremony," the holy man had explained the night before, "you will each choose a representation of the other which will be tattooed on the inner part of your right wrist. Do not reveal what you have chosen for one another until the ceremony, when the tattoos are finished."

The night before, the holy man had told them to contemplate their choice with much prayer and consideration, but Jaelle knew what Lucas was to her the moment the holy man had given them the instructions as to how their marks would work. And now she watched as one of the Taistille took up the colored sticks and began to prick her wrist again and again. The pain was worse than Jaelle had anticipated, despite being warned of the method in which tattoos were given. And yet, she gritted her teeth and embraced it. This ceremony was too beautiful, too perfect to represent what was truly taking place without some painful reminder to ground her to the truth. And nothing bound her to the truth like the image, which was slowly taking form on her skin, of the silhouetted ship sailing into the purple, orange, and gold sunset.

Away from the pier, toward the magic of the unknown that she would never know.

But after that kiss...Was there a chance? Maybe he didn't now, but could he ever wish to take her with him into that sunset?

Eventually, the two men creating the tattoos laid down their tools, and the holy man put their right hands together and held them up for everyone to see, their right hands clasped as they faced in opposite directions. Finally, after the applause had gone on long and loud, the holy man lowered their hands and allowed them to look at what each had chosen for the other.

Lucas was the first to look. When he saw the ship on her wrist, he got a strange, haunted look in his eyes. Jaelle wanted to ask if something was wrong, but it was her turn to see. When she saw his overturned wrist, however, her curiosity died as her heart sank into her stomach like a rock.

A diamond.

So many miles traveled, so many enemies brought down together. All their laughs and tears over the fire in the forest or in her herb garden while Drina was sleeping...and she was still simply an agreement of convenience. Not because she was smart or cunning or beautiful. All because of those blasted diamonds.

A feast ensued after, and more food was produced than Jaelle had ever seen in Terrefantome. Roast duck, lamb, deer, and ham were all part of one course. Other courses included apples sliced, cooked, and seasoned in every way possible. Sweets upon sweets, mostly made with honey and molasses, were served between courses, and wine flowed freely. There was music, at which the Taistille were quite proficient, and there were never fewer than eight or nine people singing. But Lucas only watched her, a worried frown on his face. And Jaelle could enjoy none of it. Not as long as he kept looking at her the way he was.

Drina seemed to enjoy herself for the first time since arriving in the land. She ate heartily of the food, and Esmeralda motioned for her wine to be watered down only an hour into the feast. Eventually they cut her off. Drina even played games with the children, a sure sign she'd imbibed far too much wine, as Lucas had once mentioned she hated playing with children.

But the day couldn't last forever, and when the sun began to set, the entire party began letting out strange whoops and hollers until the holy man notified them that it was time for the newly-weds to retreat to their wagon.

She nodded and smiled, but inside, Jaelle shook. She wasn't ready to be married. Not that Lucas planned to treat her as his wife. He'd made that perfectly clear the day before.

And yet, she seemed to hear Selina's warnings in her head. What would she do if he did take her in his arms again? What if he kissed her the way he had after their vows? Would she really be able to object? Or would she let herself be swept away into the biggest mistake of her life, falling for a man who did not love her in return?

CHAPTER 35

TIRED

As the sky began to darken, the time for dancing was announced with the beat of a drum, and dozens of Taistille raised their voices in a song in response. Several beckoned to Jaelle and Lucas to join in, but Lucas seemed lost in a world of his own. And after watching the others, Jaelle decided she would never be able to keep up. Poised and daring, their dances far surpassed any Jaelle had ever seen in creativity and expressiveness.

As exhilarating as their dances were, though, try as she might, she couldn't seem to keep her eyes open. For despite her trepidation about the wedding, she found herself dozing off several times during just the first dance. What she wouldn't give to have a nap.

"Tired?"

Jaelle jumped slightly at the closeness of Lucas's voice. But after she'd gotten over her surprise, she simply nodded.

Holding his finger to his lips, Lucas noiselessly got to his feet and pulled her behind him. And while Jaelle appreciated the escape from the loud music and constant laughter, her exhaustion fled her and was replaced once again by the hammering of her heart.

It was her wedding night, and now they were all alone.

Lucas led her to the van at the edge of the camp. It had been loaned by one of the caravan elders to the newlyweds specifically for their special night. But to her great relief, instead of going inside, he simply pulled himself up on the edge of the platform and then held his hand out to help her up beside him. Then he handed her a mugful of wine, which Jaelle gulped down gratefully.

"Rough night?"

"What?" Jaelle lowered her mug so she could see him.

He chuckled softly. "Forgive me if I was mistaken, but you didn't exactly look like you were having the night of your life."

"Well," Jaelle laughed nervously, "truth be told, I wasn't exactly expecting to marry a prince in a Taistille camp when I set out to save my sister." She glanced at him, but his expression was unreadable. "I suppose you could say the same, though."

"That I didn't expect to marry a prince?" He nodded. "That would be a correct assumption."

Jaelle nudged his shoulder. "You know what I mean. You couldn't have expected your mother to waltz up during your mission and practically force you to marry a girl like me."

He'd been leaning back on his hands, but at this, he turned toward her.

"What's that supposed to mean? A girl like you?"

The way his eyes suddenly smoldered made Jaelle's thoughts stumble as she searched for words.

"Well," she shrugged, taking the diamonds that fell into her lap and separating them into little piles by color, "I suppose I mean that you were raised with everything you could want. Servants. A palace. Everything you could desire at your whim." She studied her gown. "It's highly doubtful that an illiterate daughter of a convicted, exiled criminal would have been the woman of your dreams." Especially when she recalled everything Drina had said about his beloved Vittoria.

His brows drew together, and he looked away from her. "Yes," he said in a strange, tight voice, "my early childhood was blessed with every desire sated and two parents who adored the ground I walked on."

Even that would have put him miles ahead of her in advantage.

"But war changes everyone." His eyes returned to hers. "Especially when your grandfather kills himself because of the mess he's made, and in an effort to keep your people safe, you find blood on your hands before your seventeenth birthday." He looked at his hands, as though he might find them red and sticky now. "The color washes away," he said in a softer voice. "But the stain never really disappears."

Jaelle's chest was tight, and she was glad he couldn't see the way her face heated in shame at her assumptions.

"So, yes," he said, leaning back again. "I was born a prince, but I've learned two things in my short twenty-one years. First," he held up a finger, "no one is immune to life's sorrows." Then his eyes softened, and he tapped her nose. "Not the girl in the mask. And not the prince in the palace."

"I'm sorry," Jaelle whispered.

"Don't be. It's not your fault." He leaned back and looked up into the trees. "Second, the Maker has also made it abundantly clear to me that he often puts gems in the places you least expect to find them."

Jaelle smiled sadly, though she knew he couldn't see. "Gems don't always shine the way they're supposed to. Some are dull." She swallowed. "And some lose their luster."

"And sometimes," Lucas said, cupping her jaw in his hand, "all they need to really shine is the sun." He tucked a lock of hair behind her ear.

"Why do you keep doing that?" Jaelle breathed.

"Doing what?"

"Touching my face," she whispered as he ran the back of his hand down her cheek.

"Because I want to see you," he said with a small smile. "And this is the closest I can get."

"But why?" Jaelle pressed, at once dreading and desiring his response.

For a long moment, he didn't answer, just touched her face over and over again. Finally, he whispered back, "Because you deserve to be seen."

Jaelle grew roots and couldn't have been moved if someone had tried to drag her away. That was until a shout made them both jump. They looked to their left to find several of the Taistille staring at them.

"What are you doing?" one of the men shouted.

Lucas glanced at Jaelle.

"What do you mean?"

The speaker and the group behind him guffawed, the situation's humor probably increased by the jugs of spirits in their hands.

"It's your wedding night, boy!" the man cried. "Take your girl and enjoy it! Won't be long before you've got too many little ones running around to properly appreciate the night."

Jaelle's neck heated, and even in the dim light of the bonfire, she could see Lucas's face flush as well.

He looked at Jaelle, but his smile wasn't the same one he'd worn two minutes before when he'd caressed her face.

"I am a bit tired. What about you?"

Jaelle nodded and let him help her stand. If she had been nervous before, it was nothing compared to how she felt now.

CHAPTER 36
TO HIS WIFE

L ucas would be lying if he said his pulse didn't double as they approached the van where they'd spend the night. His vision went slightly blurry as he turned on the steps to wave to their well-wishers one more time before leading his wife inside.

It was a sweet little place. It was about twenty feet in length and eight in width with a small wooden bench on one side and a little table beside it. Across from the bench was a chest of drawers beneath a long wooden shelf that was covered in trinkets and baubles of all sorts, including a mirror, which couldn't have been easy to acquire in this part of the world. Even at home, mirrors were expensive. A faded but cheery green and pink rug stretched the length of the room. There were lots of windows for such a small space, at least two on each wall, including the one by the bed at the end of the room. Curtains, the same shade of green as the rug, were already closed over each window to cover it.

For a long time, they froze, both staring at the bed. Every inch of his skin felt like it was on fire. The plush sheets and several quilts, all that same curious color of green, beckoned to him, not having slept in a real bed in over a week. But he knew better than to take a step toward the bed.

Instead, he forced himself to turn to face Jaelle.

319

To his wife.

He had a wife. His breathing grew faster as he contemplated this. The possibilities, though he bid them leave, forced their way into his mind. They had just been wed before the Maker and many witnesses, and by a holy man from his own faith, no less. His mouth still hummed from the taste of her lips. Part of him, a voice in his head that was growing louder by the second, wondered what life would look like five years from now if they simply accepted what had just happened and embraced it to the best they were able. Yes, they were both broken and bruised. But...what would happen if they tried to heal together, instead of navigating this complicated web of emotions and rules and memories alone?

And why was Vittoria suddenly so easy to forget? Why didn't he care that she was?

Their fingers were still intertwined, and though he couldn't see them, he could feel her eyes on his face. Slowly, so slowly so as not to scare her, he raised his hands and traced her lips. They were soft and warm, and he found himself desperately wanting to meet them again. She went still at his touch and didn't move again until he'd pulled his hand away from her face.

"There's..." Her voice seemed to give out with the first clink of a diamond hitting the floor. She tried again. "There's only one bed."

Lucas felt like a bird shot down from the sky, and he had to swallow hard before he could answer. Forcing a smile felt like pushing a boulder uphill, but he somehow did it.

"I'll take the bench."

She didn't move for a long time, but when she finally nodded and moved toward the bed, her shoulders slumped, as though she'd been defeated. She took the thickest quilt from the bed and passed it to him along with a few of the smaller blankets and a pillow. But the longer he watched her, the more he realized she looked...disappointed.

Was that it? Was she disappointed that she'd married him after all?

As soon as they were in their respective beds, Lucas rubbed his eyes with both hands. This mission couldn't end soon enough. He needed the sea and sails. This was why he shouldn't get married.

Lucas knew what to expect from his ships, and even to some extent, from the ocean. Sailing and war and barking out orders were familiar and safe.

But with women, he couldn't seem to do the right thing if his life depended on it.

CHAPTER 37

IF THAT KING

The soft bed was far more luxurious than anything Jaelle had ever slept on. The blankets smelled of lemongrass, and they were soft and smooth, making her want to melt into them. They were also, however, surprisingly cold. She curled her legs up to her chest in an effort to make her little space warm. The warmth came, but for some reason, she was still close to shivering ten minutes later, even though she'd been sitting outside without even a scarf or shawl.

Sleep. She needed to sleep. Then she could forget that her wedding had been a fraud and that despite all she and Lucas had shared in the last few days, she was still alone. But her tired mind continued to churn through all that had and *hadn't* happened over the course of this journey. What could and should not have been.

What would it feel like if he changed his mind? Days ago, she wouldn't have dared to even imagine such, but something in his kiss had opened a door she couldn't and didn't want to close. Because she knew without a doubt that if he got up now and crawled into bed beside her, there was no bone in her body strong enough to tell him to leave. And she would have felt nothing but peace if he'd taken her in his arms and held her close.

Hours later, though she couldn't have guessed at how many, he did stand. She did her best to pretend to sleep as he came to stand beside her, and her heart leapt into her throat as he laid his hand on her head briefly and brushed a strand of hair from her cheek.

Just as quickly as it had sprung up, however, her hope died when he padded away and pulled a quill from his shirt and a piece of paper. For twenty agonizing minutes, she spied on him through slitted eyes, dozing off several times as she did, until she heard him pulling on his heavy boots. She opened her eyes a slit and watched him. From the way he was taking care with his movements, she could see that he was trying not to wake her, and for some reason, she found this highly annoying.

Still, not bereft of all her pride, she pretended to sleep until he took one last long look at her and then stepped out of the van. Before he closed the door, however, he folded the paper and left it right in front of the door.

As soon as the door was closed, Jaelle scrambled out of bed and threw on her shoes, and threw on her own her clothes so she wouldn't rip the borrowed gown. She paused to open the paper. Why, she couldn't say, as she couldn't read. When she did, though, his leather thong with the little shell fell out, and she barely caught it before it hit the ground. Once the shell was safe and hanging from her own neck, she yanked the door open and darted outside.

The sky was still dark, just moving into the hour in which shadows and shapes were almost recognizable. Jaelle panicked for a moment before she heard the low murmur of voices several vans down. Stationing herself behind a nearby tree, she strained to hear and was rewarded with the sound of Lucas's voice.

"...said to talk to Manfri before I left. She said he would be here."

"That's me." The man, whom Jaelle didn't recognize, grunted. "What do you want to know?"

"I need to find the king."

"What would you want to do an awful thing like that for?"

"He's threatening to loose the criminals on my kingdom. Now where do I find him?"

"Up that way," Manfri said, though when Jaelle peeked, he was still shaking his head. "Follow the path until you come to a bend that goes right then left. The castle will be visible in twenty minutes after that."

Lucas thanked the man, but as he began to walk away, the man put his hand on Lucas's shoulder.

"If you're going to see the king, you'd best get in and out as fast as you can carry yourself."

"Noted," Lucas said stiffly.

"He's trying to establish a monarchy. A lasting one, unlike the other kings who have seated themselves and unseated one another for hundreds of years." He pulled Lucas closer, and his voice was nearly impossible to hear. "Get in and out as soon as possible," he repeated. "Or you won't be getting out at all."

Jaelle had been peeking out from behind her tree, but she snapped back into hiding until she was sure Lucas was gone. Just as she stepped out to follow him, however, someone grabbed her wrist. She yanked it away and turned around ready to fight until she realized it was Drina.

"What are you doing?" she hissed. "You're supposed to be asleep!"

"I should ask you the same question." Drina glared at her. "Or rather, I should ask you why, the morning after wedding my son, you're here in the shame of the night, chasing after other men!"

"I'm not chasing..." Jaelle rolled her eyes. The diamonds that hit the dirt made thumps that seemed loud enough to wake the camp. "I'm following Lucas. He tried to sneak out this morning without telling me."

"Lucas?" Drina's eyes grew large. "But why?"

"I don't know." She held up the crumpled note. "He only left this."

Drina took the letter and began to read, for once, in a quiet voice.

Jaelle,

I've gone to finish what my grandfather started. By the Maker's mercy, I'll be back before sunset tonight. Stay with Esmeralda until I return, and whatever you do, please keep my mother at bay to the best of your abilities. I'm confident these people mean you no harm, but my mother could drive a rattlesnake mad.

Drina gasped. "That boy is going to—"

"Just finish the letter!" Jaelle pleaded.

Drina pursed her lips, but much to Jaelle's relief, she resumed reading.

Don't tell her I said that, though.

Drina snorted.

Please, instead, give her my love and share my desire that you both remain with the Taistille until it's safe to go home.

I desire nothing more than to return to you both, but we know the reality of this mission far too well. If for some reason, I don't return, please remain with the Taistille for one week. If a that time passes and you have not heard of me, ask Esmeralda to take you to the shore. Then throw the shell in the water, and my sister's people will come to find you. Ask that they take you to the Sun Crown, and tell my brother everything.

Please do not neglect to tell him of my promises to you in our agreement. He will make sure you meet the Fortiers. King Everard is a bit forward, but they have good hearts, and if nothing else, I know they will work to remove the curse from you. Even now, I take comfort in the knowledge that you will be free from this burden eventually.

I know this was not the end you wished for. I'm far from the ideal husband, and you deserve better. But as of yesterday, something my mother will bear witness to, you are my wife by all legal rights, and you'll be a minor princess of Maricanta. Use this position, I beg of you, to set yourself up for the greatest opportunities.

Bithiah will teach you to read. Arianna will teach you of the sea. Michael will see to it that you are safe.

I only give two requests in my absence. First, that you do not come after me. This is my burden to bear, and everything we went through yesterday will be in vain if you follow. Second, that you tell my brother to do the same. Under no circumstances is Maricanta to enter a second war for the sake of her second-born prince. Instead, please pass on my desire to be remembered among my family and my men as one who tried to serve.

And thank you, Jaelle, for everything. I know yesterday was not what either of us had dreamed of. But if it gives any consolation, I could not ask for a worthier woman to wed. Your honor and loyalty put me to shame, and I'm grateful to have spent my last few weeks with you by my side.

Yours truly,
Lucas

DRINA'S FACE had gone white as she read, but Jaelle didn't stay to ask what she was thinking or if she'd finally learned to see her son as she ought. Instead, she was already running in the direction the man had pointed out to Lucas. She could hear Drina calling out behind her, but she didn't stop.

The fool was going to get himself killed. And though he saw her as his wife in the eyes of the law only, she wasn't about to let her husband walk into the den of wolves alone. He might be a prince and an admiral and the most ridiculously handsome creature to ever walk the earth, but he was not from Terrefantome. Jaelle was, however, and whether or not she liked it, this land was in her blood.

Just as the man had said, the road began to bend, and soon, Jaelle burst out of the trees into a wheat field. Beyond the field was a walled castle. And only fifteen feet ahead of her was Lucas.

The wheat was only as high as her waist, so Jaelle closed her eyes and let the earth cover her until she was invisible. She hated the feeling, but there was little else to do. As soon as she'd disappeared, she began to make her way toward the familiar figure.

Unfortunately, the sounds of heavy breathing and heavy footsteps came crashing out from the woods behind her.

Lucas whirled around at the sound. Then his eyes widened. "Mother? How did you find me?"

Drina held up the letter, and Jaelle wanted to throw something at her.

"So you thought it appropriate to leave your wife a letter and not your mother?" Drina's voice was on the edge of hysterics.

"How did you get that?" Then he muttered something before calling out, "You can come out, too, Jaelle. I know you're there."

Jaelle huffed and allowed herself to return to her usual form. "You forget," she said, crossing her arms. "I can't read."

"You were supposed to take it to the sehf when she woke up. I didn't think you'd take it to my *mother* of all people!" He glowered at Drina.

"What is that supposed to mean?" Drina huffed.

"No matter who read it," Lucas snapped, "you both ignored my plea that you leave me alone."

"What did you mean about your wedding not being what you wanted?" Drina snapped. "Your letter was vague and odd, and I frankly don't like it."

But Lucas ignored her and went to Jaelle, taking her hand and dragging her away from Drina. Jaelle let him, but she wasn't about to back down.

"I expect this from my mother," he said when they were by themselves, "but—"

"Before you take that tone with me," Jaelle snapped, "remember what I told you at the beginning. This is my world, and I'm not about to let you run around and get yourself killed in it!"

"And I told you," he glared down at her, "that I'm not about to sit by and watch while some rotten king takes a liking to my wife, who happens to produce diamonds. Or worse, whatever other pleasures he might want to help himself to."

Jaelle refused to let him see the shiver that ran up her spine. "It may not be ideal," she hissed, "but as your wife, I say you're not facing the king alone."

Lucas closed his eyes and put his hands over them. After

several long, deep breaths, he looked at her again, this time looking more weary than angry.

"If for nothing else," he said slowly, "would you return to the Taistille for the sake of my mother?"

Jaelle opened her mouth to speak but found she had no words.

"I could take you," he said softly, "but you and I both know I can't bring her into a court like this one."

Jaelle stared at him for a moment longer before her shoulders slumped, and she knew she was defeated. Because as much as she was loath to admit it, he was right. Drina wouldn't last five minutes in the Terrefantomen court. If she wasn't thrown into the stocks for her mouth, she'd be taken for one of the nobles, no doubt, as she was an unusually handsome woman. So instead, Jaelle ran a hand over her eyes.

"What..." She sighed, trying to sort out her thoughts, which were chaotic and choppy. "Will you need any diamonds for this?" As she spoke, she realized she'd forgotten her scarf. But by now, she didn't care. Her stranger husband was saying goodbye, and they both knew the likelihood of her seeing him ever again.

Lucas got a funny look on his face as he began to take off his coat. It was the ratty, tattered one he'd refused to take off. When he handed it to her, she gasped.

The coat was far heavier than she'd anticipated. And when she held it up to the dim light of morning, she realized small squares had been sewn all into the coat. And in every lighter square, there was a circle.

"Coins," she whispered.

He nodded and put the coat back on.

"That's why you wouldn't let anyone touch it." All this time together, and she hadn't realized that the ransom of Lucas's people was literally the burden he carried day and night.

"I told you," he said, giving her a sad smile, "my people can't afford another war. It must be avoided at all costs." He traced her chin, and Jaelle couldn't have moved if she'd tried. "That," he continued softly, "is why I need you to follow my instructions in the letter. Once this is over and our oath is fulfilled, and the danger of the king's wrath is averted, my brother has to know that I am not to be the cause of war. If I disappear, I'm not worth all the lives such a conflict would cost." His voice hardened slightly. "I also need to know you're safe and far, far away. Because if that king tried to lay a finger on you, I couldn't trust myself not to start a war."

Jaelle's only response was the tears, hot and wet, that rolled down her face.

He cupped her jaw and leaned forward, and for a moment, Jaelle closed her eyes. But instead of feeling the burst of heat that she hoped would come with the kiss she longed to taste again, he simply brushed his lips against her forehead. Then his face hardened. He stood taller and he gave her a nod. Then he turned and was gone.

CHAPTER 38

YES

Lucas forced himself to keep his eyes on the castle as he moved toward it through the wheat field. He wouldn't look back. He couldn't. The masked eyes that he knew would be following him were a distraction he couldn't afford right now. He had one duty, and that was to get into the castle, give the king the money, get his proof of payment, and leave. He could sort out his feelings for and about Jaelle later.

Still, as he approached the gates, it was hard to push out images of the night before, how lovely she'd looked in the gown that had draped down her slim form like wisteria, hanging delicately and fluttering in the wind. Her choice of tattoo had also surprised him, and if he was completely honest, had brought a tear to his eye. No image had ever captured his soul so completely as that ship sailing toward the sunset. And the sound of her crying softly in the night had nearly done in his resolve to remain safely on the bench. He'd wanted so much to get up and cross the floor and to beg to know how he could comfort her. But the comfort of an unwanted husband was most assuredly the last thing she could have wanted.

He shook his head as he made eye contact with the two guards at the gate. He'd married Jaelle to get her safely away from this wretched place. But all that would be in vain if he got himself killed here or left any clues as to where his wife and mother were.

"Name and purpose?" the guard called as Lucas drew near.

Lucas hesitated. He'd attempted to keep his name hidden until now. But this was what he'd come for. These people needed to know his identity. Even if it meant his loss.

"Prince Lucas Gabriele Stefano Solefige of Maricanta, sent by the Sun Crown, King Michaelangelo Solefige, for the purpose of debt payment to the crown of Terrefantome."

He expected some sort of reaction from them at the announcement of his title or even the errand he'd been sent on. But for some reason, these men seemed completely unsurprised to see him. He fought the uneasy twist in his stomach as one of them turned and disappeared behind the gate. What would he do if they refused him entry? It was honestly a possibility he hadn't considered before this.

Now that he was close, he could see that the castle and its surrounding wall were ancient. Though much of it had been rebuilt, it was easy to see where the old stones had fallen from the wall and the fortress, and where someone had come and put new stones in their places. This king was trying to build a dynasty on a foundation that was crumbling. That made Lucas feel slightly better as he waited, but only just.

Old or not, the castle was of the traditional design, four round towers with walls surrounding one large square tower in the center. There were two outer walls, though these looked as though a heavy wind might blow them over. How many men were at this king's call? What kinds of weapons could they have access to in a place like this? An outer yard of yellow grasses grew between the external walls and the fortress itself, making Lucas wonder just how long the castle had been regularly inhabited.

"Says to let him in." The first guard returned and nodded to his neighbor. Lucas took a step forward, but the men blocked his way.

"Weapons first," the second said.

Lucas stared at the man long and hard, trying to discern whether or not he should take leave of his weapons. Even as they'd spoken, his hand had been near the hilt of his sword. But after sharing a long glare with them, he unstrapped his sword and handed it over. They pointed at the dagger at his side which Lucas removed as well. Much to his annoyance, only after Lucas had relieved himself of six more weapons, was he finally allowed to follow the first guard inside.

Giving up all those weapons made him nearly sick to his stomach. Rarely was he without at least three, let alone all of them, and that was in the civilized world, outside Terrefantome. Now he had only the tiniest of blades in his belt. He would have to save it as his last resort, should he need it.

For a crumbling castle, the inside was surprisingly lavish. Rugs, tapestries, and even several tables and chairs were in numerous rooms as he was led inside, past the great hall toward what appeared to be a throne room.

Inside were an assortment of several dozen guards, men, and women standing back from a dais with a throne on it. And on the throne was a man who looked to be in his third decade, perhaps ten or fifteen years older than Lucas. He had pale blue eyes and a neatly trimmed dark beard and hair that was pulled carefully behind his neck, hanging in thick ringlets down his back. His clothes looked like they cost more than half of Terrefantome had in gold.

A servant ran ahead and whispered to the man on the dais. The man, whom Lucas assumed to be the king, listened to the boy for a moment before letting out a short laugh.

"It's about time," he boomed, standing and holding his arms open wide as he made his way down the dais dramatically. "So, Maricanta finally decided to show some sense of honor."

Lucas, who had spent years of his life studying both diplomacy and intimidation, ignored the jab, simply nodding deeply as he came face to face with the self-proclaimed king.

"So," the king said, looking Lucas up and down, "the Sun Crown sent his little brother, I'm told. I'm touched by the way." He put his hand over his heart. "But hopefully, he sent me more than that."

Lucas removed his coat and asked for a knife, not wishing to give away the location of his own. The guards looked at the king, but when the king nodded, one handed Lucas his dagger. Slowly, so as not to startle anyone, Lucas took the dagger and began to tear his limp, threadbare coat into pieces.

The king's eyes, which had been half-lidded, grew wide as gold coin after gold coin rained down from the coat until the coat was no more than a pile of rags. A considerable pile of gold, however, also lay on the floor at Lucas's feet.

"Well," the king said, leaning over and picking up one of the coins. "I must congratulate you on your creativity."

"Not to insult His Highness," Lucas said dryly after handing the borrowed dagger back, "but the first several parties we sent to repay our debt disappeared and were never heard from again after crossing into your borders. We counted their disappearances to the...nature of your citizenry and chose to keep our final attempt a secret." He nodded at the pile. "It's all there, plus interest."

The king smiled. "That's very good of you."

"I'm glad you think so," Lucas said, standing straighter. "Because once we have our proof of payment with your seal, you won't be hearing from us again on this matter." He dared to breathe now that it was over, but too soon. Behind him, he heard the doors slam shut, and slowly, he turned again to face the king.

"Is that not all?"

"Unfortunately," Bartol said, steepling his fingers, "you're a day late."

"Today is the date you set forth in your letter," Lucas said.

"Yes," Bartol said. "But in Terrefantome, the date given for a contract is considered the date by which it must be finalized. You see," he said, motioning to someone concerning the pile, "you needed to have this gold here yesterday if you wished to see the benefits of your debt paid in full. Today is too late, I'm afraid."

"Then the terms should have specified such," Lucas said, his face growing hot. He knew it was foolish to argue with liars, but he was too angry to care.

The king waved at Lucas, and four guards began to collapse in on him. Lucas had his little knife out in a flash. Using it seemed nearly pointless as he was surrounded by men with swords, and yet, he held it readily as the four men converged. He wasn't about to go quietly.

The guard was not well-trained, praise the Maker. Not only were their movements clumsy, but their uniforms were also a poor cut, which was a detriment to their performance. For several long minutes, Lucas was able to fend them off, even moving the king farther back each time he slashed. But the longer he fought, the more men appeared. And just when he thought there couldn't be any more, they all smiled at one another as though sharing some private joke. He tried again to free himself from the corner he'd been driven into, ready to slip out, when one by one, they began to disappear.

Just as Jaelle had predicted, he was thrown to the ground. Kick after kick was delivered to his ribs, his legs, and even his head and face. When he was about to pass out, the abuse slowed enough for them to bind him with ropes and chains.

"Because the other kingdoms seem so reluctant to recognize my authority in their ranks," the king said, "I'm going to prove to them that I am deadly serious."

"By abducting a prince?" Lucas gasped as he tried to pull away from the invisible arms that held him. "You're going to start a war for the sake of pride?"

"If I have to," the king said cheerily, "then yes."

CHAPTER 39
MAKE THE BET

Jaelle forced herself to turn around and escort Drina back to the Taistille camp. It killed her that he was right, but Drina certainly wouldn't survive long in Terrefantome without her.

The older woman was surprisingly quiet, though, as they went, her eyes cast down, not focusing on the world around them as they walked. Every half a minute or so, a shaking sob escaped. Jaelle eventually stopped trying to console her and walked a little behind so she could hear the sounds of the forest better. Even as she made herself put one foot in front of the other, she couldn't ignore the tumultuous fight going on within her, a fight that was largely between her common sense and her heart.

Why was she placing such tremendous importance on this marriage? It wasn't real. And yet...something felt very wrong about returning to safety while her husband walked into the mouth of the beast.

Husband. Even the word made her chest hurt in a funny way.

Was there a possibility that he truly cared for her? That he valued her as a friend, she had no doubt. He'd been too kind throughout their journey not to. Or at least, he didn't loathe her and paid her the respect he might pay any woman. But there had been moments when she'd seen a look in his eyes that made her wonder if perhaps...just maybe, he might want more.

When they reached the safety of the camp, Esmeralda immediately put Jaelle and Drina to work washing clothes with the other women at the river.

"No use worrying about him," Esmeralda declared as she dropped a bucket of dirty clothes at Jaelle's feet. "What happens will happen. Might as well let it happen faster by keeping busy."

Any other day, the chores would have been a welcome distraction. Unlike the chores Chiara had forced her into, alone and under constant threat of punishment, the women here chatted loudly, their talk interrupted often with lots of laughs and the scolding of any small children who got too close to the water. Even more entertaining was the sight of Drina attempting to do laundry, which mostly involved lots of staring and a few tentative prods to the clothing in the buckets it came in. Jaelle would have found her horrified expression highly amusing if her heart hadn't sunk to the bottom of her stomach like a rock.

Though the laundry took all morning to wash and then most of the afternoon to hang, the hours dragged on. In spite of herself, Jaelle imagined every situation that might take place to keep him from returning. Once he had his gold, the king could enslave Lucas, something that wasn't uncommon for this particular king, Jaelle had heard. He might torture and interrogate Lucas for information about Maricanta's military. Or he could simply kill Lucas on the spot.

The only hope Jaelle clung to as the light finally began to wane was the fact that Lucas was a prince. And it was well known that this king, ruthless as he was rumored to be, also desired peerage with the other royals of the world. It would be foolish, when one wanted recognition, to destroy the prince of those who could give that respect.

When they'd first met, Jaelle had found Lucas's position somewhat repugnant, as though he had been the royal to banish her family. But now she pleaded with Lucas's precious Maker that his crown might be his saving grace. For though Terrefantome was a fearsome place to behold, she knew of no organized military beyond the local marshals and the king's personal guards. If they wished to pick a fight with one of the allied kingdoms in the western realm, Maricanta's allies made it a kingdom to be reconciled with. And from what Jaelle gathered of its king, Lucas's brother was likely to do exactly what Lucas feared by coming after him, should he disappear. Not that Jaelle would blame him if he did.

For some reason, she felt obligated to fetch an extra plate for supper that night. She didn't know what Lucas liked when he wasn't eating corn cakes, so she put a heaping helping of meat, bread, and just enough vegetables to keep him healthy. As the meal wore on, though, Jaelle could feel people's eyes on her as their lively banter and good-natured teasing began to die down. It didn't matter, though. As the sun sank lower on the horizon, Lucas didn't come.

By the time Drina was tucked into bed in the van Esmeralda had kindly allowed Jaelle to stay in again, Jaelle knew she couldn't wait any longer. He hadn't come home, and no good could come of it. So when night had fallen and the camp was quiet, Jaelle made her way to the van in which Esmeralda had said she would be spending the evening. She took a deep breath before rapping on the door. The Taistille had done so much for them. Could she really ask them to do more? Esmeralda had said she would give her life for Jaelle, but in asking this, was Jaelle endangering her entire troop?

As she stood there, waffling in front of the door, however, her decision was made for her when Esmeralda's captain stuck his head out the window.

"Well," he said gruffly, "are you coming in or not?"

Jaelle swallowed and nodded as the door opened for her. She climbed the blue wooden steps, the fluttering of her heart making her breathing slightly uneven.

Esmeralda, the holy man, whose name she learned was Django, and her captain were playing a round of *comorara*. Jaelle had seen the game played enough whenever she went into town, a favorite of the men. Only this time, each player had a handful of real cards made of thick parchment, something extremely rare in Terrefantome. Usually, common players used stiff bits of leather they'd scratched symbols on. Also different was that the usual common stones sitting in the center of the table had been replaced by Jaelle's gems which sparkled in the candlelight in their assorted colors.

"Comorara," Django said, tossing a blue diamond into the center of the table with a wry smile. The others groaned as Esmeralda tossed in two green gems and the captain pushed forward a yellow.

"So," Esmeralda said as she rearranged the cards in her hand, "what have you come to ask?"

Jaelle cleared her throat. "I would like to ask you to care for the queen mother when I'm gone." There. She'd said it. Or at least, half of what she needed to say.

"You're going after him." Esmeralda didn't sound surprised.

Jaelle nodded.

"I believe that's another two copper pieces." Django held out his hand. "You said she wouldn't go until tomorrow."

"I thought it was against your holy laws to steal," the captain muttered as he thrust the money into the holy man's outstretched hand.

"It's not stealing when you make the bet."

Esmeralda rolled her eyes, but she paid two copper pieces to Django as well. Then she turned to Jaelle.

"What changed your mind?" she asked.

Jaelle felt a strange catch in her throat. "He didn't come back."

Esmeralda pulled another card from the stack. "But I thought this marriage was all for show." She raised an eyebrow at Jaelle.

Jaelle swallowed. "How did you know?"

"My dear, I am the one who suggested the marriage."

Right. Jaelle forced herself not to fidget and tried to stand taller. "No matter what I feel, he's a good man." Too good to die alone.

"And if you don't come back either," Drina went back to her cards, "what should we do with your mother-in-law?" Her lips twitched. "She's such an excellent housekeeper. I'd hate to give up her services."

Jaelle produced Lucas's letter, the shell necklace tucked safely inside. "If I'm not back in three days, I need someone to take Drina to the ocean. All she has to do is throw this shell into the water, and the mermaids will come to escort her home." She nodded at the letter. It shook as she held it out. "Lucas's instructions are in this letter."

"So," the captain said as he tossed a red diamond on the table. "He wishes to bring more blood to our shores by summoning his brother's army."

"No." Jaelle's chest tightened. "He asked that they do nothing."

For once, the holy man lost his smile. "That doesn't sound like something most royals would do."

Jaelle held her head high. "He's not like most people." Commoners included.

Django nodded, his eyes probing hers. "This is true. He's not." Then he tilted his head to the other side. "But then, neither are you."

Esmeralda fingered a few of the jewels in her lap. Unlike the common Taistille, who had drawn back from Jaelle's jewels upon arrival, she seemed to have no aversion to touching them. If Jaelle had been less frightened, she would have asked why. Instead, however, she waited until the sehf raised her head once again.

"I will be honest. Our people do not go to the ocean. There's too much open space and not enough towns to justify the risk of getting trapped on the beach."

"Who could trap you?" Jaelle asked, trying to imagine anyone from the towns or even the cities having enough organization or strength to defeat even a smaller troop of the well-trained Taistille.

Esmeralda pursed her lips. "Bartol is stirring up more trouble than any of his predecessors. He's amassed more men and has been more aggressive than any of our histories tell. Even when we're not near the villages, he follows and attacks us."

That might have something to do with your marauding the villages, Jaelle thought, but she knew better than to say it. Of course, she also knew the Taistille believed the villages were theirs to begin with, so there was no use arguing the point.

"They haven't caused us any real trouble yet," the captain scowled.

"They're getting closer." Esmeralda's frown deepened. "Still, I will do my best." There was a faint turn to the corner of her mouth. "If not for Maricanta's sake, for ours." Then her smile faded. "But, Jaelle?"

"Yes?" For some reason, Jaelle's voice wavered.

"Before you skim over your feelings for this prince..." She

paused. "Stop and consider what it is that could move you to take the risk you're taking." Her eyes darkened. "Because this risk is unspeakably great."

As Jaelle returned to her van, she was haunted by Esmeralda's words. The sehf was mistaken, though. Jaelle didn't love him, if that was what she was implying. Lucas didn't make her feel the way she'd always envisioned love feeling. No, Lucas made her feel...

Confused. Lucas confused her. So often she was angry with him. And enthralled. And curious. And suspicious. And, if she was honest, jealous of every woman that looked his way.

No, this wasn't love. She didn't know what to call the emotion bouncing around inside her. She did know, however, that she'd spoken the truth to Django. Lucas was a good man, one like Jaelle had never seen. And he was too good to suffer the kind of end the darkness of Terrefantome was sure to doom him to for the rest of his life. No matter what her consternations, there was a light that came from within Lucas, the first she'd seen since her holy man had died. And no matter what it cost her, Jaelle couldn't bear to see that light snuffed out, too.

JAELLE DIDN'T KNOW how she'd sleep that night for fear of not waking up in time. But sleep tugged at her eyelids the moment she lay down, and in what seemed like mere minutes, she was waking up once again.

It was hard to tell what time of night or morning it was outside, but Jaelle put on her shoes anyway. She'd slept just enough to feel energetic about being anxious, and she knew her mind wouldn't let her rest anymore. She tiptoed away from the bench, where she'd slept to give Drina the bed, and headed for the door. But just as she opened it, she heard a voice from behind her.

"Take care of him."

Jaelle froze then turned to see Drina sitting up behind her. Instead of looking rested or even simply tired, however, the queen mother's eyes were red, and the skin beneath them was puffy.

Jaelle blanched. Drina had been crying, but for once, it wasn't the weeping, wailing tones of self-pity. Instead, she sounded just as any mother might, who was mourning for her son.

"Please care for him," she said again, her voice thin and brittle. "Maybe you can pay his ransom in diamonds or...or something like that." She met Jaelle's eyes. "Please?" she whispered.

Jaelle wanted to tell the woman that while she would pay whatever price they demanded for Lucas's life, she didn't have the heart to admit that they were unlikely to be satisfied with just a single round of generosity. After all, why take one gift when they could take all the gifts forever? Still, rather than tell Drina the odds of her son, much less Jaelle coming out alive, Jaelle simply nodded and went back to the bed to pull her into an embrace. Drina certainly wasn't the perfect mother, but obnoxious or not, the love wasn't gone.

If only Jaelle could understand where she fit into the world of love. Taking a deep breath, she adjusted her scarf and headed off into the night.

CHAPTER 40

ASK YOU AGAIN

The sky was just beginning to change color by the time Jaelle spotted the castle. She should have awakened sooner to make the trek completely in the dark of night, but she was too close to change her mind now.

As she neared the castle, however, walking through waist-high golden wheat stalks that blew slightly against her in the breeze, she didn't have much time to contemplate how she would enter. The entire building, as far as she could see, was surrounded by a crumbling but very tall wall, at least four or five feet higher than Lucas's head. A cry sounded out, and two guards were at her sides before she could think to escape. She went invisible as they reached for her, but the ease with which they gripped her arms told her that they were no newcomers. She sighed and let herself reappear as they dragged her toward the front gate.

The gate, though largely rusted over, was still impressive, made of metal curls and filigree as thick as her wrist. A thin man sat at the gate in front of a desk. He wasn't as impressive physically as the men who had taken her, but for being so very thin, even he wasn't very small.

"We found her snooping," her smaller captor said, gripping her arms until they hurt.

"And where are you headed?" the thin man said, not looking up from the worn ledger he held.

Jaelle considered answering, but then she realized there wasn't much point. Even with the scarf, she would be limited to how much she could speak without needing to empty it. They would find out about her secret soon enough. No need to help them.

"Stubborn then," the man noted, pulling her scarf ever so slightly, as though he was examining a horse. "Put her in the dungeon with the other one. We'll get them sorted out after breaking fast." The man glanced up at them again. "Victor, you take her. I need Ramon to come with me."

The smaller guard nodded and let go of her, while the larger of the two tightened his grip on Jaelle's arm and dragged her up the gravel path through a courtyard toward the castle.

The castle was bigger up close than Jaelle had first thought. As she drew closer, she could see the cracks in the mortar between the stones. Though the contours of the towers had once been elegant and intricate, most of the details had been worn away by wind and rain or were covered in moss. Jaelle shuddered as they walked beneath the main archway into a shadowed overhang, a whoosh of chilly air rushing in with them. Victor grunted at two more guards who stood on either side of the wooden doors which were only slightly smaller than the stone arches.

They opened the doors, but Jaelle didn't miss how the guard closest to her raised his eyebrows as Victor dragged her through.

"Where'd you find this one?" he asked, his eyes running appreciatively up her person in a way that made Jaelle cringe. He frowned slightly when he came to the mask.

"Snooping around the wall," Victor answered over his shoulder. As soon as they were inside and the doors were shut again, he paused in the entryway and put his mouth up to her ear. "Stay away from that one if you'd like to keep that mask on. He can be very persuasive." He paused, and she thought she could hear a smile in his next words. "If you stick with me, though, I'll make sure you don't have anything to be afraid of." He ran the back of his hand down her arm, and Jaelle stiffened.

"Victor!"

Jaelle whipped her head around at the sound of the familiar voice.

It couldn't be.

But sure enough, striding toward them was Selina, her eyes fixed and burning. Jaelle gawked as her sister came to stand beside them. Her hair was pulled up on her head in an impressive twist, a few dark strands hanging down around her face. Her dress was made of the finest material Jaelle had ever seen, peach-colored gauzy material that floated around and behind her like a ghost. The dress was well-fitted to show off not only Selina's slender, well-endowed figure, but also the defined muscles in her arms.

"I'll take this one," she said, a little toad escaping her lips as she took Jaelle by the other arm.

Victor frowned, and his grip on Jaelle's arm tightened again. It was going to be bruised tomorrow for sure.

"I really don't think the king..." Victor snapped, but before he finished, Selina opened her mouth as if to speak. Instead of speaking, though, she simply made a slight humming noise. A black snake with a yellow belly shot out of her mouth, stopping an inch from the guard's face. It hissed, its fangs moving out slightly.

Victor clenched his jaw and had the audacity...or perhaps, the stupidity to glare at Selina. He glared so long, in fact, that Jaelle nearly wondered if something deeper was going on. But after a few long seconds, he let Jaelle go, and Selina yanked her back. The snake gave one more strong hiss before sliding the rest of the way out of Selina's mouth and wrapping itself around Victor's arm and then making its way down his body. Once it was on the floor, it slithered into a dark corner and curled up into a little coil.

"Yes, madam," Victor said stiffly. He cast one more pouty look at Jaelle, nodded curtly to Selina, and stomped off.

Jaelle was still in shock when Selina yanked her over into the corner, too close to the snake for Jaelle's comfort, and crossed her arms.

"Why the plague are you here?" Her hiss was about as dangerous as that of her snake. "And while you're at it, why is the prince you were supposed to marry in the dungeon?"

Jaelle let herself exhale. He was alive. And even better, she realized, she'd found her sister. For angry as she was, Selina was here in front of her. Jaelle threw her arms around her sister and breathed in deeply, smiling when she picked up the faint familiar scent of lemongrass. The perfume was Jaelle's own recipe using the ingredients she'd picked in her garden.

Selina sighed, but she wrapped her arms around Jaelle in return and leaned her cheek against Jaelle's head, just as she had the night Jaelle's father died. And for one moment, Jaelle was safe. She was with the one person in the world that she didn't have to question how either of them felt. They were sisters, and nothing could sever that.

Finally, Selina pulled back and shook her head. "You have no idea how hard I had to work to plan that escape. Would you like to tell me why you're here now?" More baby toads, all blue and black, crawled out of her mouth and stuck to her cheeks.

How did she manage to speak clearly while all that was happening?

"It's..." Jaelle paused. So much had happened in the last few weeks. She felt like Selina's scheme to get her into Maricanta had been a lifetime ago. "It's a long story," she finally said slowly. Before she could finish, though, a guard appeared at the end of the hall once more.

"The king wishes to greet our visitor," he said with a mock bow.

Selina stiffened and grabbed Jaelle's hand. "Let me do the talking," she said, glancing down at Jaelle's scarf. A few young garter snakes slid from her mouth as they walked. "Do your best to play dumb."

Jaelle hadn't noticed when they'd first entered, as she'd been distracted by Victor's advance and then Selina's appearance, but now, as they made their way down the hall, she found herself in awe at its opulence. For while the castle was crumbling away on the outside, the inside looked as though it had never seen a speck of dust in its life. Marble the color of sand was inlaid on every inch of the floor. The arches on the ceilings soared overhead, and tapestries of rich red with tassels of gold hung from walls. The fixtures on the walls looked like bronze, and they shone almost as brightly, as if the sun were directly upon them.

Jaelle tore her gaze from her surroundings back to her sister, and a new sense of wonder and dread began to drip inside her. At first, she'd been so excited to see her sister that she hadn't questioned Selina's apparent position of power or her fancy clothes or the fact that she seemed so at home here in the dreaded regent's palace. But now, Jaelle was unable to quell her growing misgivings. How had her sister fallen into company with the king? And how had she gained so much power so fast? For his favor was the only explanation Jaelle could think up to explain such rich clothes or a seat of honor so high that even the guards listened to her.

The only comfort she found in all of this was that Selina was alive, at least, and that Lucas seemed to be for the moment as well. Jaelle could only surmise that the king didn't keep dead people in his dungeon.

They turned from the main hall into a large room. This one had a dais at the end. There weren't many people in the room, perhaps a dozen, and to Jaelle's surprise, at least five were women. The man who was sitting in the throne on the dais looked away from the man he'd been speaking to as they entered. When he turned his eyes on her, Jaelle felt her blood curdle, and she wanted to pull her mask over her entire body. The look he gave her was somehow more revealing than any she'd ever felt before.

"Selina." His voice was slippery and smooth and made her sister's name sound like a it was covered in oil. "Who is this little beauty?"

"This," Selina said in an even tone, "is my little sister."

"How delightful." The man clapped his hands together and rubbed them. With his angled face and thick, dark hair, he might have been quite handsome if it weren't for the way his pale eyes continually roved the room, like a starving man searching for a morsel. He stood and came to them before walking in a slow circle around Jaelle and Selina. Selina squeezed Jaelle's hand.

"I didn't know you had a sister," he said, returning to stand before them again, a brilliant smile on his face.

"She's a mute," Selina said coolly, a delicate garter snake making its way out of her nose. "She's only come to find me now because our mother died."

"You seem quite broken up about it," the king said, raising his eyes to Selina. "I can give you time to mourn if you wish."

"My mother was a cruel, sadistic woman who cared only for

herself." Selina drew Jaelle closer. A tiny toad made its way out to her cheek.

"Actually, Sire?"

Everyone turned to look at Victor. Selina glared daggers at him, but he ignored her.

"She's lying," Victor continued. "That's no mute. I saw them talking before I called them here." He looked rather pleased with himself, but Jaelle wondered just how many of the colorful frogs or deadly snakes he might find in his bed that night. Judging by the look on her sister's face, he might not even have to wait that long.

"What is..." The king tilted his head and squinted at her scarf. Before Jaelle could even send up a prayer to Lucas's Maker, the king had pulled the scarf off, and a handful of diamonds clattered to the ground.

For a long moment, no one spoke. But inside, Jaelle felt like her insides had been melted together in one of the Taistille's bonfires.

The king stared at the ground for a long time, looking just as confused as the courtiers around him. More had come since they'd arrived, and now Jaelle felt dozens of eyes focused right on her. Or rather, right at her feet. The king looked up again. He studied the sisters, looking back and forth until understanding lit his eyes. Jaelle could hear her sister exhale sharply when a small smile formed on the king's lips.

"So one speaks toads," he murmured, noting the toad making its way down Selina's neck, "and the other diamonds."

Jaelle had felt fear many times in her life. But never like this.

"My dear," the king said, taking her right hand from Selina and running his fingers lightly up and down her arm, "I think you and I have much—" He stopped and frowned.

Jaelle looked down to see that he'd turned her arm over. And there on her wrist was the picture of the ship.

He looked up at Selina, his frown deepening. "But she's wearing a mask."

Selina regarded him evenly, though Jaelle could read her surprise beneath her carefully constructed facade. "She's very particular about her mask," Selina said, giving him a forced smile. "I would not consider it more than a trifle."

"If you're here," the king said, turning back to Jaelle. "Then where is your husband?"

Jaelle took a deep breath. She had one chance to get Lucas home. She would have to tread carefully. "I do not know," she said, forcing herself to hold her chin up while everyone gasped at the gems while they dripped from her mouth. "I have come in search of him, but clearly, he is not here." The sound of the diamonds hitting the ground as she spoke felt deafening.

"What man would leave a creature as enchanting as you?"

A noble one, she wanted to retort. But she remained silent instead.

He studied her again before a knowing smile turned up the edges of his lips. How she would have liked to slap that smile as far as it would go.

"Come," he said, taking her elbow and placing it in his. "I can tell that this story is not going to be simple. We might as well give you a tour of my home."

Jaelle hesitated slightly but let him lead her. As if she had a choice.

"I don't know how much you've heard of me," he said, casting a sideways glance at her as they walked down another massive hallway, "but I came here on purpose."

In spite of herself, Jaelle stopped walking and turned to stare at her host. He grinned, seeming pleased by this reaction. She stood still, but in her mind, Jaelle was scrambling away as fast as she could go. What kind of man went to Terrefantome on purpose?

"I'd talked to enough of those who escaped to have an idea of what this place was like," he said, continuing their walk and pulling her along with him. Several dozen of his courtiers, men and women, walked beside or behind them as he spoke. They wore odd mixtures of fear and curiosity, and Jaelle could see them look longingly at the floor every time she dropped another gem. But no one dared to pick them up.

"As soon as I was old enough for the judge to view me as a man," Bartol continued, "I killed three travelers on a country road. That took place in Lingea." He nudged her, though she wished desperately he wouldn't. "The judge immediately sent me to the king, who banished me here. Now look there." He paused and pointed to the door, which was open, that led to another large hall. "That's the dining hall. But if you wish to eat in your chambers, you can certainly do that simply by pulling on the rope in your room."

Her room? Jaelle stared ahead as they resumed their walk. She'd been here less than an hour, and the king seemed to think that her presence was going to be permanent.

"Anyhow, as soon as I arrived, I knew the opportunity to unite the people was ripe. So I spent my first seven years moving from place to place, putting together my own group of supporters and biding my time until I could become invisible." His eyes lit up as they turned another corner. Just as with the other two, this hallway had vaulted ceilings, marble floors, and rich decorations covering most of the walls. Hundreds of candles lit what wasn't touched by the weak sunlight which came in from the outside.

"This castle was falling to pieces when I first saw it," he said, touching a wall as they walked. "The previous king had been losing his hold on the throne for years when I arrived. By then, I had a following of no less than two hundred, so taking it from him was one of the easiest things I've ever done. As you can see, we've been doing our best to restore it to its first glory."

"How?" Jaelle couldn't help asking. The king smiled widely as a large emerald bounced to the floor.

"Your sister has been instrumental in helping us as of late. But in the beginning, I used avenues that I...I suppose you could say I took care of them before getting myself banished here."

Jaelle didn't know what to say to that. She didn't have to say anything, though, because the king gestured to a set of winding stairs, and she followed him up, glancing back often to see if her sister was still with them. Selina walked slightly behind him, but for some reason, she didn't even try to meet Jaelle's eyes. Instead, she stared either at the floor or into the distance.

"This castle originally belonged to the Taistille, you know," he said as a servant ran ahead of them to light the sconces on the walls as they continued to ascend. "It was the only large permanent structure that they owned, though for the life of me, I can't understand why."

Jaelle did, but she wasn't about to enlighten him.

"But when the other kings," he continued, "walled off the land, the Taistille king had already sent too many of his men out to patrol against the criminals who had fled to the land where they could become invisible. All it took was one rebel with too many followers, and the Taistille king, or *sehf*, as they call it, could do little more than call the patrol groups back to rescue their families." He shrugged. "The Taistille were eventually forced to leave the castle to seek food. Soon after, the leader of one of the criminal mobs noticed the empty castle, declared himself king and took up residence in it. The reigning kings, each usurping the one before him, have been here ever since. Ah, here we are."

They'd climbed more steps than Jaelle was able to count, and now they stepped out onto a balcony. As he moved them closer to the edge, Jaelle realized that they must be in the tallest tower.

"I come out here to think," he said, looking around him with a serene smile. "The wind clears my head." He took another step toward the edge, and despite the wall that went up to Jaelle's waist, the height made her heart speed inside her chest.

"Jaelle," he said, taking both her hands and holding her out in front of him. How he was so composed before the dozens of people who were now crowding the stairwell, she hadn't an idea.

"I'm not one for superstitions," he continued, "but I feel as though the Maker has truly gifted me today in the greatest way possible." He took a step closer. When she instinctively fell back, his grip tightened. "Marry me, and I will provide you with every wish your heart could desire." He swept his hand over the land behind and around them. "You'll be queen to all of this! You'll birth the child who will inherit the land." He took another step closer, his dark eyes seeming determined to stare into hers. And yet, it was far more frightening than any look Lucas had ever given her. "Your words will move mountains."

"And as long as I keep speaking them," Jaelle said softly, "you'll treat me like a queen."

The king's smile held, but his eyes slightly tightened. "Pardon?"

"Let us be candid." Jaelle stood taller and hoped her trembling knees wouldn't betray her. "You have known me for the span of twenty minutes. You cannot possibly think yourself in love with anything about me except for the fact that I still wear a mask and I could provide you with more wealth than any one man could dream of seeing in his lifetime."

"Come now, Jaelle. The morning is lovely. We have been both gifted the opportunity most people even outside this land couldn't dream of. Why clutter it with unpleasantries?" He moved his grip from her arm to her hand and leaned forward, his breath tickling her neck. "Because I can guarantee you will not like me when I'm unpleasant."

Without looking away, he reached over and placed his hand on the chest of the nearest man to his left. And with a smile as serene as a pond, he shoved the young man so hard that he stumbled back and toppled over the balcony. Then, without a word, he turned her back to the stairs. One of the women who followed them let out a stifled shriek and then began to cry quietly. Based on her age, Jaelle could only imagine the man had been her son. Several of the other courtiers quietly comforted her as they walked. Jaelle wished she could have remained untouched, but inside, she was shaken, particularly for the woman. To have one's child ripped away so senselessly...Jaelle did her best not to let that fear make her hand or arm shake as he led her back down.

As soon as they were at the bottom, a female servant ran up to them, bobbing up and down quickly before addressing the king.

"Your Highness," she cried, "a young man has fallen from the tower!"

"Is he dead?" Bartol asked, his face full of concern. Jaelle gawked. Was he truly pretending to be confused?

"Nay, he's alive, Your Highness," the girl said. "But he's awful hurt."

"Good," said the king, letting out a sigh and briefly closing his eyes. "Give him all the attention he needs." He glanced back at the crowd behind them. The woman who had been sobbing was now watching them, wringing her handkerchief as though she might have need to tear it. "Take his mother out to him," the king continued in a gentle voice, "and let her minster to him for as long as she needs." Then he turned back to Jaelle. "See how pleasant I can be?"

He was mad. There was no other explanation. Jaelle glanced back at Selina, but Selina's face was impassive. How could she not only stay with this madman but aid him as well?

"Come," the king said, turning to a second set of stairs. Once again, servants hurried ahead of them to light their way. He put his right arm around her back to her shoulder and used his left to grip her elbow. "Be careful," he said. "These are steep."

Jaelle decided to do as he said.

"Back to what we were discussing, though," he said, his voice light again, "I realized that the only way our people will find their way out of this hole is through respect."

Respect? For whom? Jaelle frowned, but said nothing.

"You see," he said, continuing to guide her down the winding steps, "the other kingdoms don't respect us. And as long as they don't respect us, they'll keep dumping their worst into our borders while starving us of the trade and resources we desperately need and would be happy to share."

What resources they could offer, Jaelle had no idea. But she was getting more suspicious by the minute. How were these stairs even more numerous than the first? She felt as though they'd been descending for miles.

"They treat us like a refuse dump," he continued. "And I'm going to have to change things *here* if we're going to change their minds." As he said the words, they reached the bottom, and Jaelle looked around to realize they were surrounded by prison bars. Instead of letting her explore, he guided her to the prison compartment behind the stairs.

In this particular cell, a man lay on the floor. Blood caked his lips and chin, and awful bruises and lacerations covered his skin. Weak shafts of daylight were mottled by the bars in the small window at the top of his cell as they rained down on his skin.

In spite of herself, Jaelle's hands flew up to her mouth to hold in the scream. She ran to the bars, but he was too deep inside for her to reach. She whipped back around.

"So abducting a prince is going to garner you that respect?" she snapped. "If anything, it will start a war!"

Instead of responding, though, the king only folded his arms and watched her. And for once, his insipid smile was gone.

"So this is your husband then."

She felt her face drain of blood. "I never said—"

His smile widened. "I never told you he was a prince."

Jaelle could only stare miserably as Selina closed her eyes and shook her head slightly to herself. The king walked forward and took her hand again.

"Don't be too hard on yourself," he said, turning her wrist over to show the ship once again. "The wound is new. I noticed his mark was still healing as well when he came into my court here yesterday. Even if you hadn't said anything, I would have figured it out soon enough." He straightened. "He stood his ground, even when the invisible soldiers set in on him. And despite his obvious disadvantage, he managed to give several of them broken bones, so that should make you proud. Unless," he turned to her again, "it was a marriage of convenience." His smile widened. "In which case you shouldn't care whether or not he makes you proud."

His was an annoying smile, she decided, ugly and condescending.

"I'm supposing that he realized after arriving and somehow getting mixed up with you that you wouldn't be safe until he married you. So, being the honorable young man everyone knows the youngest Maricantan to be, he married you." The king raised his eyebrows. "Does that really sound so far-fetched?"

Jaelle couldn't get herself to answer. She couldn't tear her eyes from the still form on the cold prison floor.

"You asked what I could gain from kidnapping a prince. Well, I can tell you that holding one of the darlings of the western realm will catapult me into the height of royal and noble conversations. If nothing else, they will all know my name."

"They won't want to ally themselves with you after this," Jaelle spat.

"I don't want to make friends, Jaelle." He turned back to her. "I want respect. And respect can only come from power." He rapped on a rusty bar with his knuckles. "Holding a prince captive is a sure way to power. Before we get distracted, though, I want to remind you that my offer still stands."

"Your offer?" Jaelle couldn't bring herself to look at him.

"Marry me. I can easily declare your marriage annulled, though

I doubt it means much to you even now." He glanced at Lucas. "You couldn't have known each other for that long."

Jaelle knew better than to speak her mind, particularly considering the way he'd pushed the young man from the balcony just a few minutes ago. But she couldn't stop the words. Instead, they fell from her mouth the way the diamonds did. Angry tears made her eyes hurt.

"You demand my husband come here to pay you." Why was her voice shaking? It needed to be strong. "Then you beat him senseless when he does what he promised. And then you offer me marriage as though your actions could make all of that go away?"

"Of course not." The king's voice was cool. "Nothing could make that go away. I'm simply making a point that either way, your husband is going to be here for a long time. You can either make his stay more pleasant, or you can guarantee every minute here will be slow and full of misery." He shrugged. "It's your choice."

Jaelle found her voice caught in her throat, and all she could do was stare at Lucas.

"But should you be inclined to think me naive to your desire to escape," the king added in a low voice, "know that it will be just as easy for me to hunt and kill your prince and his mother where she stays in that Taistille camp just over the ridge," he paused as his words sank in, "as it was for me to find and kill the guides your prince brought with him when he first entered the country. You should also know that I have spies not only in my own kingdom, but in the courts of all the greatest monarchs of the western realm."

Jaelle's mouth went dry.

"So," he said again in that smooth tone, "I'm going to ask you again. Will you marry me, Jaelle?"

Jaelle was about two seconds away from losing her mind when she felt familiar hands on her shoulders.

"Before you ask her to make a decision," Selina said in her own smooth voice, "I would like to talk with my sister privately in my chambers. Perhaps, I can talk some sense into her before drastic measures must be taken."

At this suggestion, the king's smile reappeared. "That would be an excellent gesture," he said. Then he turned and clapped his hands at the people who were waiting behind him. "Come now. Let's allow these sisters some time to themselves. Everyone back up to the dining hall. Oh, is that sausage I smell?"

CHAPTER 41

LUCAS

J aelle followed Selina back up the stairs and down several corridors until they came to a wooden door that had been painted red and was adorned with a gold handle. As soon as they were inside, Selina locked the door behind them, and Jaelle turned around and gasped.

The shiny marble that covered the floors of the main halls also covered the floors in Selina's room. But rather than lying flat as Jaelle would have expected to find the floors here, there were multiple levels with steps all over the room, as space large enough to have swallowed their old cottage. A bed nearly the size of their old bedroom stood on a raised platform in the middle of the floor and was covered by swaths of transparent, peach-colored, gauzy material that hung down from the top of the four-poster bed. A wide vanity with a mirror, various divans, three wardrobes, and a few tables with lamps, candelabras, and beauty products were also scattered around the room. Four large windows with separated panes of glass were spread evenly across the wall. Dividing the windows into sets of two was a double-door balcony, which was currently open, allowing a cool breeze to float through the room.

"This is yours?" Jaelle gaped.

Selina smirked. "Slightly nicer than what Mother had for us, isn't it?"

Jaelle shook her head slowly. "I didn't know so many riches

could exist in all the world." She turned to look at her sister. "But where did you get it all?" Once again, her stomach slightly turned. What kind of services was Selina providing to the king?

"You'd be surprised how much gold the inhabitants here are holding onto."

"But how?" Jaelle asked again.

"Many of them hate snakes." Selina went to close the curtains. "We are going to talk, but I need you to stay here for a little while as I finish up some business. Can you wait for me?"

Jaelle nodded.

"Feel free to help yourself to the refreshments." Selina waved to a tray full of tarts and fruits on the bedside table. "And you can sleep on the bed if you wish to nap."

"How long will you be gone?" Jaelle asked.

"I don't know. Probably a few hours. I didn't exactly expect you to waltz into my arms this morning." Selina smiled slightly, but then her brow creased. "Stay here until I know what to do with you."

"Wait, Selina?"

"Yes?" Selina turned, her hand on the door.

Jaelle took a deep breath.

"Lucas...Is he—"

Selina's smile tightened. "He's alive. Now stay here. I'll be back."

Selina was gone for more than a few hours. The morning gray moved to the gray of the afternoon, during which Jaelle did indeed nap and eat from Selina's tray of food and then napped again. It would have been the most extravagant day in her life if she hadn't been so worried for Lucas.

Though she wouldn't have dared admit it to her sister, Jaelle tried the door several times. She was rather sure she could find her way down to the dungeon if given a few moments to orient herself to the palace halls once more. But she understood quickly that she was as much a prisoner as he was.

Blast it. If she wasn't worried for her sister, she was worried for her husband. It would be a miracle if she was ever spared five minutes without having to worry about someone.

Selina finally returned as the evening light began to wane. She brought two plates of food, but this time, all hints of a smile were gone.

"Now that we're alone," she said, handing the plate to Jaelle, "I'm going to ask you again. Why are you and the prince you were *supposed* to marry gallivanting around Terrefantome? And to make matters worse, in the presence of the king, might I add? And why," her voice grew sterner, "do you have tattoos? Maricanta doesn't include tattoos in their wedding rituals."

Jaelle's face grew hot, and she looked at the spoonful of berries she'd just scooped. "You couldn't have known it, but when you sent me with Drina, Lucas was already in here."

Selina blinked. "What?"

"Apparently, his grandfather borrowed money years back to aid his war." Jaelle spoke quickly. For some reason, she felt the need to defend Lucas in all of this, imprisoned or not. "Lucas's brother tried sending the money twice, but it disappeared in Terrefantome each time. And when the king sent word demanding payment a third time, he threatened to release the prisoners and break down the wall if it wasn't brought to him soon."

"But how did you end up traveling *with* him?" Selina looked less than impressed. "You were supposed to go to Maricanta. You could have at least waited for him there."

"His mother," Jaelle said, studying her wine, "wanted to surprise him with his new bride."

Selina closed her eyes and let loose a string of curses Jaelle had never heard fall from her sister's pretty lips. Eventually, Selina shook her head and opened her eyes again. "Then what?"

"Well," Jaelle shrugged, "he couldn't call off the mission, but when his guides disappeared, he was stuck with the deadline. So we made a deal. I would lead him to the castle, and when we were done, he would take me to meet the Fortiers."

Selina sat straight up in the divan she'd just collapsed on. "The Fortiers? Jaelle, they're the most powerful king and queen in the western realm. What in the world would you need to meet them for?"

Jaelle finally forced herself to meet her sister's gaze. "To save you."

At this, Selina's eyes, which had been hard like flint, softened.

She put her plate aside and sat next to Jaelle and began to unbraid her hair and comb it with her fingers.

"Leave it to you," she said softly, "to ruin the most perfectly laid plans so you could rescue the planner."

Jaelle didn't know what to say to that. So she stayed quiet, simply soaking in the way it felt again to have her sister beside her and brushing her hair.

"And I'll have you know," Selina continued with mock fury, "that I spent nearly a year planning this."

"But I thought you planned it after Chiara threatened to marry me off," Jaelle said.

Selina gave her a wry smile and grabbed a silver-handled brush from a nearby vanity. "I'd been planning it long before then. Mother's threat only hurried me some."

"But how did you get the message through the wall?" Jaelle asked, "Let alone to the queen?" She tried to ignore the garter snakes which seemed to be leaving her sister's mouth by the dozen.

Selina took the brush back and began to pull Jaelle's hair back again.

"You wouldn't know this because you've stayed at home so much, but there are holes in the wall all around us. A few are bigger, like the ones Bartol uses to get supplies for the castle, but most aren't big enough for people to fit through. They're big enough, though, that young boys will wait at the wall on either side to run messages to loved ones for coppers." She began to braid, wrapping her fingers in the locks of hair she'd separated. "I scrimped as much as I could before bringing my pay home to Mother. Your little tiff with her did cause me to work more than I should have preferred to raised my funds sooner, but I finally had enough. I sent ten letters, each sent with a different carrier, and was able to contact the queen. We were able to connect enough times after that to work out where she would find you and when."

"But why would you use a Taistille curse?" Jaelle looked again at the two garter snakes wandering slowly down Selina's collarbones. "Lucas says—"

"Because, as I'm sure you know by now, everyone in Maricanta knows that the queen is greedy," Selina leaned back and let her head rest on the silk pillows behind her. "I knew I would need a one-of-a-kind daughter she couldn't resist. And considering Maricanta's recent financial woes, I was right. She wrote back, enthusiastic and obviously oblivious to the dangers our land holds. I told her how to get in and how to reach us." She looked down at the black snake that was slithering out of her mouth, pausing to let it finish its exit.

"How are you?" Jaelle asked quietly, dumping her own pile of gems from her lap onto Selina's bed. "With this, I mean." She indicated warily to the snake.

Selina closed her eyes and let her head fall back onto the pillow once more. "I hated it at first. I felt like an anathema, disgusting and despised by even myself." She opened her eyes and stared at the ceiling. "But it's strange how quickly one learns to adapt. If nothing else, it gave me the courage to leave Mother and strike out on my own. As soon as I realized I controlled the creatures I produced, I knew I would be more dangerous than anyone I might meet on the road."

"But Sorthileige..." Jaelle said slowly, "Lucas says it twists and turns you into something you were not." She looked down at the new pile of gems in her lap. "I know you meant well, but I want nothing to do with this if it's going to change who you are." Then she took her sister's hand and squeezed. "That's why we need to find the Fortiers. Lucas is friends with them. He assured me that if anyone can get rid of this darkness, King Ev—"

"There's been a darkness in me for a long time, Jaelle." Selina stood and went out to the balcony. Jaelle followed.

"Receiving the Taistille curse didn't put it there," Selina continued. "It only ignited it."

"I don't understand," Jaelle said. Selina had never been cruel to her. Perhaps her sense of humor was on the cutting side, and she'd never pitied others the way Jaelle tended to. But Jaelle had never seen anything in her sister that resembled the Sorthileige Lucas had described.

"To properly enact a curse that appears as a gift," Selina said slowly, "the witch told me that she would need a source of darkness from which to draw. To make the gift appear as light, she would need even more darkness. Then she would use some of that power to create the gift..." Selina paused. "And she would take the rest as payment."

"But where did you find it?" Jaelle asked. "Lucas says it comes from the ocean." Even as she spoke, though, she remembered the cavern and the thick shadow that had chased them out.

"The sins of my parents have stained me," Selina said quietly, staring at the forest that lined the horizon. Jaelle looked out as well, and if she squinted hard, she imagined she could see the distant shine of the sea.

Selina continued. "When I asked the witch where she wanted me to find the Sorthileige for her, she touched my chest, just over my heart. Then she said I would do quite well."

Jaelle stared at her sister, her own chest suddenly tight.

"By drawing the poison to the surface, however, she made that darkness visible, and with it," Selina stopped to pet one of the serpents as it coiled itself around her wrist, "the power to change my own life." She gave a humorless laugh. "You should have seen Bartol's face when I waltzed into his court and put a cobra in his lap."

"He seems to like you now," Jaelle said, studying her sister anew.

"He was angry at first, especially when I demanded to be his closest adviser. But it wasn't long before he realized what an...asset I could be." Her lips twitched. "I can be quite convincing."

Jaelle didn't doubt that as she watched a long brown snake make its way down Selina's leg.

"Don't worry about them," Selina continued, waving at the serpents. "I told you, they can't harm you without my permission. Unless I have an errand for them, I send them all outside." Then she plopped down in one of the outdoor chairs and set her elbows on her knees. "But enough about me. I am quite interested as to how *you* became married to the prince of Maricanta *while* in Terrefantome." Her eyes darkened slightly. "And why you believe continuing such a marriage would be beneficial to either of you."

Jaelle turned her wrist over to gaze at the ship. "It's like I told you," she said, keeping her face cast down. "His mother wanted to show me off. He wanted to send me back to Maricanta with his mother. But I knew he wouldn't survive. So we made a deal." Not that the mobs had given them much choice. "I would help him find his way, and he would help me meet the Fortiers. But when he saw more of the land, he believed it would be safer if we were married."

"Which I understand. But you haven't removed your mask, so you're obviously not in love with him." Selina turned to face Jaelle and studied her just a little too intently. "Why are you hesitant to annul a marriage that's not even real?"

"The marriage was real." Jaelle shifted. "It was done by a holy man."

"Did *he* talk of getting it annulled after?"

Jaelle couldn't bring herself to answer.

"Horse hooves, Jaelle!" Selina threw her head back and rubbed her eyes. "Uttering a few words in front of a man with an education does not make you husband and wife!" She began to pace. "Look, here's what we're going to do. Bartol likes you. You're innocent and naive, and he finds that attractive. So you're going to let him annul your marriage with Lucas, then you'll marry him." She paused and shooed Jaelle back inside, closing the balcony doors behind her. Once they were back in the room, she began talking again, but her voice stayed low.

"Once you've worked your way into his heart, which I know you're perfectly capable of doing, and you have enough responsibility, I'll kill him."

"You'll kill him." Jaelle echoed. "Just...just kill him like that?"

"I'm the king's most trusted adviser, but I have no claim to the throne." Selina looked at Jaelle, her face suddenly enraptured. "But if *you* become queen, and he dies, you and I will rule together. It's even better than before." She went immediately to her writing desk beneath one of the windows and began to scribble something on a piece of parchment.

What had just happened? That Selina was desperate, Jaelle had no doubt. And in the past, it wouldn't have surprised her a bit if her sister had killed a man who had threatened either one of them to the extent that they might be taken. But to talk of killing a man in cold blood after marrying him...That was too much.

And even if she hadn't been plotting murder, there was Lucas.

"I can't," Jaelle squeaked.

Selina looked up from her parchment. "What?"

"I can't leave Lucas. Not like this."

Selina stood slowly and took off the spectacles she'd donned for writing. "Jaelle, I know he's good looking, but—"

"It's not about that."

"Then what is it?" Selina's eyes went wide. "You're not saying you love him?"

"Not love," Jaelle said quietly. "But...he cares for me. He's protected me." She spoke faster and faster, hoping to get it all out before either she lost her nerve or her sister tied and gagged her. "I know you don't believe in love, but he could have abandoned me more than once, and he didn't. Instead, he married me without ever having seen my face and came here alone so he could keep me safe." She laughed nervously. "Selina, the man spent his wedding night on a bench! And...And I just can't throw all that away. He's a *good* man, and I—"

"You've fallen for him." Selina's face had turned a deep red, and she stood, stiff as a plank of wood. "I've spent the last six years warning you of what men are capable of and what's in their nature. And it's like you've heard none of it."

"You arranged our marriage in the first place!"

"It was meant to be a marriage of convenience! Not one that had you running around the forest with Taistille and the world's most insensible queen mother! You weren't supposed to fall in love with him. You were supposed to use him!"

"But—"

"Lucas might seem kind now, but he will only hurt you. All men do. They always choose what's best for them in the end!"

"You don't know that," Jaelle shouted back. "He's different."

"He's going to leave you as soon as it's convenient for him. I can promise you that." She scoffed. "Do you know how many ladies his grandfather kept for himself on the side? There were always at least three."

"This isn't about his grandfather."

"You're right it's not! It's about men in general."

"Lucas is not your father!"

As soon as the scream had left her throat, Jaelle knew it was the wrong thing to say. But before she could try to repair the damage, a look spread across Selina's face that Jaelle had never seen, one of rage and pain. She stalked forward and grabbed Jaelle by the arm. Then she dragged her to the door.

"If you're so determined to stay with your prince," she snapped as she pulled Jaelle back down the hall, "then perhaps a night with him in the dungeon is just what you need."

"Selina!" Jaelle winced as her sister's fingernails dug into her arm. "Why are you doing this?"

Selina yanked Jaelle to a stop and pulled her close until their faces were only inches apart.

"I swore to myself that I would do whatever it took to keep you safe. Even if that means teaching you the hard way." Then Selina began to drag her toward the dungeon once more.

CHAPTER 42

RISK

Jaelle's knees cracked against the marble floor, and her palms stung when they smacked stone. She groaned as she turned over to see Selina locking the cell.

"Maybe after a night in here you'll be more reasonable," Selina said, handing the key back to the prison keeper. "Those marble floors might be smooth and even, but I can guarantee that they get grotesquely cold at night." Her eyes glinted slightly. "I saw to that when I helped the king rebuild the palace." Then she turned and followed the prison keeper upstairs.

Jaelle stared stupidly after her sister as she disappeared. She should be upset or angry or hurt. But shock seemed to be all she could find.

Selina was trying to force her to marry a cruel, spiteful man.

Selina was using her to kill that man.

Selina had thrown her in the dungeon.

In spite of her confusion, tears began to roll down her cheeks, and heaving sobs racked her chest. Unable to move from the place where she knelt on her hands and knees, Jaelle cried like a child who had been tossed aside. Her heart hurt in a way she'd never hurt before. The one person in the world who should have protected her had become her betrayer.

A sound from behind her interrupted Jaelle's cries. In her haste to turn, she slipped, and this time, her shoulder hit the stone floor, compounding her humiliation and pain. As she lay there, wishing she could just disappear, a strong hand grasped her own and held on tightly. She opened her eyes, and as they adjusted, she was able to make out a familiar face.

Dried blood caked his nose and mouth. Even in the weak light of the single torch, she could make out the beginnings of countless bruises that were forming on his face, neck, and arms as he leaned limply against the stone wall. Horror mixed with dread, and any remaining shred of dignity she'd clung to came crashing down as he drew her into his lap and held her against his chest, her sobs turning to wails.

Part of her mind, the part that was concerned with protecting herself, told her she shouldn't let him hold her like this. Not when he'd made it clear that they weren't husband and wife. But she couldn't push his arms away, nor could she find it within her to pull away from him as he made soft shushing sounds and ran his right hand down her hair again and again, his left hand gripping her tightly. She could feel him breathing as his chest moved up and down, and she realized that in this moment, she wanted nothing more than his comfort. It might be a terrible mistake, but she needed someone's love. Why not her husband's? If only for one night, why not let him hold her like the wife she was?

"Lucas," she rasped when she finally found the breath to speak again. "My sister...She—"

"I know," he whispered into her hair. "I know."

She pulled away slightly to search his eyes. "You do?"

He smiled faintly. "It's amazing what guards will discuss when they think you've been beaten unconscious."

"She's different, Lucas," Jaelle said, her voice trembling again. "She's changed. Selina would never have wanted me to marry a cruel man, and she wouldn't have wanted me to help kill someone in cold blood." She wrapped her arms around herself, trying to stop the shaking that threatened to overcome her. "I don't know what's happened to her, but she's not the sister I left behind."

"That's what Sorthileige does to people." He tucked a lock of hair behind her ear. "It poisons hearts."

"How do you know that?" Jaelle asked.

"Didn't you see my scar?"

Only now did Jaelle remember the story Lucas had told his mother outside of Norio. "I tried no to."

He gave her a strange look and moved her a little farther down his lap. Then he took the corner of his shirt, and lifted it up to reveal his stomach and half of his chest.

Jaelle's own stomach warmed and did a strange flop at the defined muscles. She stopped, however, when she saw the scar.

About three fingers wide, the scar was long and thin, whiter than the rest of the skin around it and slightly raised.

"Is that from your brother?" she whispered. She'd shied away from looking back when he'd shown his mother on the road. But now she couldn't look away.

He nodded, not moving his eyes from her face. Again, she wondered what he could think he was seeing when he stared at her like that.

"My brother was taken captive by a mermaid's siren song before he was married." His brows furrowed slightly. "The woman who bewitched him was my sister-in-law's aunt who believed she had discovered Arianna's higher purpose. And when Arianna didn't comply, the woman used her gift of the merperson's song in a way that's been forbidden for centuries. It possessed my brother enough to think he was doing good when he climbed aboard my ship. When I embraced him, he stabbed me and left me to die."

Jaelle stared at him in horror. "But how did you save him?"

"I didn't." Lucas gave her a tired smile. "Arianna did. And the Maker saved us all." He sighed and let his shirt fall. "My brother still struggles, though, with guilt. And probably will for the rest of his life."

"But he didn't choose the darkness." Jaelle shook her head. "My sister did." And she was still doing it now, embracing it rather than fighting it off.

"Yes and no." Lucas picked up her hand and traced her knuckles. "He didn't choose the Sorthileige, but he turned his back on Arianna when she was the one person who could help him."

Jaelle couldn't answer. She felt like there were no words. Instead, she reached out and gingerly touched the scar, running her fingers up and down its length. The scar was hard, but his skin was warm.

Lucas closed his eyes and drew a deep breath in slowly through his nose.

"You keep talking about the Maker and how good he is," Jaelle said. "And yet, all these terrible things have befallen you and your kingdom. How do you reconcile the two?"

Lucas tried to push himself into a slightly higher sitting position. "What do you mean?" he asked with a grimace.

"The holy man used to tell us the Maker was above all. That he'd created it all and was in control of everything."

"Do you believe him?"

"I used to." She kept her eyes on his scar. "But the longer I live here, the more I wonder how anyone could believe in so much goodness when there's so much darkness that squeezes out the light."

"But don't you see?" Lucas surprised her by taking both her hands in his. His eyes were wide, and he leaned closer. "That's exactly why such goodness has to exist."

She frowned at him. "Have you been conscious these last two weeks?"

Lucas laughed weakly and shook his head as he leaned against the wall again. "I've never seen so much evil in one place in my life. But the very fact that we all know there's something *beyond* this evil...that we yearn for the light. It means we were made with an innate knowledge that there is something better."

Jaelle frowned. Could he be right? Was it really that simple?

"The only difference," Lucas continued, taking her face in his hand, "is that this," he pointed at the barred window at the top of the cell, "is what happens when one refuses to look at the light. Terrefantome refuses to look at the light."

Evening was falling fast, though how the day had gone by so quickly, Jaelle couldn't understand.

"All you know is shadow," he said softly. "But when dawn breaks and the sun bathes you in its light, no matter how many times you've seen it, you can't help being blinded by its beauty and the beauty of the world it illuminates." He paused and looked at their clasped hands.

Jaelle couldn't have spoken even if she had anything to say.

"The problem," he continued, his voice nearly a whisper, "is that...just as you're trapped here away from the sun, we can't see the Maker's goodness until our eyes are opened for us." He chuckled. "I suppose those of us who are born into the outside world take it for granted. But that doesn't mean it's any less wondrous when the sun touches the horizon, and the world is painted orange and purple and pink and yellow and blue." His eyes were distant as he looked once more in the direction of the ocean. There was something in his face that she couldn't name as he gazed, unseeing, toward the west.

A calling. That's what it was. Like he was being pulled, in mind and body and heart back to his beloved ocean.

"But that doesn't tell me," he said hoarsely, turning back to her, "why you did what I asked you not to."

Jaelle opened her mouth to answer then paused. Why had she come? There had been a reason that morning, one she would have been able to verbalize. But as she gazed at him now, the shadows of evening casting half his face into darkness, she couldn't find those words.

"I don't know," she whispered.

He used the backs of his knuckles to trace her face, and she closed her eyes as she drowned in the bliss of his touch. Reaching up, she took hold of his wrist with both hands and held his fingers against her cheek.

"You don't know?" His voice was rough and sounded closer this time. But she kept her eyes closed as she tried to memorize the feel of his hand. She needed to remember this forever. "That's a lot of risk," he continued, "to come after someone without knowing why." She heard the slight smile in his words. "Especially a spoiled flirt of a prince without an ounce of common sense in his head."

Jaelle wanted to melt, but instead, she kept her eyes closed and focused on the heat of his palm. "I don't know who you're talking about."

"Maybe," he said, his face suddenly touching hers, his breath hot on her lips as he held her face between his hands, "I should introduce you to him. I hear he's quite the scoundrel."

"But I hear he's a married man." She laughed in spite of herself. What was wrong with her?

"That he is," he whispered, his lips brushing against hers.

"There's something I have to know first," she said as she drew back slightly, somewhat breathless. "Why did you choose a gem?"

"What gem?"

"For your mark," she said, feeling as though his response might send her soul into flight or break it into a thousand pieces. Her fate rested on whatever words he uttered next. And yet, before she gave herself to this man, heart and soul, she needed to know that he saw her for more than her gift. For more than the stolen value that wasn't hers. "You chose a gem," she said, holding his wrist up to show him. "Why?"

Understanding lit his eyes, and though she knew he couldn't see her face, she felt in that moment as if he were the first person to see her in all the world.

"You," he said, his voice like a caress, "are beauty itself, like a diamond that's caught the moon's light."

"But what about when we leave this place, and I stand beside all the other gems?" Her heart beat so fast she felt like she might pass out. "Will you still think me beautiful then?"

"No true diamond makes its neighbors any less bright." He leaned forward, and his lips traced the side of her face. "If anything, it only shines more for the light."

Something inside Jaelle broke open. Like flood waters racing out over a dusty plain, an emotion she couldn't name filled her entire being, and she pressed her mouth against his with a new kind of desperation. Warnings, like bells, pealed in the back of her mind, screaming of the danger she was placing her heart in. But as she sat there in his lap, wrapped in his strong arms, his mouth hot on hers and his hand tenderly exploring her face, her heart was too full to listen.

CHAPTER 43

NOT THIS ONE

J aelle woke up the next morning feeling gloriously rested. Without opening her eyes, she decided she would be content never to move again. Instead, she inhaled deeply, letting the sensation of his arms wrapped around her encompass her entire being. After talking for hours and kissing him more times than she could count, she'd finally fallen asleep with her head on his chest, knowing that even in the dungeon, she would sleep without harm. For the first time since her mother had held her, that vague, hazy figure she'd tried so many times to recreate in her mind, Jaelle felt safe.

He was still leaned up against the cell wall, and she was on his lap, curled up like a kitten, her cheek against his chest. She could feel his warmth through his shirt, and there was something soothing about the rise and fall of his chest.

And there was no doubt in her mind that she loved him.

She was in love with Prince Lucas of Maricanta.

Love was strange, though, she mused as she opened her eyes to study the calloused hands that held her. She'd always wondered what it would feel like to be in love. She'd asked Selina once, and Selina had scoffed. Love was the unfortunate result of humans standing too close to one another, was her reply.

Then Seth had come along, and Jaelle had been sure Selina was in love with him. He was handsome, and he'd kept the other men away from both of them, an act sure to win even Selina's heart. He'd said he wanted to marry her and had even talked often about how life would be on the other side of the wall, when they could live as a happy family should. And when Selina was really his wife, Jaelle had assured herself, they would give themselves to one another, heart and soul. And Selina would believe in love, too.

But Seth's affections dried up and crumbled compared to the attentions of Lucas. Even when they'd argued like old women throughout their journey, snipping at each other for the sake of having the last word, never once had he brushed her off like she was less than him. Even in his anger, he'd protected her. He'd put his own mission in danger and come after her when she was taken. And somehow, despite her mask, he'd seen her.

So why did love feel so strange? She wasn't giggling over him the way the girls at the well had about the men they'd hoped would ask their fathers for them. Her emotions were oddly calm, like a pond in the morning after a storm had passed in the night.

Perhaps that was just it, though. Her love wasn't one of raw feelings and emotions. She felt those, of course. But the love that now filled her heart to overflowing had been pooling inside her for the last two weeks, before she'd even known it was there. Hers was a love born of actions and a knowledge that he had meant what he said at the wedding, choice or no choice. Even if he hadn't meant to do so in a romantic way, Lucas had loved her from the start, refusing to claim her because that was a decision, misguided as it was in Terrefantome, that he'd wanted her to make for herself. Even if she wasn't his first choice in a wife, she knew deep down that he would keep her faithfully until the day he died. And that kind of love was the kind she wanted by her side forever.

If the world had been a perfect place, Jaelle smiled to herself, playing with the corner of his shirt, she would have been the one at his side forever. There wouldn't be a disparity of birth or rank, and she would be at his back whenever danger called. They would sail off, chasing the sunset until old age or stronger duties claimed them, and theirs would be a love of choice.

But it wasn't a perfect world. And where delightful peace had made her feel aglow just moments before, Jaelle knew that it would be far from perfect unless they did something.

Well, unless she did something. As strong as he was, Lucas had no power here. He had nothing to barter with, nor did he have a choice in the matter of where they put him. Still, he'd gone willingly, giving up everything for her and for his people.

But Jaelle did have a choice. And she knew what she had to do.

She stood carefully, so as not to wake him. In the hazy morning light that came through the tiny barred window, she could see his bruises turning yellow and green, and blood was still caked near his ears and forehead, though she'd cleaned him off as best she could last night. She considered placing one last kiss on his temple but then decided against it. If he woke up, he would make this so much harder than it already was.

She went to the bars, where the guard, who had reappeared sometime after they'd fallen asleep, was trying to clean his knife blade with his spittle.

"I need to speak with the king," she called softly.

He raised an eyebrow.

"Tell him..." She faltered and took a calming breath. "Tell him I have a deal to offer."

The guard left, probably under orders to expect such a request, and returned quickly.

"Come with me," he said, unlocking the door and staring back at the diamonds strewn all over the ground.

She followed him back up the stairs, through the marble halls, and to the highest part of the castle's keep, her heart threatening to make her knees buckle with each step. The guard knocked at the large wooden door, this one painted red also, and called out, "Your Highness, I have the girl."

"Bring her in!" the king called back, his voice far too jovial for Jaelle's taste.

The guard opened the door and gestured for Jaelle to go inside. She raised her chin and forced herself to walk in resolutely, but the click of the door behind her nearly ruined her determination to be strong.

"Over here," the king called. He was sitting in a lounging chair out by the balcony, which was twice the size of Selina's. Jaelle forced her feet to carry her forward over the thick red and orange rugs, past the raised bed, which she couldn't look at for fear of getting sick to her stomach. Past the gilded mirror, past the wardrobes, and out to the balcony.

"Come," he said with an easy smile, gesturing to the plate of food on a small table beside his chair. On it was a bowl of grapes and blackberries. A few fancy bread rolls sat beside it, along with a slab of cold bacon.

"Have some. My cook seems to think I'm three men instead of one." He patted the slight paunch that was sticking out from beneath his robe, which showed far too much of his legs for Jaelle's taste, as they were splayed in a rather ungentlemanly fashion. She forced her eyes to stay on his face so she wouldn't gag as she contemplated what she was about to do. But then, she might as well get used to it.

"I have a proposal for you," she said, keeping her eyes focused on his.

"So you said." He grinned so widely she wanted to slap it off his face.

"Let my husband go free, and count Maricanta's debt paid. Then give him and his mother safe passage back to the ocean." She willed her voice to stay steady. "And I will stay here with you. I will give you diamonds for the rest of my life." Deep breaths. "I won't even try to leave."

He leaned back and studied her, and for once, his eyes stayed on her face. Or where her face should have been. Then he put down his goblet and folded his hands across his chest.

"How do I know you're telling the truth? What proof do I have that you won't try to go with him?"

Jaelle's stomach had a nearly painful tickle in it, as did her shoulders. *Don't do it!* her body seemed to scream at her.

She'd been so tempted last night. If anyone deserved to see her, it was Lucas. But even as he'd kissed her over and over again, his lips tracing the face he couldn't see, she'd known deep in her heart that this was the only way. She might not be able to be his princess, but she could keep him safe.

Her hands shook as she reached up to her face. Touching her temples with her third fingers, her cheeks with her forefingers, and her chin with her thumbs, she closed her eyes and felt a slight rush of air blow tendrils of hair across her face. When she opened her eyes, she sucked in a sharp breath.

The world, which had been full of dull hues of orange, red, and gold, was suddenly glowing. Her chest tightened as she looked around the room, drinking in the color and light as though she'd never truly seen before. How had she forgotten this? Had the world always been this brilliant?

"Well."

Jaelle refocused on Bartol, blinking rapidly, as if her new vision might make him go away. Unfortunately, he was still there, and by the upturn in his mouth, he seemed more than a little pleased. Her heart fell.

"Selina was right. You did turn out well." He stood and walked over to her, leaning in close. She did her best not to flinch when he reached up to touch her jaw. Lucas had done the same the night before, and she'd eaten it up like she was starving. Now she just wished he would stop.

"You're not beautiful in the traditional sense," the king was saying as she roused herself from her sorrow. "But there's something...unusual about you." He stepped back, and as he studied her again, his smile began to grow, and his eyes grew brighter. "Yes. Like East meeting West. You'll do perfectly!" He clapped his hands like a little boy and whirled around, bellowing at the top of his lungs. "Call Selina! And find someone to prepare the wedding. I want this wedding to be a proper enough to rival any other. The most well-attended in the western realm." He dashed off, seeming to forget Jaelle completely.

Several minutes later, a familiar hand lifted her face. Jaelle didn't realize until she looked into the eyes of her sister that she was crying. She braced herself for the onslaught of advice and scorn she was sure to receive after their parting before. Instead of haughty words or condescending admonitions, however, Selina did what Jaelle had expected from her yesterday. She wrapped Jaelle in her arms and held her as Jaelle sobbed into her shoulder, smoothing her hair and whispering soft words of comfort. Finally, when Jaelle had cried what felt like every tear she had, Selina leaned back and studied her.

"You're more beautiful than I imagined," she whispered,

touching Jaelle's face. Her own eyes glistened and she moved a lock of hair off Jaelle's forehead.

"Not for the one I want to be." Jaelle burst into another round of tears.

"Why?" Selina asked, taking Jaelle's hands. "What made you change your mind?"

Jaelle sniffed. "Maricanta doesn't need another war right now. They can't afford it, Lucas says."

Selina's eyes hardened slightly. "Did he ask you to give yourself up to the king?"

It was a strange question, considering Selina had been the one to send Jaelle to the dungeon in the first place. But Jaelle wasn't in the mood to argue.

"No. He would have done everything in his power to stop it if he'd known." She squared her shoulders. "He sacrificed everything on this journey, for me and for his country. And if I can keep it from all being in vain, at least I'll know I had a purpose for once in my life."

"You've always had a purpose," Selina said, taking her hand and leading her back toward the door. "But you're doing the right thing in this."

"I traded a good man for an evil one," Jaelle said bitterly as they left the king's chambers.

Selina smiled sadly. "All men are the same. Some just mask it better than others."

Jaelle shook her head. "Not this one."

CHAPTER 44

CHOICE

After they left the king's chambers, Selina informed Jaelle that she was free to explore the castle. Selina even offered to show her the room she'd been preparing for her. Apparently, Jaelle was that predictable. But Jaelle declined and said she needed to go back to the prison.

Selina pursed her lips. "Bartol won't like that. He's already jealous that the prince marked your wrist first."

"I need to convince Lucas to leave me be," Jaelle said in dead voice. "Or he'll keep trying to come back."

For once, Selina didn't argue. Instead, she wrote a little note on a small, square piece of parchment. Then she poured a little circle of orange wax and sealed it with a signet ring before giving it to Selina.

"This will get you down into the dungeon. Be quick."

Lucas was awake and standing when Jaelle came down the stairs, and he was grasping the bars with both hands.

"Jaelle!" he shouted, standing on his toes as though that might get him closer to her.

"I need to speak with him alone." Jaelle told the guard. The guard gave her a skeptical look until Jaelle produced Selina's seal. "The king is allowing him to go free."

The man looked at her like she'd asked him to swallow one of Selina's toad, but after taking a long look at the paper with the wax seal in her hands, he nodded and unlocked the cell. Then he went to stand at the top of the stairs while Lucas rushed out and gathered her up, crushing her to his chest.

"I didn't know where they'd taken you." He sounded like he was choking. Jaelle pulled back enough to see tears rolling down his face.

He met her gaze and stared into her eyes with the purest intensity she'd ever seen. After several seconds, though, his mouth dropped, and he grasped her face gently.

He'd realized the mask was gone.

"You're so beautiful," he whispered, tracing the outlines of her cheeks, nose, forehead, and brows. "Just like I imagined you." Then the joy melted from his face and he took a step back, and dread washed over Jaelle. "But your mask," he said slowly. "When did you take it off?"

Jaelle just swallowed.

"Jaelle." His jaw twitched. "What did you do?"

This was it. She'd gotten married to a man who might be the most loyal creature in the world...and she was going to have to bring that loyalty to an end. It hurt her chest and made her dizzy.

Her voice was unsteady.

"I've decided to stay with my sister."

For a moment, he looked a lot like a lost little boy. "But—"

"I've arranged for the king to give you and your mother safe passage to the ocean," she said, keeping her voice flat. It was easier than maneuvering around the emotions battling inside her. Fear. Regret. Loss. Anger.

Shame.

"And what," he stepped closer again until his face was right above hers, "was the cost of such a deal?"

So he knew it was a deal. For some reason, this brought Jaelle more relief than she could say. At least he knew she hadn't wanted to betray him. She hoped.

She shrugged and kept her eyes fixed on his neck instead of his face. "Does it really matter? Everyone wins this way. I've found my sister. You're going home, and Maricanta will avoid war."

"And the mask?" His jaw trembled slightly.

Jaelle looked away. "Just part of the deal."

"No." He took her chin and tilted her face up, forcing her to meet his gaze. His wonderful, murderous gaze. "I won't let him do this."

"Do what?" Jaelle tried to look away, but he wouldn't let her.

He pointed at the door. "That man is going to hurt you!" he shouted. "He is going to hurt my wife!" His voice broke on the last word, and the next thing Jaelle knew, he had cupped her face gently. "We'll run away." His voice trembled , but he gushed on anyhow. "I'll figure out a way...something. And we'll all go. The Taistille will help us." Tears began to fall even harder until he was sobbing, and Jaelle felt something inside of her crack.

"Hurry up," the guard called from the top of the stairs.

"You need to go now." Jaelle's voice sounded strange, even to her. "I don't know how long Bartol will wait."

Lucas took a step back, and Jaelle prayed he wouldn't see just how much it hurt to say those words.

"You're giving me no choice, then," he whispered.

Jaelle looked at the ground. "Everyone has a choice. I'm just making yours more clear."

Neither of them spoke until the guard called down a final warning.

When Lucas spoke again, his words were sharp enough to shred leather. "Just so you know, I meant it."

She looked up at him miserably.

"That's right." His voice wavered as he glared at her through wet eyes. "I meant every word I said when I made those vows."

Jaelle closed her eyes. This was too much. Her resolve was slipping, and if she wasn't careful, she'd let him see just how much this hurt. How much she wanted him to stay. How much she wanted to go with him.

But wishes wouldn't keep him alive. Her sacrifice, however, would.

"You meant the words," she said stiltedly, "because you didn't want to sully your honor."

"No." He lifted his hand, and she flinched. But his touch, of course, was gentle as he put his hands on her face and turned her toward him once more. "I meant them because in the short time I've known you, I've realized that you're what I want—"

"No!" she sobbed. "No, you don't want me. I'm not royal. I'm an ignorant girl who's known nothing but a world without color. You might think you want me now, but one day, you'll wake up and realize you regret it." Her voice fell to a whisper. "You already said so yourself."

"So that's what you think of me?" He scoffed. "And when did I say that?"

She willed herself to glare at him. "You said we could get our marriage annulled."

"That we could, not that we would!"

"Just get your mother and go, Lucas! Unless you think she'll be happy to live as a Taistille for the rest of her life!"

Lucas stared at her. His hands fell to his sides, and he was breathing hard. Jaelle meant to stay strong as he stared at her, but she only sobbed harder. Calloused hands took hers.

"Please don't do this," he whispered. "I beg you."

Hating herself for the pain she was about to cause them both, Jaelle stood on her toes and wrapped her arms around his neck. He met her lips willingly, but his mouth trembled, and she could taste tears. For one second longer, she kissed him. Then two. Then three. Then, with a pain that was nearly crippling, she let go.

"Goodbye, Lucas."

And while he protested, taking her by the shoulders and begging her to give him a chance to think of something new, she called up to the guard. "He's ready."

The guard came down and tried to escort Lucas forcefully, but Lucas yanked his arm away and said he could walk by himself. She walked behind him in silence, trying to ignore the way he continued to shoot glances at her until they came to the main entrance.

The guard held the door open, but Lucas paused once more to look at Jaelle.

The door is open, she thought as they shared one last gaze. *I'm not making you walk through it.* If she was honest, some foolish, silly part of her heart wished he would stay. To what end, she didn't know. She just wished...

She didn't want to let go.

"Think of me," she said instead, "when you see the sunset on the water."

He watched her for another moment longer before turning slowly, as though in a dream, and walked out the door.

The moment the door closed, Jaelle fell to her knees, strange, guttural wails building in her chest.

He was gone. And this time, she knew it was forever. And though she knew she had forced his hand, for she truly had left him no other choice, the sight of him walking away was more than she could take.

Before she could fall apart completely, though, Selina's strong arms were lifting her to her feet.

"It's better this way," she whispered in Jaelle's ear. "He would have gone eventually."

Jaelle shook her head and pulled out of her sister's embrace. "Where's my room?" she choked out through her tears. Selina studied her for a moment before nodding and leading the way.

When she was finally in her new chambers, Jaelle began to cry all over again. The room wasn't bare and empty the way Selina had made her believe. Instead, it was nearly as furnished as Selina's had been. This only sickened Jaelle more.

They had known she would do anything for Lucas, including forcing him to go. And she had.

CHAPTER 45

TOO LATE

Jaelle tried to fall asleep, but the moment she lay down, she knew sleep would be impossible. Pulling herself off the bed, she ignored the mirror on purpose and forced herself over to the little balcony that was already open to let in air.

For one short night, she'd been sure happiness truly existed. All Lucas's words about the Maker's goodness and her innate knowledge that something better existed had awakened a faith she hadn't touched since the day the holy man had died. For now that she thought about it, she remembered nights of lying awake in her little bed, long before Selina or Chiara had ever entered her life. Each night she'd spent talking to the Maker about all she'd seen and done that day. And she'd nearly always fallen asleep in peace.

But those days had been simple and full of the lies her father had fed her about the future. Now her eyes had been opened to all the danger and pain the world had to offer. Her father and the holy man were dead. Lucas was gone. Selina was being transformed before her, and Jaelle was no closer to saving her than she had been before. And after being so close to reprieve only to have it snatched away time and time again, Jaelle knew she'd never have such childlike faith again. Not after what the Maker had done to her and everyone she loved.

She leaned against the doorpost to look at the forest she'd

somehow left only the morning before. But instead of wind in the trees, she saw movement just below her balcony. She straightened and went to the edge to see better.

The clouds were thicker than usual that morning, but even so, she was able to make out movement against the waving grain. Sure enough, there was Selina. Instead of her flowy garments, though, she was wearing men's trousers and a shapeless tunic, and her hair had been tucked up beneath a hat. Jaelle might have mistaken her for a man, except that Selina had often used the same disguise to sneak into town when they were younger. And this time, she was holding a shovel.

But why was she leaving the castle under disguise? And why was she walking the same direction Lucas would have gone?

Jaelle looked around her balcony to realize with great glee that the architectural design had created natural holes in the walls that were just the right size for footholds. Tying her skirt into a knot, she climbed out over the balcony's edge and dug her hands and feet into the soft mortar and exposed brick. It seemed a long way down at first, but she knew they had only placed her on the second story of the building. She'd climbed higher trees as a child, trying to get the dry, wrinkled apples at the tops of the branches. In just a moment, she was on the ground, and her heart soared as she took off after her sister.

Only to run right into the guard gate.

"Going somewhere?" He raised his eyebrows.

Jaelle stared stupidly up at him, trying desperately to come up with an excuse. He'd taken her arm and was about to march her back to the main door when she remembered something.

"This is my sister's!" She yanked the paper with the broken wax seal from her gown and shoved it in his face. "She left just a few minutes ago, and I need to catch her!"

The logic of this, of course, was absurd, but it was all she could think of. The man glowered at her for a moment, but after examining the wax seal for himself, he thrust it back at her, and she breathed an inner sigh of relief that he, too, seemed unable to read.

"Follow her," he growled. "I'll be watching you, though. You'd better be back soon, or I'll have these forests crawling with the king's men, and that prince and all those Taistille will be bleeding in their beds tonight."

Jaelle shuddered and nodded before taking off through the open gate. She just hoped that whatever she was running toward, she wasn't too late.

CHAPTER 46
POISON

Lucas barely had enough time to scramble up a tree when the search party made its way into the clearing. He wasn't surprised, as he'd been listening for footsteps since he'd left the castle. Unlike Jaelle, he knew better than to trust the king.

"He's here." He heard Selina's voice through the leaves below him. "We only spotted him a minute ago. He couldn't have gone far."

"Want us to search?" a man asked.

"Prince Lucas," Selina called. "I know you can hear me. So I suggest you come out so we can have a civil conversation."

Lucas only crouched deeper in the leaves. If she'd wanted a civil conversation, she wouldn't have brought three men with her.

"If you don't," she continued, "you should also know that we know where your mother is. And I'll not hesitate to burn down this entire forest. We'll see what your Taistille think of you then."

Lucas closed his eyes and cursed. *Why must you give them the upper hand at every turn?* he asked the Maker. There was a reason he'd refused the king's escort. There he wouldn't trust the king enough to escort him to the garderobe, let alone back to his own country. Of course, the only reason he'd been willing to walk out of that dungeon at all was because of his mother. Jaelle had known how to corner him completely. And, it appeared, her sister did, too. There was no way the Taistille would be able to pack up their homes and families and escape from a fire. Their vans were impressive, but by no means fast.

With a silent groan, he dropped from the tree.

"There you are." Selina smiled, and Lucas could see why Jaelle had described her as beautiful. Of course, that had probably been before snakes started poking their forked tongues from her mouth. How did she even talk like that?

As if answering his question, she waited until the snake, which was unusually long for the ones he had seen her produce, had slithered out of her mouth and wrapped itself around her outstretched arm.

"I knew you could be reasonable. Jaelle wouldn't have been infatuated with you if you weren't."

"What do you want?"

"I wanted to tell you that I know your kind."

Lucas snorted. "My kind?"

"I don't know if Jaelle mentioned it, but my mother and I are from Maricanta. In fact, I saw you often as a child. My father worked in the shipyards, and you would sometimes ride down with your father to inspect the cargo."

A sharp pain flashed in Lucas's chest. He'd loved those excursions. It had been his father's way of getting him close to the naval ships when his mother threw a fit about their impropriety for a young prince.

He cleared his throat. "And?"

"I watched you. And I'll admit that you're different from many of the other men, even in Maricanta."

Lucas gave her a wry smile. "You must not have known me well, because I was renowned throughout the court as a flirt from the time I turned ten."

"Perhaps." She pursed her lips. "But you were loyal before you were a flirt. And from what I see, that hasn't changed."

Lucas gave a start. She really had watched him. It was the trait his father had most praised him for as a child.

"I also know," she said more quietly, "that you're going to try to rescue my sister."

"But why go through all the motions of betrothing us if you didn't want us to marry?" he asked, exasperated. It was a question similar to the one he'd been asking the Maker. *Why give her to me and then yank her away?*

"At the time, my proposition was ideal. I'd made contact through some of my customers at the tavern and was able to purchase a way to send out letters. You were one of the least objectionable men I could think of, and I knew you'd be able to provide her with everything she would need to thrive." She frowned slightly as a burst of toads made their way down her chin and looked down at the serpent, which was still sliding slowly down her arm. "She deserves to thrive." Then she looked back up at him. "But things have changed. I can make her a queen now. Not even you can offer her that."

"What if she doesn't want to be queen?"

"She doesn't see what's best for her. Not yet." Selina's eyes softened. "She's young. But she will one day when all of this is done." She straightened and met his gaze once again. "And I can't have you coming back for her."

The hairs on the back of Lucas's neck stood on end.

"The king let me go free."

"This," she said, "is between you and me. I've been working since I was fourteen to keep my little sister safe. She was my gift after everything I loved was torn from my hands. She gave me a purpose, and I'm not about to abandon my duty to her now."

Talking. He needed to keep her talking. He'd managed to back up about six inches as she spoke. He just needed a few more feet so he could get enough of a proper head start to hide and take the guards out one by one.

"You wouldn't have to stay here, either," he said, slowly easing his right heel back. "You could return to Maricanta as well."

"To what?" she spat. "The father that abandoned me when my mother was exiled? The one who let her take me into this land of filth and sin?" The snake hissed.

"With Jaelle," he said, keeping his voice calm. "That's all she's ever wanted. She wants to see the world with you. That's the whole reason we made the deal for her to be my guide. So she could help you be free of the Sorthileige—"

"Maybe she wanted that once. But after the way she looked at you, I know that I'll never be enough for her now. Not anymore."

Selina's voice cracked. She swallowed hard and lifted her arm with the snake. "But I'll be cursed if I let any man break her the way my father broke me."

"So how long are you going to force her to live with that lecher as his wife?" Lucas spat. "You don't think *that* kind of cruelty will break her?"

Selina gently unwound the snake from her arm and held it, slowly rubbing its scales.

"When my mother dragged me here, I was afraid and angry. But Jaelle taught me to be strong. And now I'm going to be just that for her."

"By hurting her?" Lucas cried. The flame in his chest roared as he imagined the kind of pain Jaelle would go through as her dreams were broken and her heart was shattered. She was so fragile already. Would there be a way to even pick up the pieces by the time he made it back?

"Sometimes love is poison," Selina said. "But sometimes the poison is necessary." And with that, she flung the serpent at Lucas.

CHAPTER 47

CONTRIBUTE

Jaelle followed her sister and her guards at a distance. She couldn't tell how many there were. Two? Three? Enough to stay a long way back.

They walked along the path Jaelle had taken to the castle until they reached the forest. She had to follow at an even slower pace then, hopping from tree trunk to tree trunk for shelter until they came to a stop in a clearing. If she wasn't mistaken, they were no farther than five or ten minutes from the Taistille camp. She crept closer to the voices until she could make out the figures of Selina and Lucas facing one another in the clearing.

Selina cradled a snake in her hands, and Lucas looked as though he were about to bolt. Jaelle prayed that he would. Before she could finish the prayer, though, her sister threw the snake at Lucas.

The snake sank its fangs into his ankle and held on tightly. Jaelle screamed, and her knees buckled. But as soon as the shriek left her mouth, along with a very large gem, a meaty hand muffled the sound. When she tried to break free, the guard grabbed her, wrestled her arms down, and held them behind her back.

"Best to let the king's adviser attend to royal business," he whispered in her ear. Jaelle fought, doing her best to step on his feet and kick him in the knees, but the guard held on, pressing her against him so tightly that she couldn't move.

Selina turned, and when she saw Jaelle, her eyes widened slightly. But then she lifted her chin stubbornly and waved in the direction of the palace.

"Seamus, stay here and make sure he's good and dead. You can start digging a hole while he dies." She tossed him the shovel, which had been leaning against the trunk of a nearby tree. "Throw him in and bury him as soon as you're done. I don't want the Taistille finding him and interfering. The rest of you, come with me."

Jaelle hung limply in the man's arms as he dragged her back to the castle. Never in her life, not even after the holy man or her father had died, had she felt such mind-numbing pain.

The man she loved was dead. And the woman who had loved her was gone. For while the tall, graceful figure walking before her was still very much alive, she wasn't the sister Jaelle had cherished and chased. This creature was entirely new.

And Jaelle was alone.

CHAPTER 48
WEDDING PLANS

T'll take her to her room," Selina said to the guard after they'd arrived back at the castle. The guard handed her over, but he gave her a long look before leaving them. He needn't have bothered, though. Jaelle couldn't have fought if her life had depended on it. It was all she could do to let them drag her along as she relived the way his face had looked the second the snake dug its fangs deep into his ankle.

Her mind went in circles as she tried to work out just how he might have died. The arms that had held her the night before had been too strong for death. The lips that had whispered gentle, soothing words into her hair and kissed her face were too soft and warm to grow cold and stiff.

How could you? Jaelle screamed silently at the Maker. *He trusted you. And you let the evil of this land devour him. You let it devour everything good and light!*

Maybe that was what hurt the most. Well, after losing Lucas. She'd been so ready to believe. She'd wanted to embrace the Maker and the hope that Lucas promised0. Not only had she lost the man she loved, the kind of man she thought didn't exist. She also lost the one she'd believed to carry him.

"This way, Jaelle," her sister said gently, ushering Jaelle toward a part of the castle she'd never seen before.

Jaelle, too tired to fight, let her sister lead her down a few corridors and out into the weak sunlight of a courtyard nearly the size of her room.

She looked around as her sister bade her, but inside, she felt like her mind had been separated from her body and was watching from somewhere above.

In vain. It had all been in vain. Removing her mask for the king. Sending Lucas away after breaking his heart. Spending the rest of her life in this prison, a future of being mined for her jewels and paraded about by her soon-to-be husband. Everything had been for naught. Jaelle slumped into one of the benches and then laid down on it and shut her eyes tightly in an effort to fight the memory of death on his face.

"I know it's not the garden you had at home." Selina said, her voice suddenly shy. "But I've already ordered my servants to find me all your favorite seeds, as well as some new ones." Jaelle cracked her eyes open to see Selina's eyes, bright with the excitement Jaelle had once loved. She gestured to the rows of soil that had already been turned. When Jaelle didn't respond, she stepped closer and began to wring her hands. "Jaelle?"

But Jaelle just hugged her middle and glared at the sky. She could have been gardening in the sun if everything had gone as it was supposed to. A real garden with sunlight and rain and clean air and a view of the ocean Lucas loved so much.

"Jaelle." Selina came to stand beside her. "Do you like it?"

Jaelle ground her teeth and kept her eyes straight ahead. This work couldn't have been done in a single morning. No, Selina must have ordered it completed as soon as Jaelle had appeared. As if she had known Lucas was going to die.

Jaelle's breathing became strained.

The way Selina's face fell would have filled Jaelle with shame and remorse three weeks ago. Yesterday, it would have filled her with fear. But now, all she felt was...nothing. Jaelle was simply numb.

"I thought you would be pleased," Selina said, wringing her hands even harder as she looked back at the garden.

How had things changed so fast, Jaelle wondered, not sparing her sister a second glance. Her entire journey had revolved around saving Selina...until it hadn't. When had Lucas become the center of her world?

"Say something," Selina whispered.

"You want to know what I think?" Jaelle's voice was nearly inaudible even to herself, but Selina somehow heard and nodded.

"I think," Jaelle said, letting her voice harden as she finally brought her eyes down to meet her sister's, "that you took the man I loved and used him against me. And then you toyed with him. And then you lied to me..." She was shouting now as she sat up and faced her sister. "And you killed him like a coward where no one could see!"

Selina stiffened. "It was for your good."

"You killed a man who was trying to save his people!" Jaelle shrieked. "And me! He wanted to save me!"

"Jaelle, it's—"

"It's wrong," Jaelle snapped. "It's all wrong."

At this, Selina, who had been staring at her like she was speaking gibberish, smacked her lips and rolled her eyes. "Who's to say what's right and what's wrong? And that man is far from innocent. If you knew the number of men he's killed—"

"Selina, we have staked our entire futures on what's right and wrong! Everything we worked for was to get out of this...this... cesspool of evil!"

"Is it?" Selina sighed and clasped her hands in front of her. "I know," she said in a low voice, "you want to leave so badly, but is there really a difference between here and there?" She went to Jaelle and took her hands. "Love, the men outside these walls can be just as evil and conniving as the men here. They just have to be more underhanded about it, but that doesn't make it any more tolerable."

"But why?" Jaelle laughed without humor. "*Someone* made the laws that force them to be underhanded in the first place, instead of committing their sins out in the open without shame like they do here."

"Jaelle, you can't—"

"We know there's more than this!" Jaelle leaned forward as Lucas's words came to her mind unbidden. "Or we wouldn't be fighting the king and all his men. You wouldn't have saved me all those times from Chiara, and you wouldn't have schemed out all of this for my sake if you didn't believe."

Selina's lips thinned. "The longer I live, the more I'm realizing that good is nothing more than a point of view. You'd do well to learn the same."

Jaelle squeezed Selina's hands. "But if that's true and no one set boundaries for good and evil, then how can you talk about deserving and undeserving and innocent—"

"I hope," Selina said in a low voice, "that you're not referring to your husband's superstitions."

In spite of the anger she'd felt for the Maker just moments before, Jaelle's anger at her sister was even greater. She lifted her chin.

"And what if I am?"

"You've known the man for what, two weeks?"

"Look around us, Selina!" Jaelle gestured to the towering walls surrounding the courtyard. "Have you ever met a man on this side of the wall like Lucas?"

Selina glared at her.

"Well, have you?"

Selina huffed. "No."

"Think about it!" Jaelle pleaded. "The people here believe in nothing more than putting themselves first. But Lucas is different!" Her mind wouldn't allow her to say *was*. Not yet. "He has done nothing but put others before himself. And if believing in the Maker makes him different from everyone else, then..." She let her hands fall helplessly as the conclusion became inescapable. "I want that."

For as much as she wanted to deny the god that let Lucas die, she could not.

"Then you're a fool." Selina turned sharply and headed for the door. As she slammed it shut, Jaelle thought she heard the distinct sound of crying.

She went back to the bench and let herself collapse onto it. What had happened? How had she gotten here? Then her heart stopped. She wasn't the only one in a dire place.

Maricanta was now without its youngest prince and military head.

King Michael would probably go to war.

Terrefantome was about to become the richest kingdom in the realm.

And Lucas was dead. It always came back to Lucas and the stabbing awareness that he was dead.

But...what if he didn't have to die in vain? What if this trek yielded something good and beautiful after all?

In an instant of clarity, Jaelle knew what she needed to do. She stood and ran to the door. Before going through, however, she forced herself to slow. Sprinting the length of the palace would be preferable, but that would draw attention. So she forced herself to walk until she found her sister's chambers. As she knocked, she put together an excuse that might convince her heartbroken sister to let her in. But when no one answered, her heart lifted. Even better was when she tried the handle to find that Selina must have forgotten to lock her door.

I wish I knew more about you, she prayed to the Maker as she stepped silently inside and closed the door behind her. *But if you do care about goodness and justice, please let me find something I can use to stop them.* It felt silly, thinking to the air. But Jaelle was too desperate to question Lucas or his "superstitions" now.

Selina was somewhat ridiculous about parchment. She hoarded piles of it wherever she could. Back at home, she'd slip it beneath their mattress whenever Chiara came to check on them. For while Jaelle couldn't read or write, Selina could. She'd tried to teach Jaelle once, before Chiara had caught them and forbidden it. Selina was meticulous about keeping lists and notes. At home, she'd even made notes to herself of how much meats cost in the market during the different seasons. If she'd written that much at home under her mother's watchful eye, Jaelle knew there was no way she would have left her plans unwritten here.

Jaelle headed to with her sister's desk, for want of a better place to start. Sure enough, there were piles of paper all over the desk and inside its drawers. Plans for the castle, for Jaelle's room, and lots of other papers that were identifiable to Jaelle only because they had lots of drawings on them along with the words. But nothing that seemed of the dangerous sort.

The longer Jaelle searched, the faster her heart beat. Selina could come in at any minute. But with Lucas's death painfully fresh in Jaelle's mind, assaulting her memory every time she blinked, Jaelle was beyond remembering any excuses she might make up for going through her sister's things. So instead, she searched faster.

Just as she was about to give up, Jaelle noticed a pair of stockings on the vanity. And only then did she recall.

Selina and her socks.

Running over to the vanity, Jaelle nearly shouted with relief when she felt the crackle of paper within the socks. Just as she was about to open it, however, she heard voices at the door. With nowhere to escape to, Jaelle dove under the bed and prayed her sister wouldn't see her since it sat on a raised platform.

"You said it would only take a minute."

Jaelle frowned. That sounded like the guard, Victor. The one that had made her uncomfortable on the first day and had raised Selina's ire on more than one occasion.

"It will. I left it..." Selina's steps stopped beside the vanity. "Where did it go?"

Jaelle realized with dread that they must be looking for her prize, and she greatly wanted to kick something. She couldn't read, but the Taistille could. If she could deliver Selina's plans to them, they might be able to stop her. But now Selina wanted those plans back. And it sounded like she might start looking in earnest at any moment.

With only seconds to make her decision, Jaelle rolled the socks gently just to the edge of the platform, where they stuck out from under the bedding. Selina searched for several minutes, but just as her voice was becoming laced with panic, she noticed them.

"Here it is!"

"Finally," Victor muttered. His heavy footsteps came to stand beside Selina. "Oh, I meant to ask you. Has Tumen confirmed that they'll recognize us?"

"Yes. If we agree not to open the gates in their direction."

"What did they want in return?"

"They want to plunder Destin, which I gave them the sole right to, at least from our end. It's not like we'll need the Fortiers' treasures with my sister here."

"Speaking of your sister, will we have enough to purchase the weapons soon?"

"I'll make sure we do. And I've got agreements worked out with arms dealers at holes four, five, and seven." Paper crinkled. "See? They should have them here no later than the wedding."

"Which is..."

"In four weeks. Or so Bartol says." She paused. "And you're sure we have enough with invisibility?"

"We do. I counted at least a hundred last night. And we were missing some. Not that we need that many. I could take down an entire army myself if I went up against it invisible."

"What about——"

He growled. "And before you ask again, yes, the invisibility works outside Terrefantome as well. I've told you that time and time again."

"You forget." Selina sounded pouty. "Unlike *some* people, I haven't yet been here seven years." Then she sighed. "Now I just need to convince my sister."

"Sister or not, I don't understand why we have to hide things between us from the king." Victor took a step toward Selina.

"I told you," Selina said with a laugh. "He's a bit jealous."

"But he's getting a wife."

"He also likes to be the center of attention. Besides, it's only for a little while longer. Soon my sister will be queen, and we can do as we wish." She giggled a little. "Well, I can. *You* will still be beneath me. Oh, and while we're on that subject," she stepped back, her words suddenly clipped, "never go above my head to Bartol again."

Victor sighed. "What are you talking about?"

"With my sister. I had everything under control until you got sleazy with her and then turned me in."

"Are we still talking about that?"

"I'm just warning you that when it comes to my sister, you leave her out of your games."

"Very well." He huffed. "But it's not like you don't flirt with my men."

Their voices faded as they made their way out of the room, their conversation turning to another topic completely.

When they were finally gone, Jaelle climbed out from under

the bed and searched desperately until she found the sock, the paper folded and stuffed back inside. She pulled it out and looked at it longingly.

If only she could read!

But it didn't matter. If she could get this to the Taistille...or someone who might help...

But even as she contemplated possibilities, she knew they were all impossible. The guards would never let her leave again, and there was no one here she trusted enough to send the paper with. She stole out of the room, and as she walked aimlessly, her sister's conversation with Victor went through her head again and again.

So they planned on murdering the king soon after the wedding. That she gathered easily. But what would they need weapons for? And why were they so happy to let Destin fall to... What was that kingdom's name again?

Whatever their schemes, Jaelle understood one aspect of their plan with perfect clarity. They were going to use their invisibility against their neighboring kingdoms. And Victor had been right. A single invisible soldier would be able to take out a hundred from any other army.

Jaelle grieved, and her steps slowed. The Selina she knew wouldn't have spoken of murder with such composure.

She wouldn't have killed Jaelle's husband in cold blood, either.

In her musings, Jaelle wasn't looking where she was going, and as she turned down a new corridor, she caught her toe on a corner and stumbled. Instead of getting up, though, she remained on all fours, tears filling her eyes again as she saw Lucas on the ground, writhing in pain from the serpent's bite. A long, low sob tore itself from her chest.

She had come to save her sister. But in the end, it was her sister who was tearing apart every good thing Jaelle had come to know and love. And yet...

But no. It wasn't her sister who had done all this. Selina had only been trying to save her. It was the Sorthileige within her. Lucas had told her of all the dangers such evil could bring about, but only now did Jaelle see it clearly.

As she wiped the tears from her eyes, she also saw the small, clear diamond that had fallen against the marble floor as she'd let out her cry. It was smaller than even the smallest coin and would have been easy to miss if she hadn't already been on the ground.

And with brilliant clarity, Jaelle knew what she had to do.

Picking herself up off the floor, she turned toward the king's chambers for the second time that day. But this time, she couldn't get to him fast enough. She would save her sister, and with her, Terrefantome and all those kingdoms around her. The darkness might have taken her husband, but Jaelle would die before she let it touch anything else.

"Your Highness!" Jaelle burst into the king's study. With only a few books and even fewer pieces of furniture, it hardly looked like a study. Not that Jaelle cared.

The king looked up at her, surprise on his face. When the jewels from her outburst rolled onto the carpet at his feet, though, he gave her a saccharine smile.

"What can I do, my love?" he asked, coming to her from the other side of his desk.

Jaelle wanted to recoil from his touch as he took her wrists in his hands, but she forced herself to remain still.

"Is the wedding really to take place in four weeks?"

He nodded. "It is. I would have preferred it to be sooner, but the nations around us need to know what kind of wedding we're capable of hosting." His eyes glinted. "I've even invited foreign dignitaries from every kingdom in the realm to come and witness our day themselves." He lifted a finger and ran it down the side of her face, leaving what felt like an trail of ice wherever he touched. "Does that agree with you?"

As much as Jaelle knew she should say yes, she did her best to simply smile and thank him for his time. When he'd gone back to the parchment he was writing on, she walked as slowly as she could manage until she made it to the door. Then she found a nearby servant and asked them to take her to the laundering room.

The room was large and surprisingly full of windows, which were all open. She understood why, though, when she saw the laundry flapping in the littles breezes that blew through the clothes they had hung from the ceiling.

"Pardon me," she said, approaching the oldest servant in the room, a heavy woman with brown hair and sharp blue eyes. "I'm afraid I don't have much to do here until the wedding, as my sister's taking care of most of the preparations. Would you..." She paused, glancing around the room until she saw what she was looking for. "Would you be able to send up some of the laundry that needs darning and mending to my room?"

"You want to darn and mend?" The woman looked at her as if she were mad.

But Jaelle did her best to smile anyway. "I grew up mending my own clothes, and now that I'm here, I feel as though I have nothing to do."

The woman glanced at the door. "Um, what do you want to start with?"

Jaelle pretended to look around. "What about the guards' uniforms?" she asked after a moment. "They seem simpler than some of the ladies' fashions."

The woman studied her again, this time, with more than a hint of skepticism.

Jaelle needed to do something fast. So she leaned forward and dropped her voice to a whisper. "I know it's not expected, but there has to be *something* I could contribute in my gratitude for your aid. You would really be helping me avoid boredom."

"Contribute?" The woman looked long and hard at the large pink diamond that had just rolled out of Jaelle's mouth and landed on a pile of unfolded satins. "How so?"

With a grin, Jaelle picked up the diamond and handed it to her. A minute later, she was answering all sorts of questions from the other laundering girls, who seemed determined to squeeze every word possible from her as she waited for the first servant to gather the uniforms. Still, even if it was only the diamonds that changed their minds, Jaelle must have been convincing enough, for a few minutes later, she and a servant carrying her load of uniforms were headed up to her room.

Once the servant was gone, Jaelle pulled out the needle and thread that the laundering mistress sent up in the mending basket.

Then, carefully, she unpicked a hem that had been sewn into one of the legs.

They could all think they were using her, her sister included. But Jaelle was making this decision for herself. And hopefully, it would save them all.

Maker, she prayed as she attacked the uniform with needle and thread, *I...*

She what? *I wasn't sure I wanted to believe in you after you made me mad?* As if her desires had anything to do with whether or not the Maker existed. She sounded like a fool even to herself.

I feel like a fool. But if you can forgive me...for Lucas's sake, don't let his death be in vain. Please free my sister from this darkness. She paused. *And me as well. And please don't let it ever touch us again.*

CHAPTER 49
SO BE IT

Lucas drifted in and out of consciousness, though for how long, he couldn't tell. At first, whenever he was awake, he was only aware of the sharp pain in his ankle. Soon, though, the pain faded away and he felt like he was burning up from the inside. He heard voices sometimes, one in particular that sounded familiar and strangely comforting, but he couldn't make out who it belonged to.

As he floated through dreams, though, he knew somewhere deep down that someone special was missing. She'd been taken from him because he'd failed to protect her. He should be running back, snatching her up and whisking her home. That's what a good man was supposed to do. But he wasn't a good man because he wasn't going to find her. She was fading away, and all he did was lie there, fighting with the heavy clouds of confusion as his memories and fears circled in an eternal loop.

The first time his mind began to reconnect with his body was when the pungent scent of brine filled the air. A cool, wet breeze caressed his face, and for the first time, he realized he wasn't burning up anymore. Instead, he was propped up in the back of a cart, and the cart was moving toward the ocean.

This was good. Lucas couldn't remember where he was or what he was doing, but the ocean was always good. Now, where was his ship?

"Well, look who's alive."

Lucas looked to his right to find Esmeralda riding a horse beside him. She wasn't smiling. Then Lucas remembered.

Esmeralda.

Bartol.

Jaelle.

Lucas looked around wildly for any other reminder he might have missed, but before he could see much of the beach, his mother had wrapped him in her arms and was holding him tightly, her tears running silently down her face. But his mother never cried silently.

Lucas was briefly so surprised by his mother's unusual display of emotion that he let her do as she wished and looked back up to Esmeralda for an explanation.

"You were bitten by a serpent," the sehf said, still unsmiling. "Some of our children found you dying in the woods."

Lucas vaguely recalled the sharp pain in his ankle, which, now that he looked at it, was all bandaged up.

"You would have died had it not been for your mother," Esmeralda continued. "None of our healers had ever seen such a bite. But she insisted on using grass, and much to our surprise, you lived."

Lucas coughed. "You don't seem thrilled with that."

Esmeralda glared down at him through cold eyes.

"I truly thought you might save her. But then you came back. And she didn't."

Lucas could say nothing to this. His throat only grew thick, and his limbs, as they began to regain their feeling, felt flushed with the shame that threatened to consume him.

"I tried." His voice was so rough even he had a hard time understanding his words. "But she made a deal with the king to save me and my mother."

"And you chose to take it."

Lucas had been studying the horizon, where he was fairly sure he saw a ship, but at her words, he looked back up at the sehf.

"I didn't want to."

"But you did."

Lucas stared up at her miserably. Yes, he did have a choice. He could have refused to go and remained in the dungeons. What he would have done there, he didn't know, and he was certain his brother would have started a war over his disappearance. Nevertheless, leaving Jaelle behind had been his choice.

"I'm not saying it was the wrong choice." Esmeralda's voice was gentler this time, and she glanced at his mother, who was clinging to his arm, and for the first time in her life, seemed to be out of words. "As the prince, you had to choose for your country. As a son, for your mother." At that moment, one of her men rode up to her and claimed her attention. But her unspoken words hung in the air.

As a husband, he had to choose for his wife. And he'd hadn't chosen her.

"I'm coming back for her." He tried to sit up straighter, but to his surprise, the sehf shook her head.

"I'm afraid that's out of the question."

"What?"

"You've already brought enough unrest to our shores. Because of you, my friend's daughter has become the prisoner and mistress to a cruel man." She shook her head. "I cannot allow you to risk any more of my people in one of your quests."

"But you said—"

"*If*," she gave him a hard look, "in the unlikely chance we are somehow able to get her back, we will find a way to send her to you. Or at least, to send you word. But under no circumstances, are you to return." And before he could argue, she held up her arm and called for the group to stop. "This is where you go home, prince. And I can honestly say I hope to never see you again."

Lucas's mother helped him from the back of the cart, and she didn't even complain when his knees buckled and he nearly knocked her over. His body was beginning to regain its strength, but with it came pain and stiffness. Only with her help and the aid of a horse was he able to shuffle to the water, where Esmeralda rode up beside him to hand down the familiar shell necklace. But when he took it from her hand, she didn't let go. Instead, she leaned down.

"Mourn your wife, Lucas. Miss her. Learn to forgive yourself and move on. Perhaps the Maker will grant you love one day that will fulfill those hopes you had with her."

Lucas met her gaze, but for the first time in his life, he felt no urge to pacify. No thanks rose to his lips, nor did he try to play the part of an ambassador. Instead, he simply took the shell.

"You know I can't do that."

"We will have to kill you if you return."

He gave her a sad smile. "Then so be it."

Bold words for a man without a plan or even a safe way back into the country where his wife was being held hostage. But the sehf's threat of death couldn't stop his spirits from soaring as the water swirled around his feet. Cool and wet, it lapped at his burning skin and renewed his determination.

He would be back. Just as he was doing the impossible in escaping now, he would do the impossible and get back in. The Maker had made a way, and Lucas trusted that he could do it again. Then Lucas hurled the shell into the water.

Nothing happened.

A minute passed by. Then two. Then three. The small contingent of men and women that had accompanied the sehf glanced at her uneasily, and her mouth was drawn up tightly as she stared at the place where the shell had landed. Dread turned his veins cold as Lucas began to imagine all the reasons the shell might not have worked. Perhaps the rain had ruined it and already used up the magic. Or he hadn't thrown it far enough.

But before he could worry too long, a ripple went out from where the shell had plopped down in the waves. The ripple swelled as it moved out, faster and faster into the open ocean.

The water all along the coast burst into a swirling mass of colors, a rainbow glowing from within. And a hundred yards out from where he stood, a wave rose higher than any of the others. But rather than moving toward the shore, it stayed in the air. Ten feet, twenty feet, thirty feet high. And resting on the wave's crest was Arianna, the crown on her head shining like the sea in the midday sun. The water lifted her up in a continually flowing fountain that covered all but her shoulders and head. Her platinum hair blew back in the wind that seemed to come from the water, and her face was hardened as she slowly pointed her golden triton at the shore.

The water a few yards ahead of Lucas and his mother began to boil, and the rainbows moved toward them, tendrils of beaming color. The horse he'd been leaning against snorted, and Lucas barely missed being trampled as it scrambled away. Thankfully, by this time, he'd grown strong enough to stand with only his mother's help. And as soon as he was stable again, the water at his feet began to burn even hotter than his fever had. He looked back up at Arianna, who caught his eye and nodded.

He turned to his mother. "We have to go in!" he called over the roaring of the water.

She gaped at him. "We can't go in there! We'll boil alive!"

"It's safe!" he shouted. "Ari will take care of us. The Maker will take care of us. But we have to do it now!"

"I can't do it, Lucas!" His mother shook her head as tears streamed down her face.

"I need you, Mother!" He begged her with his eyes. If ever he'd needed his mother, it was now. "I can't make it without you."

She studied him for a long moment. And for a second, there was a glimpse of the soft, gentle mother he vaguely recalled as a small boy, back when his father was alive and they were happy. Finally, she nodded.

"Very well," she said, her voice nearly inaudible. "I'll try."

As they took their first step away from the shore, she stumbled under his weight. Lucas was by no means heavy, but he had a sturdier build than his brother. They recovered and managed to stay upright, though, and continued their trek. Slowly, slowly they shuffled forward, the water deepening around them. Soon it was up to his calves, then his knees. When it was around his waist, his mother slipped. Panic filled him as they fell backward, fear for his mother more than for himself. She didn't know how to swim, to his knowledge, and he was in no shape to save her. But just as his face sank below the surface, big hands lifted him by his shoulders, and a string was slipped around his neck. Lucas looked back to see a female mermaid taking hold of his mother as a large merman swam beside him.

"Just breathe," the Protector said as he began to propel Lucas deeper. "The charm will keep you safe."

No matter how many times Lucas wore one of the merpeople's charms, it felt wrong to take that first breath underwater. But as always, his lungs filled with air just as they would have on land, and he relaxed.

Only for a moment, though, for as they went deeper, he became aware of the thick billows of black smoke rising up in the water around them. He tensed, and had the cowardly urge to cry out as they moved closer to one to avoid another.

Despite his recent close encounters with Sorthileige, he felt no more comfortable with it than he had the first time he'd seen it up close. His skin crawled every time they came within feet of one of the black columns. He'd always heard his brother and Ari speak of the darkness that billowed up in the deeps, but never had he imagined it could be so visceral even beneath the sea.

After what felt like years, they made it into open ocean. Relief made him weak. But to his dismay, he almost instantly felt himself slipping back into unconsciousness.

CHAPTER 50

IF ANYONE CAN

The next time Lucas awoke, he was in his own bed. He didn't have to open his eyes to know where he was. The scent of bougainvilleas, Bithiah's favorite flowers, hung thick in the air around him. He could also just make out the smell of salt from his open window, through which he could hear the sound of the crashing waves.

Unfortunately, not all of him was at peace. From the stiffness in his limbs and the heat that radiated from his body like the midday sun, he could only guess that he'd fallen ill.

Again.

"You're awake."

Lucas opened his eyes to find his mother sitting on a chair beside his bed. The light of the late afternoon sun poured through the window on his northern wall, hitting his face and nearly blinding him. He'd been so long without the real sun that he briefly shied away before remembering how much he loved its touch.

"Jane," his mother called, ringing a small bell on the table beside his bed.

A young servant girl appeared at the door.

"Fetch the queen," his mother said, "and let Cook know we'll be needing some bread for my son's soup tonight as well."

Lucas blinked at his mother. But perhaps it was his ears, rather than his eyes that needed clearing. Fetch the queen? His mother hadn't called Arianna the queen since the day she'd taken her vows.

"Mother," Lucas tried to say, but it came out more like a croak than a word. His mother lifted a glass of water to his lips and let him drink until he was full. Not a muscle twitched, nor did she seem to mind the length of his sip. Instead, she waited patiently, and when he was done, helped him move to a sitting position.

Lucas regarded her suspiciously.

"How long have I been ill?"

His mother picked up a bowl of soup and began to feed him. Usually, Lucas would have shuddered at the thought of letting someone else feed him. But he was too interested in the state of his mother's senses to object.

"We've been home a week," she said, her brows slightly furrowed. "We thought you were out of danger when we reached the ship, but the poison must not have been all gone. And since we don't grow such grass here, we very nearly lost you." Her voice hitched, and she swiped at the corner of her eye.

"What changed?" Lucas asked, unable to look away.

"Arianna has had those merpeople...What does she call them? The ones with the healing songs?"

Lucas smiled. "Healers?"

"Yes, those ones. She's been giving them charms, and they've been coming up every night to sing to you. And when you started to falter during the day, when they couldn't be here, she sang to you herself."

That made sense. The merpeople's healing songs, or *koroses* as Arianna called them, were known throughout the world for their power. Their magic was usually reserved for their kind only, but at the moment, it seemed Lucas was entitled to special privileges. Of course, that probably had something to do with his being the brother-in-law of their queen.

They would have used their special charms infused with their powerful songs, like the one he'd worn, to give them temporary legs so they could come to the palace to sing to him at night. Unfortunately, Arianna was the only merperson able to expose her skin to direct sunlight, so she would have been the only one able to sing to him during the day, ill or not. He would have to remember to thank her later.

"Lucas," his mother said slowly.

He pushed himself slightly higher. She hadn't used such a genuine tone with him since his father had died.

"I'm..." She stared down at her hands. "I keep thinking about everything that's happened, and I...I wish to the Maker I could take it all back."

He could only watch her. Where was this coming from? And could it be real?

"And I mean *all* of it." She waved a hand at the window. "Going back to before I was married to your father, all the way to when I was a girl."

The servant girl came in with a bowl full of steaming hot bread. His mother thanked the child, another strange act in itself, and waited until she was gone and Lucas was chewing on the bread to continue.

"I wasn't a dramatic child by nature. It may seem impossible to believe now, but...I was really quiet. Sure, I've liked parties and pretty gowns since I can remember, but I wasn't the silly woman I'm sure you've come to know me as now."

If Lucas hadn't been stuffing his face with bread, he would have rung for someone to examine his mother for a fever as well.

"But I wasn't very old," she continued, "when I realized that my father was prone to dramatics. And hysterics. And as my mother died quite soon after I was born, I learned quickly that if I wanted him to see me or to pay heed to my needs, I had to cause a scene. So," she shrugged, "I learned to cause a scene, and my father learned to listen, and it wasn't long before I forgot that I was pretending."

Lucas shifted. "You weren't that way with Father."

His mother smiled gently at the ocean through his western window, her eyes shining slightly. A tear rolled down her face, followed by another.

"No, I wasn't. Your father was good for me." She laughed, a broken sound. "He didn't chase all the silliness out that my father had planted within me, but he brought back that part of me that I'd forgotten existed." Her jaw tightened, and the smile disappeared, and for the first time, Lucas saw pure pain on his mother's face. He reached out and took her hand, and she didn't pull away.

"When your father and your sister died," she said, her tears falling faster, "I felt like the sun had fallen out of the sky. Everything real that your father had brought with him was gone, and to make it worse, I'd lost my first baby, too. And all I knew how to do was fall back into the arms of my father and all the ridiculousness he required. He even told me once..." Her voice cracked, and Lucas squeezed her hand, far too close to tears himself to trust his voice. "My father told me that I was dishonoring your father's memory by keeping so quiet. He said if he didn't know better, he'd have thought me glad to be rid of him."

At this, true sobs broke through, but for once, Lucas didn't mind holding his mother as she cried. In a way, he felt like he was seeing her for the first time since he was a boy. Like his mother was coming home.

"I'm so sorry," she rasped between broken cries. "I knew it wasn't fair to you and Michael to make you carry the burden. But I didn't know what to do. And by the time I tried to fix it, I'd become as silly and useless as you ever accused me of being." Tears still fell, but she leaned back and took his face in her hands. "It wasn't until I saw your scar, though, that I really began to understand what I'd done." Her lips trembled again, but instead of wailing as she would usually do, her voice came out in a whisper, and her dark eyes were clearer than they'd seemed in years.

Lucas knew he should let it go. But years of pent up frustration and anger weren't quite ready to be gone so fast.

"But Michael told you—"

"I know." She squeezed her eyes shut and bowed her head. "He told me again and again, and I thought I understood. I just..." She looked up and met his gaze, her eyes still wet. "I didn't realize how deeply you'd suffered for me and for everyone else until I saw that scar. And then it all came crashing down. But I've been too foolish to know what to do about it since."

Lucas's thoughts and feelings warred within him. He was still angry. And yet...he needed to forgive her. She was contrite. Her thoughts were deeper and clearer than he'd believed possible.

For once, he didn't want to pacify his mother. He wanted to do just the opposite. But he knew, deep down in his heart, that for once, she not only wanted to hear words of kindness. She needed them.

"I suppose..." He cleared his throat. "Esmeralda said you're the one to thank for saving me."

His mother laid her face in her arm, and a shudder ran down her body. "When we heard you yell, some said it was merely young men roughhousing in the woods. But I knew your voice. And when the children found you and they brought you to me, all I could see was Maura's body washed ashore again. And I knew I couldn't lose another child. Not when I had the chance to save you." She trembled violently once more.

Lucas swallowed hard at the sound of his sister's name. "That was quick thinking, remembering the grass."

His mother wiped her nose. "Well," she said, her voice growing slightly petulant. "I wasn't about to let that awful event at the pond go unused. I figured that if the Maker had forced me to survive the worms and then Mila, he would want me to use that confounded knowledge I'd gained from there, too."

At this, Lucas had to laugh. And as they talked long into the night, little by little, Lucas began to truly hope that his mother...his *real* mother had returned to stay.

"What will you do?" she finally asked after he'd eaten his supper and the sun had fallen from the sky.

"About Jaelle?" he asked.

She nodded with a small, sad smile.

He huffed. "I'm not leaving her if that's what you mean."

"I knew you wouldn't."

"No." He shook his head. "I just have to come up with a way to get back in. And that's not going to be easy."

"Well," she said, squeezing his hand, "if anyone can, it'll be you."

Lucas smiled back, but as she busied herself ordering more food from the kitchen, he prayed desperately that she was right.

CHAPTER 51
HELP

Unfortunately, after his mother had kissed him on the head and wished him a good night as if he were a little boy, the feelings that had nearly consumed Lucas on the cart when he'd first awakened returned with a vengeance.

There were many to choose from, should he grow bored from one. Pain. His ankle felt as though someone had beat it with a bent nail sticking out of a long piece of wood. Dread over how long it would take for him to heal enough to attempt a return. Angst over what Jaelle might be suffering tonight on the other side of the wall.

But the worst was the guilt.

The unconsciousness was bad enough, periods of slumber where his mind continued to run in circles. But perhaps worse than the sleep was being awake. Because at least in his sleep, he was confused enough to temporarily forget the shame he wore like a robe when he was in his right mind. Because every time his mind was clear, he saw her again, the fear on her face as he'd walked away, the terror in her rich brown eyes. And he hated himself for it. He had his fair share of what others would call acts of bravery on the seas. But he hadn't been able to protect the one person in the world he was most responsible for. And guilt reigned supreme.

The next day, he woke up and immediately knew the strength had returned to his legs. After getting dressed, he made his way to his brother's study. Michael wasn't going to like what he had to say. But he knew his conscience would smite him until he did what was right. He only prayed that Michael's love for Arianna would soften his heart toward Lucas's cause.

"Lucas!" Michael jumped up from his chair and pulled Lucas into a fierce embrace. And Lucas held him back. He'd been sure at one point he would never see his brother again. When Michael let go, he took Lucas's face and studied him as one might look for cracks in a porcelain bowl after it's been dropped.

"You look like someone beat you with a dull knife."

"Thank you." Lucas gave his brother a sardonic grin when he let go. As Michael went back to his desk and leaned against it, Lucas let himself fall into one of the soft chairs and nearly groaned. Everything hurt. "Is Mother all right?" he asked as he tried to find the least painful position in which to sit.

Michael stopped. "I thought she'd come to see you."

"Oh, she has. She's spent nearly every hour of every day with me. I just..."

Understanding lit his eyes, and Michael nodded. "Oh, you mean with her sudden burst of clarity. Well, I can't read her mind or her heart, but I can tell you that she's definitely shaken up." Michael stood behind his desk instead of sitting and rubbed his eyes. "She hardly talks to anyone, just stares out at the ocean." He shook his head, a thoughtful frown on his face. "She's even been spending time with Claire and Lucy. And not once has she complained about their noise or their terrible jokes." He ran a hand across his face.

"Have you been eating?" Lucas asked. "You look thin."

"Searching for Mother has kept me slightly busy." Michael made a face. "And you're one to talk. Bithiah nearly fainted when she saw you."

Lucas took a deep breath and squeezed the arms of the chairs. "What did she tell you?"

"That she'd been contacted by a woman in Terrefantome claiming she had the perfect wife for you and that she snuck out to find the girl and bring her to you." Michael shrugged. "She *seemed* oddly transparent and...penitent. She's even been nicer to Arianna." He narrowed his eyes at Lucas. "Care to explain?"

Lucas paused. Had he only been gone a a month? It seemed like a lifetime. He felt like another man compared to the one who had sat in this very chair to plan his venture into the heart of evil itself.

"We made it into Terrefantome exactly as planned. The first night I was there, my guides were murdered. Apparently, Bartol has informants not just in Terrefantome, but in the surrounding kingdoms as well." Lucas gestured back at the door. "Including here."

Michael's head snapped up from the paper he'd been browsing. "Here?"

"He knew enough to have everyone in my group but myself murdered the first night I was there. He knew Mother was with me and where I left her when I went to deliver the money to the castle."

Michael kicked the leg of his chair and began pacing. Then he sat down and leaned over his desk.

"So what in the oceans was Mother doing in Terrefantome? Really. I want to know if she was telling the truth."

So Lucas recounted how Selina had contacted their mother, which led to his first meeting with Jaelle, and their subsequent pact. He ended with his successful payment to the king, but he left out the most vital detail, watching his brother carefully as he did. Michael was a good king, far better than Lucas would ever have been, a shining example of patience and grace. But even Michael had his limits.

"So..." Michael frowned. "The girl led you to the king. What happened next? I can't imagine Bartol took kindly to one of his own helping you out."

"He took her." Lucas's throat squeezed so hard it was difficult to talk. "And he's still got her in his castle." He cleared his throat. "She agreed to stay with him so I could go. She didn't even give me a choice." He tightened his grip on the armchair. "If it hadn't been for Mother, I would have stayed."

Michael covered his eyes and let out a gusty breath. After a long moment, he finally said, "I'm so sorry, Lucas. I know that must have been..." He shook his head. "I'm sorry."

"I'm going back for her though."

Michael looked up. "You're what?"

Lucas squared his shoulders. "I'm going back for her. You can do without me for a few months, and—"

"What are you not telling me, Lucas?" Michael leaned forward, the green in his hazel eyes standing out more than usual. "And don't bother trying to lie."

Lucas drew in a long, slow breath. "I'm going back because Jaelle is my wife."

Michael stared at him. Then his eyes flew open wide. "You mean you actually married her?" He stood and started pacing again, and this time, Lucas knew there would be no talking him down.

"I did."

"And what in the...What possessed you to do that? You didn't have to do what Mother planned for you. I mean..." He squeezed his eyes shut and pressed his fists against his nose. Then he opened his eyes as if he'd just remembered something. "And what about Vittoria? I thought you were desperately in love."

"So did I." Lucas turned his wrist to look at the gem that would be with him now for life. "But her father said no." He smiled faintly. "And I'm glad he did."

Michael gaped at him. "When I forbade you from bringing one home with you, it was a joke! I didn't think you'd actually take me—"

"Jaelle would have been claimed without it," Lucas said quietly. "As it was, she was almost taken from me twice." His voice was shakier than he wanted it to be. "And I couldn't watch it happen a third time. I just couldn't." His voice cracked, and he buried his face in his hands. "But it did. And I was the one who walked away."

Michael's mouth fell open slightly. "You really love her," he whispered. "Don't you?"

Lucas nodded miserably, and all he could think about was the way her lips had felt on his. The way her brown eyes had followed him as he'd left her there with the self-made king.

Michael closed his eyes and grimaced. "Leave it to you," he groaned, "to find a woman in the only place where men outnumber women ten to one."

"But I *am* going back for her," Lucas said again.

"No," Michael said, pulling out a new sheet of parchment and opening a bottle of ink. "You're not."

"I am." Lucas stood. "Maricanta can't afford a war, but you can afford me." Jaelle, however, could not.

But his brother ignored him as he began to write on the parchment.

"Michael!" Lucas banged on the table. "I'm serious about this!"

"So am I." Michael didn't look up.

"Then what the kraken are you doing?"

Michael huffed and looked up. "Apparently, we have a princess being held captive in Terrefantome. Now," he dipped his pen again and went back to writing. "I'm not sure if you were paying attention to our tutor, but the imprisonment of a person of the royal family is considered an incident of international interest."

Lucas's heart thundered in his chest. "But you said we can't afford a war right now."

"You're right. We can't."

"So what are you doing?"

"I'm writing Everard."

"What for?"

Michael looked up, and this time, he smiled slightly.

"Help."

CHAPTER 52

AND IF

Lucas fidgeted on his horse, unable to find a comfortable position. In the three weeks since his return home, he'd recovered from most of his injuries. But today he felt sore all over as if his injuries were returning along with the clouds that were constantly overhead once more. But one question drove him on, past the pain in his rear and the stiffness of his joints.

What if he was too late?

They'd been saved in a way by the cocky wedding invitations Bartol had had the audacity to send to all the surrounding kingdoms, including the one from which he'd stolen a princess and nearly killed the king's brother. This had assuaged Lucas's fears slightly, as he at least knew when the wedding would take place.

Still, his initial relief began to wane as plans were drawn together. It had taken days for Michael's letters to make their ways to the other kingdoms. Of the fifteen kingdoms he sent letters to, seven had come back and agreed to join him in their fight. This was far more than Lucas had dared to hope for. Destin's involvement, of course, was the least surprising, as King Everard liked to keep a close eye on the realm as a whole. As far as the other allies went, most shared a border with Terrefantome, so their involvement made sense as well. Lucas was of the opinion that this was far more about the danger Terrefantome posed to their borders than about the Maricantans' youngest prince's missing bride. But that was fine with Lucas. All he cared about was getting her back.

And possibly gutting the man who had dared take his wife.

After the initial joyous day when the responses of Destin, Ashland, Lingea, Ombrin, Giova, Vaksam, and Staroz had come back, however, the waiting had become agonizing. Armies were not quick to move, especially when they had to move all the way around countries like Tumen to meet Michael and Lucas with their men. Two weeks passed from the time of their responses to the day everyone was gathered at the gate.

Entering Terrefantome the second time was far more gratifying than the first had been. Lucas pulled his horse to the front, between Michael and Everard.

"Ready?" he asked the Destinian king. Everard turned to him, the rings of blue fire dancing in his gray eyes, and nodded. In turn, Lucas nodded down at the gate guards, whom he'd spoken with several times as plans had been made. They saluted and began to remove the gates.

"So what exactly are we doing?" Giova's captain asked nervously as the first gates were laid to the side and the guards began to loosen the second set. "Won't some of them escape?"

"No," Everard said, folding his powerful arms over his chest with a smirk.

"But how?" the man pressed, frowning at the gates.

"I promise." Queen Isabelle, or Isa, as her close circle knew her, reached out and gently squeezed the man's arm, the flame in her blue eyes briefly burning brighter as well. Lucas watched curiously as a hint of blue flame passed from her hand to his arm. The captain startled, then relaxed before looking at the queen in open awe.

"I see," he said softly.

She smiled sweetly at him and then turned back to her husband, and Lucas marveled at how the two monarchs wielded their power while remaining humble. And he couldn't help feeling more than a little jealous as they shared a look of adoration, as if there were no one else in the world but them.

"Hold!" A shout went up, and Lucas stiffened. They were nearly ready. Everard raised his hand, and a wall of clear blue flame engulfed the two final doors. The guards loosening the doors cried out at first and jumped back. When they saw that the flame did not consume them, however, they went back to their work.

Lucas placed a hand on the hilt of his sword. This could get quite messy. Sure enough, as the doors were pulled back, they could see the dozens of people waiting on the other side. And from the way they were standing, no small number were planning their imminent escape.

But clearly, such people had never seen the legendary Fortier fire. Everard kept his fingers slightly lifted as he grasped the pommel of his saddle. And though the people let up a great cry, and many rushed the entrance, every single one fell back. They gripped their arms and legs, whatever touched the wall of fire first, and howled as the allies' soldiers began to pour through, unaffected as long as they went the way they were directed. Several villagers tried to attack the soldiers, too. But as the king had covered them with a thin layer of blue fire as well, no one was able to touch them.

Michael went ahead with several of the generals to direct the men, and Lucas remained behind with the king and queen. As King Everard worked, his wife sat proudly on her horse at his side, reading the hearts of the villagers as they moved close, relaying any alarming emotions to her husband. Eventually, they were all through, and Lucas followed the monarchs as they moved to return to the front of the armies.

None of the contingents were above thirty men, as the king could only cover so many with his fire at once. The numbers were relatively small, but Lucas knew from past experience that Everard could protect them from any harm the residents of Terrefantome might wish to cover them with, particularly involving invisibility. The queen, who could sense deception, was even better at detecting those under the cloak of invisibility, thus eliminating much of the greatest danger Terrefantome posed.

To say that King Everard of Destin was imposing was a gross understatement. He wasn't quite as tall as Michael, but he was powerfully built with arms far thicker than Lucas's, and legs like tree trunks. Even without his legendary blue fire, he was the most formidable warrior Lucas had ever seen, and though Lucas had spent an entire summer training with him, he could only last a minute or two at most in mock combat. He was a proud man, and guarded even around those who knew him best. His goodness, though, was his greatest asset of all.

Queen Isabelle was no less formidable, though one wouldn't know it simply at a glance. With copper hair and dark blue eyes, she was tall and slender and the most graceful creature Lucas had ever witnessed walking the earth. She looked more like a dancer than the living weapon her husband had trained her to be. But Lucas knew better, as she'd bested him more times than he wanted to admit in the training ring as well. And when the situation called for it, she could also summon the legendary blue fire. But her strength lay in her heart. And when she chose to employ it, she could make truth the most frightening weapon of all. If anyone was going to answer the call of his brother, Lucas was glad it was them.

And so their journey into Terrefantome began. In the night, the king and queen took turns sleeping, the king rescinding his blue fiery cover only when the queen stood guard, alerting her men to any unfortunate souls that approached the group under the cloak of invisibility, for she was the only one among them, aside from Lucas's guards, who could see the invisible with her own eyes. In the mornings, she would retire to the single coach they'd brought along, built specifically for speed and defense, and sleep as they prepared themselves for yet another day.

Even with the stops to rest their horses and men, every man rode a horse, so their speed was far greater than Lucas's first journey had been. But as the days pressed on, it wasn't fast enough.

Every time Lucas closed his eyes, he saw her. Though he'd only seen her face for a few minutes, every detail was burned clearly into his memory like the brand one might use on cattle, or the mark he bore on his wrist. He imagined all the ways Bartol might have hurt her by now. Four weeks, she'd suffered at his hand, each day spent alone and defenseless in that awful castle.

Would she hate him when he found her?

They were less than a day's ride from the castle when they reached the forest in which the Taistille had found Lucas, Jaelle, and his mother. The path through the forest was only wide enough for four horses to fit through at once, so progress was slowed significantly. But just as Lucas was about to jump off his horse and run out of desperation, Queen Isabelle threw up her hand and closed her fist. Everyone came to a halt just as the Taistille revealed themselves on every side. And every one had his or her weapon drawn.

"Prince Lucas," Esmeralda called out from the front. She spat his name like a curse, and she kept her bow stretched tightly. It was aimed right at his face. "I told you very clearly that you were never to return." The sehf's face was devoid of any friendship or familiarity. Instead, it was cold and hard as she glared up at him.

Lucas nudged his horse forward. He could feel Michael push up beside him.

"I told you I was coming for my wife," Lucas said, willing his voice to stay even.

"I told you never to come back." Her eyes flashed. "And not only do you return, you bring more bloodshed to our land."

"Lay that charge on me, my lady." Michael nodded. "It was my doing to gather allies. Not my brother's."

"She's testing you," Isabelle murmured.

"So you come to ignite a war?" Esmeralda continued, glaring only at Lucas. "We brought you in. We sheltered you."

"And for that I'm grateful," Lucas said.

"It seems not. Because you know that the moment you turn tail and run, Bartol will send his men after *us*. And where will we go?"

"Who said anything about running?" Everard grumbled.

"And you are?" Esmeralda snapped.

"Most honored sehf," Lucas held his hand out. "I would like to introduce you to my brother, King Michaelangelo, Sun Crown of Maricanta."

Esmeralda snorted.

"And this," Lucas turned, unable to keep from smiling, "is King Everard and Queen Isabelle Fortier of Destin." As he said the words, Lucas wondered if such an introduction would reap the same benefits as it did everywhere else in the world. Even in the far east, the Fortier name was known and feared.

Esmeralda's jaw dropped.

"And if it helps," Lucas said, taking advantage of her shock, "I left my mother at home this time as well."

Esmeralda stared at Everard and Isabelle for a long time, but when she seemed to blink herself back to consciousness, the angle of her bow lowered slightly.

Beside him, Lucas could feel Isabelle relax.

"I suppose," Esmeralda said slowly, glancing back at her captain, "that would be a way to begin."

"I also," Lucas said, the humor draining from his voice, "plan to smash the man who stole my wife until he has nothing left with which to pursue you."

Esmeralda lowered her bow until the end of it was touching the ground. And for the first time, her own mouth quirked up as well. "Leaving your mother behind would have been enough."

"Would you join us?" Michael asked, leaning forward. "My brother has told us what you've done for him, and we wish to rid you of this king once and for all."

"Thank you," Esmeralda called back, finally letting her bow drop completely, "but this is the wrong of *your* ancestors and your duty to right." She glanced at the leaders. "All of you."

"Not us," the Vaksam commander called out, a little too gleefully. "We're just here as doers of good deeds."

Everard ignored the cheeky commander. "You're too kind," he grumbled to the sehf.

Isabelle flicked a look of annoyance at her husband before addressing the sehf herself.

"We are grateful for passage." She paused. "And perhaps when all of this is done, we can find a way to leave authority to the proper figures."

The sehf studied Isabelle for a moment before looking back at Lucas.

"I like this one. Bring her back with you when you're done." She stepped aside, and the other Taistille followed her example.

Several minutes after they'd resumed their journey, Everard cast a sideways glance at Lucas. Only then did Lucas realize he'd forgotten to drop back to where he'd been with Michael. But now Michael was chatting with the queen, and before Lucas could move back very far, Everard shook his head.

"Stay," he said. "And tell me what's bothering you."

Lucas tightened his grip on the reins. "I'm worried about her. That man is a monster."

Everard nodded slowly, and not for the first time, Lucas found himself desperate to know what the king was thinking. Everard had always been one of the wisest and smartest men Lucas had ever known, even when he was only a prince. But after being in their presence for several days, Lucas was even more astounded with his former mentor. Being married to Isabelle had changed him in a way his controlling father never could have. He was gentler now, less quick to judge. And yet, the tender glances he often sent his queen, the little teasing and their quiet whispers somehow made him stronger. Lucas knew that this man would go beyond the edge of the world and back for his wife and children. If anyone understood this mission, Lucas knew it would be him.

As if reading his mind, Everard gave him a hard smile. "You're a courageous man, Lucas. But don't be afraid to be dangerous."

"A few months ago, one of my father's friends told me I should stop making peace at the cost of my gifts." Lucas studied the road ahead of them. "Now not even that seems to be enough."

"Explain."

Lucas rubbed the side of his neck.

"I know I've been quiet for too long, telling people what they want to hear instead of what they need to hear. I've been what others wanted me to be rather than who I needed to be. And I know he was right," Lucas hurried to explain, though why he wasn't sure. "But now you're saying I need to be dangerous. And I know you're right. And I want to be. I just..." He sighed. "If I know anything about her sister, it's that one of us isn't going to make it out of this alive. I just hope I can do what I need to when the time comes. I want to be the man Jaelle needs me to be...instead of who she'll want me to be in that moment."

Everard frowned. "From what you've told me of her sister, you'll have to watch out for more than just a dangerous woman. You'll be dealing with the Sorthileige now. It's had a long time to fester, and she'll be nearly consumed by it."

"Meaning?"

The king gave him an unhappy look. "When the time comes,

and you have to make that decision, you'll have to make it fast. You won't be able to hesitate. Make a decision, go for the heart, and know that no matter how Jaelle feels about you after, you did what you had to in love."

"Could you help Selina? If we were able to bring her back somehow?" Lucas held his breath. It was what Jaelle had wanted all along.

The king's eyes dropped to the road. "If she doesn't want to be helped, I can't force her to be helped."

Lucas nodded and tried to steady his voice. "And if Jaelle disowns me for it?"

Everard's face hardened slightly. "Love isn't following an emotion of infatuation, Lucas. If you really want to love those around you, your father's friend was right. You'll do what they need, which isn't always what they want."

"And if she leaves me?" Lucas's chest was tight.

King Everard gave him a sad smile. "You'll just have to leave that in the Maker's hands."

Lucas stared at the road ahead. The part of him that was inclined to please was still there. But for the first time in his life, it was submissive to the rapidly changing part of him that knew he couldn't always do both. And when it came to Jaelle, he loved her too much to try. Whether or not she wanted him back when this was all done would be up to her. But he was going to make sure she had the chance to make that decision herself.

The sound of a trumpet echoed through the forest. It was thin and nearly inaudible above the sounds of the many hooves behind them. And Lucas's heart nearly stopped.

"The wedding," he said, looking at the king as he felt the blood drain from his face.

"Quickly," Everard said, nodding at the road. "If what you tell me about her sister is true, she's not going to leave Jaelle with the others for long. We'll draw them out into the open, but I don't think she's going to give us much of a chance. You'll have to find them." His fiery eyes searched Lucas's. "Are you ready for that?"

Lucas knew he was talking about more than tracking the sisters, but he didn't have time to answer. So instead, he gave him a sharp nod and sent his horse flying. If only they arrived in time.

CHAPTER 53

THEY HAVEN'T SAID

J aelle's sleep the night before the wedding was hardly enough to call sleep. Now and then, she would wake up and realize she'd been dozing, but more than not, she simply lay in her bed and stared through the nearest window up at the purple sky where the moon tried to shine fruitlessly through the clouds. She often worried about whether or not her plan would work. She'd sewed tirelessly through the last four weeks, often till her fingers bled, in the thin light of candles even after darkness had fallen. The castle staff, while numerous enough to always have someone at hand, wasn't large, four or five dozen people. And despite the king's personal display of wealth, most of them had few clothes. The only difficult part had been the guards. They had more than doubled in number over the last few weeks, and Jaelle prayed she'd been able to get to all of their uniforms. After the wedding, she wasn't sure if the king would continue to let her sew, or if he would consider her above such things.

Between short bursts of sleep, she also thought about Drina, and prayed to the Maker that the clueless, hapless queen mother might get home to her living son, and that she would treasure him for the man Lucas had believed him to be.

Jaelle was also painfully aware that this was her last night of sleeping alone.

It was funny. She'd wondered once if she would ever find

someone she wanted to sleep beside, someone she could trust to keep her safe even when she was at her most vulnerable. But now, she just wanted to keep her solitude. She stayed far away from the thought of what tomorrow night would bring. And she most definitely refused to think of Lucas.

Except she did think of him. And she wished with all her heart she hadn't let him sleep on the bench.

The morning gray chased away the night's purple clouds hours before Selina knocked on Jaelle's door, but Jaelle didn't bother to get out of bed.

"Jaelle? Are you awake?"

I was hoping you would have freed us by now, Jaelle prayed as she stared miserably at the ceiling. *I thought you wanted me to save her, but I can't save her if she won't let go of the darkness within.*

The door clicked open, and Selina let herself in. "I thought you might like to sleep in this morning, so I came later than usual." She held up a gown. "I brought you something."

Please make her let go now, Jaelle pleaded. *I've prepared the uniforms and nearly every article of clothing in the palace. It will be ready when you are. Just...Please don't make me do this.*

"Jaelle," Selina laughed, "wake up."

Jaelle was going to ignore her completely, but the flash of color caught her eye, and she found herself rolling over for a better look in spite of herself.

"I know you didn't like the gown the king commissioned," Selina continued, smoothing out the thin, nearly transparent layers of lilac purple and pale pink material she was holding, "so I had another gown made with your measurements instead." Even her creatures seemed benign today. Only a couple snakes escaped her mouth, mostly frogs and toads instead. And even the poisonous ones were few in number.

Jaelle inwardly sighed. As usual, her sister was doing her best to cheer her up, despite the circumstances.

Then it struck her.

Yes, Selina was trying to cheer her up. But she was doing so in a way that masked her motives. Her control. Because Selina was always in control.

Why did someone else always have control over Jaelle's life?

The king, his men, the marshals, every man in Terrefantome, from the butcher to strangers in alleys, Chiara, Drina, Mila, and even Selina. Especially Selina. The only one who had never tried to control her was Lucas. And Lucas was dead.

"Jaelle?" Selina asked, holding the dress up in the light. "What do you think?"

Jaelle pushed herself out of bed and stood so the servants could change her, but she didn't answer. Hurt showed in Selina's face as the servants adjusted the many layers of skirts around Jaelle's hips, but Jaelle was too engaged in her revelation to speak.

Selina might think she was in control now. But she didn't know what Jaelle had done. And she didn't know that Jaelle was planning to save her from herself. All Jaelle needed was the right moment. And the darkness that had taken control of Selina would lose its foothold forever.

In the meantime, Jaelle was going to tear down the darkness of this kingdom one piece at a time.

"I'm so glad your mask is off," Selina said, leading her over to the vanity. Turning her away from the mirror, she picked up several little clay bowls, some of powder and others that looked like a paste, bright and shiny. "I've been dreaming of this day since you were fourteen." She took a small brush with long hairs at the end and dipped them into a bowl that smelled of ash. Then she told Jaelle to close her eyes and began to paint the ash onto her eyelids.

"The day you hand me over to a corrupt king to be his wife?" Jaelle asked coolly.

The brush paused, and Selina sighed.

"Everyone out," she snapped. "I want to be alone with my sister." When they were alone, she began painting again, this time covering Jaelle's lips with something wet that smelled of berries. "What I *mean* to say is that I've wanted to present your beauty to the world for years. But your attachment to your mask prevented that." She laughed a little then sighed again. "Mother always said you were ugly because she knew the opposite was true. You were a beauty like we'd never seen. She didn't want you competing with me for the more desirable men."

Jaelle opened her eyes and gently took her sister's wrist to stop her as she tried to powder Jaelle's cheeks.

"We don't have to do this," Jaelle whispered. "There are ways to stop him that don't involve murder." She shuddered. "Or marriage."

"You still believe the Maker will help, don't you?"

Jaelle leaned forward. "We can send messages to the wedding guests. Bartol's been going on about the guests who decided to come. I know they'll help us if they knew what's happening here today. Lucas says they believe the Maker—"

Selina put her finger on Jaelle's lips with one hand while she brushed her hair out of her face with the other.

"I love you, little sister," she said with the gentlest smile Jaelle had ever seen on her proud, handsome face. "But if you ever bring up the Maker to me again, I will make sure that is the last time you ever speak his name. Do you understand?"

Jaelle searched her sister's dark eyes once more, praying to find some hint of sorrow or turmoil. But there was none. A cobra forced its way out instead, rearing and hissing at Jaelle until she nodded. But inside, she felt as though someone had closed her coffin.

All too soon, guards, including Victor, arrived at her door, and Selina and Jaelle were escorted to the throne room. And as Selina took her arm and prepared to walk her down the aisle, which was surrounded by people in fine clothes, and decorated with wilting flowers that had been tossed haphazardly on the ground, Jaelle couldn't help the memories that flashed through her mind.

The rough skin on the tips of Lucas's fingers and across his palms. The way those fingers had felt as they'd traced her face while kissing her gently in the dungeon. The warmth in his lips as he brushed them against her brow and then her temple and then her mouth. The way her heart had leaped in her chest as his hands had pressed against the small of her back when she'd whispered that she loved him.

The man at the end of the aisle she now walked would never be her husband. But he did have the power to hurt her and everyone she loved. Her heart ached as she came to stand before him, wishing with all her might to be in the forest once again, looking instead into the face of her prince.

Bartol's black hair had been gathered and tied at the nape of his neck, and he was clean-shaven. His long, black coat looked as though it had buttons made of real gold, and he wore a brilliant smile.

"My bride," he said, taking her hands and kissing them both. "You look like a sunrise." He led her over to a small table that had been placed before the thrones. On it were two pieces of parchment. He turned to their guests and held out his hands.

"I don't know how familiar you are with our wedding customs," he said, picking up a quill pen, "but in Terrefantome, weddings are less ceremonial and more...legal, I suppose you could say. But here in my court, I am hoping to marry the two and bring out a little of both." Then with a smile, he handed her the quill. "All you must do is sign," he whispered, "and we'll exchange the rings."

"Rings?" Jaelle echoed, staring at the parchment full of indecipherable ink. She heard a few gasps from the guests as a large ruby hit the floor, but she ignored them. Was this truly even a wedding? While she could fully admit to being ignorant of marriage traditions for Terrefantome, Jaelle had relived her Taistille wedding over and over in her head. The ceremony and the weight of the holy man's words had touched a place deep in her heart. And yet, here in the palace, where the king might have had any traditions he could have asked for, he'd chosen to sign papers.

Oh well, she thought darkly. *At least they aren't asking me to give him my heart.*

"While I chose to honor the usual custom of our people," he spoke to her, but he turned to the court and grinned, "with these as our witnesses, I have also decided that the tradition of your late husband's people of exchanging rings would be an elegant way to unite our traditions with the cultures of—"

"Late?"

"What?" His smile was frozen on his face.

Jaelle dropped the quill and took a step back from the table. "You said my *late* husband." She studied him anew. "You...you knew Selina killed him?"

Bartol stared at her for a long moment before casting a nervous glance at their audience. From what Selina had told her, there were several emissaries and ambassadors from various kingdoms in the western realm who had grown curious enough to accept Bartol's invitations. And from the way the king had glanced at them just now, Jaelle realized he didn't want them to know.

She could help with that.

"Terrefantome," she said loudly, "has one rule. One cardinal rule that above all must not be broken. That a man must not claim another man's wife while that first man is still living. And yet, *you*," she turned back to Bartol, "not only threatened my husband with harm while I was in your home, on the day after *my* wedding, you made a deal with me, allowing him to go free if I would marry you and give you my diamonds."

Those who were part of Bartol's court shot their king horrified glances, but the guests looked like they were about to fall over.

"My dear," the king said, picking the quill up from the floor and placing it roughly in her hand. "We have a lovely feast prepared, and it would be a shame if we allowed it to grow cold." His pale eyes bored into hers like icicles, but as he put one arm around her waist and held her tightly against him, leading her back to the little table, she shouted over her shoulder, pushing her words out as fast as she could go.

"He swore my husband, Prince Lucas of Maricanta, would arrive back at his country unharmed. But then he allowed my sister to kill him as he tried to bring his aging mother home!"

Bartol continued to drag her forward, his silence worse than any threats he might have otherwise uttered, and Jaelle wondered how much pain she had just cost herself. But before he could force her to sign the paper, they were interrupted by the sound of a soft voice from the audience.

"Your Highness."

The entire court turned as a man with gray hair and a slightly stooped back stood. He looked around nervously, but he addressed the king anyway.

"My name is Jos Hennah, and I am the emissary from Eliah." He paused and glanced about again. "I was sent by my king to see whether this land truly had a king who might bring the country to light. But this..." He gestured to Jaelle, who Bartol was still holding tightly against him. "I cannot condone this, nor can I recommend our alliance to my king should you force this girl into matrimony."

"And I'm afraid," a well-dressed woman in the back stood as well, "that I cannot commend your alliance to Ashland either." She sent Jaelle a nod and a meaningful look.

Whispers broke out in the room. Jaelle turned back to the king, unable to keep a slight smile from her face.

Several other visitors stood as well and made their dissent known, but he ignored them, glowering down at her and gripping her waist until it hurt.

"Sign the papers, and stop making a scene," he growled. "Or I will forgo making you queen and lock you in the dungeon forever. Your gems will be mine when I torture them from you by drawing your screams every day until you die." He shoved the pen at her again with his other hand. "This is your last chance. Sign."

Jaelle leaned forward, a triumphant, hard smile spreading across her face. "I. Can't. Write."

"You're a foolish woman," he whispered back. But just as he turned her away from the audience, slyly delivering a sharp knee to her thigh, a guard ran in panting so hard he nearly fell over as he bowed before the king.

"What is it now?" The king rolled his eyes then cast another glance back at the audience, which had become even more unruly.

"Sire," the guard gasped, "we're being surrounded."

"By whom?" The king gaped.

"They haven't..." He swallowed and faltered as a strange sound moved through the windows from the outside. Jaelle had never heard it before, but it sounded much like music. "They haven't said."

CHAPTER 54
HOLD ON TIGHT

Jaelle felt as shocked as the king looked.

"And exactly where are they?" the king roared.

Instead of answering, the guard pointed to the long row of windows on the left side of the throne room.

The king let go of Jaelle and stomped over to the nearest window. Guests jumped up from their chairs to see as well, and even Selina ran to the window.

Instead of joining them, Jaelle removed her heeled shoes and let herself go invisible. She wouldn't be hidden from Bartol or his men, but none of the guests, even those from the king's court, seemed to notice as she slipped through their ranks, quietly making her way across the room.

"Wait!" Bartol's shout echoed through the chamber. "Where is she?"

Jaelle didn't look back to see what he was doing or if he'd seen her. Instead, she took off as fast as her feet could carry her. She didn't know who the army outside was or what they were doing, but she would rather chance her survival with them than stay here, waiting for the inevitable. If she died today, it wasn't going to be at Bartol's hands.

She could hear the guards shouting for her to slow down, but it was her sister who caught her first. Selina had always been a faster runner than Jaelle, and Jaelle nearly choked when Selina caught her by the thin cloak that had been fastened around her neck. Instead of stopping, though, Jaelle loosened the pin that held it and kept running.

"Jaelle, please!" Selina cried out as she fell, and Jaelle felt guilty as she pressed on faster toward the doors. But she knew her sister would get up and continue to follow...which was exactly what she needed her to do. She just had to get outside before Selina caught her again.

She was almost to the main entrance when she realized that the doors were guarded even more heavily than usual. In her haste, she pivoted so fast she nearly fell over, but she somehow kept her balance as she ran for the nearest open window.

"Jaelle! Just stop for a moment!" Selina was gaining on her once more.

Let us make it outside, Jaelle prayed as she pushed herself over the last few yards to the window. *Please let this work.* And with that, she leaped through the window and stumbled out onto the grass.

Unfortunately, she'd forgotten about the wall that ran around the castle. Letting out a groan, she picked herself up and ran again for the nearest gate. Thankfully, the guards, whoever they were, weren't paying attention to those on the inside of the wall as they stared at what Jaelle guessed to be the army on the outside. One even had his hand on the gate, holding it open as though they couldn't decide whether they should stay or go.

Jaelle made up their mind for them as she ran through at top speed.

Just as the guard had said, the field outside the castle was covered with men. Unlike Bartol's men, however, who wore shoddy uniforms that mostly matched, these men, bearing the flags of many lands, all wore well-fitted armor, and their colors were organized to perfection. Forbidding and disciplined, they stood or knelt or rode in lines, weapons drawn as they stood motionless. And at their center three figures sat proudly upon magnificent horses.

One was a beautiful woman in dark trousers sitting astride her beast like a man. Beside her, in the middle, was a very large, very muscled man sitting on a giant of a horse. His helmet was under one arm, and his sword was in the other. The man on the right looked painfully familiar, only slightly leaner and taller than the man Jaelle had said goodbye to a month before.

Jaelle's heart twisted and leaped at the same time. Did she dare hope?

"Come out, Bartol!" that man shouted. "We need to talk."

Before Jaelle could decide whether she should run toward them or simply make a scene where she was standing, someone grasped her wrist and yanked her back against the wall.

Jaelle turned to see her sister glaring at her through bloodshot eyes. Her head had a red mark on it, and Jaelle wondered if she'd gotten that when she tripped on Jaelle's cloak. But even if she had, there was no time for regret now.

"Jaelle, what are you doing?" Selina gasped. "Why are you running into a battle?"

"I know who they are!" Jaelle nearly jumped with excitement as she pointed at the three figures. "That's Lucas's brother, King Michael! And those are—"

"Yes, I know who they are! But what about our plans?"

Jaelle took Selina by the elbows and drew her close.

"Forget the plans, Selina. What we need to do is get you to someone who can help you!" She gripped her arms more tightly, as though Selina were the one who might run away. "We need to get rid of the Sorthileige inside you!"

Selina looked like she might cry. But before she could answer, hoofbeats approached and slowed. When Jaelle looked up, a snorting horse came to a stop beside them. Two hands reached down and grasped Jaelle by the shoulders before yanking her up and putting her in the saddle behind the rider.

Selina let out a shout of rage, but when she reached for Jaelle, the rider's ungloved hand stretched out, and the blue flame that sprang from it made Selina fall back. Then the horse began to ride again. Jaelle was nearly ready to throw herself off when she realized that the rider wasn't a soldier or guard, but a woman with a long copper braid.

Was it possible?

She got her answer when the woman turned around. Her face was lovely, but the blue fire in her eyes was slightly more than unsettling.

"You're Jaelle, yes?" the woman asked.

Jaelle somehow managed to nod. She had never been on such a fast horse before, and never one so high. If the shock of being abducted hadn't stolen her voice, the speed would have.

"Good." The woman grinned. "I'm Isabelle Fortier, and your brother-in-law sent me to get you. Now hold on tight."

Jaelle had barely enough time to wrap her arms around the woman's waist before the horse shot forward, somehow even faster than before.

She wasn't able to find her words again until they had come to a stop beside the other two figures Jaelle had first seen in the field.

"I am King Michaelangelo, Sun Crown of Maricanta," the man that looked like Lucas was still yelling to the castle. "And I wish to speak with you."

"Please," Jaelle addressed the woman, "I need to go back and get my sister!" But as she spoke, a grating, familiar voice floated out onto the field.

"And what gives you the right to invade my kingdom?" Bartol held his arms out as he made his way onto the field to where Selina was still standing. "After sending thousands of criminals into my borders, you come now to get one back?"

"Abducting a princess generally leads to an international conflict," King Michael called out. "Not to mention poisoning their prince." His face darkened, making its sharp angles stand out even more.

Jaelle stared at him. How did he know about all of that? Had Drina actually gotten to the ocean? Then her heart fell. The Taistille must have found Lucas's body.

"We need to send him the signal," Queen Isabelle murmured to the heavily muscled man beside her.

The man pointed his sword up into the sky, and Jaelle ducked and shrieked as three rings of fire blasted up into the sky and exploded above them.

"I sent you invitations," Bartol called. "You could have just accepted those."

"I didn't know how to dress to celebrate the man who schemed to kill my brother to marry his wife," King Michael called back dryly.

"If that's the case," Bartol held his hands up helplessly, "all I can say is that apparently, our reputation hasn't properly preceded us." Even from across the field, Jaelle could see him smile as soldiers began spilling out of the castle behind him. They lined the walls, and Jaelle drew in a sharp breath as she tried to count their numbers. There were far more than she had originally thought. She'd tried to find all the uniforms she could, but now there were so many...

"We came," Michael said again, "to offer you the chance to give up our princess without a fight and to talk in terms of your dishonest behavior as of late. It seems, though, like you prefer different methods."

"So," Bartol sneered, "you really just needed to go find help."

King Michael's face turned to stone. "My pride isn't worth the lives of my people." His jaw twitched. "Nor that of my brother and his wife."

Jaelle's chest squeezed tightly. Lucas had sworn his country couldn't afford another war. And yet, his brother had not only come back for her, but he'd brought friends. What she still couldn't understand was...why.

"So you brought men from seven kingdoms to get one girl and die for his memory?" Bartol's tone was acidic. "How romantic." He straightened. "In that case, we shall appreciate your horses and weaponry."

"The western realm isn't about to be cowed by a bully," the large man, who Jaelle could only guess to be King Everard, said tersely.

"They're preparing," Isabelle said, her voice still low but sounding slightly alarmed. "I can feel them flickering."

Jaelle looked back at the queen in amazement. For Isabelle was right about the soldiers. They were preparing to disappear. But how could she *feel* them?

The queen's gaze didn't waver as she stared out at the hundreds of soldiers standing around the castle wall. Jaelle turned back as well. This was it. She hadn't quite expected her plan to work out this way, but if she failed now, she would be responsible for the death of seven armies.

Bartol's grin widened. "Now!" he shouted. Several of the men flickered, just as the queen had said. But not one disappeared. Only Selina was gone. But Jaelle knew better than to think her sister had given up. Now it was just a question of where she would spring up. And when.

Please let me save her, Jaelle prayed with all her might. *Or Lucas's death will have all been in vain.*

"What's happening?" Bartol looked back at his men. "Why are we still visible?"

In spite of her angst, Jaelle couldn't help smiling slightly. As if hearing her thoughts, Bartol finally locked eyes with her. And as they stared at one another across the field, his eyes grew wide, and he began searching his clothes. He finally understood.

"You!" he screamed, pointing his sword at her. "Conniving woman!" Before he could get another word out, though, King Everard muttered something to the young man who had come to stand beside him. And the young man lifted an object, gold and shiny, up to his lips and blew into it. The strange sound she'd heard in the throne room rolled through the valley again, and the soldiers behind them swarmed the field toward the castle.

Jaelle watched in awe as Everard raised his left hand and pressed it palm out toward the battle. He closed his eyes and bowed his head, but she could see his fingers moving slightly. Even more astonishing were what looked like thin tongues of blue flame that surrounded each armored knight. Bartol's men far outnumbered them, but the armored knights sliced through their ranks like a butcher cutting meat.

King Michael lifted a large golden object that looked like a gigantic fork and raised it to the sky. Briefly, he held it aloft, his lips moving as though uttering some sort of chant. Then he brought it down, again and again, aiming its prongs at the battle. Balls of yellow flame rained down on the wall itself and anyone that stood too close to it. And to Jaelle's amazement, where each ball of flame fell through the clouds, a golden shaft of light followed, as though the sun were touching the earth itself.

"I didn't think there would be so many," Michael called out over the chaos.

"He must have been planning something all along," Everard answered. Jaelle shrieked and pointed as one of Bartol's guards, a giant of a man, broke through the line of armored soldiers, leaving a trail of bodies behind him. He set his eyes on her and began to barrel toward the queen's horse. Without lowering his hand, Everard's eyes opened, and his force charged out and met the man head-on.

The man swung his gigantic axe up at the king, and Jaelle was sure his horse would be killed at the very least. She glanced back at the queen, but Isabelle's eyes were distant, as though she weren't even seeing the danger her husband was meeting right in front of her.

King Everard met the man's axe with his sword. Instead of merely blocking it, the king shot another thick wave of blue fire up his sword and into the man's axe. The man shouted and fell backward. And as the king reigned his horse back in, his opponent didn't get up.

Jaelle couldn't believe her eyes as guard after guard fell or surrendered. None of the monarchs seemed surprised, though. King Michael wasn't able to send out as much power, it seemed, as Everard, but his flames from the sky herded the enemy together and broke down the outer walls, and Everard continued creating the shields of fire around his men. Just as Jaelle was beginning to feel as though they might actually survive and possibly even win the battle, Queen Isabelle's eyes widened, and her hand shot out to her husband's shoulder.

"Ever! They're coming!"

The king's face tightened. "Where?"

"Behind us!" The queen turned her horse to face the field and distant treeline behind them.

"I can't see anyone!" Michael called.

"Because they're invisible!"

King Michael may not have been able to see them, but just as the queen had said, hundreds of men and women raced toward them, weapons, homemade and traditional, raised as they approached the battle.

"How many?" Everard grunted.

Instead of answering, Isabelle leaped lithely off her horse and ran over between Everard and Michael's horses. She pressed a hand against each of their legs, squeezing her eyes shut tightly.

Fear wreaked havoc with Jaelle's breathing as Everard's eyes popped, and Michael raised his triton higher than he had since the battle had started. Were they seeing the invisibles, too? But how?

Everard made a sharp motion to the young man, who raised the strange round thing to his mouth again and blew three times, two short and one long.

The armored soldiers on the field turned from the guards, who were nearly all motionless on the ground or hostages, and most of them began to race back toward their leaders.

"Maker," Jaelle breathed, "help them."

Michael broke the clouds open again to deliver more flame. Instead of a single burst, though, he created a line of fire to separate them from the hordes rushing toward them. "It won't last long!" he called. "Just a minute or so before they're able to get over it!"

"Acelet!" Everard barked.

One of the men, older than any of the monarchs, ran up to Everard.

"What is it?" he asked.

Everard pointed to the field behind the flame. "These fields are full of invisibles."

The man, who looked to be in his early fifth decade, gave a start. "How are we supposed to fight them?"

"Leave that to me," Queen Isabelle said. She looked up at her husband. "You'll have to lift the shields to help me magnify my sight."

Jaelle frowned. Her sight?

But Everard only hopped off his horse. Sword still drawn, he took her hand and nodded at her.

Even in that short nod, Jaelle's heart hurt as she glimpsed the deepest look of love she had ever witnessed pass between them. Well, the second deepest. The first belonged to Lucas.

The queen took a deep breath. Her jaw tightened, and her arms flexed as she stared into the field once more.

Jaelle gasped as the hundreds of men and women came into sight once more. The man who had addressed Everard let out a curse and ran back to his men, shouting orders as they regrouped and prepared to run out again.

"Jaelle," the queen called over her shoulder without looking, "if something happens and we can't protect you, I want you to take my horse and flee to the forest."

Jaelle looked at the queen in horror. She'd never ridden a real horse on her own before, let alone a queen's warhorse. And worse, if something happened to the three powerful monarchs, how could she hope to get away?

The queen continued, still without turning. "If you must go, flee to the forest. Seek the Taistille, and we'll find you when we're done here."

Jaelle wanted to remain. It felt wrong to run from danger when Lucas's brother and his allies were facing it all for her sake. But just as Jaelle was about to say so, she glimpsed a movement at the edge of the forest, a fluttering of something the same color as a peach.

Shame and guilt welled up inside her for disobeying the queen but not enough to stop her. She had one more chance to save Selina. And she wasn't going to waste it.

Jaelle did her best to turn the horse in the direction she wanted to go. She took a few tries, but eventually, she got the beast to canter toward the forest. Thankfully, as most of Bartol's men had been dealt with, Jaelle made it to the forest safely. But when she got there, she realized the peach-colored gown was nowhere to be seen.

"Selina?" she called out as the horse slowed to move into the woods. "We need to talk. We can't go on like this."

Before she finished, however, something grabbed her by the wrist and yanked her sideways. She slid off the horse and landed painfully on the ground. When she opened her eyes, she was staring up into Selina's face.

CHAPTER 55
RESPITE

Without giving her a chance to recover from her painful fall, Selina tied Jaelle's hands behind her back and fit a gag over her mouth, leaving just enough space for her to spit the gems out so she wouldn't choke. Then she began dragging her deeper into the forest. Jaelle tried desperately to scream, but the gag was too tight to get any sort of true shriek out. No one who could have helped was close enough to hear her, anyhow.

She tried to resist, but Selina was too strong. When she let her knees collapse so that she was a dead weight, Selina simply turned and lifted her in both arms and continued toward the forest. How had her sister gotten so strong? She'd always been bigger and stronger than Jaelle. That was why she'd become Jaelle's protector when they were young. But when Jaelle looked into Selina's eyes, she knew. The white surrounding Selina's pupils was gone, and her eyes were now an inky black.

"I can't say I'm not furious with you," Selina said as she walked, a long, thin white snake making Jaelle shudder as it slithered from Selina's mouth down Jaelle's back. Instead of dropping to the ground, however, like most of her serpents did, this one moved up her shoulder and wrapped itself around Jaelle's upper left arm. "But this is going to work out better than I thought. Once Bartol is gone, it should be easy for us to get out unnoticed." She came to a horse that was tied near the edge of the forest where

Jaelle had stayed with the Taistille. She put Jaelle on the horse and then climbed up behind her.

Jaelle wanted to beg her sister to go back. After witnessing their actions on the battlefield, she was convinced the Fortiers could save them both from the darkness inside. But she also sensed that if Selina didn't get help soon, there would be no sister left to save. She fought the gag until it slipped off.

"Selina!" she gasped, looking back when she'd finally worked it free. "You're going to die if you don't get help!" She tried to look behind them, but what she could see of the receding battlefield was too full of smoke to see who was winning. "The Fortiers can help!"

"They shouldn't be a problem much longer," Selina continued as though Jaelle hadn't spoken. She didn't even seem to notice the gag had slipped off. Not that it mattered, as a slightly thicker brown snake wrapped itself around Jaelle's other arm. "Their son is young, not even nineteen years of age. He'll be too busy assuming the throne to pay us much heed here."

Jaelle could hardly breathe as she stared at the snakes. "You think he won't care that you killed his parents?"

"I think that the Fortiers are so focused on the purity of their own throne that he'll sacrifice revenge to keep his crown unstained." Selina shrugged. "And even if he does come, like I said, he's young, and everyone knows his father has protected him from most real exposure to war. Either way, he shouldn't be much of a problem." She glanced at Jaelle. "Especially now that I know how closely I'll have to watch you." She smiled slightly and looked back up at the road. "I have to say, though, I'm proud of you. I wish you'd been that creative around Mother. We might have escaped ages ago." This time, a round snake with black, yellow, and red stripes came to rest on Jaelle's lap. And this one opened its mouth and hissed, revealing two long fangs.

"I was trying to save hundreds of lives!" Jaelle whimpered.

"You chose poorly." Selina pulled the horse to a stop. They'd gone about a hundred yards into the forest. She dismounted beside a particularly knotted tree. Jaelle was tempted to throw herself off the horse, but the snakes kept her in the saddle.

"Here's what we're going to do," Selina said as she grabbed a large spade from the horse's saddlebag and knelt on the ground. Then she began digging. "In order to get the armies into Terrefantome, the Fortiers and Solefiges must have had to rearrange the process for letting people in and out of the gates quickly. And with their armies still within the walls, we shouldn't have that much trouble taking advantage of the disruption. Getting out should be fairly easy. There." She pulled out a large brown bag and opened it to glance inside. "Perfect. It's all here."

"Selina, please!" Jaelle sobbed. "I can't do this anymore. I just can't."

Selina stood slowly. "What do you mean?" For the first time, she seemed to hear Jaelle's desperation. "This is all we've ever wanted. Now we don't even have to kill anyone!"

"Do you hear yourself?" Jaelle cried. "You aren't yourself!"

Selina jabbed a finger at her. "You take that back!"

"Selina!"

"For the first time since my mother brought me to this place, I have power. I can decide who lives and who dies."

The striped snake in front of Jaelle hissed, and for the first time, the other two revealed their fangs as well.

"I know what's best for us," Selina continued. "And I'm going to keep us safe."

"I'm not going with you," Jaelle cried. "Not like this." She pleaded with her eyes, willing Selina to see the truth. "I can't."

Selina stared at her for what felt like forever. Then she looked down at the bag in her hand. "You don't want to come with me," she said slowly.

"I want to be with you," Jaelle wept. "But I can't be with you when you're like this."

"What do you mean like *this*?" Selina's eyes narrowed.

"I loved who you *were*! You were funny and sweet, and you protected me. You wanted me to be happy!"

"I'm making you happy now."

"You're controlling me!" Jaelle screamed. "You're worse than Chiara ever was. And I'm done being your puppet!"

The moment the words were out of her mouth, she regretted them, but it was too late to take them back. Selina dropped the bag, and the striped snake coiled back. Jaelle closed her eyes as she waited for the snake to spring.

"Then if I can't have you," Selina said through gritted teeth, her voice shaking, "no one can."

"Let her go, Selina."

Jaelle nearly fell off the horse at the sound of the familiar voice. She had to be hearing things. Maybe the snake had already bitten her, and she was hallucinating. But when she turned to her right, there he was. He was even limping slightly, just the way he should have been in real life.

He also had his bow drawn and an arrow nocked, and the arrow was aimed straight at Selina.

"How in the oceans—" Selina whispered, but Lucas cut her off.

"Because I love Jaelle," Lucas said, continuing to inch forward, "I'm going to warn you again so you have one more chance. Get rid of the snakes and let her go."

"Or what?" Selina spat.

"Or I'll kill you. It's as simple as that."

"No, Lucas," Jaelle pleaded. "She doesn't need to die. There's been too much death already." She turned to Selina. "No one has to die!"

"I'm afraid," Lucas said, his voice slightly softer, "that I can't promise you that, love."

"Please," Jaelle cried, tears filling her eyes, "don't fight. We don't have to fight. Either one of you!"

"What are you going to do, Selina?" Lucas asked as he and Selina walked slowly in a circle. "You say you love your sister. If that's true, give yourself up and let us help."

"You say you love Jaelle," Selina said, "but you threaten to kill her sister. Hardly the kind of love she wants."

"Perhaps," Lucas said. "But it's the kind of love she needs."

"Don't," Jaelle breathed. "Please. Don't take her from me."

"You heard her, Selina," Lucas said, keeping his bow poised. "If you love your sister, you'll let her go and come with us."

"I'll not be powerless again," Selina snapped as she continued to circle.

"No one said you would be," Lucas replied evenly.

"You don't know what it's like," Selina roared, "knowing that your mother is too selfish to leave you behind in her exile, and pleading with your father to keep you. And having no way to save yourself when he pulls his hand out of yours and walks away." She turned to Jaelle. "If I knew what I know now, I would have escaped them both and made my own way in the world. Then I wouldn't have come here with you only to have you betray me, too."

Jaelle winced, but Lucas was as steady as ever.

"That's the Sorthileige talking. Come with us, and we can bring you back to your right mind. Then you and Jaelle can go wherever—"

"As if you'd let your wife leave."

"I'd let her go wherever she wished to go," Lucas said quietly.

For a long second, Selina stopped walking and stared at him. "You're just saying that because it's what she wants you to say."

"I'm telling the truth," Lucas said. "I'm also telling the truth when I say that I will not hesitate to loose this arrow through your heart if you don't let her go."

"And I," Selina said, the vein in her neck darkening as it throbbed, "will tell you what I told her. If I can't have her, no one can."

"No one has to die!" Jaelle heard her voice growing louder. She turned to glare pointedly at each. "If either of you hurt one another now, I'll never be able to forgive you!"

"I know." He stopped and met her gaze. "But you need to live."

The snake on Jaelle's right arm hissed. And before Jaelle could reply, the arrow sprang from the bow. Four thumps sounded as four bodies hit the ground. Three long, skinny bodies and the body of one human.

Jaelle tried to scream, but nothing came out. Instead, she could only watch as Selina went still. She scrambled off her horse and pulled her sister's head into her lap. Seconds stretched on, as Jaelle counted the nearly imperceptible rising and falling of Selina's chest. But just as Jaelle was sure those would stop, Selina's eyes fluttered open, and as the ink drained from them, she sucked in a sharp breath.

"Selina!" Jaelle tried to lean down to embrace her, but Selina held her hand out, a slight, sad smile on her face.

Surely this was a dream. A nightmare that had gotten caught

up in a dream. Because her beloved was alive. And he was standing over the sister who had just tried to kill her.

He was also saying something. Jaelle tried to hear him, but her head swam with memories and confusion and the way her sister's face grew whiter by the second.

"Jaelle!" he called, finally breaking through some of the noise in her head. "Jaelle, I need you to listen!"

She looked up at him, some familiar notion of emotion rising to the surface. He reached over and brushed a lock of hair away from her eyes.

"You only have a few minutes," he said softly. "Talk to her while you still have the chance."

Jaelle shook her head. "We need to get my bag." Her mind worked faster than the rest of her suddenly clumsy body seemed able to move. "If I stop the bleeding, we can move her to—"

"Let me lie here," Selina panted. "The magic...the magic is draining, but if you move me, it might stop."

"Is it..." Jaelle stuttered. "Are you back?"

Selina nodded and gave her another tired smile. "Silly idiot. And why are you still here? You should have run when you had the chance."

"I couldn't leave you!" Jaelle sobbed. "But you wouldn't listen."

Selina looked up at Lucas, who had come to stand several feet away.

"He was right. The magic..." She paused to swallow, and Jaelle hurried to get her a sip from the waterskin that had fallen from the bag Selina had dropped. When she was done, she took another deep breath. "The poison I allowed her to bring to the surface of my heart...It changed me. And there was no way I could have escaped it on my own."

"Why did you do it?" Jaelle asked, taking her sister's hands and holding them to her face.

"I thought I was strong enough to suppress it. Beyond the snakes, I mean."

Only then did Jaelle realize that for the first time since the curse, Selina was speaking, and nothing was coming out.

Selina looked up into the trees, and her eyes wandered slightly before returning back to Jaelle. Then she smiled again as she traced Jaelle's cheek with her finger.

Jaelle shook her head. "I don't understand."

"The witch said whatever was in our hearts would become visible for the world to see." She drew in a shaky breath. "It was how I paid her without money." Selina coughed, and this time, a small drop of bright red blood stained her lip. Jaelle hurried to wipe it away with her skirt.

"She said she could see the darkness inside me, and she was impressed because that kind of potency is hard to come by."

"But what darkness?" Jaelle asked. "You were always good to me!"

"That seed of darkness was there long before I talked to the witch. The one my parents...my parents put there before I ever met you." Selina let her head fall back against Jaelle's legs. "All she had to do was draw it out." Her eyes remained open, but her breaths were beginning to grow shallow and her words began to slur. For some reason, though, her smile grew as she met Jaelle's eyes once more.

"That's what I loved about you. While I was growing more and more bitter on the inside, you were always there with some sort of light." She chuckled, which turned into more coughing. "You nearly drove me mad when we first moved in. You always had something sweet to say or something fun for us to do. But no matter how I looked at it, I eventually had to admit that the Maker had put a light inside you that couldn't be snuffed out."

Jaelle's heart jumped. "But I thought you didn't believe in the Maker."

"Love, you can lie yourself into believing anything if you try hard enough." She swallowed again then licked her lips. To Jaelle's surprise, she then threw a glance at Lucas, who nodded once.

"Don't be angry with him." She turned back to Jaelle. "I'm glad I got to see your face without the darkness masking my sight." She touched Jaelle's cheek. "You truly are beautiful. I always knew you would be." She drew in a long, shuddering breath then let it back out. "Pray for me, love. Pray the Maker will give me respite from the darkness."

"Selina!" Jaelle cried as her sister's eyes fell shut. "Selina, come back, please." She held her sister tighter. "You're supposed to be with me. We're supposed to live outside the wall." Her voice grew higher and her words spilled out faster and faster. "I did all this for you, so you can't leave me now!"

But Selina didn't open her eyes again. Instead, her chest fell once more. And it didn't rise again.

Jaelle had no idea how long she wailed as she pressed her face against her sister's shoulder. She was vaguely aware of Lucas standing beside her, but she couldn't meet his eyes. All she knew was that her sister was truly gone. And she didn't even know where the Maker had taken her.

THEY STAYED THAT WAY, frozen in time, until they were discovered by the Fortiers, Lucas's brother, Esmeralda, and several of her Taistille warriors. Isabelle gently took her by the shoulders and pulled her back from the body. Jaelle let her, too tired to cling to it any longer.

"Lucas," Everard said, crouching beside Selina's head, "I need you to lift the body, but don't touch the wound. Put it in that pit over there, and I'll take care of it in a moment."

Lucas nodded, and he and his brother bent to lift Selina's body. When they did, Lucas's arrow fell out, and Jaelle felt her mouth fall open. The arrow that had pierced Selina's skin had been corroded down, like an axe left for years in the rain. The ground beneath her was covered by a thick, stringy liquid, the same color as the inky substance that had filled her eyes.

"Is that..." Jaelle whispered.

"Sorthileige, yes," the queen answered, her voice tight as her eyes went back and forth between the dark spot on the ground and her husband, who was now bending over the ground with the palms of his hands stretched out toward it.

"Everyone, step back, please," he said. "And I would advise you not to look."

"Be careful, Ever," Isabelle murmured, her brow creasing. Jaelle wanted to keep watching, but the queen carefully angled them so they were facing in the opposite direction.

The others present followed her example.

"You don't want to see this," she said softly to Jaelle as a hiss and pop sounded from behind them.

"Wait." Jaelle grabbed the queen's hand. "You mean I won't get to bury her?"

"I'm sorry." The queen's eyes were sorrowful as she took Jaelle's hands and squeezed them. "This kind of darkness has to be destroyed or it will devour everything around it."

"But if she's been touched...what about me?" Jaelle had to force herself not to turn and get one last look at the body, though it was what she wanted to do most. "I've been affected by the curse as well. Does that mean—"

"No," the queen said, shaking her head. "You weren't the one to choose the darkness. That was your sister's decision. Not yours."

Jaelle frowned as she considered this. It didn't seem fair that her sister would take such evil for Jaelle's sake, just so she could escape unscathed.

She considered arguing again that she deserved to see her sister one last time. But when she turned to address the queen once more, there was an ancient look in the queen's eyes that kept Jaelle quiet.

There was also the strange heat that was beginning to warm Jaelle's back. It itched and prickled and made her skin feel as though she was too dirty to ever be scrubbed clean. The air was thick with a sweet, cloying smell that made Jaelle want to retch. Everyone remained silent after that as the air continued to grow hotter, despite the day's light waning. Every so often, they would hear a groan or even a whimper from the king behind them, and Jaelle became more convinced that she didn't want to look upon the power that could challenge such a powerful man.

Finally, the king gave an audible sigh.

"You can turn around now. It's gone."

Immediately, Isabelle let go of Jaelle's shoulders and went to her husband. And Jaelle could see why as soon as she turned as well. Selina's body was gone, but the air around them was black and smoking, as though it had been scorched by one of the Sun Crown's fireballs from the sky. That wasn't the frightening part, though. Rather, it was Everard himself who made her hand fly to her mouth.

The great king who had stood so proudly at the beginning of the battle was bowed as though he might fall over. He swayed until Isabelle put her shoulder under his and steadied him. She spoke soft, indiscernible words as her hands, now alight with the same blue glow, were pressed against his heart.

"Come."

Jaelle turned to find Lucas holding his hand out to her.

"Let's give them some privacy."

JAELLE DIDN'T NECESSARILY WANT to take his hand after all that had just happened. But as everyone else was leaving, she accepted with a sigh and let him lead her back to the field along with the others, where the Taistille had, apparently, set up camp just outside the castle's scorched walls.

"Will he be all right?" she asked in a dead voice as they walked. Twilight had fallen, and for some reason, everyone around them seemed to be compelled to whisper, just as she was.

Lucas gave her a tired smile. "Of course. Everard's the only one in the realm who can outright destroy Sorthileige like that." His smile slipped slightly. "But it takes a great deal of healing every time he does." Jaelle felt his fingers tremble slightly.

"It doesn't seem fair," she said, staring at the bonfires they were approaching.

"It's not. But I'm just grateful the Maker has given them to us. I'd hate to think about what our world would be like without the light of Destin."

Jaelle looked around at the ancient broken castle to their right. "I think I have a good idea."

A stiff silence fell between them as they walked, and Jaelle felt as though she were holding the hand of a wooden board. Or maybe she was the wooden board. She had no idea of what she felt or how she felt it. All she knew was that Lucas was alive. And Selina was dead.

Thankfully, Esmeralda was approaching them, so she didn't have to think about it for too long.

"So you decided to join us, it seems," Lucas called.

She gave him a wry smile. "Once we saw that you and your friends were in earnest, we thought you might use a helping hand." She surveyed the groups of prisoners the armored men now had lined up against the wall. "Once we got here, though, it seemed you had already taken care of it."

Lucas motioned up to the castle. "Isn't that yours?"

Esmeralda grinned, and for once, it was free of sarcasm or scorn. "This was the home of my mothers and fathers before the criminals chased out the Taistille." She paused. "Before we became wanderers, we were the children of kings."

"Well," Lucas said, "maybe it's time your children held that name once again."

Esmeralda stared at him for a moment before letting out a shout of a laugh. When she was done, she gave Lucas's arm a playful shove. "Why couldn't you have been born first? You would have made a good king."

"Because he's too much of a stubborn fool." Michael appeared out of the twilight and elbowed Lucas's arm. Lucas chuckled.

"It's true. If I'd been born first, I would have signed the crown over to my nieces within two weeks for sheer boredom."

"And you," Michael said, letting go of his brother and walking toward Jaelle, "must be my brother's lovely wife."

Jaelle gave a small start at the word *wife*, but not wishing to offend Maricanta's king during their first meeting, she simply did her best to curtsy.

He took her hand and bowed to kiss it before standing beside his brother again. But this time, his face grew grave. "I'm sorry we weren't able to get to you any sooner. We did our best but..." He looked back at the field behind him. "It was very nearly too late."

It was too late, Jaelle wanted to say. But instead, she did her best to smile and thank him.

Over the course of the evening, Jaelle was introduced to a number of other kings and generals from other countries, and she was treated to another one of the Taistilles' flavorful meals. But she tasted little and heard even less. All she wanted to do was sleep. If only she could escape the reality of what was for a little while, maybe she could sort out what it was that she was truly feeling inside.

Even more pressing than her exhaustion, however, was Lucas. Though he didn't ask for details of what had happened while she was gone, or worse, demand they talk about their present situation, he hovered at her elbow, and the glances he continued to cast at her were alternately full of hope and shame.

She should talk to him. They would have to talk sometime. But instead of getting the awkward, painful conversation over with, Jaelle contented herself with settling on the outskirts of a group of soldiers gathered around a young man with bright red hair. He seemed to be giving a dramatic reenactment of the battle. Lucas followed her example, but she could still feel his eyes on her as she listened.

"I been on the front line several times," he cried in an accent she was unfamiliar with, "but I never seen anything like it before! We nearly took Bartol and his goons when the generals started ordering us to turn around and move ranks to the other side. And I can tell you I's more confused than I ever been."

"See what we get for signing up as cooks?" one of the younger men muttered to the man standing beside him. "We miss all the fun."

"They tell the archers," the red-haired man continued, "to nock their arrows, and we're all looking at each other aghast. But Destin's queen," he pointed at Queen Isabelle, who was eating beside her husband on a log at the edge of the camp, "suddenly goes all aglow, and blue flame streaks from her eyes! And before we know it, all the invisibles appear! Hundreds, there are, and we're nearly too shocked to do any good but be run through by their blades."

"Aye," someone else called, "and the world might have been a bit quieter for it." The group chuckled as the storyteller scowled.

"As I was saying," he made a face, "that's when the nomads burst onto the valley behind the invisibles. And before our archers can let a single arrow fly, they're hemming the baddies in from the back. Our commanders tell us to get them from the front. And what with the kings throwing their flame, yellow and blue, all over the field, 'twasn't more than five minutes before everyone was done."

Someone touched Jaelle's elbow. She turned to see Lucas.

"We..." He took a deep breath. "We need to talk."

Jaelle panicked, but before she could utter a breathless word, she was saved by a deeper voice calling out into the night.

"All right."

Everyone turned to see Everard and Isabelle stand. Esmeralda stood beside them. The king's face still looked haggard, but he was upright again, and to Jaelle's relief, a little of his color was back.

"We'll sleep here tonight. The Taistille are going to keep watch while we rest," he called out. "Tomorrow we'll set out with a contingent of their men to escort us as we make our way back to the gate. But we need to move fast before word spreads about who is here and what we can and can't do." He looked around expectantly, as though he were used to being obeyed. Sure enough, as soon as he'd seated himself to eat, men jumped up and scurried.

"You'll be riding back with us in the coach we brought," Lucas said, pulling Jaelle's attention back to him. "One of us will ride with you at all times." He fidgeted slightly and wiped his hands on his trousers. "We'd give you a horse, but since you're not used to riding, we figured you'd prefer something at little easier for the journey back."

Jaelle nodded as someone handed the each a plate of food. And for a few minutes, she was spared the necessity of conversing as they ate.

For this short respite, she was grateful. Even as they ate, she was torn between wanting to cling to him and wanting to push him out of her life forever. Not because she didn't love him. Lucas would always be her first love. But even the simple act of sitting beside him stirred all sorts of hopes and questions and disappointments inside inside of her, emotions and questions buzzing at her mind and heart like hornets whose nest was disturbed.

When she looked at him, every inch of her heart hurt.

"Lucas?"

He looked up from his food. "Yes?"

Jaelle paused. Her lips trembled and her voice threatened to fail her, but she had to ask.

"How did it feel when you thought the Sorthileige was going to kill him?"

She didn't say who she was speaking of , but she didn't have to. Lucas looked at Michael, who was sitting across the fire, talking with Everard and his general. When he looked back at her, all signs of mirth were gone from his face.

"In truth?"

She nodded.

"I wanted to die."

Jaelle nodded again then cleared her throat.

"Could Queen Isabelle ride with me?" she asked in a lighter tone. "I...I'd like to get to know her better before we part ways."

For a short second, his face fell, but he covered it well and nodded quickly. "If you want that, I'm sure she can."

Jaelle felt bad for asking such a question. Of course it would hurt him for her to ask if someone else could ride with her. But she wasn't sure she could trust herself to say what was wise when her heart was too broken to know what it wanted.

CHAPTER 56
WHERE THEY NEED TO BE

'm sorry you have to ride with me, Your Highness."

Isabelle raised her head from where she'd been resting on her hand and slowly opened her eyes. "I'm sorry, what was that?" Then she waved her hand. "And please. Call me Isa."

Jaelle wasn't sure she was ready to go that far, but she could at least drop the title, she supposed. Clearing her throat, she tried again.

"I said I'm sorry you have to ride with me." She chuckled nervously. "I can't imagine spending days on these roads is what you imagined when you came to fetch me." Even as she spoke, they hit a bump in the road, and all the benches they were seated on creaked loudly.

"Oh." The queen rubbed her temples. "It's quite all right." Then she sighed. "Actually, if I'm being honest, I much prefer it this way. This place gives me a headache, and at least in here, I don't have to look at it."

Jaelle didn't know what to say to that. The queen did look as though she had a headache. Her skin was a shade too pale, and her brows were constantly furrowed. Jaelle rummaged through her bag of healing ointments until she found the dried lavender. Pulling a sprig from its jar, she handed it to the queen.

"I don't know if this will help, but lavender often helps my patients with headaches." At first, she was afraid she might be insulting the woman. Queen Isabelle was surely powerful enough, even if Jaelle didn't understand that power completely, to find wellness without her help. But to her surprise, the queen took it eagerly and inhaled deeply, and the furrow in her brow relaxed as she closed her eyes.

"Thank you," she said, keeping her eyes closed. "This is perfect."

Jaelle wondered whether or not she should keep talking. She liked the queen and wanted to know more about her. Never had she seen anyone so refined and still so comfortable around commoners. She was fascinating, and Jaelle felt strangely inclined to trust her, despite practically being strangers. Jaelle also still needed this woman and her husband to remove the curse. As relieved as she was to be moving to the other side of the wall, she had no wish to live the rest of her life as a target for the greedy, no matter where she lived.

"A number of people I've seen get headaches from the constant cloud cover," she added hesitantly. "They miss the sun."

The queen chuckled dryly. "I'm sure they do." She shifted until she was lying across the bench opposite where Jaelle sat. "Unfortunately, I'm afraid the only relief for me is going to be when we leave this place. Then perhaps I'll get some peace and quiet."

"Oh," was all Jaelle could say.

The queen opened her eyes again and studied Jaelle closely, her head slightly tilted.

"What has Lucas told you of my gift?"

"Your gift?" Jaelle echoed.

Isabelle smiled. "You don't need to feel embarrassed. Most people don't know what I'm talking about."

How had she known Jaelle was embarrassed?

Isabelle paused and bit her lip for a moment before a small smile lit her face, and she sat up a little against the cushions. "What your sister tried to get for you is known in other lands as a *gift*."

Jaelle raised her eyebrows. "It doesn't feel like a gift."

At this, the queen laughed. "No, I don't suppose it would. What

I mean, though, is the ability to do something others can't. Yours isn't a true gift because it wasn't given by the Maker."

Jaelle stared at her, more confused than ever.

"I'm explaining this badly." The queen pursed her lips and huffed. She entwined her fingers as she looked around. When her eyes rested on the window, they lit up. "You saw what my husband did yesterday with the fire?"

Jaelle nodded.

"The Maker gifted my husband's line with an unusual strength. That strength is manifested through his fire. With it, he can burn, destroy, protect, and heal. My son, though he's our nephew by birth, comes from the same line, so his ability is similar to my husband's." She nodded at the window again. "Michael is the Sun Crown. When he was crowned king, fulfilling an ancient prophecy with his wife, he gained the ability to rule the sun, to an extent, the way his wife rules the seas."

"And what is your gift?" Jaelle asked. "How did you see the invisibles yesterday? No one can do that without having lived here at least seven years."

Isabelle gave her a knowing smile. "My gift manifested when I broke the curse the Maker had laid over my husband for his disobedience. But that's another story entirely." She waved a hand. "I was gifted, though, with the gift of the heart."

"What does that mean?"

"It means I see the heart of truth, and to an extent, I can force others to see it as well." She glanced at Jaelle's filthy gown. "People can tell you that the truth is subjective all they want, but no matter how hard one might try to tell you that your dress is clean, I can see otherwise." She leaned back. "Likewise, I can see through most lies, and if I wish to, I can press the truth into the heart of the liar. Which, from what I'm told, is often more painful than the lie itself."

"So..." Jaelle said slowly, "you could see the people even though they didn't want you to."

Isabelle grinned and nodded. "Exactly. Unfortunately, in a place so broken as this one, it can be difficult to focus. No matter where I go, I feel the constant needs and pain pushing in from every side." She touched her temples again and winced. "Ever can help with the pain, but I'm trying to let him be after yesterday's escapade."

Jaelle forced a smile and nod, but inside, she wanted to melt. If the king couldn't even help his wife—

"Jaelle."

"Hm?"

The queen gave her a gentle smile. "Why do you think I'm letting my husband rest?"

Jaelle shrugged sheepishly. "To help me?"

Isabelle nodded and reached out to place her hand on Jaelle's. It was warm, and the feeling was...comforting, as though the queen had placed a warm blanket around Jaelle's shoulders and handed her a cup of tea. It was one of the strangest, most delicious sensations she'd ever had.

"Tell me about your sister," Isabelle said, leaning back once more. "You were obviously close."

Jaelle looked at the ground. "If you have a headache already, I don't want to—"

"Please." The queen said. "It's different when I'm asking." She gave Jaelle a wry smile. "It also helps when I focus on one person instead of letting it all come to me."

Jaelle got the feeling it wasn't a request so much as a command, but she was fine with that. So she told the queen about how Selina had come to be her sister, how Chiara had treated them, how they'd been betrayed by Seth, and finally, how Selina's desperate attempt to get her out of Terrefantome went horribly wrong.

"I just..." Jaelle's voice trailed off as she traced the little windowsill. "Selina and I were supposed to see the world together. It was going to be just us. Her and me." Everything she had lived and breathed for for so long had been for them.

"Why?" the queen asked.

"Well," Jaelle said slowly, "we were all we had."

"And you loved her," Isabelle said softly.

For some reason, this made Jaelle's eyes prick. "Of course," she choked. "She might not have been my sister by birth, but she was as real as any sister ever was."

Isabelle nodded softly. "And do you love Lucas?"

Jaelle's head snapped up. "What?"

"I asked if you love Lucas." She raised an eyebrow. "Even after he killed your sister."

Jaelle leaned back in her seat and tried to gather her thoughts enough to answer. If she'd been asked that question the first week she and Lucas had met, in spite of how handsome he was, she would have vehemently denied any and all feelings of even neighborly affection for the man. If she'd been asked on the eve of their wedding, her answer would have been less confident. If she'd been asked the night they spent in the dungeon, she would have laid her heart bare. But now, after he'd killed her sister in front of her, even though he believed he was doing the right thing...

It didn't matter. As much as she might deny it, there was love inside her that was meant only for him. That would only ever be for him.

"You do," Isabelle said softly.

Jaelle nodded miserably.

"Then why are you trying to hide it? And before you deny it, I've been watching you. You've hidden yourself away every time he walks within twenty feet of you. You might as well still be wearing a mask."

"I..." Jaelle faltered. "I don't know how much more I can lose."

Isabelle said nothing, just watched her with those eyes so deep they seemed to have their own stars behind the rings of fire that burned continuously within them.

"My sister and I were supposed to be together. Forever. But she's gone now. And Lucas was the last person I wanted in my life, but somehow, he's become ensnared so deeply I can't get him out." She sat up straighter. "The two people who were supposed to love me the most tried to kill each other, one of them succeeding. But even he hasn't been able to give me his word."

"He gave you a vow, didn't he?" Isabelle nodded to Jaelle's tattooed wrist, which lay in her lap.

Jaelle shrugged helplessly, pushing the diamonds in her lap into piles of different sizes for want of something better to do.

"He did," she finally said miserably. "He also gave me the assurance that we could get the marriage annulled." She turned sideways and flopped back on the bench, regretting it as her spine hit the wood. "I have lost everyone that ever meant anything to me. I'm not going to promise myself to anyone again until I know they truly intend to stay." She sat up and looked at the queen, "I mean," she continued, briefly forgetting what rank Isabelle occupied, "how do you know your husband truly wants to stay with you forever? There's no way to tie him to you. And what if he wanders, or better yet, dies? What then?"

"My husband has nearly died more times than I can count," Isabelle said softly. She turned to stare out the window at the brown drudgery passing by, and her eyes grew distant. Then they focused back on Jaelle. "But then, so have I." She chuckled slightly. "I suppose it's a hazard for occupying the Fortress thrones."

"I don't know how I could live with myself if I lost him again," Jaelle whispered. She thought back to the holy man and her father, Selina, and now Lucas. And though Lucas was currently on a horse between his big brother and the famous king of Destin, Jaelle could recall with instant clarity how it felt the moment she thought she saw him die.

"I don't know what you know of the Maker," Isabelle said, standing up and coming to sit on the bench beside her. Jaelle watched her warily. The way she took Jaelle's hands was familiar, much in the way Selina had once done. There was a steadiness in the queen's eyes, however, that Selina had never held.

"But," the queen continued, "I do know that the Maker is faithful, and I have been reminded again and again since I was nine, that because he is always with me, I am never alone. And second," she said, "I have learned over the course of my lifetime that he puts in my life those who need to be there for that season." She looked up from Jaelle's hands into her eyes. "Just like trees with their rings, we are given hours, days, months, and years of growth to become the people we were meant to be. And in season, he will provide those who will shape us appropriately. And I must be content to know that even in my seasons of loss, the void isn't the Maker's betrayal. It's his way of directing my path."

"But how do you know which way he wants you to go?"

Isabelle's eyes softened.

"In my experience," she said gently, "he'll put you and

everyone else in your life exactly where they need to be." With that, Isabelle sat back and looked out the window, as though she hadn't shattered what little order Jaelle had managed to put back in her life since the night before.

Jaelle wanted to groan. Now she had a headache, too.

CHAPTER 57

THE REAL MAN

After two nights and three hard days of riding straight through Terrefantome, a speed which could only have been aided by Everard's power, Lucas released a heavy sigh of relief as he exited the gates himself, and an even greater breath when the gates were back up where they were supposed to be. From the edge of the field that stood between his own city and Terrefantome's gates, he could see the lights of the palace shining out into the night.

The captains, generals, and kings had already agreed to spend the night encamped on the field, rather than to overrun the Sun Palace with soldiers only to uproot them again the next day to begin their respective journeys home. There was plenty of food and wine left, and having lost only a handful of men to their enemies, the soldiers themselves were in good spirits. Lucas turned a blind eye to the drinking games his men played around their campfires, laughing a little too loudly and most likely taking bets. He would keep an eye on the younger ones, but as a whole, they had served well and had earned a night of celebration.

If only, he thought to himself as he walked back up the hill to where the monarchs and captains and generals had made camp, he could rejoice such himself. True, their objective had been completed. Michael had been the one, much to Lucas's surprise, to slay the evil king with his newfound powers. Selina would never manipulate Jaelle again, and Jaelle was no longer lost. Instead, she was now sitting at Queen Isa's side, probably the safest place in the world for anyone to be. But Lucas couldn't quell his fears as he gingerly sat beside her, leaving a healthy distance between them.

She sent him the same polite, guarded smile she'd been sharing since they were reunited. And yet, as always, she stayed close to Isa's side, her knees pulled up to her chest as she listened with wide eyes to whatever was being discussed around the fire.

The fire played with the shadows on her face, tossing them around like a million masks that fought for dominion. There was something unusual...something alluring about her, the way her almond-shaped eyes and shiny dark hair contrasted with her olive skin and thin face. She truly was east and west in one. He ignored the urge to draw closer and take that face in his hands and kiss it until she looked him in the eyes the way she had the morning he left.

His heart thumped unevenly, and his blood ran warmer as he remembered the kisses they'd shared that night in the dungeon. She'd followed his lead then. But since then, he'd left her alone with a power-starved madman and killed her sister. Who knew how she would react if he tried to do such a thing now?

Other eyes followed her as well. Lucas wasn't thrilled about this, but he got the feeling that much their curiosity was aroused by the gems falling from her lips. He would have been more wary, of course, without the Fortiers nearby. No one would dare cross them. Still, he had the ridiculous urge to take her by the hand and drag her the rest of the way to the castle, where Bithiah could fuss over her and she would be away from all this attention.

To the place that he prayed she might one day call home as well.

"Jaelle," King Everard said, dusting his hands on his trousers and turning to her. "I hear there's something you'd like to discuss with me."

The group, which had quieted when he spoke, as they always did, began to chatter again as Jaelle nodded and moved to sit closer.

Lucas watched as they spoke. They were far enough from him

he couldn't hear what the king was asking her. Whatever it was made her pause, and for the first time, she looked directly at Lucas.

Hope sprang into his heart and had him halfway to his feet when she looked back at the king without smiling and nodded, and disappointment chased his hope away.

Since they'd made their deal, he'd believed he would have weeks before she spoke with the Destinian king. At first, his agreement to take her to Everard had been an annoyance, yet another errand to run in the time he already didn't have. But as he'd gotten to know her, he'd grown more and more excited about the promise of getting to know her outside of her nightmarish land. They would have others with them, of course, as it only would be proper to take a contingent of guards as well as some of Arianna's maids for escort. And yet, he'd believed himself perfectly capable of creating an excuse to get her alone enough to hear her thoughts unhindered. And perhaps, to have even stolen a few kisses beneath the stars.

Just as exciting would have been the chance to watch her explore the world. There were few people Lucas knew who loved to travel as much as he did and understood the thrill of leaving the familiar behind to dive headfirst into a new adventure. Vittoria had never understood his delight in new lands and foreign wares, but the more he'd gotten to know Jaelle, the more he'd been convinced *she* would understand. Perhaps, he'd hoped, he might convince her to come with him.

"You're feeling guilty."

Lucas turned to see Isabelle seat herself beside him.

Lucas picked at the grass beneath him, shredding the blades into fibers. "That I do."

"And it's keeping you from her."

Lucas put the grass down and turned to face the queen. "I killed the person she loved most in the world. And I did it in front of her while she begged me not to." He plucked another thick blade and began tearing it, too. "I'd say that makes me more than just a little guilty."

She smiled sadly. "In your defense, Selina nearly did kill you."

"And I think that's the only reason Jaelle hasn't tried to kill me herself." He shook his head. "Not that it matters."

"Why is that?"

When he looked at her again, Destin's queen was studying him directly, not even bothering to hide her searching. Her dark blue eyes seemed to pierce his soul, and he fidgeted. Of course, it wasn't that he didn't trust her. He trusted the Fortiers implicitly. But the way she was looking at him made him feel as though his chest had been turned inside out, and everything he tried to hide from the world was there for her to see.

"I'm not enough." As he said it, he felt his carefully constructed walls come crashing down.

"And by that you mean..."

He huffed. "I mean I've spent my whole life trying to be who everyone else wants me to be. To my men, I'm an admiral. To my family, I'm a smile. To the court, I'm everyone's beloved jester, and I have a pocket deep enough to sate any lady's needs. To the rest of the western realm, I'm my brother's errand boy." He shrugged, staring at his hands. "I've got the depth of a tide pool, and to make it even messier, my hands are stained with the blood of more lives than I could count. And if that weren't enough to drive her away, the one time I did what someone needed instead of what she wanted, I made her hate me."

"How do you know she hates you?" Isabelle asked softly.

"You've talked to her more than I have." He nodded at Jaelle as she spoke with Michael and Everard. "Does she seem like an enthusiastic lover?"

Isabelle tilted her head to the side and studied the girl the way she'd studied him a few minutes before. Lucas tried to keep his heart steady, but his breath hitched slightly as he waited.

"She's conflicted," she finally said, the blue fire in her eyes blazing as she turned back to him. "What she knew and what she knows are battling." Then she leaned toward him. "But I can guarantee you this. If you don't act, you're going to lose her."

"I don't know how," he said, hating the way his voice broke. How did he reach a woman who had been bruised and battered her whole life, like a storm beating against a reed?

"I'm not a mind reader," Isabelle said, giving him a wry smile. "I only see the truth as it's revealed to me. But...I will say that now would be a wonderful time to see that man inside who's been hiding for so long." She gave him a sad smile and stood. Before she left him, though, she paused and looked back down. "And in case you're wondering, you're not enough."

He stared up at her. Was that supposed to make him feel better?

A small smile played on her lips. "You're never going to be everything she needs in this life."

Lucas looked at Jaelle again as the pit of his stomach developed a hollow feeling inside.

The queen's smile widened. "And no matter how beautiful and perfect she looks to you now, she'll never be enough to sate your soul either. No one person can be all that." She paused. "Selina can attest to that."

Lucas frowned. He hadn't thought of that.

"You can be, however, the perfect tools the Maker uses, each to shape the other. Because there's nothing in the world that feels like knowing she was made just for you, and you for her." And with that, the queen squeezed his shoulder and left.

Lucas watched the queen resettle herself beside her husband and felt a pang of jealousy as he pulled her into his side. They had been that way when he'd trained with them as well, fitting just like two pieces of those annoying ancient stone puzzles his brother liked to play. Not that they got along perfectly. In the summer he'd stayed with them when he was younger, they'd had some of the most intense arguments he'd ever heard between royals, each as stubborn as the other. But no matter what their disagreement, there had never been any question of their loyalty to one another. There was an unspoken understanding that no matter what, they would face their demons side by side.

He wanted that. But did Jaelle?

Everard stood and motioned for Jaelle to follow him. They went to stand about ten feet from the group, and Lucas wished once again for the two weeks he was supposed to have with her. They shriveled up, however, as Everard placed his hand on Jaelle's head and closed his eyes. Soft blue flame enveloped her entire body, and with the curse, Lucas's hope of keeping her near went up in flames. She wanted to be a healer, not a princess. After he killed her sister, what could she truly want from him that would make up for such a deed? What did he have to offer her that she couldn't find on her own? Still, he put on the best smile he could muster as she sat down beside him again.

"So," he ventured, "how does it feel to be free?"

"Well," she said slowly, staring down at her outstretched hand. When nothing fell out, a real smile touched her face. "It shall be fantastic not to trip over or choke on my own words again."

He laughed along with her. Then they settled into an awkward silence.

The real man. Isabelle had said he needed the real man. So he gathered his courage and turned to her once again. When he made eye contact with her, however, he felt the air go out of his chest. She looked terrified. Like one little word might send her running. So he traded in his courage for conversation.

"Well, you got what you wanted." He sent a forced smile at Everard. "So what's the plan this time?"

She blinked at him a few times. "The plan?"

"You always have a plan." He tried to give her a flirtatious grin. "You're free now. So where do you go from here?" *Stay with me,* he wanted to plead instead. But fear of what she would say kept his mouth tightly shut.

She stared at him for another moment before biting her lip and looking down at her lap. "Well," she said slowly, fingering the edge of her dress, "I suppose I—"

"Ladies. Gentlemen." Ever interrupted her, his deep voice booming into the night. "As we all have rest to achieve before we begin our journeys homeward tomorrow, I think it would be prudent to discuss the obvious question of what is to be done about what we just witnessed."

Lucas wanted to groan. But this conversation was inevitable, so he tried to put his angst on the shelf long enough to concentrate on what was being said. For while he had no desire to be a king on display as his brother always was, he did love a good strategic conversation.

"What do you mean *do* about it?" Vaksam's general called out. "I say we leave the place and let it bury itself."

Ombrin's king snorted. "If you think someone else isn't going to take up that man's schemes and try again to do what he failed, then you're an ignorant donkey."

Usually, Lucas liked the king of Ombrin about as much as he liked staying in bed with a rash, but for once, he agreed.

"Terrefantome is on the western border of Tumen," the Ombrin king continued, "who I'm sure would be more than accommodating to to any schemes that might involve us, particularly Destin." He gestured at their circle. "What makes you think hardened criminals like that would be satisfied with settling in Destin and never stepping any farther south?"

"We have proof that Tumen did contract with Bartol for weapons and safe passage," Isa called out in a low voice. "And I have no doubt they would agree again in a heartbeat, no matter who was giving the orders."

"So suppose we choose to do something about it?" Vaksam's general scowled. "What exactly do you do with generations of dangerous criminals and their spawn?"

Lucas had determined not to say anything and just to listen. But when Jaelle flushed, his heart got the better of his mouth.

"I think," he snapped, "you begin by showing some respect and compassion for those who don't deserve to be there." He met the man's gaze. "And if that's too much to ask, perhaps you ask the Maker to put a little mercy in your heart."

"You're not suggesting we simply let them out!" A female ambassador from Ashland gasped. She'd been unfortunate enough to have been sent by her pig-headed king, Lucas's uncle, King Xavier of Ashland, to attend Bartol's wedding. She'd also been among those they'd rescued after taking the castle. Or so Lucas had been told.

"My brother isn't suggesting that at all," Michael said in a soothing voice. "He simply means this is a delicate situation that cannot be canvassed in all manners the same."

Lucas shot his brother a grateful smile, which Michael returned, tired as it was.

"That," Ever said, taking control of the conversation again, "is why we need to discuss this and to ask the other kings what long-term solutions are both righteous and feasible." He glanced around the circle. "It was a mistake and sin on the part of our fathers to believe they could simply dump their filth on another man's property and come out unscathed. I believe we can do something to help."

"It's a cold, sunless, muddy hole of a land," a general from Lingea grumbled. "I'm not sure what can be done with it."

"The darkness that covers the sky," Isa said, staring into the fire, "is the darkness that fills the land." She finally looked up and at her husband. "If we can lessen the concentrated evil, I have no doubt the land itself will be fruitful again."

"But that would merely let the evil spill out into other kingdoms, wouldn't it?" the Ashlandian ambassador asked.

"We won't come to any conclusions tonight." Ever turned to Jaelle. "But I think we would be wise to hear from the only resident expert on Terrefantome in our midst. Jaelle, what do you think ought to be done about your kingdom?" He stared expectantly at Jaelle, along with the rest of the circle, but it was a few seconds before Jaelle seemed to understand they wanted her to speak.

"Oh," she said, glancing at Lucas. He gave her his most encouraging smile and a nod, so she turned back to Ever. "I suppose I could try." She turned her body toward the group, but her address was to Ever. Lucas couldn't help feeling proud. She was in the midst of some of the most powerful men and women in the entire world, and she was willing to speak. As always, she was full of courage.

"Many of the people in Terrefantome are rough and dangerous," she said slowly, "not because of their criminal pasts, but because they've been born and raised in a world where they know nothing else." She paused. "Some leave, but many cannot or are afraid to." She glanced at Lucas.

He wondered what she saw there as she held his gaze.

"What do you suggest we do then?" someone called out.

Lucas mourned when she turned away from him to look at the speaker, her deep brown eyes no longer on his.

"Oh, it won't be easy," she said quickly. "And for some...for many, it will be impossible."

"What makes you believe that it will be possible for anyone?" the Lingean general asked.

"Well," Jaelle said slowly, tucking a lock of silky hair behind her ear, "take my sister, for instance. She was plucked from her life in Maricanta and forced into exile with her mother through no fault of her own."

"Are you saying she wasn't responsible for what she did to you?" someone asked.

Jaelle shook her head. "No," she said slowly, "she chose to seek out the witch. She knew better, but she did it anyway. And to make things worse, she gave in and chose to embrace the darkness, even when help was offered. But...I can't help wondering what life would have looked like for her if her world hadn't been so dark."

The group was quiet for a moment, the only sounds the distant voices of men and the pop of the fire. Finally, the man from Staroz said, "As lovely as the sentiment sounds, how do we put any of this into practice?"

"I don't know for sure," she said. "But I do think...I *know* that the Taistille deserve their land back, and perhaps, if we start with the families of children, we'll be able to stop the next generation from growing so tainted so young." She looked up, and for the first time, her eyes sparkled just a little. "And if we could get the help of the Taistille, I think it could be even better." Her words sped as a slight smile came to her face. "There are many who don't want to leave. Terrefantome is their home. If we could help the Taistille restore the light, many wouldn't even need to come your lands. They could build a new world together."

"Thank you," Isabelle said with a kind smile. "We appreciate your insights."

The group broke into quiet conversations of their own, and Lucas took advantage of the break to take Jaelle's hand and squeeze it.

"You did well," he mouthed, and the corners of her mouth curved up slightly, but it didn't touch her eyes.

"I think," Everard said over the noise, "that this is a good place to stop for the night. We can go home and continue to consider this while we prepare for a more formal meeting of the realm to create a plan and move forward with it." He met everyone's eyes. "Agreed?"

There were no objections, so everyone mumbled a goodnight and left the circle to find his or her tent, which had been set up by some of the soldiers earlier in the evening. Lucas's heart beat in his throat as he and Jaelle stood at the same time. This was it. He was going to speak. He had to.

Before he could say anything, though, it was she who spoke.

"I've been thinking," she said in a low voice.

Lucas couldn't have moved if he'd wanted to.

"I'd like to meet you in that..." She paused and frowned. "The place with the holy man tomorrow."

"The chapel?" he guessed.

She nodded.

He took a step closer, and reached out slowly, so slowly, to touch her face.

"Do you want to tell me what this is about?" He did his best to smile. "I'll listen to anything you want to say."

Coward. Tell her what you're really thinking. And yet, Lucas waited.

She opened her mouth but then seemed to think better of whatever she was going to say. Instead, she swallowed and looked at the ground. "Just be there."

CHAPTER 58

WHAT SHE SAYS

Jaelle woke before the sun the next morning. She'd expected to have some time alone to think, but when she ventured out of her tent, despite the early hour, the men were already moving out of their respective camps. So instead of waiting for the awkward invitation to walk together that she knew Lucas would extend, she followed the steady stream of soldiers who were winding their way down the hill to the city by the sea.

She was more than a little hesitant to walk beside so many men, particularly without Lucas, Michael, Everard, or Isabelle. But as they sent her no more than curious glances, she decided the risk was worth it. Walking with Lucas would be worse. He would throw her those impish, dimpled smiles, and she would get lost in the depths of his hazel eyes as he talked about whatever it was that struck him at the moment. And she would lose her nerve and allow his charms to dissuade her.

But no. This was her decision, and no one, not even the man she loved, could change her mind.

Well, what mind there was left to change. Inside, Jaelle felt like a pile of the meat scraps the butcher threw out for the dogs at the end of every day. A part of her had died when she thought Lucas died. And then, after her brief moment of bliss at his return, the two people she loved more than life had tried to kill each other. Again. And this time, one had succeeded.

The journey to Maricanta had been a difficult one. Though her conversations with Queen Isabelle had allowed her more insight into the outside world than she'd ever gained before, twin clouds of pain and disillusionment had hung over her the entire time, and she'd felt herself drifting farther and farther from the man who bore her mark with each mile as endless questions revolved in her mind.

Now that Selina was gone, Jaelle had no idea of what she was supposed to do with her life. Yes, she was gaining her freedom. But at what cost? Every time she shut her eyes, she saw the granite determination in his face as he'd loosed the arrow, and the night she'd slept soundly on his chest in the dungeon seemed more distant than ever. Then, of course, there was the fact he'd suggested the annulment.

Still, for a while, she'd faintly hoped after their night in the dungeon he wanted her and that he wanted their marriage to work. But her doubts had all come crashing back during the night before when he'd asked her what she was going to do next. As if he hadn't pledged his life to hers and whispered that he loved her over and over again between kisses on the one night they were happy.

What did you want him to do? the annoying voice in her head asked. *You agreed it was only for your safety that you got married in the first place.* Besides, he was pampered and always out at sea and, it seemed, had a knack for landing in dangerous situations. He admitted as much. Even if they stayed together, what good would it be to spend the rest of her days on the shore looking out at the sea, praying that he would come home?

No. It would be best this way, parting as friends while she moved on to see what life was truly meant for her without all the fear and danger and complication that Lucas brought with him.

She sighed as she neared the top of the final meadow. Despite knowing that she was making the right decision, she felt like she was seeing the world through a mask again, all the colors of the grass and sky and sea muting as they ran together in various shades of gray. She'd left the land of darkness behind her the evening before. But now it felt like she was running from the sun all over again.

Lost in her thoughts, Jaelle wasn't paying attention to the sky, and she crested the hill just as the sun peeked over the horizon behind her. She only thought to turn around when the world around her erupted in color.

The city.

The sky.

The palace.

The sea.

Everything burned her eyes, as though it had all been set alight by a thousand torches. The sky was an explosion of blue, yellow, purple, orange, and pink. The grass beneath her feet was greener than her clearest emeralds had been. The ocean glimmered like a million sparkling sapphires, and the walls around the palace grounds shone brighter than her clearest gems.

The palace itself was no less blinding than the ocean, many of its walls made of glass. Columns that must have been at least ten times her height stood at the its distant entrance like soldiers.

And even better than the sights were the sensations. A warm breeze played with her tattered purple gown, and she closed her eyes to soak it up. She was warm. Without a blanket or extra layer of clothing, Jaelle simply stood and soaked up the sun's rays, and she promised herself then and there that she would never live anywhere cold again. Not when there were places like this that warmed one simply by going outside.

Her chest squeezed, and tears filled her eyes. This was why her mother had died of heartache. Leaving all this behind for a place like Terrefantome...

Jaelle forced herself to open her eyes and resume her walk. The rest of the world was out there. She couldn't chain herself to one place. *Breathe, Jaelle.* She needed to breathe. Yes, she would be leaving this wonderful man. But this was only the beginning of her life. She glanced at the tattoo on her wrist. Not the end.

Maybe if she thought it enough, she would believe it.

When she reached the city, the market was crowded and livelier than any Jaelle had ever imagined possible. Countless kinds of seafood and baked delicacies filled the air with their sweet and salty aromas. Children dashed about without seeming to care where their parents were. Neighboring stall owners gossiped as they sold their wares, and Jaelle couldn't even count the number of trinkets and baubles she didn't know the names of. That familiar pain inside gave another twinge, and she promised herself she would come back here one day, Lucas or no Lucas, to experience this land to its fullest. But for now, she thought as she frowned up at the winding road up to the palace, she needed to get to the chapel.

The climb was long and took her nearly an hour, but as she chose to follow a group of soldiers, she never feared getting lost. It was strangely exhilarating to be so close to a group of men, knowing none of them could legally pounce and claim her as they would have in Terrefantome. Her heart squeezed. What she wouldn't do to stay in this new world with the man she loved, sharing its delights with him day by day. But it couldn't be.

When she finally arrived at the top, she had to take a moment to bask in the glory of the palace, which was nearly blinding in the light of the sun and the golden sand of the beach below. If she'd had a box of paints and unlimited easels, she would be happy to never move again. The white of the palace, along with its countless windows, decorated in flourishes of gems, shells, and stones, was like music to the eyes. Even more breathtaking was the vastness of the ocean.

But she wasn't here to stand agape at the beauty of her new world. She was here to make everything as it should be for herself and for the man she loved. Jaelle swallowed hard and turned away from the glory of the morning to ask one of the older soldiers nearby where the chapel was. He pointed to one of the little white buildings nestled near the foot of the palace, and she turned her weary steps toward it. After a moment of hesitating, her hand on the golden handle, she pulled.

A small boy darted out before she had the door all the way open.

"Can I help you?" he asked in a sweet sing-song voice.

She gave him a tired smile. "Is the holy man somewhere nearby?"

The boy nodded and dashed off, but before she could breathe in relief, she heard a voice that was all too familiar.

"Jaelle! I've been looking for you."

She closed her eyes and sighed as Lucas pulled up. He hopped off his horse, and came to stand beside her. And though Jaelle was perfectly aware that she needed to begin distancing herself immediately, she couldn't deny the pleasantness of being so close. It took every ounce of her self-control not to lean against him and relish the safety she felt as he took her hand in his.

"Isn't it magnificent?" Lucas's eyes shone like a little boy's as he gestured behind him. "I can't wait to show you everything! Michael has me gone much of the year, but he does his best to give me a little time between each voyage. And I know we can arrange for you to come on the diplomatic missions as well. You'll see bazaars, markets, trading posts, and orchards full of foods you never imagined. And I'll introduce you to kings and queens and some of the most powerful people in the world. And since we planned several joint ventures, patrolling the coast for pirates, you'll probably meet Admiral Starke soon. And Elaina, of course, too."

"Who are they?" Jaelle murmured, doing her best not to look as wilted as she felt inside. All this joy, and she was going to crush it.

But it was for the best. Because he didn't love her the way he was convinced he did. Not really. And she needed to find her footing.

"Admiral Starke is Ashland's supreme admiral. He commands the king's flagship, and Elaina is his daughter."

"Why would I meet his daughter?" For some reason, this was morbidly intriguing. Jaelle might as well know about all the other beautiful women Lucas would spend time with and admire after she was gone.

"Oh, she lives with him aboard the *Adroit*, the Ashlandian flagship. Funny little thing. She's only fourteen years, and she's already been on the seas since she was six."

"Oh." Well, fourteen wasn't so bad. And it was interesting that she lived on the ocean with her father. Lucky girl.

"Unfortunately, I need to run inside and talk with a few of my captains." Lucas tugged on her arm, seeming to forget that she'd asked him to meet her at the chapel in the first place. "Want to come with me?"

Pulling her hand from his was possibly the hardest thing Jaelle had ever done, and the spark in his eyes dimmed as she shook her head.

"I actually wanted you to speak to the holy man with me." She felt sick as she whispered the words.

"Oh." His smile faltered before it was replaced with a polite one. "Of course."

Jaelle took a deep breath as he held the door open for her. She went inside and made her way slowly down the aisle that ran between the seats toward the altar.

If she ever grew to miss her diamonds, she would need to come here. This room was somewhat reminiscent of the handfuls of gems she'd buried all throughout Terrefantome. The windows had no holes, but instead of being filled with clear panes, the glass was a conglomeration of every color imaginable. The countless five or six-inch pieces that were crammed together had no discernable pattern, but they looked so lovely side-by-side. Again, her heart twisted. Oh, to be married in a place like this.

She wasn't allowed to be alone with her peace, though. The altar itself seemed to mock her, and Jaelle turned to glare at it.

You are *married,* it seemed to say, a newer, cleaner copy of the Holy Writ than her own lying open upon it. *And that hasn't seemed to make a difference either way.*

But hers wasn't a real marriage. It was a business agreement made by acquaintances who had each hoped to give the other his or her best chance of survival. Real marriage was...

Ugh. Jaelle shook her head. More proof that she wasn't ready to be Lucas's wife. Maybe, after she'd gone into the world and found where she belonged, she would find another man. He wouldn't be Lucas. There would never be another Lucas. But he could be kind, and she could live with that. And Lucas could find himself a wife who would actually know how to be a princess.

Lucas had followed her silently to the altar, but now, as they stood before it, he took a deep breath and licked his lips. "Um...Is there...Why are we here?"

She had to cast her eyes down, unable to look at him as he spoke. If she did, he would drive her mad with the way he was looking at her. Like a little boy desperate to please.

"I was informed," she said softly, "that the holy man would be the one to oversee the annulment."

He stared at her for a long time. Then his eyes widened. "Jaelle, wait—"

"This was what we agreed to." Her voice was too high and too thin. "This way we all get what's best for us."

He stepped back and put his hands behind his head as he started to pace.

"It wasn't supposed to be this way." He stopped pacing and stood beside her, cradling her neck in his hands, searching her eyes with an intensity that made her heart break. The warmth of his hands on her skin was better than the rays of sun. "I'm sorry. I'm sorry I didn't stay with you." His breathing began to grow faster, and his voice began to crack. "I wish I could do it all over again, but if you give me the chance to prove that I want you with me for the rest of my life, I promise, I will do anything you wish."

"It's not about you or your failures." She smiled sadly and touched his face. "Or mine. This is about life and me...trying to find where I'm supposed to be."

"You're supposed to be here. With me." His eyes burned the way they had in the firelight the night of their wedding.

"Lucas," she said, pushing him back slightly, loosening his grip from her arms where he held them, "we knew this wasn't meant to be when we decided to get married. You're a prince, and I'm a commoner who can't read."

"That doesn't matter." He leaned closer, and the proximity of his lips nearly broke her determination. "I meant every word of those vows," he said, taking her hands. "I planned to take you forever and keep you as mine."

"Because you're a good man." She felt a tear squeeze its way out of her eye and down her face, but she ignored it. "Not because I was meant to be your wife."

"Please don't do this." He took her hand in his and held it tightly to his chest. Then he grabbed her wrist and placed their wrists together, as though she couldn't see them on her own. "You see this?" he said, pointing to the tattoos as he held them side-by-side. "These were meant to be permanent. Just like any couple that takes those vows." He paused, looking at her once again. But when she didn't answer, he seemed to finally understand what she was saying. "You...you really mean to go."

She nodded, unable this time to produce even a false smile. "Our worlds weren't meant to collide, Lucas. You're the busy prince...an admiral of an entire fleet, and I'm..." She shrugged. "I don't know who I am. Or where I'm supposed to be. Or who I'm supposed to be with."

"Be with me! I'll help you find your way—"

"Oh really?" Her laughter sounded strangled. "And what happens when your beloved ships bring you to an early grave? What am I supposed to do then? Wait here for months or years, hoping you didn't get washed away and will miraculously appear one day?"

"I know you can't have read it yet," Lucas said, his words rushed as he searched her face, "but the Maker considers marriage to be a sacred bond. Even...even if you don't love me now, he'll give us what we need to make this marriage. I swear it." He drew in a shaky breath. "Just give me a chance. I can be the man you need me to be. He can make me that man, I promise."

At that moment, the holy man walked in. Instead of greeting him, Lucas took her face in his hands and leaned in until he was close enough to kiss her.

"Before you do this," he whispered, "tell me you don't love me."

Jaelle stared at him for a long time, soaking in the way it felt to have him so close to her once more, so close they could kiss if she wanted.

"Do you love me?" he whispered fiercely.

Desperately.

Instead of speaking that one simple word, the word that could change the course of her life, she squeezed her eyes shut and uttered the lie she knew she would regret for the rest of her life.

"No."

"Good morning, my lord." The elderly holy man smiled up at Lucas and then at Jaelle. "And this must be our new princess." He took her hand and bowed. "It's lovely to meet you, my dear."

Lucas looked at Jaelle as though she'd stuck a shard of glass in his back. "It doesn't—"

The boy who had gone in search of the holy man ran in again. This time, he was accompanied by a sailor Jaelle didn't recognize.

"I have word from the king, my lord," the sailor said, slightly out of breath. "We're to cast off first thing tomorrow. Pirates have been reported down the coast. They're pillaging the barrier isles. Admiral Starke has just dropped anchor, and he wants to speak with you immediately."

"I..." Lucas turned back to Jaelle and swallowed.

"It's all right." She gave him the best smile she could muster and placed her hand on his cheek once more. "I have to go anyway." And with that, she gave him a soft kiss on the cheek before turning to the holy man. The anguish in her heart felt like it was hollowing her out one blow at a time, but deep down, she only knew all the more what she'd known all along. Lucas was owned by the sea, the crown, and his own wandering spirit. And there was nothing left for her here.

"Your honor," she said. "Prince Lucas and I wish to have our marriage annulled."

The holy man's expression went from a benevolent one to gaping horror. He turned to Lucas.

"Is this true?"

Lucas and Jaelle locked gazes for what felt like an eternity. And even now, just as when he'd hesitated at the door of Bartol's castle, part of her wished he would fight. Really fight. Not beg. Not say what he thought would please her. If he loved her as much as he said, he would fight for her with the tenacity that she knew burned inside him.

Finally, Lucas withdrew his gaze and turned to the holy man.

"Do what she says."

And as the little old man shuffled off, muttering to himself about finding the right papers, it took everything in her not to cry.

EPILOGUE
THE ONLY SUNSET

The next three hours dragged on. Jaelle insisted she would be able to find passage on a ship herself, as she'd hidden enough diamonds on her person to last a lifetime, but Lucas was rather dogged about getting her a particular captain that he knew could be trusted. In seeing how determined he was, from the hard set of his jaw to his short, clipped sentences, Jaelle let him. Aside from the fact that she didn't actually know anything about finding passage on a ship, she knew he'd passed the point of being dissuaded. He was hurting, and she was to blame. If letting him help allowed him to think he was fulfilling his promise to take care of her, she might as well let him have it.

But when it came time to say goodbye, and she somehow dredged up a smile, though there may or may not have been tears, he simply stared at her for a long time before turning and striding back down the planked walkway toward the palace. Not a word of farewell. Not even a glance behind. And once he was gone, Jaelle realized just how alone she was.

The captain Lucas had gotten her passage with looked to be in his late fourth decade, with thick, graying red hair and a bushy beard, and his boat, though small, was large enough to host about five passengers. Most of his business, he told Jaelle as the other passengers boarded, came from the larger companies in the north who wanted merperson products.

"Pearls, fish, they even harvest kelp," he said as he neatly wound a thick rope. "But they don't like to trade where it's cold. Maricanta's about as far north as they'll go if they're planning on coming to the surface."

Jaelle looked longingly out at the vast blue expanse, which made her eyes burn. She'd really wanted to meet Queen Arianna, but her hasty departure had ensured she miss all of Lucas's family.

Mermaids included.

"The northern kingdoms can't get enough of their stuff," the man went on. "Even the big ships aren't enough to keep them sated, so smaller boats like mine can do well if we're quick about turning cargo."

"And we won't be quick if you don't get to preparing for launch," his wife called, playfully swatting his arm. The captain laughed and shrugged before standing up and walking away. His wife took Jaelle gently by the arm and bade her to follow her downstairs.

"The rest of our guests are gentlemen, so I've put you in the room next to ours. I hope you don't mind."

"No," Jaelle said shyly. "I'm actually quite grateful."

"The prince was adamant that you not be left alone with any of them while you were under our care." She turned and gave Jaelle a curious look as she unlocked the room, but Jaelle only smiled and thanked her for their attentiveness.

"Very well, then," the woman said with a resigned smile. "I'll let you rest. We'll be putting off soon."

As soon as the door clicked into place, Jaelle turned to examine her new room. Hers, at least, for the next few weeks. They would make their way up the coast to Giova, the captain had told her. It would be slow, as they would make port often to trade, but she would see many of the coastal towns this way. They would even pass, from a distance, the dreaded Terrefantome. Jaelle shuddered at the thought.

Once she was in Giova, she would seek out any living relatives her father might have left behind. She would open a healing shop of her own and get a dog. And a cat. She detested the haughty felines, but Selina had always wanted one. And with her pets and her business and her new life, she *would* be happy. Yet for some reason, Jaelle had to grit her teeth to hold back the tears as she turned in a slow circle to examine her room.

So this was what freedom looked like. One small bunk bed shoved up against the wall, each mattress with a faded but thick quilt and pillow, took up the majority of the room, which was even smaller than the one Jaelle had shared with Selina. In the morning, a bowl of water would be brought in for washing, she'd been told, but it wasn't any use to keep one in the room for the likelihood of spilling it when the weather got choppy. A small circular window that was too tall for her to see through sat in the middle of the outer wall opposite to the bed.

Jaelle dropped her worn bag in the middle of the bottom bed and went to the window to stand on the tips of her toes, but to no avail. So she trudged back to the bed and flopped down on her back. She could have had a more luxurious journey, to be sure. Lucas had offered to pay for whatever level of comfort she desired. But Jaelle wanted nothing to do with expensive beds or pampering service. She didn't deserve that kind of treatment after breaking his heart.

Not that she regretted her choice. It was better this way. Lucas was infatuated, the product of losing Vittoria. He seemed to have convinced himself he was really in love, but Jaelle knew better.

Likewise, Jaelle knew better than to listen to the weeping in her own heart. She loved him, yes. But everything else she had known was gone now. Every scheme and hope had been dashed when Lucas had put that arrow through her sister's heart. Or maybe the real arrow had been loosed much sooner. Jaelle really couldn't tell. All she knew was that the Maker had confused every plan she'd ever made. She felt as though a *manka* had opened up beneath her and swallowed her whole, and everything she knew had faded into the black.

There was a light, that nagging little voice in her head piped up. *And you left him behind.*

Real love, she argued with the voice, would have fought. Real love would have lit that same spark in his eyes that he'd worn whenever his bow and sword were in his hands. It would have filled him with the passion he spoke with when discussing sailing. It would have had him burning with the same desire he expressed for the safety of his country.

But he had let her walk away. He'd even helped her. And that was all the proof she needed.

What was it that Queen Isabelle had said? *He'll put you and everyone else in your life exactly where they need to be* .

"Is this where you want me?" Jaelle whispered into the still, quiet air. "Alone?"

No one answered.

"I want to go the right way," she tried again. "And for a while, I thought I could. But then he died. And she died. And everything is..." She paused. Everything was what?

"Everything is wrong," she whispered into the silence. Left in ruins, the chaos of it enveloped her. No matter what she did, she would be lonely. Selina was gone, and even if Jaelle had stayed with Lucas, she would have been left behind time and time again as he sailed off into the sunset. There was no safe harbor, as she'd always envisioned on this side of the wall. No matter what, she would be lonely.

Back in Terrefantome, Lucas had assured her that the knowledge of something better was proof of the Maker's goodness. And at the time, it had made sense. After all, it was easy to hope for something better when you were in a deep, dark valley. Then she'd come out of the valley, and Queen Isabelle had said that the Maker would put her exactly where he wanted her to be. But how could one be in the right place if one was just drifting? How did she know if she would ever reach that place of *better* that Lucas had spoken of?

"I don't understand what you're doing," Jaelle sobbed as she buried her face in her pillow. "Just tell me what you're doing, and I'll follow. Just...just don't leave me alone."

JAELLE DIDN'T MEAN to fall asleep, but the next thing she knew, she was rubbing her eyes and waking up to shouts from the deck.

Before she could make out what they were saying, someone knocked on her door. Jaelle went to answer it and found the captain's wife waiting for her.

"Beg your pardon," the woman said, worrying the folds of her skirts with her hands, "but it appears we're being boarded."

Jaelle blinked. "Boarded?" What did that mean again? She was sure Lucas had told her at some point...

"Aye," the woman said, glancing behind her at the stairs that led to the deck. "Shouldn't be anything dramatic. Just a quick on and off by some of officials, I'm sure." But the furrow of her brow said otherwise.

"Who is boarding us?" Jaelle asked, wishing again that she could see through her window.

"That's just it." The woman paused. "We've been hailed by the Ashlandian flagship. And... and it seems their entire armada as well."

Jaelle stopped. "Ashland? Isn't their navy big?"

"The most powerful in the world." The woman glanced at the window as well. "And the *Adroit's* admiral, Baxter Starke, is the most powerful man on the seas."

"What does he want with us?"

"We haven't the slightest idea unless they're doing random searches for illegal cargo."

"I should come up with you to the deck," Jaelle said, grabbing her cloak from its peg on the wall.

"I only came to inform you. I don't think you need to bother yourself—" the woman began, but Jaelle was already throwing her cloak on.

"Lucas knows him. Perhaps I can convince him to let us go." Not that she had any way to prove who she was or that she knew the prince. But Jaelle would drown before she let someone else take her captive again.

On their way up the narrow wooden steps, the ship shuddered so hard Jaelle nearly fell backward down the stairs.

"They're coming now," the woman muttered behind her.

Jaelle hesitated for a moment longer before forcing her feet to carry her up the rest of the steps. What would she find at the top?

Lucas's awe for the Ashlandian admiral seemed to border on obsession, so he couldn't be that bad...could he?

When she got to the deck, a man in a blue uniform with dark hair that was beginning to gray was standing and speaking with the captain. Though he stood tall, he didn't look particularly uptight, and the captain, thank the Maker, didn't appear distressed. But when Jaelle turned to study the young man who stood to the admiral's left, she froze.

His uniform was a forest green, and the sharp, angled lines of its cut made her breath hitch. His broad shoulders were straight and proud, and his polished black boots reached up to his knees, making him look taller than she remembered. Curly dark hair was brushed back neatly, the curl above his right eye barely visible. A silver sword hung at his side, and when he turned, his eyes were sharp and resolute.

"Lucas," she whispered for lack of anything better to say.

Instead of responding, though, he marched over to her and grabbed her by the hand. She was in too much shock to resist as he dragged her to the railing, away from the others.

"Lucas," she breathed again, but he held his hand up.

"Before you say anything, I'm going to speak first this time."

Jaelle stared at him. "Um...very well."

"Now I know you don't want to hear this, but I'm going to say it, and you're going to listen."

She nodded faintly.

"I have spent almost my entire life being who others wanted me to be. I measured my words, I held my peace, I played the fool. But in doing so, I lost the man I should have been."

Jaelle's heart was beating so fast she thought she might pass out.

"I thought my world had ended when Vittoria's father said no. But what I didn't understand was that the Maker was making way for you. Because I have never needed anyone or anything so much in my life as I need you. And because I love you, I fell right back into that damnable hole of shutting my mouth when I needed to use it most."

"You need me?" she whispered.

"You," he said, touching her face, "are the life I've been searching for. You are adventure and sunrises and sunsets. You took my broken, bleeding soul and placed it back in my chest so I could breathe like I had before."

Jaelle felt dizzy as she tried to comprehend the magnitude of what he was saying.

"You may not need a prince to live happily ever after," he said, his voice low and rough, "but I will need you until the day I die."

"Why?"

"Because you," he said, holding up his wrist, "are my gem. And if it hadn't been for the light the Maker placed in you, I would still be stumbling around in the dark, praying for the morning star." And before she could say anything more, he dropped to his knee.

"Jaelle, will you marry me? Forever this time?"

Jaelle put the back of her knuckles to her mouth as she laughed, trying to take it all in. Just when she'd been sure the Maker wanted her alone, Lucas had returned. And he was fighting for her with a fiercer determination than she'd seen in him yet. The word yes was nearly on her lips when she saw a young woman, probably four or five years younger, standing on the deck beside the admiral.

"Is that her?" she asked.

"Who?" Lucas frowned and turned. "Elaina Starke?"

Jaelle nodded. "The one who lives on the ship with her father, right?"

He looked back, his brows knit together. "Um...yes?"

Jaelle felt bad for ruining his sweet proposal, but she had something she needed to say as well. For at the sight of Elaina, Jaelle had received a flash of inspiration...and the answer to her prayers. Gratefulness enveloped her as she briefly closed her eyes and mouthed *thank you* to the sky. Then she grasped Lucas's hand in both of hers and looked down at him.

"If I'm going to marry you, I'm not staying behind."

"Oh?" His eyebrows shot up, but she continued.

"I want to go on your adventures with you." She squeezed her hands tightly to keep herself from hopping up and down like a little girl. "Let's sail into the sunset together. Every night. We won't have to say goodbye when your brother sends you away, and I'll be right here at your side whenever you need me."

He stood and put his hands on his waist. "And what in the depths am I supposed to do with you when we run into pirates and have to go to battle?"

Jaelle rolled her eyes. "I'm sure no admiral *ever* needed a healer in the midst of battle. Besides." She pointed to Elaina, who was eyeing them with bright curiosity. "She does it."

Lucas stood and pinched his nose. "I knew it would be a bad idea to introduce you two."

"Take me with you," Jaelle said again, stepping closer and placing her hands on his chest. "Let me be your helper."

"Do you know what kind of men I deal with?" He scowled down at her.

"Do you know what kind of men I grew up with? Besides." She reached up on her toes to place a soft kiss on his lips. "You'll be with me. And the Maker. So I know I won't have to be afraid."

"You don't fight fair," he growled as he wrapped his hands around her waist and leaned down to kiss her.

"Because I want to win."

"So," Admiral Starke said as he walked up to them, "am I marrying you or are we all just going to watch?"

Lucas pulled out of the kiss to scowl at the admiral.

"I already married her once."

"Well, in that case," the admiral said, folding his hands, "I'll just wait here until it's time to christen your children."

Lucas huffed and straightened, but kept one arm firmly on the small of her back, and Jaelle laughed. He'd been right when he'd spoken of looking for something better. And Queen Isabelle had spoken true when she said the Maker would put her right where she needed to be. For better than riches or being a princess or traveling the world or even being wed a second time to the man of her dreams, Jaelle knew she was loved. And, Jaelle thought as she prepared to say her vows once more, what a powerful love it was.

"Here." Elaina Starke held out a large folded blanket. "You'll need this this evening."

"Thank you," Jaelle said hesitantly as she took the gift. Then she leaned closer. "But Lucas won't even tell me why we're here. How did you know what we needed?" No sooner had she been transferred to the *Adroit* and the admiral married them than Elaina had announced that the pirates could wait, and Lucas and Jaelle were going to get their honeymoon. That the girl had the audacity to make such a bold statement had been surprising enough, but then the crew had shocked Jaelle even more by doing exactly as she said, including the admiral. They'd set sail for the nearest port, which was known far and wide for its pristine beaches and excellent market, according to Lucas. Three hours later, they'd arrived as though it had been part of the plan all along.

"Apparently," Lucas said dryly, arching his brow at the girl, "you don't understand what a *surprise* means."

"Oh, a little birdie told me." Elaina's blue-green eyes sparkled. Then she turned to Lucas. "Three days now. Understand? And not a moment sooner."

"Yes." He rolled his eyes. "I've only heard you the first four times."

"Good. The pirates can wait."

"Don't you have something to do or someone else you can bother?" He tried to reach out and poke her shoulder, but she danced out of his reach.

"Bothering you is fun! But yes, I'm going to the market. The last time I was here, one of the cobblers was selling a silver pair of shoes that was calling my name." She beamed and bounced away.

"What was that about?" Jaelle chuckled as Elaina began to good-naturedly boss the sailors around as she went. "And I thought we were chasing the pirates, not meeting them."

"We were, but Elaina says they'll not hurt anyone if we wait a few days first."

Jaelle laughed. "Do you usually take your orders from girls of fourteen years?"

"Elaina Starke is..." He hesitated. "Unusual. After her mother was killed when she was young, her father took her aboard his ship. After that, they seemed to stumble upon a string of good luck that has yet to be broken."

"Is she gifted?" Jaelle asked in a low voice, studying the girl anew. Being gifted would account for the girl's strange behavior.

"It wouldn't surprise me a bit." Lucas shrugged. "They've never actually said so, though, so I figure it's best to keep my thoughts to myself. Besides." He gave Jaelle an appreciative glance, and her cheeks heated pleasantly. "I'm rather sure Elaina didn't call off our entire joint mission so we could talk about her."

Jaelle's skin tingled, and she shivered with delight. Any fear she'd harbored about his passivity for her went up in smoke as he lightly ran his fingers from her shoulder down the length of her arm.

"Take this." He put his hand on the blanket she was still holding. "And meet me out on that beach in an hour." He caught her around the waist and kissed her hard enough to leave her red-faced and giddy before making his way down the gangplank. Several of the sailors snickered, and even Admiral Starke smiled, but Jaelle didn't care. She just put her hand to her mouth and grinned like an idiot.

An hour later, she made her way down to the beach and spread the blanket out on the sand. Then she lay on it and closed her eyes, soaking in the golden, rays of the sun as it moved closer and closer to the ocean. Its warmth bathed her in bliss, and the smell of the sea and the sound of the waves felt as though they were washing away the stains Terrefantome had left on her soul.

"Peaceful, isn't it?"

Jaelle opened her eyes to see Lucas standing over her with a bag. He'd removed his shoes, and even more impressively, his shirt. The sunset, which had been so alluring a moment ago, couldn't hold a candle to Lucas.

"Sorry about that. There were a few things I needed to find." He sat cross-legged beside her and laid the bag down beside him. Then he pulled her into his lap.

"What kind of things?" Jaelle sounded like someone had whacked her in the chest and chased all the breath from her lungs.

"Three tokens." The deep timbre of his voice made her turn to study him more closely.

"Tokens? What for?"

"I know," he said slowly, "that it probably seemed to you like I was just trying to do the right thing in marrying you, and that honor was all that bound my heart to yours."

Jaelle could only nod slightly, her throat too sticky to speak.

"But I want you," he said, taking a lock of her hair and twirling it around his fingers, "to know that when I vowed to marry you, I meant that I would love you for all of my days. Because even though I was confused after the Maker shut the door on Vittoria, I quickly began to realize that he might have opened the gate to something better. And by the time I took you as my wife, I'd spent enough time with you to know that you had the kind of heart I wanted to share for the rest of my days. And I know," he said, holding up a hand when she opened her mouth, "that I did a poor job of showing that. So these are my tokens to show you that I listened when you spoke. And I want to prove to you that the hopes and dreams that were once yours are mine now, too."

Jaelle could only sit there as she tried to keep herself from hyperventilating. *It can't be real*, she told the Maker. *This day has been too good already. Nothing this good can truly last.*

He reached down and pulled a long, thin box out of the bag. Then he handed it to her.

"Open it."

Jaelle did so and let out a cry of delight.

"Paints!" She turned to look at him before looking back at her gift, as though it might just disappear. But sure enough, they were still there, ten little squares of bright paints in every color she could think of.

"I want you," he said, keeping his eyes on her face, "to paint every sunset you come across. And then we'll hang every one in my chambers in the palace."

Jaelle's stomach warmed at the thought of his chambers, but he was already pulling a second item from the bag.

"This," he said, handing her something much larger than the box, "is going to fulfill my second promise."

"It's a book!" she gasped as she turned the thick, crisp pages. Bright paintings adorned the pages, along with large symbols.

"It's one the governesses of the wealthy often use with the

small children they tutor," he said, taking the book from her hands and turning a few pages.

"I'm really going to read." Jaelle laughed.

"I had planned on teaching you on the way up to the Fortiers' Fortress," he said, nuzzling her neck with his nose. "But I think I'm going to prefer teaching you alone in our room ever so much more."

Jaelle gave him a look. "I may not know how to read, but I'm pretty sure you have to actually look at the book."

"Sometimes, I suppose." He softly placed a kiss behind her ear.

"Well," Jaelle laughed breathlessly, "then I can guarantee you that we won't be doing any reading when you do *that*."

"Why? Do you like it?"

"Perhaps a little too much." She giggled again. In the whole course of her life, she couldn't remember laughing as much as she had that day. She nodded at a few of the other beach visitors, who were probably a good hundred yards away but staring as if they were invisible. "Some of our neighbors also seem to be enjoying it as well."

"Aw, them." Lucas glowered at the figures dotted along the shore. "They can mind their own business."

"I thought you had three tokens for me." She gave him an ornery look. He kissed her arched brow and then reached into the bag a third time.

"This," he said, pulling out something that glittered, "is to remind you of what you are to me."

In spite of her excessive exposure to diamonds, Jaelle inhaled sharply as he held the necklace out for her to see. It was simple, and yet, she was dazzled. The thin golden chain came down to her collarbone, where two white gems, long and thin, continued in place of the chain. Each side led down to a little round amethyst. Then at the bottom hung a single delicate white gem that was shaped like a teardrop.

"It's beautiful." She gingerly reached up to touch the gems as they glittered in the dying sun. Then she looked at him. "But what are they for?"

He took the necklace and draped it against her skin and

fastened it at the back of her neck. The hairs on the nape of her neck tingled as his warm, rough hands lingered close to her skin.

"I know your gems felt like a curse," he said slowly, lifting her out of his lap and turning her to face him. "But I firmly believe that what felt like a curse was a gift. In disguise."

"You nearly died for my gems," she said softly.

"But without them, I wouldn't have found you." He trailed his fingers along the cool lines of the necklace then began tracing her collarbones. Jaelle closed her eyes. She'd never imagined a feeling so heavenly as his touch. And even more, the innate knowledge that she didn't have to be afraid.

In an effort not to cry at the sudden, nearly overwhelming sense of wonder, Jaelle traced the scars on his abdomen with her own hands. They were warm and surprisingly hard. "These weren't treated properly." Her voice sounded too high. "They shouldn't have scarred like this."

"I think my men were more concerned with my survival than my vanity." Lucas chuckled. "Besides, I kind of like them." He straightened and gave her an ornery smile. "Quite attractive, don't you think?"

Of course she did. "I'm just glad I'm going to be the one patching you up from now on." She nodded to herself.

Instead of laughing, though, he only looked at her, his hazel eyes suddenly large and sad.

"What is it?" she asked.

"We nearly missed this," he whispered, running his thumb across her lips.

That they had. Jaelle sighed and dropped her gaze to the ground. "I'm sorry I ran," she said, unable to meet his eyes.

"Why did you run?" he asked, pulling her back into his lap and kissing the top of her head.

She closed her eyes and leaned back into his warmth.

"I felt...I felt as though the world had crumbled. The plans we'd lived for, the dreams we had...even my sister was gone. And you..." She picked up his hand and placed hers against it. "You were too good to be true. And since you were getting over Vittoria, I was sure that one day you'd wake up and know you'd made a mistake. I didn't want your honor to be all that tied you to me. And when you let me go, I knew I must be right." She paused. "Why didn't you come after me?"

He groaned and wrapped his arms around her. Then he placed his chin on her head.

"It killed me to let you get on that boat. But I'd seen what you lived with, and I didn't want to force you to stay with me against your will. So many decisions had been taken from you already..." He cleared his throat. "But as soon as you were gone, I knew I'd made a mistake. And the moment Starke's ship was sighted, I jumped in a dingy and rowed out to meet him. And I told him that pirates or none, I had to follow you."

Jaelle chuckled. "He must have thought you were crazy."

"He was married too, once." Lucas's voice was low. "And as he still carries her locket with him at all times, I get the feeling he knew exactly what I felt." He shook his head. "But back to you. I realized as I raced after you that in order to truly give you the freedom to make the right decision, you needed to know how I felt. And no matter what you thought you wanted, I couldn't stay silent any longer."

"Isabelle was right, you know," she said, fingering her necklace.

"She usually is. But how so?"

"She told me on our way back that in her experience, the Maker puts us exactly where we need to be. And it wasn't until I resigned myself to his plan that I was able to understand and trust your love when you came running back to me."

"And I hope," he said, kissing her temple, "that you never doubt either again."

She smiled. "Never." Relief rushed through her veins, and before she stopped to consider the prudence of such a display, she'd turned and sat up on her knees and wrapped her arms around his neck. Then she placed her lips on his and gave him the kiss she prayed would prove to him the passion he had ignited within her.

Without breaking the kiss, his hands moved from her waist to her arms and shoulders. Without breaking contact, he stood then lifted her off the ground and turned to face the ship.

"I think," he mumbled into her kiss, "that the good admiral has reserved one of the larger rooms for us to rest in."

Jaelle pulled back and grinned. "Only as long as we can see the sunset from inside the room."

"The only sunset I'm going to be needing tonight," he breathed in her ear, "is right here in my arms."

"And it will be yours," she smiled, "for the rest of our lives."

Neverland Falling

A Clean Fantasy Fairy Tale Retelling of Peter Pan, Part I

Wendy, isn't it?"

Nana barked, and Wendy whirled around once more to see the young man with green eyes watching her with an odd mixture of curiosity and humor. He was standing in the shadows under the eve. Wendy's heart pumped hard with a combination of shock and thrill.

Nana would have run up to him to warn him away, but Wendy grabbed her by the collar and dragged her back a few steps.

"Nana!" she hissed. "You're being embarrassing."

Nana glared at her for a moment before glaring back at their visitor. Then she went to stand behind Wendy as she was supposed to, though this was done by sticking her head between Wendy's ankles, where she could clear just enough space to see from beneath Wendy's skirts and robe.

Only then did it occur to Wendy that she was outside in front of a stranger in her nightdress, robe or no robe. And for one long second, her voice was caught in her throat. Even amidst her embarrassment, all the questions she wanted to ask him bubbled up in her mind. Were you the boy from four years ago? Where have you been? Can you really fly?

Of course, asking any of those questions would be the perfect way to convince him she was downright addled. So instead, she managed a nod.

"I am. And you are?"

"Name's Johnston."

Wendy's heart cracked slightly. For some reason, she'd been sure he would say Peter. But she kept her face straight. Talk. She had to talk. She needed to do something to get this strange silence over with because it was suffocating.

"My brothers and I heard something at our upstairs window," she blurted out. "I came to see if I could find what it was."

If he knew anything of the anomaly, he gave nothing away. Instead, he looked up to the attic of the house, where Wendy and her brothers slept.

"That's a rather long way for someone to come up and knock."

"It wasn't you, was it?"

Wendy had meant the words to come out as a tease. But instead, they sounded desperate and tightly wound. Fool. If he hadn't thought she was daft already, he certainly would now.

But to her utter shock, he didn't deny the question, only tilted his head in the other direction as he studied her.

He certainly wasn't as tall as the new magistrate was, nor was his figure so broad or thick. And yet, there was something attractive in him that Wendy had never seen in a young man. It was as if he had all the marks of manhood, at least in his size, but with a strange, familiar light in his eyes that could only belong to a boy who still believed in the magic of life.

"I saw you leave with your family," he finally said, breaking the silence. "You looked as though you were going somewhere quite fine."

Memories of the embarrassment and indignation of the evening, which Wendy had somehow managed to temporarily forget during her little escapade, came crashing back in. She shook her head and groaned, which elicited a laugh from him.

It wasn't a cruel laugh, but rather one of surprise. "That bad, huh?"

She grimaced. "My parents thought I might be a good match for the new magistrate."

He leaned against the side of the house and crossed his arms. "I take it the meeting didn't go so well?"

"No, it went quite well. All up to the point where I contradicted him to his face not once but three times."

He squinted and tilted his head, his messy hair falling slightly over his forehead. "You seem a bit young for marriage, don't you?"

Wendy stood taller. "It'll not be long before I'm eighteen."

"Well, then," he said, not even attempting to hide his smile. "I'm afraid you've cost yourself your future happiness forever. Whatever oaf the man must have been to arouse your ire, a life of misery with him must be found superior to anything otherwise." His grin widened. "Especially since you're so close to becoming an old maid."

"You should watch your tongue," she laughed as she glanced around. "If my parents heard you speaking with so much impertinence, you'd lose your job."

He shrugged. "Wouldn't matter. I'm not much good at doing as I'm told."

"Then why are you here?" Unable to hold back her curiosity, she took a step forward to see him better. Nana, seeming to sense Wendy's curiosity, slipped around her and became an immovable statue that would trip Wendy if she tried to move again.

A grin slowly spread across the young man's face once more as he stood taller and straightened his shirt. "Good night, Wendy." Then without another word, he walked back to the barn where all the men slept.

If Wendy's curiosity had been aroused before, her entire mind was ablaze now.

To find out who Wendy's mystery man is, read Neverland Falling: A Retelling of Peter Pan, Part I.

Thank you so much for reading A Curse of Gems! I hope you loved it! You can find more free stories about Lucas and Jaelle if you become one of Brit's Bookish Mages by signing up for my newsletter. There, you'll get download links to free books, the password to bonus stories, coupon codes, and more! I also send out book updates and sneak peeks at books before they're published!

Also, if you liked this book, please consider leaving a rating or review on your favorite ebook retailer or Goodreads so other readers can find it, too!

NEVERLAND FALLING

A RETELLING OF PETER PAN, PART I

ABOUT THE AUTHOR

Brittany lives with her Prince Charming, their little fairy, and their little prince in a ~~sparkling~~ (decently clean) castle in whatever kingdom the Air Force has most recently placed them. When she's not writing, Brittany can be found chasing her kids around with her DSLR and belting it in the church worship team.

Facebook: Facebook.com/BFichterFiction
Subscribe: BrittanyFichterFiction.com
Email: BrittanyFichterFiction@gmail.com
Instagram: @BrittanyFichterFiction

A CURSE OF GEMS (THE CLASSICAL KINGDOMS COLLECTION
BOOK 7)

Copyright © 2019 Brittany Fichter

A Curse of Gems / Brittany Fichter. -- 1st ed.

Edited by Kimberly Kessler